*YELL-*Oh **Girls!**

Emerging **Voices** Explore Culture,

Identity, and Growing Up

Asian American

YELL-Oh **Girls!**

Vickie **Nam**

✒Quill

An Imprint of HarperCollins*Publishers*

FIRST EDITION

Designed by Ruth Lee

Library of Congress Cataloging-in-Publication Data
Yell-oh girls! : emerging voices explore culture, identity, and growing up Asian
    American / Victoria Nam.
        p.   cm.
    ISBN 0-06-095944-4
    1. Asian American teenage girls—Psychology.   2. Asian American teenage
    girls—Physiology.   3. Self-esteem in adolescence—United States.   4. Body
    image in adolescence—United States.   5. Youths' writings, American.   I. Nam,
    Victoria.

E184.O6 .Y45   2001
305.235—dc21

                                                                2001018164
01   02   03   04   05   ✳/RRD   10   9   8   7   6   5   4   3   2   1

Additional Praise for *YELL-Oh Girls!*

"A diversity of younger Asian American writers carrying the banner forward. I think this is great."

> —Claire S. Chow, author of *Leaving Deep Water: The Lives of Asian American Women at the Crossroads of Two Cultures*

"Finding your voice has to do with writing and practicing writing until you become attuned to your own rhythms and poetic sensibilities, until you write like yourself and no one else."

> —Young-Adult author Marie G. Lee, author of *Finding My Voice* and *Necessary Roughness*

"*YELL-Oh Girls!* gives voice to an energetic group of young Asian American women. The collection is alternately poignant and funny, tender and tough. The diversity of young voices and accompanying mentor pieces, written by various Asian American women leaders—including journalist Helen Zia, novelist Lois-Ann Yamanaka, and U.S. Representative Patsy Mink—belies the notion that any culture can have only one spokesperson. This book is valuable not only for its insights—which are sharp—but perhaps more importantly, as an inspiration to any young person seeking self-expression."

> —Elaine Mar, author of *Paper Daughter: A Memoir*

in loving memory of Grandma

Myung-Kun **Chey**

(1903–2000)

Contents

Orientation: Finding the Way Home

Family Ties

Dolly Rage

Finding My Voice

Acknowledgments

In addition to thanking the Lord for guidance, I'd like to show my deepest gratitude to those whose support made *YELL-Oh Girls!* happen.

My real-life "Woman Warrior" and mother, Ok-Hee, my sister, Lisa, and my father, Kwang-Joon, for helping me realize my dreams and convert thoughts, words, and passion into action. Best friends, therapists, and consultants all rolled up in one: Amy Athey, Marc Chow, and Ashley Im. *YELL-Oh Girls!* made it because you always believed.

My passionate interest in Asian American girls and women's issues originated in college. A million thanks to professor of women's studies at Wellesley College, Elena Creef, for triggering my first major awakening, and for teaching me new ways of seeing. Also to Phoebe Eng, my all-star mentor, for her insight, wisdom, and endless encouragement.

Heartfelt thanks to my editor, Sally Kim, who challenged me to make the anthology sing from the first page to the last. And many thanks to the people at HarperCollins who championed the project: Gail Winston, Elizabeth Pawlson, Jennifer Hart, and Christine Walsh. Doris Michaels Literary Agency's Faye Bender, my friend and agent, not only for embracing a "rad" concept and mission of the anthology, but also for recognizing the possibilities of our endeavor from day one.

All of the contributors to *YELL-Oh Girls!* would like to thank Asian Avenue (www.AsianAvenue.com) for building the girl-powered channels of communication, for sponsoring creative writing scholarships aimed at empowering Asian American girls through self-expression.

The Web site (www.yellohgirls.com), which played a key role in inform-ing and mobilizing the community of Asian American girls throughout the duration of the anthology project, was created by Sze-Ho Hsu. And thanks also to Michael Chen for his artistic contributions.

In pursuing my professional goals, I have been blessed to meet many strong female visionaries. They have given me opportunities that have helped me to re-create and redefine my dreams, while offering me sterling words of wisdom to guide me on my journey. A special thanks to: Mary Athey; Maria Baugh and Cara Shultz/*Teen People*; Hillary Carlip and Maxine Lapiduss/VOXXY, Inc.; Sherry Handel/Blue Jean Media; Jeannie Park/*InStyle*. The individuals and organizations who helped spread the word about *YELL-Oh Girls!*: Quang Bao/Asian American Writers Workshop; Jim Cho and Dina Gan/*aMagazine*; Lindy and Jessie Gelber/Korean American Adoptee Network; Pam Hayashi; Risa Mori-moto/Asian/Pacific/American Studies Program and Institute; *New Moon* Magazine; Danny Seo; Beau Sia; David Song/HardBoiled. And to the countless women whose work made space in the literary arena for our anthology, and who share our hopes for progress—namely, Nora Okja Keller, Elaine Kim, Patsy Mink, Wendy Mink, Janice Mirikitani, Lois-Ann Yamanaka, and Helen Zia.

Thanks to long-distance angels who made it their business to keep me focused at every crazy twist and turn: Jenny Han, Hera and Alex Hong, Annice Kim, Joyce and Sandy Law, Lillian Lee, Angie Maximo, Amy Yee, and Connie You. Also thanks to Alex Hong, Frank Huang, and Rob Cerwinski for brotherly love. A shout-out to my LA gal pals for pep talks, coffee breaks, and late-night calls during the long haul: Ophelia Chong, Evelyne Kim, Ginny Kim, and Amy Rardin.

And finally, I wish to acknowledge the hundreds of brilliant girls who contributed to *YELL-Oh Girls!*, some of whose names do not appear on these pages. Special props go out to Cerissa Francisco, Yu Gu, Teresa Hsu, Shirley Man, Elizabeth Nguyen, Kanya Panyavong, and Annie Than for their diligence. Your bold creativity, determination, and supersized dreams continue to unveil the locus of our collective power as Asian American girls. Continue to draw strength and support from each other—we will be heard.

Foreword

Themes of women, power, and community have always been interesting to me. And so, as I write and lecture around the country, I am
thrilled and inspired when I meet women who live on their own terms,
unbound by rules and false limitations.

One woman's story that is particularly special is Patsy Mink's. She is
the first and only Asian American woman member of Congress, representing the Second Congressional District of Hawaii. When she was
younger, and at the urging of her high school principal, Patsy became
the first girl student-body president of her high school class. Later, as a
young woman, Patsy knew she could represent the views of her community on Capitol Hill. And so, shortly after Hawaii became a state in
1959, Patsy Mink ran in her first congressional election . . . and lost.
That didn't stop her from trying again, however. Reconvening her loyal
base of supporters, she tossed in her hat a second time, and in 1964,
won a congressional seat. Once in office, Patsy made good use of her
time. Among her many victories, Patsy was instrumental in the passage
of Title IX, one of the most important antidiscrimination laws for
women. Her life story reminds me that, with chutzpah and tenacity, little by little, big things can happen. From high school president to pio-
neering U.S. congresswoman, Patsy showed that our dreams and sense
of personal possibilities take shape when we are young.

Big things happen through the collection of small occurrences,
such as the small occurrence of my first, casual meeting with Vickie

Nam. I met Vickie after an awards ceremony one cold spring day in New York when she first told me about her project, *YELL-Oh Girls!* In Vickie, I saw a smart, directed younger sister who understood what it meant for women to speak out. I could see that she was driven by big visions and took on large goals, that she worked hard, and that maybe I could help her.

We agreed to meet for lunch. Over the years, that lunch extended into several more, where we talked about our shared vision, our sense of Asian American community, race, our families, our wardrobes, even hair coloring—the kinds of things I talk about only when I know that I am in the company of a friend.

In our conversations, we also talked strategy. How to get things done. How to relax when the pressure is on. I gave her suggestions for people to contact and tried to make sure that her calls would be answered. I recommended girls that she might want to talk to. I did these things for many reasons. The first is that, in doing so, I was honoring my own teachers—professors, friends, big sisters, committed activists—who have helped me make right and moral choices, and who have continued to inspire and support me when I've stumbled. I wanted to pass on to Vickie the vital vision of community that my mentors instilled in me. The second reason is that I knew that Vickie had the kind of raw energy that I had when I was younger, full of optimistic conviction and an innately practical sense of what was required to get things done. I wanted Vickie to succeed. I also wanted her to know that what she was doing was so very important.

In my book *Warrior Lessons: An Asian American Woman's Journey Into Power*, I ended with these words of hope for Asian American women:

May we look inward to find the truth . . .
May we give words to that which is not yet spoken.
My strength, is your strength, is ours . . .

Those three phrases are "crucible" ideas—simple, essential terms that define a "warrior's" power, where deep introspection, courage to incite, and confident sisterhood are essential. In *Warrior Lessons*, there is no power without community.

Vickie practices those words in this book that you now hold. She has given a new generation of young Asian American girls a chance to speak in ways that they have never been asked to before. In collaboration with hundreds of girls across the country and the support of supportive members of the community, Vickie has given us the first anthology of Asian American teenage girls' writings, which is destined to become a cornerstone resource for Asian American girls, their parents, teachers, and those involved in young Asian American women's lives.

In *YELL-Oh Girls!* Asian American girls have attitude. Their stories show that they are trying to find ways to make their voices count. Some are tenuously balancing between the past and the future. Some are directed and determined, fists poised to strike. All are willing to continue exploring for answers. These young women could not have found it easy to write these pieces, some of which are poignant and heart-wrenching. For, in doing so, they are exposed, named, held accountable to life's large questions. In revealing their stories, these young girls have begun a hero's journey—that long-term and arduous testing of what gives their own lives meaning and power.

As I said, little by little, big things can happen. And as I've found time and time again, what gives life to "big things" is the choices that we make. Will we choose to speak? Will we choose to listen? Will young Asian American women choose to approach and demand of their mentors? As mentors, whether Asian American or not, will we choose to respond and follow through? An affirmative answer to each of these questions is a small step, which, taken collectively, can catapult a whole lot of our younger sisters into the places they want to be.

Patsy Mink shows us, as does Vickie Nam, that big things can never be accomplished by sheer will and talent alone. Instead, it requires the collusion of hundreds of people who also believe in you, who want you to thrive, and will do what is necessary to lift you up to that place where, finally, you have what you need to fly on your own.

So with *YELL-Oh Girls!* let us learn to testify. Let us learn to listen. And for Asian American women, let's work on making our voices and dreams big and impactful. The result will be nothing less than a powerful kind of sisterhood we've been wanting for a very long time.

—Phoebe Eng

Introduction

Like most of the gals I grew up with back in Rochester, New York, I had a sticker collection. I bartered and stole until I had finally amassed the entire puffy glitter scratch-'n'-sniff series, and that was it. I lost interest. My next obsession was stuffed animals, but this craze petered out as soon as my precious poly-fills had paired off and had their own "kids." The family was complete.

Then I turned nine. And with the help of my older sister, who was thirteen, I became addicted to teen magazines. Throughout my growing-up years, I discovered that collecting 'zines was the only hobby that could keep up with me.

Until recently, I had forgotten all about my old magazine collection. My mother was cleaning out her shed when she came across a mountain of musty old boxes, covered in dust and spiders, the ones I'd packed the old glossies in before moving away to college. She quickly made a cross-country call: "If you don't mind, I'm going to throw your old magazines out," my mother huffed into the receiver.

I grew silent. Those boxes were filled with at least ten years' worth of history. I insisted that she leave the boxes alone until I came to visit. Then I could decide what I wanted to keep and have shipped, even though I knew there wasn't enough space in my Los Angeles apartment for a 200-pound pile of magazines. My mother was annoyed that I was even thinking about holding on to the stinky, lopsided boxes.

"Don't be ridiculous, why do you want to keep those junks, anyway?" she inquired, half knowing the answer to her own question.

And how couldn't she? My mother knew "those junks" were symbolic mementos of my childhood. On lazy Saturday afternoons, I would sit on my bed for hours, picking through the pages of *Seventeen* or *YM* (then *Young Miss*). Sometimes she'd walk into my room to find me sketching pictures of the girls I saw on the pages. Other times she'd see my sister and me partaking in odd beauty rituals. Like when we took turns applying strips of tape across each other's eyelids, so that when we opened our eyes, we would have the pretty folds that made white girls' eyes big and round. And when my mother caught us with our hair flipped over the gigantic metal tub, which she used to season kim chee, to catch the excess Sun-in lightening solution that dripped off our dried, fried split ends.

During prom season, I would spend days leafing through the magazines because the March issues were the fattest. I fantasized about going to the prom when I was fifteen—my date would look like Jordan Knight from New Kids on the Block, and my dress would be white with black polka dots and a black bodice that had red bows trailing down the back. By the time my first formal dance rolled around, my mother made sure I got the dress of my dreams; she spent two whole days pedaling her old sewing machine, and the dress swished exactly as I imagined it would when I twirled. My date, however, was no Ken. I liked and resented Charlie, one of the only Asian kids in my town. I couldn't deny that I thought he was cute, but the fact that he was Korean and that my peers teased us every time they saw us together ("You look *so right* together—you guys'll get married someday!") left a bitter taste in my mouth about the entire fanfare.

The Ken guys were taken. Most of them went for the popular white girls at school who looked like the models in my teen magazines. How I yearned for the carefree way in which they talked, laughed, and moved around! Seeing them gallivanting in delicious clothes, flirting with cute guys, and coming back sun-kissed from their tropical vacations reminded me of the whimsical fashion spreads that I scrutinized on the weekends. My close friends, who were white but weren't part of the popular crowd, were leading totally "normal" lives, too; they were dating, going to parties, eating hamburgers and maybe Brussels sprouts (if they were unlucky) for dinner. My parents, on the other hand, were nothing like everyone else's parents. Every night, mine turned into human metronomes, keeping time as I practiced violin, but only after stuffing me with rice, spicy stews with fish eggs, and vegetables that my friends said smelled "gross." My family was getting on my nerves, and I was growing frustrated with myself in the process of trying to blend into the world outside.

Any one of those magazines was the closest thing I had to a journal. I collected every issue, marked important pages, and kept track of the names of recurring faces that appeared in consecutive issues. There were holes where I'd cut out certain blurbs or images, and those pages were wrinkled and torn, but all of the marks were still there, including my answers to the featured quizzes, "Are You Jealous?" "Are You Too Insecure?" "Are You Boy Crazy?" Looking at the scoring columns, I noticed that I always fell somewhere in the middle. If the scale was 1 to 3, I was a 2. If it was A through C, I was a B. That was me—too stable, too levelheaded, *too boring*. And of course these quizzes fed my magazine addiction. I waited for my character analysis, and my life, to change.

Then one day I found something of myself represented in the magazine, but not in the way I'd ever expected. Niki Taylor, whose big break came when Revlon made her a superspokesmodel, was debuting in *Seventeen*, showing off a fall wardrobe in a big fashion spread. Niki's makeup artist had committed black eyeliner abuse, drawing her eyes out to mimic Asian eyes. She wore saris, silk pants, and all sorts of decadent "Oriental" bangles and garments. The text described the "spices" of the Far East, the mystery, the exotic appeal of the Orient.

I sent a letter to the editor of the magazine. It was never published, but this was major. It was the first time I challenged a medium, which I perceived to be the authority not only on reflecting fashion trends, but on reflecting society. It was also the first time I questioned the depiction of Asianness in the mainstream media. I wrote, "If you were going to portray Asian clothes, why didn't you at least use Asian models in the fashion spread?" At that point, it didn't occur to me that the language used in the editorial was equally if not more problematic than the photographs. I was just pissed off that girls who looked like me never appeared in the magazine and, as far as I was concerned, we were invisible to the rest of the American population.

This critical observation was a turning point for me, and I would never again be a passive receptacle of the written word. My eyes probed the text and pictures for errors, and I was cognizant of the fact that the media wasn't speaking to me. Although this realization could have crushed my girlhood fantasy of becoming an editor of some swanky New York fashion magazine, my list of grievances led me to visualize a revolution. I formed a habit of checking the mastheads in all of my favorite publications, hoping that I'd recognize names that sounded like they belonged to women and minorities. Suddenly, it all seemed to make sense. With so few Asian American staff members involved in the production process, no wonder there was a lack of representation in the editorial content. Thinking about my own future, I knew that having zero contacts in the industry would mean that getting my foot in the door would be difficult.

At Wellesley, I majored in history and women's studies with a concentration on the representation of Asian Americans in the media. The college didn't offer a journalism degree, so I found summer internships that gave me experience in the field. During this time, my parents tried to dissuade me from making a "huge mistake" by choosing a career that wasn't proven to be an industry where people like me would flourish. I tuned their comments out, fearful that their anxiety would erode my own self-esteem, and insisted that I was determined to give this goal my best shot, with or without their support.

While I began to feel more confident about the direction in which my professional future was headed, my inner self was caught in never-ending conflict, and I was wrestling with questions that plagued me as a girl. Pieces of my past were slowly congealing to form what I thought was a more definitive ethnic and gender identity. The term papers I generated for class along with the presentations I gave in senior seminars were helping me understand "that token Asian Girl," who was still trying to make sense of the contradictions of being Asian, American, and a girl. I had grown up feeling invisible, yet conspicuous, at the same time and all the time.

My magazine archive at home became a warehouse of academic artillery. I churned out dozens of term papers citing articles, images, and advertisements to bolster my argument that Asian American women were dismantling stereotypes, and defining themselves as strong, *not weak*. Proactive, *not passive*. Bold, expressive, and self-aware. Before graduating, I told my professor, Elena, that someday I would edit an anthology by and for Asian American girls. This book, I said, would bring our academic dialogue back to where it began—when we were teen girls on the journey toward finding our place in society.

I left college in a whirlwind, ready to go out and change the world. But I didn't know that my own journey toward self-discovery was far from over. It was while I was working at one of the top national teen magazines that I started to rethink my adolescent experiences.

Nothing could have prepared me for the fast-paced corporate publishing industry. As a magazine staff member, the mystique of behind-the-scenes moments of superstardom quickly faded to reveal the not-so-glamorous routine of handling administrative tasks. It was no different from being an entry-level assistant at any other successful company that manufactured popular consumer products. The only distinction was that magazine clients are a bit unusual; on any given day at work I might encounter one of the Backstreet Boys, a cast member of *Dawson's Creek*, or an A-list designer like Todd Oldham. But, believe it or not, even they seemed to blend into the background of the editorial office after the first few weeks.

When I started, I felt sorely out of place. The look and feel of the office contrasted with the college atmosphere I'd grown accustomed to. At school, at least 50 percent of the faces in my classes or in my dorm were nonwhite. Here, I was the lone woman of color. To make things worse, I didn't feel as if I and the other assistants, who were also recent college grads, had any interests in common. The sensation of being "the token Asian Girl," something I thought was a thing of the past, wriggled back into my consciousness every time the assistant clique passed my workstation. Three assistants, in particular, would stand in front of my desk after returning from their lunch break. They giggled, gossiped, cracked inside jokes. And they pretended I was dead. The fact that this high school scenario bothered me suggested that, at age twenty-two, I still hadn't completely worked through my identity crisis, having grown up Asian American in a conservative, predominantly white town. At the magazine, everything that happened in college was dreamlike; it was as if the self-knowledge and confidence I'd gained through academic rehabilitation were vapor.

During awkward moments with the other assistants, I would try to look busy, fixating on my reflection amid the millions of glowing white dots on my computer screen. I realized then that my journey was far from over. In the company of my college sisters, I knew exactly who I was and where I belonged, but in the midst of these strangers, who didn't show any interest in getting to know me, I was thirteen, invisible again, and trying to look normal, whatever *that* was.

I hadn't felt as close to that girl as I did then, or so keenly aware of once gaping wounds that now slept under a canopy of scar tissue. What was going on? Would I ever stop tripping over girlhood "trau-maramas," which seemed so silly on second thought, as a postcollege, professional, young woman?

There I was, stuck sitting near the assistant who most resembled the archetypal Popular Girl. On more than one occasion, I caught myself staring at the back of her head as she thumbed through her trusty thesaurus. I looked for dandruff on her little black sweater, a zit on her forehead, a misplaced strand in her otherwise perfectly curled coif. And then, out of nowhere, I was revisited by memories of Scotch tape, the hair dye, and Niki Taylor wearing "Oriental" eyes.

One evening, back in the fall of 1998, I had a revelation. Well, it was more like a critical kick in the ass. Right before packing up my things at the end of a long workday, I received an e-mail from my college professor. The message read:

Dearest Vickie, How are things at the magazine? I think it's the perfect time for you to go forward with your teen anthology project. A book about growing-up experiences among Asian American teens would be a success!
Love, Elena

It was fate that Elena sent me that note, right then, and in a voice that bore such conviction. Elena reminded me of my dream: to collaborate with Asian American teen girls on a book that, for once, would privilege their voices and perspectives on issues that might otherwise never be discussed at length in any mainstream teen-oriented TV shows, books, or magazines. Something that had more to do with my reality than Jennifer Love Hewitt's radiant, carefree grin.

My dog-eared copy of *Making Waves*, a groundbreaking anthology of writings by Asian American women, looked lonely sitting on my shelf. The book I envisioned would serve many purposes, in addition to being a resource for teen girls. It would fill the void that existed on Asian American girls' reading list; it would address issues that wouldn't be discussed in an anthology for mainstream, Euro-American girls. And it would be an Asian American book from the standpoint of girls who were growing up in contemporary society—something I wish I had during those years in Rochester. I wouldn't have stayed awake at night, wondering if I was alone in facing these challenges.

The anthology would build on the lessons I was still learning at the magazine about the multiple transitions we experience as individuals who are always evolving, and always growing up. It would blur the boundaries between the different generations by suggesting that all of us—girls, young women, and mature women alike—have legitimate questions to ask and insight to offer one another.

Turning my pie-in-the-sky idea into reality would require some quick thinking. I was overwhelmed by the size of the project, but as I saw it, my only choice was to move forward. The first task on my agenda was finding other girls who were interested in taking this journey with me. When I envisioned my travel companions, they were girls who were sick of stockpiling their untold stories, and who wanted to speak out about obstacles, self-reaffirming victories, or anything else that helped them gain a fuller understanding of who they are and how they see the world. *This book was going to happen.* That evening, before going to bed, I called my sister and my mom. They listened to me brainstorm an elaborate plan to launch the first-ever teen anthology by Asian American girls, mumbling something on the lines of "You go, girl!" and "You should go to bed, it's late."

The title of the anthology came to me after a long, restless night. When I opened my eyes in the morning, the first thing I saw was two words: yellow girls. The sleepy fog that engulfed me retreated, and these words slowly diverged to form three: yell-oh girls. Thus *YELL-Oh Girls!*—the title of the anthology—was born.

It is the radical act of reclaiming and redefining the word *yellow* that thrills me. In the context of our anthology, "yellow" takes on a new meaning. Old newspapers, magazines, and travelogues reveal phrases like "yellow peril," "yellowface," and "yellowskins," which remind us of the ways in which "yellow" has historically been linked to negative stereotypes of Asians. Society has reinforced these images, pushing Asian Americans to the periphery in all areas of our culture. "Yellow" has been used to define skin color (even though Asian skin comes in a wide range of colors and hues), and carries with it other racist assumptions. On our terms, however, the hyphenated "yell-oh" does not define or create barriers between Asian Americans. Simply put, the term "*YELL*-Oh" is a call to action.

During the next couple of weeks, I funneled my creative energy into getting the word out about the anthology. I revised the submission guidelines over and over. I concentrated on the first line of the message: *There is no single, prescribed way of growing up an Asian American girl.* SEND. With fingers crossed, I waited for replies.

The wires linking girls and women on the Web were on fire. The news spread between cities, states, and countries. I rented a P.O. box to handle the influx of mail I was receiving. Soon I had gotten over 500 poems, essays, and illustrations—the work came to me on torn journal paper, fluorescent stickies, and pretty stationery embellished with Sanrio paraphernalia and all sorts of wild, supportive testimonials.

If the publishing companies needed proof that there was a pressing need for the anthology, this was it. Liz, seventeen, of Monterey Park, California, wrote: "This book means so much to me. I can already hear my sisters speaking, and I realize I'm not alone anymore. I've never been so attentive, so ready to hear people talk as I am now." My heart sang! Kira, sixteen, of Chicago, Illinois, wrote: "You have no idea how long I've been waiting for a book like *YELL-Oh Girls!* to be dreamed up!" Our dream was finally becoming a reality, and other notable Asian American women were stepping up to bat for the book as well. When I met Phoebe Eng, she instantly took me under her wing, taught me her "Warrior Lessons," and told everyone she knew, "*YELL-Oh Girls!* will give us a message that America needs to hear—Asian American girls can and will speak for themselves, with power, attitude, and inspiring artistry."

Submissions rolled in, forming a heap on the floor of my cramped apartment, and my roommate Hera marveled every time she walked around it to get to her bedroom. I sat on our hardwood floor, writing postcards to girls, who sent in stories and poems, which unveiled intimate aspects of their lives.

Each piece struck a familiar chord. For example, we talked about the first time we heard the word *chink*. And the first time we saw our parents being harassed because they were immigrants or because they couldn't speak English. Grace Song, twenty, submitted an unsent letter she wrote to her father, and the tears streamed. We identified with Grace, who didn't know how to express affection and love toward her ailing father. It always came time to lighten the mood, though, so I tried to end each sitting on an uplifting note—perhaps with a story about triumph. I played some funky tunes from a CD that a girl named Mia from the Midwest sent to me. She was a badass Korean American drummer of an all-girl rock band, who was out to show audiences that Asian girls could crank out some mean lyrics and jam with the best of 'em.

By corresponding with girls throughout North America, we were forming alliances. Every day we alternated roles, back and forth, from the role of student to the role of mentor. Being Asian American girls didn't mean that we espoused similar perspectives. How could we? The fact is, we're growing up in vastly diverse settings—our parents aren't the same, we have different family histories and socioeconomic backgrounds. And yet, in some ways, we are like every other young person in America. To say that our stories don't reveal threads of shared experiences, however, would be inaccurate. We empathized with each other's joys and frustrations.

While each girl's perspective is unique, common themes echo throughout, evoking the group's subtle yet distinctive collective consciousness. Early on, I refused to categorize the selections according to rigidly defined chapters. It was plainly obvious that there were intersections between them, so the challenge was to create a structure for the anthology that would create space for themes and pieces to interact and overlap. The issues we address in *YELL-Oh Girls!* are markedly distinct and, arguably, more complex than those discussed in other mainstream books on adolescence. Our stories appear "typical" only from the surface, but, because our writings reflect the consciousness of girls who are of Asian descent, our realities spin on a completely different axis.

In the first chapter, we come closer to mapping our locations. Girls explore the meaning of Asian America, and they articulate the feelings of being lost, then found, and searching for home. You'll notice that throughout the anthology, we offer a loose interpretation of Asian America, as many of our contributors have lived in various parts of North America during their growing-up years. In "Family Ties" we examine complex relationships with siblings, parents, and grandparents. "Dolly Rage" is comprised of poignant, brutally honest, nostalgic stories about adolescence. Here we discuss issues that many girls deal with, not only Asian American girls—everything from body image to peer pressure to racial prejudice in school. In "Finding My Voice," girls discover the power of the pen, using language to shape their own identities. They pass the torch in the next few pages to sisters who are fed up, are tired of staying put, and are setting out to change the rules. Girls riding the activist tide speak out in the last chapter, entitled "Girlwind: Emerging Voices for Change." We've organized the selections so that readers can take the journey along with us, experiencing every ebb and flow of our lives.

Throughout history we've witnessed countless Asian American women who have overcome adversity and celebrated personal triumphs. The best way to recognize our many triumphs as Asian American women is by paying homage to the women who spearheaded the Asian American literary movement, filling the empty space in the "American" consciousness with our stories, visions, and dreams. To celebrate their work, we have peppered our pan-Asian collection with their cherished girlhood stories, which many of us have stashed in our hope chests—magazine clippings and book excerpts that we will refer to frequently, reread, and pass on to our sisters, girlfriends, mothers, and daughters.

The women mentors whose work is featured at the end of each chapter have, in some way, demonstrated a strong commitment toward nurturing young women and infusing our imagination with colorful possibilities. Their bricks-and-mortar stories reflect patience, honesty, and compassion and create a solid foundation upon which meaningful dialogues can occur.

On the verge of a new millennium, we are thriving in a rich, contemporary landscape. And *YELL-Oh Girls!* is long overdue. Our collective mission is to increase cultural awareness, to teach each other the importance of self-love, and to promote self-expression. This anthology will be a lasting resource claiming a spot on our bookshelves that will serve as a reminder that we are not invisible, and we are not alone. Together, we can find our way home safely and successfully. My dream is that these writings will inspire girls everywhere to speak out or—if they want—to *YELL like hell*.

Janice Mirikitani is a Sansei, or a third-generation Japanese American, born in California, interned as an infant with her family in Rohwer, Arkansas, during World War II. She has studied at the University of California at Los Angeles, the University of California at Berkeley, and at San Francisco State University. She is currently the Executive Director of Programs and President of Glide Church, a major multiservice/multicultural urban center and church in San Francisco, where she lives with her husband, Reverend Cecil Williams, and her daughter, Tianne.

Who Is Singing This Song
BY JANICE MIRIKITANI

Who is singing this song?

I am.

a child in dark streets,
seeking a home,
a woman who needs safety
in a world of shadows.
I am the one struggling to be free,
a dancer, astronaut, teacher, anyone

I want to be,
longing for clean drink of water/air to breathe deeply.
Who is singing this song?

   I am.
breaking silences, a witness, storyteller.
We survived by hearing.
We discover one another . . .
each of us yielded by hands of the transplanted,
adventurers, escapees, pregnant with dreams.
We explore our similar histories,
Light surrounds us, our hands
are warmed, alive . . .

Who is singing this song?

   I am.
pulled by hands of history to not sit
in these times, complacently,
walkmans plugged to our ears,
computers, soap operas lulling our passions to sleep.
We are required by legacies of grandparents, parents,
our enslaved and servant ancestors, our heroes and sheroes,
our fighters for freedom, to be
now the storm of hands
that wave in protest against apartheid, racism, classism, sexism,
   war, hate crime violence and indifference to the poor.

   (We are required by these hands of history
   to extend our hands to save the children,
   from Howard Beach and Stockton playground massacres,
   from Harlem to Wounded Knee,
   Honduran sweatshops to Haitian detention centers,
   Atlanta to Delano, Ethiopia to Enowetok,

Birmingham to Bosnia,
Tiananmen Square to the Tenderloin)

Who is singing this song?

   I am.
We survive by hearing.
We speak to each other,
offering choices,
to love, to dream,
to extend our hands, to dance,
to cringe, to kiss, to not kiss.

I DARE YOU,
dare you
to love, to dream, to kiss . . .

Who is singing this song?
   I am.
       You are.

Our music is beautiful.

The day after my high school graduation, I boarded a plane. Next stop, Korea. My parents waved good-bye with nervous yet hopeful smiles, and my mom yelled, "Behave yourself!" like she always did when I was flying somewhere to visit family friends or relatives.

My parents had enrolled me in a cultural immersion summer program—a "discover your roots" pilgrimage, of sorts—at Yonsei University in Seoul. For five weeks I lived in a dormitory with hundreds of other second-generation Korean American girls and guys in their late teens.

Week one of the program flew by, and not without knocking my self-confidence down a few notches. My language skills were poor, and I was having a difficult time adapting to the climate. I didn't know where to begin when I called my mother to tell her about my first days, but there was something I'd been dying to ask her ever since stepping off the plane at Kimpo International Airport. At the time I tried squeezing an explanation out of my grandmother, but she didn't seem to understand my question.

"Mom, what does 'gyo-po' mean?" Had I said hello to her yet? I couldn't remember.

"Gyo-po" is what the natives—taxi drivers, waiters, saleswomen, and the like—were calling me everywhere I went. I could tell that it was a noun, and I also noticed that people sometimes uttered the word quickly and impatiently in passing. But beyond these observations, I knew nothing.

My mother cleared her throat. "It means foreigner."

She asked me where I'd heard the expression. I told her, everywhere, and that gyo-po had become my nickname here in Seoul.

So that I didn't have to linger by the phone booth for too long, I got into the habit of writing down all of the things I needed to tell my parents in advance of calling them. It was boiling, inside and outside; the thick, soupy air felt hotter than my own breath. In a letter to my friend in the States, I told her that here you didn't move from one place to the next, *you swam.* Although I was ashamed to admit it, central airconditioning was definitely one of the things I missed most.

"Oh, it means foreigner?" I echoed. I didn't have much else to say to my mom that day. Nothing on my list seemed important anymore.

So for the next two months, I was a gyo-po, a foreigner. Viewing the city streets from above, stringy black dots bobbed up and down and darted from side to side. On ground level, I noticed that it didn't matter that I looked like everybody else; I was still singled out for being different. The pictures that were taken of me my first day in Seoul tell an interesting story. Now, all I can see is that my Western stance, my Kodak camera, and my Doc Martens were dead giveaways; I might as well have draped myself in an American flag. The thing is, and all of the other American-born kids agreed with this conjecture, even if we weren't wearing Western clothes, the natives still would have pegged us Americans. We joked constantly about our unique gyo-po status; this erased the sting of rejection by the Korean community. To the locals, we smelled funny, we talked funny, and we just didn't belong.

A few days before the program ended, one of my girlfriends and I were coming back from a long day of shopping. We wanted to stock up on all necessary foodstuffs, souvenirs, and rip-off Gucci handbags before going back to the States. Exhausted, we hailed a cab. It was too late before we found out that we'd hailed one of the few taxicabs in the city that didn't have an air-conditioner. But this wasn't the worst part.

The driver, a fifty-something man, glared at us in the rearview mirror. He was angry. Shaking his finger in the air, he grumbled, "You kids are not Korean, and your parents are traitors for having left their homeland."

He drove in circles around the Yonsei University campus, and my friend and I wondered if he was ever going to stop lecturing, or stop driving. We were terrified. We could accept that the man thought we were unappreciative, ill-mannered, stupid Twinkie kids (yellow on the outside, white on the inside), but was he eventually going to stop the car and turn us loose? My girlfriend grabbed my arm and whispered through the side of her mouth, "Do you think he's going to kidnap us and sell us into slavery?" I assured her that the driver would drop us off as soon as he was done bitching. But when we reached a red traffic light, I yanked the car door open and threw a couple bills over the seat. We jetted.

The previous few weeks had been filled with similar experiences. My friends in the program and I were kicked out of night clubs because there were "already too many gyo-pos" inside, received poor service at restaurants, were snubbed by women at clothing stores and salons—in some cases, the discrimination we faced in Korea had been far more intense than anything we'd confronted in America. Even though our friendships were growing stronger, many of us couldn't wait to get back home.

But when I finally arrived home in Rochester, I remember weaving through crowds of people who were milling about the baggage claim. It just didn't feel like it was my life I was returning to. After being home-sick for the warmth and security, I was depressed that it felt like I was visiting another foreign country.

Being that I was one of few Asian girls who lived in my hometown, I was accustomed to feeling like the outsider. But in Korea, where everyone shared the same (or almost the same) skin and eye color, I thought that somehow I'd magically fit right in. Instead, I felt more estranged strolling along the streets in Seoul than I did hanging out in the predominantly white, conservative suburb where I grew up. I was a gyo-po in Korea, a foreigner in the States. So, where was my country?

In the fall I began my first year in college and felt myself being shifted from one location to another. I was like an Asian Dorothy, clicking my heels together, and trying to envision a place that felt like home. I remember my literature professor giving a lecture one afternoon, in which she defined the word *liminal*—as in a liminal existence. After hearing her description, I thought my picture should appear next to that word in the dictionary because I was suspended between two worlds, sitting on a hyphen that bridges and separates. Asian-American.

It was during that first semester in college that things were slowly beginning to gel. The summer of 1993 was a benchmark in my youth. I learned more about myself in Korea than I had in all the years I had stayed in the tiny little town in upstate New York. Now I no longer expected that the fragments of information I'd collected throughout my childhood would neatly snap together to form some definitive cultural identity. Instead I discovered that welding irregular pieces and edges together often created beautiful patterns. I also learned to stop trying to find a "home" in the traditional sense—either in Asia or in America—but to embrace my unique situation as being in Asian America.

In the following chapter, called "Orientation," young pioneers explore the Asian American landscape and share their travel journals with us. Coming home seems like an easy thing to do, but when you're rooted in two worlds that are oceans apart, finding your way home can take a lifetime. These contributors are fine storytellers. They are world-class navigators who rely on the things they've learned about history (written and oral), their cultural heritage, and their personal experiences, to guide them on their adventures.

In the short story "The Train," Meggy Wang writes about the East-West divide. She harnesses the feeling of being torn between two cultures and of wanting to find validation as someone whose home is neither in Asia nor America. "The Train" is a story about a girl who finds herself only after she gets off at the wrong stop.

I met Jennifer Sa-rlang Kim, a poetess from Pennsylvania, at a coffee shop in New York, where we discussed her works in progress. In one of her poems called "Where are you from?," which you'll find in this chapter, an elderly woman asks her to reveal her ethnicity. Jennifer turns the tables on her inquisitor. By raising her own unexpected questions during the encounter, Jennifer makes it impossible for either of them to ignore the complexity of a person's ethnicity, race, and cultural orientation. And while she volunteers new ways of thinking about and answering the obligatory question "Where are you from?" Jennifer also embraces her Korean American identity.

When I first started this project, I wasn't sure whether girls were thinking about the thousands of immigrants who arrived in America prior to the twentieth century. My "call for submissions" flyer didn't suggest that writers should submit essays that were written from a historical perspective. But girls' responses indicated that they were doing their own research to fill in the gaps; clearly, their mainstream American history books were glossing over the Asian American experience. Last year I came across a compelling piece written by Gloria Ng. Gloria paid tribute to the Asian immigrants who, after beating the odds in coming to America, were detained on Angel Island, the immigration station located in San Francisco. She recently visited the monument for the first time, and she talks about why the island is meaningful to her in "Distance, Time, and Wingspan."

And you've probably heard this before: Hawaii is the home of tourists. Well, according to whom? Not Elena Cabatu. In "Paradise Ain't Shit So Why Don't You Jus' Shut Yoa' Mout'," Elena has a few choice words for travelers and other nonnatives who can't shake the media-driven, stereotypical images of "paradise" long enough to imagine Hawaii (Hilo, to be exact) as a home, *her home.*

Activist and writer Helen Zia's book *Asian American Dreams: The Emergence of an American People*, a groundbreaking book that encourages us all to examine the changing presence of Asians in America by rethinking our histories, came out while I was collecting submissions. I immediately called my editor to tell her that we had to include one of Zia's memoirs in our anthology. We chose a personal memoir, which begins the sixth chapter of her book, entitled "Welcome to Washington." Zia offers us an earnest and insightful piece that makes sense of many of the questions we are asking ourselves about finding our way home.

Currently I am a student at Columbia University in New York City. My writing is inspired by the struggles that I have experienced in realizing that my "culture" is neither completely Korean nor American but a combination of both. Although this blend of cultures is unique and a very significant and cherished aspect of my life, it sometimes comes with the burden of feeling like I do not belong anywhere or relate to anyone. In spite of it all, I would not trade my culture or my experiences for anything.

Two

Raised in two separate cultures
Growing up in a world with customs
Familiar at home and foreign in society

Reaching, roaring,
Rocking between things that surround
And lessons of a homeland farther away

Seeing crowds of endless faces different from your own
Hearing English words mixed with native tongues
Tasting foods loaded with thick flavor and warm spices

Scarlet passion
Craving, calling
To accept a blend of opposites
To create an experience unique to you
A struggle to convey thoughts to those who cannot understand
Despite the
Searching

Studying what cannot be taught or read in lines

The experience that only comes from
Living, loving
Leaving one behind
The choice to abandon one completely for the other
Causing betrayal and ignorant hatred
Compulsions that wrench you violently from both sides
Fighting, fearing,
Fitting into two places
Two cultures
Or maybe none.

meggy**wang**17
Los Gatos, California

I was born in a blustery Michigan environment and raised in northern California. Seventeen years later, I am finishing my senior year at Los Gatos High School, not necessarily unscathed, but certainly worn and torn in rather beneficial ways. What makes this essay similar to other "identity pieces" is what also makes it important. Looking back, I wrote "The Train" in a doldrum-ic state; however, in contemplating one's own existence, thoughts are bound to come in ups and downs.

The Train

"Where are we going? Where are we going?"

My brother was pestering my mother for the hundredth time as we walked through the train station. The air was hot and muggy, making him louder and my mother more irritable. We were toting two cans of guava juice from the vending machine by the ticket stand, but even they were beginning to lose their cooling effect as beads of condensation dripped down the sides. Guava juice is practically the only thing I drink in Taiwan; it's fresh, not fake-tasting like Chinese orange juice, and it's not a warm beverage.

"Tainan," my mother replied sharply. "We're going to Tainan."

Public transit in Taiwan is much more popular than it is here in the United States, mostly because Taiwan is about the size of California, putting less emphasis on private vehicular transport. There weren't enough seats for us to sit together, so my mother placed my brother and me into a passenger car by ourselves.

"When we reach our stop, I'll come get you," she said. "Don't leave."

We nodded obediently. I was thirteen, already headed into the depths of adolescence, and my brother was nine years old. Being in Taiwan made me nervous because while my brother could easily pass as a native youth, I was obviously American. I couldn't quite pinpoint what it was about me that screamed "American-born Chinese!" but whatever it was, everyone could sense it. It was in the way I spoke, my mannerisms, my skin, even the way my face developed in the absence of a true Chinese environment.

Approximately two hours later, after watching numerous cows and rice fields roll by, the train made yet another stop and the loudspeakers blared: *"Dau luh. Tainan tzan." (We have now arrived at the Tainan station.)*

My brother, who had been extremely antsy throughout the train ride, leapt out of his seat. "It's Tainan," he said. "This is our stop!"

I grabbed his arm. "Hey. Wait until Mom comes to get us."

I kept my hand on his arm as we watched people go by: old women with their graying husbands clutching suitcases, young women with their trendy Western clothing, children and their doting mothers, all very frazzled and tired-looking. As the people trickled away, we grew more and more nervous.

"Last call for Tainan," the announcer blared.

"Maybe she got off the train already. Maybe there wasn't time for her to come to our car," my brother piped nervously. "We should go."

Allen shoved me into the aisle. We stood by the door, craning our necks to peer down both sides. The irritated man by the door asked, "Are you getting off at Tainan or not?"

I blinked and turned my head to look at him. In my accented Mandarin, I said, "Yes, but——"

"Well, then," he answered shortly, "Get off. This isn't a vista point."

Under the glare of the doorman, we stepped off the train and looked around anxiously at the depot. There were about thirty people milling around, but my mother was not one of them. As the people dispersed like so many globules of oil in a pot of soup, and as the train pulled away from the station, it became obvious that our mother was nowhere to be found.

"I think we're lost," said my brother in a moment of pure wisdom.

"Yeah."

"I don't see her," he continued in a more panicky voice.

Thank God for kindergarten safety education, which I hearkened when I spotted a man in a uniform by the tracks. Pulling my brother behind me, I said to him (in more accented Mandarin), "Excuse me, sir, but my brother and I seem to have gotten off the train without our mother. . . . She said we were getting off at Tainan, but we can't find her. She's not here."

He peered at us curiously, then cast an eye over the area around us. "Come with me."

We followed him into the station itself. Allen was near tears as he led us to the Information section. Two other men were there. They were also in uniform, and peered down at us from their stoops.

"Now, tell me again what happened," the man said.

I told him again, quicker this time, as if to achieve a greater illusion of fluency.

"And is your mother especially old?"

"No."

"Well, then, she couldn't have forgotten you out of senility." He grinned with amusement. "I'll call the station ahead, then." He went behind the booth to where the phone was, made a phone call, and turned to us again.

"Your mother is worried sick about you two," he said. "She's taking a taxi from the next stop to Tainan. Just wait over there with the rest of the passengers and she'll be coming shortly." My brother exhaled a long, relieved sigh.

"Thank you," I said, feeling proud of my ability to remain calm and communicate in a foreign country. "We're from America, you see, so we don't really know what we're doing."

"Oh, really?" The other uniformed men stared quizzically at us. "You're from America? What state?"

I didn't know how to say California, so I stuttered my way through. "We're from near San Francisco," which literally translates to "Old Golden Mountain" in Chinese.

They started laughing. I wondered if I had drool leaking out of the side of my mouth, or if I had just called my dead ancestors something obscene without knowing it.

"You don't know how to say *California* in Mandarin?" one finally asked.

My pride sank. "No, I don't."

More laughter. Allen, who had since calmed down upon realizing that we were going to be recovered, walked over to the passenger area while my cheeks burned with embarrassment. I was reminded of my male cousin, who had laughed at my inability to read the Chinese newspaper outside of a few words like *you* and *China*.

As I played with the unraveling thread on my skirt, I also recalled an incident in Seattle a few months earlier, during which my father and I had visited the Lake Washington botanical gardens. He had asked an elderly male to please take a picture of us beneath a large white tree.

"Oh, sure," he said with a charitable smile. Picking up the camera, he asked, "So, are you visiting the country?" I almost cried.

It was there in the train station in Tainan that I realized that I was a foreigner everywhere I went, no matter how fluent I was in English or how un-American my facial features were. I could be mistaken for an Asian tourist as certainly as I could be laughed at for being an ill-spoken A.B.C. (American-Born Chinese) out of place in her parents' homeland. When my mother finally came to the station, her eyes red from frantic crying, she told us that we were really going to Shinying, not Tainan, and that we were at the wrong place at the wrong time.

I couldn't help but agree.

There's a very Western view in which somehow you need to resolve the tension between any two things, to want things to come to a kind of conclusion . . . whereas I've been wondering where this whole idea of fluidity comes from, and I think it's because I grew up with an [Eastern] idea of yin/yang, sweet/sour. Opposites don't fight each other, but belong together and can intensify each other, and are simply in the nature of the world.

—Author Gish Jen, in an article that appeared in *AsianWeek* (September 27, 1996)

jennifer sa-rlang**kim**20
Glen Mills, Pennsylvania

I was born in Lima, Pennsylvania, to Kim Chon Tae and Kim Sun Hui. Failing to be true to the sheer superficiality of my suburbanite background, I found refuge in bitter and sarcastic conversations with myself. Apart from this blatant confession of "weirdness," I have come to treasure the written and the spoken word. It is only inside those blue and pink lines that I'm laughing and crying, mesmerized by the silent sound of sincerity.

Where Are You From?

Where are You From?
a sweet
elderly

German-Polish
woman
inquires
Glen Mills.
    oh,
    but
    Where are you
    Really
    from?
Glen Mills.
    No,
    You must be
    mistaken
    I mean originally.
Where are You
Originally from,
I
inquire.
New York.
No, I mean Where are you Really from?
Fluster, fluster, fluster.
Two women unable, refusing to answer a simple question of
Origin.
I suppose you mean
Originally?
    Yes.
Germany and Poland.
Well, then I guess I'd have to say
Korea
America.

sarah**chang**17
Douglaston, New York

A seventeen-year-old senior at Hunter College High School, I am listening to Simon and Garfunkel's "The 59th Street Bridge Song (Feelin' Groovy)" as I write this bio. I am the product of two people whose families originate from North Korea—and, the product of my own self-reflection. In this story, I rode a Greyhound bus from Seattle to Ellensburg, Washington, with this Coke can to keep me company. I experienced a modern version of the American western movement, except that I wasn't a pioneer battling Mother Nature and the harsh laws of the land. I was a teenage girl wondering why the open land was appealing to the American heart, and why we as a society consume so much Coke. I sank into my seat, exhausted, wishing that something or someone would break the flat horizon.

Watching America with a Coke

I scratched a line into the sun-baked gravel that looked too clean to be public. The line I just made, it looked like the West Coast. Gray stones gave way to a dirt brown palette as I continued to dig with my toe. This activity certainly wasn't working. I could still see the monstrous bus with its monotonous sighs and grunts just 10 feet from where I stood. That bus was too stuffy, too silent, and too empty for me to reenter eagerly.

I was on my way to Ellensburg/Washington/U.S.A. It's a great place, really it is, this America we speak of. But traveling America was not my primary concern. My primary concern was the stink of dusty bus seats, painfully decorated with primary colors in a background of dark gray that failed to achieve sophistication. No, I take that back. My primary concern was the empty soda can in the back of the bus that refused to be picked up and continued to roll, roll, roll, and roll some more. Hell, I just didn't want to be indoors with people who twisted themselves into positions I thought never possible in order to fit on two bus seats they would have liked to call "bed," or "home," or "creative freedom."

I woke up two hours later, twisted. Great, I thought. I've become one of them.

The bus rolled on past flat ground whose only comfort seemed to be intrusive telephone poles that told no tale, so randomly placed that dogs wouldn't even piss on them. The can was still rolling, the seats still stank of miles of concrete, and America continued to roll past my window of monochrome.

The man with the tight jeans and balding arms sitting across the twelve-inch aisle from me said, "Arigato go jai mas." I thought, for what? I should've said smartly, "You're welcome" and shut him up. But I didn't. So he didn't shut up. Hearing no response he said, "Ah! Nee-hao mah." This time, I didn't even bother turning my head. I said, "No English." I hate this country.

I closed my eyes, swearing that I'd go pick up that can at the next service stop.

I woke up an hour later. My ass was asleep and the image outside my window had come to a halt. It was a service stop. Great, I could use some Coke.

The small mom-and-pop store had the TV mounted on a makeshift shelf that looked two days old. And as I wrinkled various plastic packages looking for those stupid Twinkies, the people of Seattle/Washington/U.S.A. threw out the first ball of the last game to take place at the Kingdome. Pity—another all-American moment.

I got back on the bus last and walked past the greasy bus driver, the tight jeans man, and numerous other shapeless lumps. The smell had just gotten worse. The rubber flooring squeaked under my sneakers in fifty different pitches and then I remembered the can. It was a Coke can smiling a cheerful fire-engine red, bubbling with American commercialism gone child-friendly.

I picked it up with two fingers and only two fingers. I tossed it into an empty seat, making sure it had a view with a window. I wanted it to watch America go by with the rest of us.

gloria**ng**21
Davis, California

I come from Nine Dragons, Fragrant Harbor, in my birth year of
the Horse. I first tapped into my feminist-of-color consciousness in
college away from the still limited U.S. K–12 public school educa-
tion system. As a queer feminist of color, I find natural alliance
with various activisms and oral histories. Perhaps others' politi-
cization will, in the future, take less than the two decades it took
me. I still see my mainland Chinese and Hong Kong-nese parents in
San Francisco and my relatives abroad.

Distance, Time, and Wingspan

What comes to mind when you hear the word *angel*? Many of us
may easily conjure images of guardian angels or angel-like characters we've seen on TV sitcoms, but for others—especially for Asians
who grow up in San Francisco—the word *angel* carries a more significant meaning. It's more than a reference to a spiritual protector
in flight. When I hear the word, I think of a neighboring mass of
rock, dirt, tree, and gravel jutting into the surface of pacific waters.
As a young, Chinese American, immigrant woman, the legacy of
Angel Island is highly significant to me at the turn of the century.

I came to the United States with my mother and father in 1979,
when I was one y-squared (one year young). We settled in Saam
Fann See, where a significant amount of Chinese people resided.
My parents didn't know how to speak English, and for the first six
months in the States, they remained unemployed. Due to immigration laws in the late 1970s, only my nuclear family was allowed to
immigrate.

They came in a wave of Southeast Asians who were immigrating
to the U.S. They believed they could start afresh in the "land of
opportunity." In the late 1970s, my extended family was still
barred from immigrating to this country with my father. According

to the law, my relatives weren't considered part of our nuclear family. In a desire to appear the "savior"—the country that provides sanctuary for refugees fleeing violence and persecution in their homelands—the U.S. admitted only my parents and me. I imagine the immigration officials thought they were admitting two adult non-English speakers, who wouldn't be vying for the same jobs as the white population; they imagined my parents perhaps working at the Chinese restaurants in "Old Gold Mountain."

In college I learned the history of immigration, and I examined the restrictions that were passed by the government to control the number of Asians who were entering the country—the Chinese Exclusion Act of 1882, for example, which banned all Chinese laborers from coming to the U.S. And I discovered that between 1910 and 1940, the U.S. government, alarmed by the sudden influx of Chinese, started to interrogate as many as 175,000 of them to ascertain information regarding the newly arrived immigrants' familial relations with U.S. Chinese citizens. All of this took place at Angel Island, which the government saw as a protective entity, a structure that policed their borders in order to achieve a necessary good, perhaps by securing a necessary commodity, like cheap labor. What I realized is that my Chinese American elders saw Angel Island from the "other" perspective; it was a reminder to safeguard secrets of actual family relations for fear that they might otherwise be deported. It also warned them about the possibility of being separated from their family members.

The first time I'd ever visited Angel Island was shortly after graduating from college. I decided to go out on my own in search of the Immigration Station. The day started out cloudy with occasional sun that winked through the clouds.

The salty bay winds clashed with the UV light, and the combination gave me a pulsing headache by the time I had reached the topmost deck of the boat that would bring us to the island. Energetic grade school kids in summer camp sat with me on the hard gray-blue benches. Girls teased each other about crushes and kisses. Boys competed with each other to make the most sound with palm-to-armpit suction flaps. Some grade school experiences transmit from one generation to another, I thought. The noise and banter, though, only made me begin to doubt whether I had chosen the right boat, the right deck, the right day for this adventure. I was relieved to step onto the dock. Somewhat dizzy and dehydrated after the ferry ride, I trudged forward to the Northridge Trail, intent on reaching my destination: the Immigration Station.

Toting a couple bucks and a bagged pink bakery box of Chinese pastries for lunch, I continued walking past the sign marking the trail. Dust rose behind my soles as I started up the slope. On the way, I found an angular staircase of tiered vertical wooden panels with packed even dirt. Even though the clouds had parted by that time, a lot of trees still sheltered me from the abundant sunlight. I heaved after two flights of stairs. *Dang it, I should have kept a regular exercise regimen in college*. I paused momentarily and revved up again. I made sure to breathe through my nose. I sighed in relief as the trail's top loomed into sight.

Where the trail's terminal met a winding gravel road, I turned left and realized that there was more shelter from the sun. I heard gravel grinding against gravel, and felt the pieces get wedged in the grooves of my tennis shoes. The grinding was rhythmic and slow as I advanced toward the station. I occasionally paused during the long walk and glanced out at the bay to restore my patience. A speedboat rides the crests, its posterior foam reminding me of the train of a wedding gown.

Finally, I spotted the welcome sign. I approached the largest building, went up two flights of stairs, and joined a gathering of other tourists at the door of the Immigration Station Museum. A white male docent greeted us. We entered the front lobby, where we saw a year-round exhibit that educated visitors about the Immigration Station: what it was built for, when it existed, what people did there. My eyes delighted at the "Protest and Poetry" information plaque, which contained information I hadn't been aware of from reading the two-line descriptions of Angel Island in U.S. history textbooks. Some of the people detained here did not passively accept U.S. immigration policies, living conditions, and poor treat-ment—many spoke out against the injustices. Thinking we'd reached the end of the exhibit, I was disappointed that it didn't take up as much space as I thought it demanded.

But the exhibit went further. The docent told us that we would enter rooms where we would see sculpted people. He told the kids not to get scared, and not to touch the walls, which were becoming worn over time. We went into a room where dozens of bunk beds lined the floor almost from wall to wall, floor to ceiling. Linen hung from clotheslines. A sculpted woman on one of the topmost bunks was folding linen. Did they have soap to wash their clothes? Or only water? I breathed deeply—if I tried hard enough, maybe I could actually smell freshly washed linens. Instead, numerous paint-shedding poles that buttressed the ceiling let off metallic plumes, which assaulted my nostrils and fed my wavering headache. I imag-ined the winter cold seeping through cracks, summer heat baking the topmost bunks, and rain raising the humidity of the rooms. I imagined people who, in their old age, probably had arthritis.

The docent briefed us on living conditions, including police surveillance, strict room entry and exit rules, gender-segregated rooms, children residing with their mothers. And we went on to see poetry carved on the walls, which expressed anger, despair, sadness, and criticism of U.S. hypocrisy. The guide mentioned that when new poems appeared on the walls, law enforcement officers would paint over them as if the writing were graffiti. The poems that existed for public viewing had been carved into the walls. Afterward, we went into an interrogation room, where a sculpted Chinese male was being questioned about his familial relations. The interrogation process could last from several days to several years. I start to feel ashamed about having been so impatient to walk the gravel road on the way to the station.

Perhaps my perception of my trip to Angel Island seems far-fetched, a flight of fancy. But if we don't grow wings, how can we imagine a more holistic Asian America, one rich with history? I dare to imagine our wingspan stretching across time. And we can quill our own histories, seek truth, and discover angels within us. Later, as I sat down to write in the comment book, I gazed through an open window and my eyes rested in the distance. The woven metal fence was meant to keep people inside, not keep people out. The thought made me shudder, and I grieved for those who were survived by spirits as a result of this enforced genocide. I recalled one man's story about people who would lure birds to the window so they could smoke them and keep starvation at bay. I wished that I could hear more stories.

In the meantime, imagination is a tool.

Comfortable enough in America, Chinatown, and even Hong Kong or Taiwan, we seem to belong everywhere. And because of this, we might also belong nowhere. "Home," it seems, ends up being a mixed-up notion that must be redefined if it is to have meaning for many of us.

—Author Phoebe Eng, in *Warrior Lessons*

jean**chow**17
Aiea, Hawaii

I was born in Taiwan, but my family moved to the island of Oahu, Hawaii, when I was eight months old. I recently moved to Palo Alto, California, where I am a student at Stanford University. I originally wrote "Memories of Chinatown" for an English assignment, but enjoyed it so much that I continued to revise and edit it even after it was due. Writing about my childhood really sparked a new interest in learning more about my Chinese culture.

Memories of Chinatown

The pig's hollow eyes stared at me. I stared right back. Around this intense staring contest, sounds of excitement whirled. Shouts of "sau ji, sau ya!" (roasted chicken and duck), mingled with "char siu bau!" (roast pork buns), were everywhere. A mix of strange smells in and out through the city streets. It was a typical Saturday morning in Chinatown.

Each weekend my mom, my brother, and I piled into our shiny red Buick and headed to Chinatown while my dad went to work.

"Why do we have to go there? I don't want to go there!" My brother and I would whine and complain during the seemingly long drive, but Mom knew just how to handle us with sweet and tasty bribes. A cold strawberry Icee for each of us was usually enough to keep us quiet.

As a child, I didn't understand why we went to Chinatown. The truth is, I was both fascinated and terrified by the place.

We would walk down the main street, stopping at every market, shop, and stand. The pungent smell of fish, the noisy chatter of shoppers, the sight of panhandlers . . . every aspect of Chinatown filled my world on Saturday mornings.

"Mom, what's that? Look, Mom! Mom, let's go over there!"

This came out in a childish rambling of Mandarin as my attention darted from one thing to the next. What thrilled me most were the boxes lined up in the seafood sections. Live crabs scrambled over each other in an effort to climb the walls and escape from their confines. I peered into the boxes to investigate the scratching sounds and shrieked in fear and delight when one clawed upward at me. I'd hide behind my mom before deciding to make my daring moves once again.

Upon reaching the end of the street, I was tired, thinking about my Icee, which, by then, had long disappeared. Hearing us start up with new complaints, my mom knew just what to do. It was time for lunch—a dim sum lunch. I had never been one to turn down good food. Rattling carts, which sporadically passed the tables, intensified the din of the restaurant. I eagerly awaited the carts, making sure I didn't miss a single dish. After dim sum, we'd pile back into the shiny red Buick and return home in a ride that didn't seem quite as long.

I never understood the significance of our weekly trip to Chinatown. Now I see that it was a way to keep the Chinese culture instilled in me. I was raised in American society, but my parents didn't let me forget or lose the Chinese values that they had been taught. They, too, had taken trips to the market (not exactly "Chinatown" since they actually *lived* in Taiwan!) with their parents when they were young. Someday I hope to continue this tradition and share these experiences with my own children. I have grown up and matured since the days of pig-staring contests, but I will never forget being deeply immersed in the Chinese culture during our weekly Chinatown excursions.

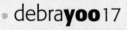

debra**yoo**17
Schaumburg, Illinois

This poem is based on an experience I had while vacationing in New York. I had encountered racism before, but not while I was with my entire family. My parents, who are Korean, attempted to laugh it off, but it put a strange cloud over us as we drove on. I hope this poem will widen the views of those who don't know how racism affects those of different origin; my parents and siblings could not even enjoy a family vacation without being plagued by prejudiced beliefs.

Family Trip

Driving down the road,
    cars cramped and crawling,
fumes sputtering, turning the sky gray.
    A deep breath;
"So this is what New York is like."
    Her almond eyes lit with excitement.

The miles pass at 5 mph,
    searching for a crack, a space, a gap,
A missing stitch
    in the path of a needle,

Big enough to fit
    Five people in a mini van.

Finally, the door slides open,
    kids, parents, pile out,
like black-haired clowns from a car.
    A lasting glance;
Buildings touching the sky,
    Like a child's slender hand reaching for cotton-candy clouds.

A look down the street,
    two animals step forward,
with spotted hair and nose rings like angry bulls.
    They stop and stare,
Stare at the 5 brown-eyed clowns piling out of the car,
    And laugh.

An accusation spat out like venom,
    "Chinks."
Burned a hole in her spirit.
    Almond eyes lose their sparkle,
Everything suspended in a single moment;
    "So this is what New York is like."

elizabeth**kao**21
Kendall Park, New Jersey

Made in Taiwan and marinated in New Jersey for twenty-two years, I am Li-Tze to my relatives and Liz to the rest of the world. If you think I am confused about my identity, however, you are mistaken, for I come from a strong Taiwanese background but have benefited from being an American. During the second year of my undergraduate days at Cornell University, I took a personal writing class and was loosely requested to write about a personal experi-

ence. The product of this assignment was "Re-orienting the Self," a personal essay that I never thought I would share with the reading public. And if you would like to know what came to pass, I will tell you when I find the right words.

Re-orienting the Self

Already halfway through telling her story, my mother burst into the house talking about the great deal she came across at work. From the tone of her voice, I could tell that she had been waiting all day to share the news with me. The unique, familiar mix of Taiwanese, Mandarin, and English filled the quiet house.

My mother's exuberance was contagious. She explained that a coworker had won a round-trip ticket to Taiwan in a raffle, but since the coworker did not have time to take advantage of the soon-to-expire plane ticket, my mother seized the opportunity and purchased the ticket for half the actual value. She stood there grinning proudly and answered my questions before I had a chance to ask them. Soon I learned that I would be traveling alone to visit various relatives and family friends. It would be the first time I would be back in Taiwan since we left ten years ago. As I stumbled upon this realization, I couldn't help but recall the experience I had when we first moved to the United States.

I was nine years old when we left Taiwan. No one explained to me why we were all packing, or even where we were moving. My brother, being the older one, understood a little more and told me that we were going far across the beach to a place where they make "real" hamburgers and speak "gibberish."

"You don't have to go to school tomorrow if you don't want to," said my mother a few days before our departure.

Being a carefree child, I didn't think twice before accepting the offer. My quiet and calm days of walking to school suddenly turned into days of packing all of my belongings into boxes and then watching them disappear. The disappearance of my boxes was followed by the disappearance of my friends and classmates, as well. By enthusiastically deciding to stay home from school, I had inadvertently severed all ties with my childhood companions.

All I had with me when I stepped off the airplane in California was my torn, dirty doll purse, which I clung to with a sense of security. Adding to my confusion, a group of very friendly strangers pinched my cheeks and patted my head as we exited the terminal. Later, I learned that the strangers were actually friends of the family; they drove us to their home, where I met other friendly strangers. We spent the following week going to restaurants where they served food similar to the food in Taiwan, and where everyone spoke Mandarin. I did not understand why nothing had changed. People were speaking a familiar language, and the only gibberish I heard was on television. And we did not eat any hamburgers or foreign foods except for Jell-O. All the store names were written in Chinese and people who strolled along the streets looked no different than the bustling market shoppers in Taipei. When I confronted my mother and told her about my confusion, she laughed at my innocence and explained that we were in a special place called "Chinatown." I smiled back and nodded, even more confused than before.

Our temporary hosts had two kids, who were the same ages as my brother and I. Their names were too difficult to pronounce, so we called each of them "cousin" out of convenience. Our cousins looked no different from my brother and me, but they spoke gibberish to each other, and spoke in Mandarin with a strange accent to us. The language barrier became apparent when they tried to translate Saturday morning cartoons to us, which turned out to be, again, a very confusing experience. The little Mandarin that our cousins knew was insufficient to explain the humor that could be expressed only in English. Like my childhood classmates, my new cousins became a distant memory once my family left California.

In the months that followed, I almost became comfortable with the constant feeling of disorientation. It did not matter that my teacher scribbled seemingly useless characters on the board. It did not matter that my brother's classmates pushed him in the playground because he could not understand the rules of a game he was forced to play. I stopped asking questions because the answers were equally puzzling.

I snapped out of my reverie as soon as I started remembering the intense frustration I felt due to my past inability to communicate. Having returned to the security of my bedroom, I thought about the emotions that had been triggered by my mother's news. Curiosity consumed me as I visualized events as they might unfold upon my arrival in Taiwan. My aunt would bring me a big red apple, like she'd done years ago. My grandmother would bring me tiny slippers that would be worn by me only during my visit. As I imagined possible settings and individuals, I unrealistically pictured myself engaged in fluent conversations with relatives, addressing each one of them according to his or her proper title.

As I get ready for the voyage, a fear of estrangement underlies happy anticipation. Feelings of alienation will surely return when I encounter my relatives speaking in a different tongue and I am unable to fully express my affection. As hard as I might try to imitate the words, which are familiar to my ears, but not to my lips, I will be the isolated American relative who bears the burden of my Taiwanese family's elevated hopes and expectations. They will understand little of the obstacles I faced in order to be like the "cousins" whom I was once in awe of. As my relatives, they will take pride in my American labels and hear only my heavily accented and poorly spoken Mandarin. Despite my effort to explain, they will not understand why I now desire to regain the part of myself that I lost a decade ago. I do not fear what I will find when I make my trip back to Taiwan. I only fear what I must find in myself.

elena**cabatu**21

Hilo, Hawaii

Currently a Washington, D.C., resident, I'm a first-generation Fil-ipino and third-generation Japanese removed from Hawaii's sugar plantation. I rediscovered the local girl in me when I wrote one of my first Pidgin poems, "Paradise Ain't Shit So Why Don't You Jus' Shut Yoa' Mout'." I was fortunate enough to incorporate my cul-tural growth with my course work at Georgetown University by producing two collections of poetry called Try Try *and* Rememba Da Time, *and a collection of short stories called* I Like Try Tell You Something.*

Paradise Ain't Shit So Why Don't You Jus' Shut Yoa' Mout'

Oh, Hawaii,
You're so lucky,
They say.
What island?
The Big Island,
I say.
Oh it must be nice,
They say
With a blank look that asks,
What island is that?
The one with the volcano
The one with snow.
I'm from a town called Hilo.

How did you study?
They say.
I would not be able to do anything in paradise.

Easy, I just live there.
I say.
I don't even like the beach.
I get seasick too.
But you are surrounded by water,
They say.
No shit.
I think.
You stupid dumb ass.
I guess you are going to ask me how close I live to the beach.

How close do you live to the beach?
5 minutes by car.
10 minutes by bike.
Everything is relative.
They say.
It must be so nice to have everything so close.
Not the car.

You must not need a car.

Oh my GOD!
I think.
What else are you going to say or ask?
I don't live in a grass shack.
Gas costs about 80 cents more there.
Our washers and dryers are outside.
We eat food that you wouldn't even touch.
And I have cousins my age pregnant on welfare.

You want to know about paradise.
I think.
You wouldn't know.
I think.

Paradise is made up.
We prey on tourists.
We suck them dry.
So we can buy can of Spam to fry.

Paradise ain't shit so why don't you jus' shut yoa' mout'.
Don't put me on display.
I am not for sale.
Hawaii is my home.
I think.

And with a *shaka* and a smile,
I say,
Nice meeting you.
Enjoy your trip.

> "Asian America" is a frame of mind, a spiritual place that is located neither in Asia nor America, but hovering somewhere above, between and around the hearts and souls of the people who belong to it. Especially for those of us who were born here—we feel alienated in America and estranged in the countries our parents came from—Asian America is the closest thing to a place to call home.
>
> —Dina Gan, Editor in Chief of *aMagazine*

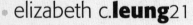

elizabeth c.**leung**21
San Francisco, California

Studying abroad in China was an experience that led me to discover the complexity of my identity as an Asian American. I wrote "My Country 'Tis Not of Thee" as an extension of my never-ending journey toward understanding exactly what it means to be a girl who was raised in America yet bears cultural roots across the Pacific Ocean.

My Country 'Tis Not of Thee

I was that little Asian girl who sat in the front row of the kindergarten classroom portraits. You know, the inconspicuous one who *had* to sit in the front in order to be noticed at all among the vibrant little faces, the one who was placed first in line for any classroom activity requiring the participants to line up in height order. That was me—the one who always got tagged "it" by every kid, knowing that I was easy to catch. Yes, the one who was always last to be picked for any team for any game—dodgeball, kickball, handball, warball, you-name-it-ball.

My family emigrated from Hong Kong when I was four years old. The day I arrived in America, I was unaware that there was such a thing as linguistic differences between English and Chinese. My parents, who were patting themselves on the back for having accurately answered "yes," "no," and "thank you" in English, could not explain it to me. Simply put, we knew zero English.

So that year, I sat timidly among all the other little ones whose last names were Johnson, Thomas, and other familiar and pronounceable Anglo-Saxon sounds. My teacher was gracious enough to correct and reprimand me for apparently mispronouncing my own surname; he insisted that I sever it into two, harsh, distinct syllables, *Le-Ung*, after I had pronounced it as the word *learn* followed by a light *g* sound. I had learned the Romanized version of my name from my teachers in Hong Kong, but I suppose my teacher Mr. Smith-or-Taylor-or-what-not probably knew better. He was, after all, an American. And he was a man.

I was a good student, extremely docile. That is what girls were supposed to do: obey and be quiet. I sat there attentively and learned how the white man, Columbus, was a great hero for "discovering" America, and how John Hancock and fifty-some-odd other great white men blessed our nation with the Declaration of Independence. I also learned how the great white men of America have been kind enough to educate the wretched countries of the Third World about the glories of democracy and capitalism.

The years passed. I graduated to middle school, then high school. Every fall, I received new textbooks, new teachers, and promises to learn new facts and skills, but it was always the same old story. There were no noteworthy Asians or women involved in the Battle of Bull Run, the Emancipation Proclamation, or the invention of the light bulb. While my lips were singing, "This land is your land, this land is my land," my heart was finding it increasingly difficult to resist the notion that this might not be my land after all. I perhaps was not meant to contribute anything remarkable to "my country 'tis of thee, sweet land of liberty."

Where were *my* role models? With whom was I supposed to identify? Where were the prominent Asians in American history? Where were the women? Where were the Asian women? Why didn't my textbooks mention their triumphs?

I scratched my head and wondered if I had fallen asleep in class during the lessons about the contributions of Asians and women. Then I contemplated cutting class, thinking in my delusion that those missed lectures were coincidentally the ones that were about Asians and women in America. Perhaps the curriculum did, after all, include us. Yes, I could very well think that.

Last year, I abandoned this hope in the educational institution and psychologically absolved myself of my American nationality. I signed up for a one-year study abroad program in China to "go back to my roots," as the saying goes. I was anxious to saunter among fellow descendants of my ancestors, to savor every morsel of authentic Chinese cuisine, and to breathe in the natural aromas of my motherland. Instead, to my dismay, "saunter" did not quite describe the trampling that I experienced in the overpopulated streets. The authentic cuisine was authentically unsanitary enough to send me sprinting to the toilet after every meal for the first two weeks, and the aromas of my motherland turned out to be a horrendous potpourri of fecal odors and pollution that aggravated my asthma. I felt as if my body were having an allergic reaction to my motherland and I wanted to return to the comfort and familiarity of America.

My interactions with the Chinese locals proved to be the biggest disappointment of all; they did not welcome me with open arms, and they mocked my American style of dress and my English-accustomed tongue. Until then, I had received much praise at home for my language skills. To the locals, I was a foreigner, a Westerner, an American. After all, I had grown up pledging allegiance to a different flag while my Chinese counterparts were reciting Mao-isms from the *Little Red Book*.

I had thought that I would find my place in my mother country. I was confident that Chinese history, written by the Chinese, would include me, a Chinese woman. Sure enough, it did. The women were documented as uneducated, submissive concubines, mistresses, fieldworkers, housewives, servants of men, or any combination of the above. They were bundled up in a petite, rosy-cheeked package with bound feet. And these women spoke only when given permission. I detested being a woman and resented men for, well, simply not being women. Apparently, women had no glory or status in both American and Chinese history. Regretful and flustered, I realized that I had fled America only to find no sense of belonging in either country.

How foolish I was to think that I could immediately assimilate into a society that I had left as a child. How foolish I was to think that I could drain away the blood that runs through my veins, the blood that is an all-American blend of Cracker Jack, hamburgers, baseball games, Madonna's music, and political correctness. I am not as "Asian" as I thought; then again, I am not as "American" as expected. Perhaps something happened to me on my way across the Pacific. My Asian roots must have gotten tangled or torn, so I never blossomed into the *true* Asian I would have been had I stayed.

It was a struggle for me to realize the paradox. It is okay to be somewhere in between—to be a so-called Asian American. As the years passed, I met more and more female Asians in America who faced the same challenges with identity, or lack thereof. We grow up being taught that all men are created equal. We are told not to worry because that statement implicitly includes us. We begin to wonder if Asians or women deserve more than they have received in the form of a few meager pages and minor footnotes in American history. We fail to take pride in our predecessors' contributions. We feel neglected in this melting-pot nation. We almost melt away. We then try to be "Asian" instead. We fail. We remember that some great white man once said that all men are created equal. We want to be men but cannot. We feel condemned as the non-Asian-non-American race and the nonimportant gender. We are confused, until we learn that there is a term that describes who we are— Asian American women. We like it. We find comfort in each other. We find pride. We find the term *Asian American women* more in the American history we are making.

ronaluo 16
New York, New York

I am a senior at Stuyvesant High School, where I am an active writer. I was born in Canton, China, and moved to New York City at the age of seven. When I was younger, I believed Asians shouldn't just write about being Asian. No matter how hard I tried, my culture still appeared in my pieces. I have come to realize that being Chinese is an unavoidable and fascinating part of my consciousness.

Flushing

The last time I saw my father *chow* our dinner, we were living in Queens. "Chow" is Chinese for cooking with a wok, except the verb *cooking* is too gentle. Chowing is a fierce activity. Vegetables and chopped pork or rice are dropped into sizzling oil and continuously shoved by a long steel spatula. Chow is a noisy homonym; indeed, the loud clanging of the spatula against the charcoal-covered wok was my signal to return home every evening.

When my friends and I went outside to play, we rode our bicycles up and down every driveway on the block. Without ears to guide us, knowing it was dinnertime would still be easy. My driveway would lure me with the smell of soy sauce and scallions. And curry fragrance would emanate from Rumana's house next door. I always looked forward to getting invited to her house for dinner because her family ate with their hands.

Soon our small block would be filled with mingling aromas. The scent was so inviting no mothers or fathers ever had to call for us to come home. Slowly, we'd straggle off.

At home I would visit the kitchen first. Peeking into the wok offered a preview of that night's meal. That evening gray shrimps turned bright red as they tried to fall back into the wok, only to be shoved into the air again by the spatula. I wanted to stay and watch my father, but he bumped into me while he was scurrying between the counter and the stove, and he promptly asked me to sit down. Instead, I left. I didn't know that we would never chow our dinner again.

My family moved to Manhattan. We stopped using the wok for fear that the noise and strong smell would offend our sophisticated neighbors. And we stopped eating shrimp as well, because Dad's arteries were getting clogged from too much cholesterol.

We have adopted our neighbors' cold air and cold food for so long, I wonder if my parents even remember how our dinners used to be. Perhaps, this weekend, I will surprise everyone. I will buy fresh shrimp and take out our lonely wok and chow and chow and chow until our home is filled, once again, with the wonderful fragrance of soy sauce and scallions.

> *Helen Zia, an award-winning journalist, has covered Asian American communities and social and political movements for more than twenty years. Born in New Jersey and a graduate of Princeton's first coeducational class, she lives in the San Francisco Bay area.*

"Welcome to Washington" from *Asian American Dreams*

BY HELEN ZIA

In kindergarten, I learned the Pledge of Allegiance. Or rather, I learned to imitate it. The words spilled out of my mouth in one long jumble, all slurred and sloppy. I'd stand tall and put my right hand over my heart, mumbling proudly, like a 5-year-old on a drunk. Even then, I understood that " 'Merica" was my home—and that I was an American. Still, a flicker of doubt was ever present. If I was truly American, why did the other American people around me seem so sure I was foreign?

By the time I was a teenager, I imagined that I was a "dual citizen" of both the United States and China. I had no idea what dual citizenship involved, or if it was even possible. No matter, I would be a citizen of the world. This was my fantasy, my way of soothing the hurt of being so unacceptable in the land of my birth.

When I got to college, I decided to learn about "where I came from" by taking classes in Asian history. I even studied Mandarin Chinese. This had the paradoxic effect of making me question my Chineseness. Other students, and even the teachers, expected me to spout perfectly accented Chinese. Instead I sounded like some hick from New Jersey, stumbling along as badly as the other American students next to me. Still my fantasy persisted; I thought I might "go back" to China, a place I had never been, as rude detractors so often urged.

President Richard Nixon's historic trip to China in February 1972 made a visit seem possible for me. That summer, China cracked open the "bamboo curtain," allowing a small group of Chinese American students to visit the country as a goodwill gesture to the United States. I desperately wanted to be one of them, and I put together a research proposal that got the support of my professors. With a special fellowship from Princeton, I joined the group and became one of the first Americans, after Nixon, to enter "Red" China.

In China I fit right in with the multitude. In the cities of Shanghai and Suzhou, where my parents were from, I saw my features everywhere. After years of not looking "American" to the "Americans" and not looking Chinese enough for the Cantonese who made up the majority of Chinese Americans, I suddenly found my face on every passerby. It was a revelation of sameness that I had never experienced in New Jersey. The feeling didn't last long.

I visited my mother's eldest sister; they hadn't seen each other since 1949, the year of the Communist Revolution in China, when my mother left with their middle sister on the last boat out of Shanghai. Using my elementary Chinese, I struggled to communicate with Auntie Li, who seemed prematurely wizened from the years of hardship. My vocabulary was too limited and my idealism too thick to comprehend my family's suffering from the Cultural Revolution, still virulently in progress. But girlish fun transcended language as my older cousins took me by the hand to the local "Friendship Store" and dressed me in a khaki Mao suit, braiding my long hair in pigtails, just like the other young, unmarried Chinese women.

All decked out like a freshly minted Red Guard in my new do, I passed for local. Real Chinese stopped me on the street, to ask for directions, to ask where I got my tennis shoes, to complain about the long bus queues, to comment on my Shanghai-made blouse, to say any number of things to me. As soon as I opened my mouth to reply, my clumsy American accent infected the little Chinese I knew. Suddenly the speech that, in English, drew compliments in America brought gasps of fear and disapproval in Chinese. My questioners knew immediately that I was a foreigner, a Westerner, an American, maybe even a spy— and they ran from me as fast as they could. I had an epiphany common to Asian Americans who visit their ancestral homelands: I realized that I didn't fit into Chinese society, that I could never be accepted there. If I didn't know it, the Chinese did: I belonged in America, not China.

When I got back to the States, I took my new appreciation of my Americanness and went to Washington, armed with a degree in public and international affairs and a minor in East Asian studies. After a lengthy application and interview process that included months of FBI security checks, I landed my dream summer job as an intern on the China desk at the State Department, created as a result of President Nixon's historic visit. As one of the first Americans to visit the People's Republic of China, I was eager to contribute to the efforts of my country—the United States—to rebuild diplomatic relations.

When I reported to work on the designated day at the State Department monolith in Foggy Bottom, the personnel officer greeted me with "We have no job for you." He offered no explanation about the job I had worked so hard to get. I was stranded in a strange city with no money, a scholarship student whose livelihood depended on summer earnings. The urgency of my financial situation forced me out of shock and into action. I walked to Congress and found the offices of the two senators from New Jersey, Harrison Williams, Jr., and Clifford Case. Their staff members kindly listened to my plight and went into action for their young constituent.

With this congressional assistance, I learned why the job had suddenly vaporized. I was told that the State Department had a policy that no persons of Chinese descent should work at the China desk, no matter how many generations removed from the ancestral bones. This would protect America in case some genetic compulsion twisted my allegiance to China.

I was incredulous. Hadn't they noticed earlier that I was Chinese American? Surely the FBI agents and State Department folks hadn't missed that minor detail. I was terribly disappointed that I wouldn't have a chance to do the one job I felt perfectly qualified to do. At least the senators managed to extract another internship offer from the State Department. My anger and disappointment gave way to practicality, and I went to work at my first writing job: researching and writing State Department briefs, reports, and various propaganda.

As I became more certain of my Americanness, my government again asserted its ambivalence to me. But I understood what the Pledge of Allegiance meant—that America was my home.

Family Ties

During junior high school, I needed only to step into the yellow bus in the morning to notice how entirely different my family was from the other kids'. A boy on whom I had a crush prattled about a movie he'd seen with his parents the previous night. Other girls confirmed their after-school agendas; they were hanging out at the mall, going to rock concerts, or watching MTV. When asked to talk about my life, I lied. I didn't want to tell them the truth. And besides, who really had the time to explain the myriad reasons why there was a world of difference between my leisure time—or my family life, in general—and theirs?

Arguments between my parents and me always seemed to stem from the same place. I was disobedient and rude. I made careless mistakes on a science exam. I didn't practice violin long enough (my mom usually claiming that I took three ten-minute "rests" during my hour-long sessions instead of two). Or I was immature, unthankful for their efforts. My parents lectured me, and I remember their grievances well. They would say:

You don't know how fortunate you are. When we were your age, we never had [fill in the blank]. There are things in life you just have to accept—you just have to do without complaining—because life isn't about what you WANT, it's about sacrifice. And we don't care how other American people think; we're not them, and as long as you're living with us, you follow our rules. Are you blind? We shouldn't have to say we love you or we're proud of you, because you should know this. What kind of daughter speaks to her father in such a disrespectful manner? You have to work ten times harder than other people if you want to succeed. If you're not going to put 110 percent of your effort in something, then just quit now—it's just as well. You think you know everything, but you're just a little girl; do you really think you know more than your parents do? You don't understand why we push you right now but in time you'll know why.

And the kicker, the bottom line that closed any topic, no matter what, was, *Everything we do—everything we've EVER done—has been for you.*

After hearing their side of the story, my responses always sounded somewhat frail, foolish, even if I was a drama queen and delivered a good tearjerker every now and then. It wasn't that my points weren't convincing as to why, for instance, they should allow me a small amount of independence because being shackled to my violin stand every evening was preventing me from assimilating into the social environment at school. But most of the time, my arguments started sounding the same, too, and I'd have these surreal, out-of-body moments when I'd catch a glimpse of us around the dinner table. My father's clenched fist knocking the same spot in front of him to add emphasis to his words, my hands waving through the air, crooked mouths, and the sound of our desperate voices overlapping and colliding. I challenged every word that fell from their lips and, although I'm ashamed to admit it, I copped a vicious, disrespectful, arrogant attitude in our conversations, something I regret to this day and cannot erase. My end of the argument sounded something like this:

Tell me again how NOT living in a democracy makes me so fortunate. You didn't have a lot of things when you were growing up, but this isn't Korea—this is America—and even if I feel guilty for having opportunities you didn't, I still want to explore them. My friends, their parents allow them to explore the things they want. They talk about things and make compromises. And when they're proud of each other, or they feel love for each other, they show it—why can't you ever say you're proud of me? The minute I disagree with you, I'm the disobedient, ungrateful, silly girl. You don't listen to me when I speak. And it's not that I don't try hard, you never acknowledge my accomplishments. You think you know everything, but you don't, and if you saw what I see going on around me, then you'd agree. Why can't you understand me?

And of course my winning line was, *Nothing I do is ever good enough for you.*

The submissions I received from girls about their relationships with family members far outnumbered the ones depicting the other general aspects of their day-to-day lives. And while we all remembered and focused on various fragments of past family blow-ups, the statements above, which were transcribed from debates I had with my own first-generation, arguably conventional Korean immigrant parents, turned out to be surprisingly "normal."

What I discovered was that our experiences were as diverse as were the cultural, racial, and socioeconomic landscapes of our youth. These factors were critical in the girls' understanding of the conflicts encountered while getting to know their families, and coming to terms with their "place" in the home, as well as in the world outside. Although many would probably claim that we don't share much in common with one another based on the fact that we have so many differences, after reading the hundreds of writings that filled my in box, I suggest that, as Asian American girls, we identify with each other on many levels.

There were four main themes that emerged in our poems, journal entries, and essays, and I interpreted this as a sign. Although it was going to be impossible for me to discuss all of the challenges we face in our families, perhaps we would be able to start raising some fundamental questions in our dialogue—the biggest one being, to what extent have our Asian American families played a role in shaping our beliefs and our self-image?

The first theme I noticed was our curiosity when it came to deciphering our family history. I hadn't predicted that girls would use this anthology project as a way to spur a conversation that, under any other circumstances, probably wouldn't occur. I would have given anything to see this happen. One of the most obvious goals of our collective endeavor is to open channels of communication, which have widened the gaps separating girls and women, and girls and their loved ones.

Some reported back to me with wild stories after unearthing fascinating trivia, lost histories about relatives who were both alive and deceased, and ancestral legends. Lauren, thirteen, was among the most diligent history hunters. She sent me an e-mail saying that, a few nights earlier, her mother told a suspenseful story about her great-great-great-grandfather, who was the district judge of Canton during the Ching Dynasty. Lauren also discovered that her great-grandmother had come within inches of losing her life to the Japanese when she decided to stay in her little village to protect the family jewels.

Knowing one's family roots was important for reasons that went beyond curiosity. I heard from girls who said that they felt distant from their parents, that their parents' unwillingness to open up about their past made it impossible for them to gain a sense of belonging. Understanding what happened to their parents in the past, they said, would help them find their own identity as people of Asian descent. Jessica, fifteen, an Asian Canadian, wrote: "I know nothing of the trials my mother and her family endured when they emigrated from the Philippines. I don't know how my father's family ended up here. I don't know how my parents started a family, and whether they were accepted by society. I cannot understand these critical links, which leaves me without a familiar culture."

Another recurring theme was the way in which girls reconciled values that were taught to them at home, and values that were championed in their "all-American" outer world. Early in life, Asian American girls learn what's expected of them at home. When I was growing up, my mother made it perfectly clear that there was a distinct boundary between how I was to behave at home, and what behavior was acceptable outside when I was around (and in competition with) my white peers. At home, I was supposed to conform to the mold of the well-disciplined, obedient Korean daughter. At school, I was supposed to speak out, to learn how to be self-reliant and aggressive like the other "American" kids.

Well, the girls spoke out, and it was loud and clear. The ideal Asian daughter mold was stifling. The most powerful metaphor that resurfaced in their short stories and poems—that of silence. Silence consumed our lives; we were obsessed with it to the point where it seemed to take on a human form in our writings. While to some girls silence represented a deep, friendly, familiar connection that characterized family dynamics, most felt trapped in it. We felt like silences—the lack of communication between parents and daughters—rendered us voiceless, repressed, and incapable of truly knowing the ones who were responsible for us. In an essay entitled "Quiet Is My Name," Kanya, fifteen, offered a most powerful, yet disturbing perspective on silence. She wrote: "Must I give up free expression and conceal my voice when what I truly want is to be as true to them [my parents] as I am to myself? If I speak out, I will bring shame to them. But can I remain quiet, even when my heart is on fire and I'm compelled to speak?"

Jina, eighteen, agreed with Kanya, but emphasized the fact that she was expected to be quiet at home first and foremost because she was female. She wrote in a poem: "Staring into the silent night I sometimes wonder who I am/Am I who I choose to be/Or am I someone my family has forced me to be/I'm severed in two/Which path to take/One foot at home/Where silence pervades/Chores await/And men speak/I hide my knowledge/While within me desire grows/An urge to be free/To make my own choices/To speak out/To be/FREE."

But the silence went both ways. Our parents weren't responding to our need for validation; many of us couldn't remember the last time we heard the simple phrases that seemed to tumble out so naturally from the mouths of our peers' parents: "I love you," or "I'm proud of you," or even "Good job, you deserve it!" I related strongly to girls who said that when they asked for recognition, their parents just stared at them, bewildered, as if we were out of our minds.

In addition to being teenagers who had to deal with the usual pressures of school and grades, we also felt an intense burden to make our parents' unfulfilled dreams come true. Most of us had some inkling about the extreme sacrifices that our parents made for us; many of our elders had left their lives behind to immigrate to the States, where they started anew with few possessions. They invested their energy in our education, and tried to provide everything we needed to be successful. When my parents told me all their hopes were in me, I heard another translation that sounded like, "You are all we have—we've made sacrifices for you, and our success depends on your success." Even if I knew that what my parents meant was that they wanted me to try my best, I was always aware of unspoken expectations. Dana, sixteen, talked about the stress of letting her parents down: "My parents are disappointed when they see me. I have my own car, my own cell phone, while my dad keeps telling me that he was too poor to afford shoes when he was little. They see a girl who's not achieving her potential (getting a 1400 on the SATs, for example), and they've concluded that I'm too lazy. And that money's a bad thing because it saps us of the drive that we need to be successful."

The last theme I was able to discern from my submissions: As we get older, our perspectives change. The way we see our parents, our siblings, and our other relatives is transformed as we come into our independence. Girls who had just left home after high school contemplated their experiences and had an insight that they'd gained as a result of being on their own, and out of the protective confines of home. Viewed from a distance, the parent that seemed almost freakish while they were in the throes of adolescence now appeared to be, well, human. During my first year in college, I felt that I was beginning to see my parents in a different light, perhaps because I was starting to hear my own voice. And I was surprised. As I started to draw distinctions between my beliefs, my passions, and my goals, I slowly discovered the unexpected. We were on the same side after all. A similar discovery came to many of the writers, who were on their own for the first time, and for whom the sheltered home environment of their youth existed as little more than nostalgic memories; distance became a catalyst in creating new depth to their relationships.

This chapter evidences the fact that cultivating robust family ties demands unyielding patience, love, and understanding. You will read heartwarming, emotionally stirring accounts by granddaughters, daughters, and sisters, who testify to the ways in which family members are playing a critical role in influencing them and inspiring them to imagine life's possibilities. And others who haven't found the strong relationships and connections that they desperately crave write about absence, confusion, and loss. All of us are growing into our independence, while acknowledging that, even if in subtle ways, our families continue to guide us on our journey toward finding our place in the world.

carolyn**feng**18

Fremont, California

I was born in Beijing, China, and my family moved to the United States when I was six years old. Since then, I have lived in Florida and various cities in California, including Fremont, where I have lived for six years, and Berkeley, where I currently attend college. Growing up in America bound by Chinese convention made me often question the fairness of life, but as I grew older, I began to appreciate the standards my parents set for me. They've helped me succeed whereas otherwise I would have failed to grow as an individual as well as in accepting my cultural background. This piece is dedicated to my mother, who has sacrificed so much for me.

Bristled Affection

Most Chinese parents aren't very affectionate toward their children. There is no kissing, no hugging, no declarations of love. When I see Chinese parents and their children in public, I see children getting yelled at, being schooled on what to do and what not to do, and being asked not to touch things.

Growing up, I was used to my mother roughly waking me from my sleep and scolding me for sleeping so long. I stumbled into the clothes she held out for me, and I would walk half asleep into the bathroom to brush my teeth and wash my face. When I came back to my room, my mother would be waiting on the bed with a brush in her hand. As I sat on the bed, she jerked my head side to side, pulling every strand on my hair so hard that I would turn around to see if some still remained in her hand—only to have my head jerked back into place.

"No time to play around!" she would tell me.

While she pulled, wove, and tucked my hair, she would often have me recite poems or songs, which I had to memorize for class that day. If I made an error, my mother chided me for not being prepared.

I would be subjected to my mother's cruel hands before any occasion where people would see me. At these times, she would tell me what I should say and not say, what I should do and not do. She would tell me about the aunt I was going to meet, the history behind the parks we were going to, or an amusing story she remembered about cats and fish. And sometimes she would sing silly nursery rhymes to make me hold still.

As I got older, my attention span started to shrink. I could no longer endure those sessions of hair pulling. I was eager to be outside playing with my friends. One day when my mother came into my room with a brush, I told her that I was old enough to do my own hair, and I no longer needed her help. As I ran outside with my newfound power of independence, I saw a look of surprise and sadness on my mother's face. That image soon left my carefree eight-year-old heart, and I gave it no second thought.

Today I realize how valuable that time was. My mother was trying to show me she cared about me and loved me. I realize those torture sessions were her chance to connect with me. I may have been too blind to see this at the time, but recently I have made an effort to get to know my mother. I talk to her more, and I tell her about what's happening in my life. She, in turn, tells me about her day or about events she has learned about in the news. She also tells me about her childhood and how her mother used to braid her hair when she was little. Once I asked her about the lack of affection that she has shown me, and she looked bewildered. She smiled and then scolded me for confusing American and Chinese cultures, but she also told me that she would try to be more open with her affections. As time passed, my mother learned to endure my kisses and hugs, and I learned to look forward to our hair-pulling sessions. And I know that when my children grow enough hair, I will be there with a brush in my hand.

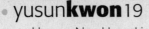
I'm currently studying studio art at Dartmouth College in Hanover, New Hampshire. My parents emigrated from South Korea right before I was born, and I was raised in a hardworking and loving family. My family suffered tragedy when my father died suddenly at the age of fifty, leaving my mother and two older sisters to live on in his memory. This piece serves as a tribute to him in remembrance of his constant love and affection. It is also a reminder of the pain that my family still endures despite the healing powers of time.

Knowing

Nothing bad had ever happened to my family. No house fires, hospitalizations, or hell-raising had ever dared set foot through the door of my sweet suburban home, and after seventeen years of life the thought of anything tragic happening in my family was simply inconceivable.

That simplicity was shattered one cold December night.

"Hurry! Put your clothes on and come downstairs—your dad needs to go to the hospital. . . ."

The lights came on, waking me from dreams, as my mother rushed toward me and pulled the covers off my head. She left the room as quickly as she had come in, saying only "Hurry" with fear in her voice as she left. Suddenly alert, I bounded out of bed and went to the closet to throw on a warm sweater and the dirty jeans that I had worn the day before, the ones with the button falling off. *Oh, I'll have to have Daddy fix this for me*, I thought.

I walked out of my bedroom. The next time I would ever sleep in that room again would be on the floor beside my sisters, with our arms around each other for comfort. After that, I would sleep beside my mother in the bed that would soon be too big for her.

Desperation. Hopelessness. Regret. Those were what awaited me at the foot of the stairs when I saw my father lying lifeless on the den floor. Had I said it? Had I said, "I hope you feel better, Daddy" when he went up to bed after complaining of back pain just hours before? I couldn't remember. But now he was lying on the floor, his leg at an awkward angle, his eyes partially open. My mom was putting socks on his feet, trying to massage some warmth into them. I took his hand. It was cold. I thought to myself, *He's already gone*.

My eldest sister had to call our other sister at school and tell her that our father had died of a massive heart attack. She had just pulled an all-nighter. I think she screamed when she heard the news.

Before my father passed away, I had never heard my mother weep. But now it seemed as if her eyes might never be dry again. She wept as I wanted to. I wanted to weep, choke, and have shuddering waves of sorrow engulf me, but that storm of mourning never came through. Instead, I had that look on my face; the kind of look that one has when one is unsure whether the present is reality or nightmare.

They said, "At least he had a quick death. He didn't have to suffer." I never had a comment to that remark. Those people didn't know my father. They didn't watch him breathe in carcinogenic dry-cleaning fumes for eighteen years, be denied a college education because he wasn't an important son, or see his ungrateful children look at him with eyes full of shame because he couldn't be an all-American dad. He never took a vacation from his life of work, work, work, just so that his family could live better than he had. But I would rather have my father than a three-car garage.

"Whose little girl are you?" he would ask, smiling and giving me a sloppy kiss on the cheek.

"Yours," I would reply.

"I love you, my daughter," he would say sweetly in his English.

"I love you too," I would reply.

I didn't even know the meaning of the word. I had never experienced such an all-encompassing pain in my heart like I did that drizzly December day, staring down into my father's grave. Some

days that pain will creep up on me and revive that feeling of hopelessness. The days when I hear about someone suffering from a
heart attack, or when I witness a classmate faint and fall to the
floor, I relive the awful feeling. I walk around with that look on my
face again. I am standing there, staring at the fresh pink roses laid
on the newly opened muddy earth, knowing the bitterness of that
cold winter.

jenny**yu**20

Albany, New York

*When I was eleven, I crossed the Pacific and moved to a remote
suburb in upstate New York. Despite learning the ABCs and sur-
viving culture shock, I reunited with parents from whom I had been
separated when I was born. Though born and raised in Shanghai,
I've spent my most impressionable years humming to* TRL *(MTV's*
Total Request Live*) and watching* Ally McBeal. *I wrote "Her
Three-Inch Feet" as a self-reflective piece back in tenth grade. Chinese lotus feet and urban Manhattan, as mentioned in the piece,
exemplify the East-meets-West complex that I dealt with frequently.*

Her Three-Inch Feet

She is different. Not just different, her presence in this big city
seems anachronistic. She has a benign grandmotherly smile with
skin like a piece of crumpled paper flattened out with lines revealing her age. She has a petite, almost childlike body, and tiny bound
feet only three inches long.

It is difficult to get a close look at her feet since she likes to move
about constantly. She can never and will never stay in one place
long enough. For most of her life, Great-Aunt Yeung worked dili-
gently; first for her parents, then for her husband, and later for her
children. In the seventy-six years she has lived, she has been bur-

dened by responsibility. And, as a result of life's challenges, Great-Aunt Yeung possesses vigor that exceeds a teenager's.

If you have ever seen her feet, you will never forget them. They are small and pale. They are like two pieces of sponge cake that have been accidentally mashed and tortured. They are painful to look at, for I wonder how excruciating it must be to walk on them, yet they are fascinating. They represent the ancient world of the East, a place of a thousand emperors and fabled dragons.

It is always a treat for me to visit Great-Aunt Yeung, though it means a three-hour drive to New York City. She lives on Mott Street, only three blocks from the heart of Chinatown. Her apartment isn't very big; in fact, it appears somewhat cluttered and unimportant compared to a typical, suburban, four-bedroom Colonial. It only has one bedroom, one bath, and a small open space that one might call a living room. There isn't much to see in the living room—just a chair, a few pieces of furniture that she might have gotten from local church sales (since they don't quite match), a thirteen-inch TV, and a table.

But it's not just a table. It's the table of Chinese gods. The burning incense on it perfumes the whole apartment. The twice-daily ritual of worship consists of kneeling, lighting the incense, and then bowing to the gods while holding up the incense with both hands above the head. It is quite a lovely scene. I like watching her and pretending to be lost in the world of yin and yang, Confucius, and fortune cookies. But deep down, I know I can never be a part of that inscrutable world.

That is how I feel about my Great-Aunt Yeung. The combination of her and New York City is as odd as eating rice topped with rocky road ice cream. She prefers bamboo mats over soft mattresses, medicinal tea over creamy cappuccino, and cooked vegetables over raw salads. Great-Aunt Yeung will always have her own ways. The East and the West will always remain apart, and the best proof of that is seeing Great-Aunt Yeung plod the streets of New York in her size 1, black-cloth shoes.

lei-ann**lawi** then 15
Honolulu, Hawaii

Born and raised in Honolulu, Hawaii, I have fond memories of hot summers of shaved ice and days at the beach. But these memories are so much sweeter when shared with family and friends. It is hard to forget the times when my brothers and I would sleep over at my grandparents' house and just do what kids do best—laugh, play, and have fun. I have better appreciated my grandparents' love for me and will forever cherish those "Monopoly Nights."

Monopoly Nights

I would look forward to Monopoly nights
with swirls of cocoa wisps
that almost burned my tongue
and salty crackers dunked so much
that there was a mush surprise at the bottom of the cup.
We'd fight for Boardwalk until we were too tired
to laugh anymore or until our eyes hurt
from trying to watch TV at the same time.
We'd end the game (just for the night, we'd always promise)
and then stay awake making forts and tunnels
out of our fuzz blankets and cloud pillows.
Then Grandma would hush us to sleep
and we'd snuggle into slumber within our walls of
    protection.

We would wake to the smell of waffles luring us in
and destroy our pillow castle in a frenzy
to claim the best seat for morning cartoons.
We always poured too much syrup in the crispy open grids
Grandma would say, "Aiya!" but smile.

I miss those Monopoly nights
filled with cocoa and laughter.
Somehow we grew out of our blanket towers
and realized they would never be strong enough to hold our
  dreams.

mai-linh**hong**21

Annandale, Virginia

My family left Vietnam as refugees when I was ten months old and resettled in the Washington, D.C., area. I just graduated from Yale University, where I studied literature and led the Asian American Women's Group. At twenty-one, I am realizing how much the women in my life, of all ages and backgrounds, have inspired and shaped me with their creativity, intelligence, and nerve. "Burnt Rice with Fish Sauce" is a reflection on how far my family and I have come in our lives, literally and figuratively; it's about the gains and losses of achieving the "American Dream."

Burnt Rice with Fish Sauce

Long before my family found the suburbs, before the little rambler by the church, before even the peeling duplex where I played one season between a wooden and a wire fence, there was a crowded third-floor apartment on Randolph Street, in south Arlington. During steamy summer mornings I watched my mother cook. She alternately stirred, sweat, sliced, and gazed tiredly out a window. A damp washcloth clung to one hand, and my baby brother perched on the opposite hip. My uncles slept, sprawled across the living room. Playing alone, I wound about them, listening for my father's footsteps on the stairs. I waited, too, for the happy smell of burnt rice. It came up in leathery strips, sometimes long, always brown or black. My mother scraped the burnt rice carefully from the aluminum pot once the "eating rice"—the fluffy, white rice—had been removed. Vegetable scraps lay scattered on the counter, orange, green, and dripping. From above, a small jar of brown fish sauce emerged. The heavy scent quickly filled the damp, hot air. Soup simmered slowly to a boil, and meanwhile, my brother was tucked away to a nap. In that slow and savory pocket of time, between the bustle of morning and the long haul of afternoon, my mother and I rested our elbows on the yellow, plastic-covered table. We ate, with our fingers, burnt rice dipped in fish sauce.

If my father came home then, haggard and sleepless, I could be charming, he receptive. He made faces at our snack when I waggled my wet and odorous fingers his way. The sight of his solemn, young wife seated at the flimsy table, far from home and tired already with the difficult years that lay ahead must have quieted his usual grumbles.

Sometimes he sat with us. Other times he ran one hand over my thin hair before peeling off his stained factory clothes and leaving to shower the sawdust from his face.

Years later, while I packed for college in our quiet suburban house, my mother—a little more stout now, and graying—came to me with a smile. She pulled me into our large, white kitchen, where the familiar smell of burnt rice hung in the air.

With her pleated sleeves rolled up, she teased, "An di."

I laughed, and shook my head, "No."

The smell of fish sauce didn't please me anymore. My mother, too, turned on the kitchen fan while she cooked.

"The steamer is broken," she explained. "I had to make rice like old times on the stove. Too bad about the burnt parts."

I fingered the plate of burnt rice and tasted a grain. It was cold, plain, but the sweet and slightly bitter scent was disconcerting. It made me think suddenly of the days of summer, soon to shorten, and of the slow, satisfied way a clothesline sways when strung haphazardly above a city street. I heard the comforting creak of an old, scratched, wooden floor, and across it, a tiny dark child walked, singing to herself.

I was real fortunate to grow up in a wonderful family, where I don't know if I would call it dreams, but I would call it expectations and hopes that I could meet my parents' demands, which were to do my best.

—Avon CEO/President Andrea Jung, in an article on CBS.com

belinda**wong** 17
San Francisco, California

As a seventeen-year-old living with both parents and a sister in the eclectic city of San Francisco, I aspire to find my voice. "Who is that reflection looking at you from the mirror? What could you possibly have in common with Chinese immigrant parents from Vietnam?" my mind frequently inquires. "Tainted" allows me to delve into myself and to seek the answers to the questions the "real" Belinda poses.

Tainted

"Your daughter is so perfect."

This is the phrase most favorable to the awaiting ears of my mother and father. For the last sixteen years, they have molded me into their own piece of pottery, exquisite and pure. I am my parents' masterpiece: a daughter who leads a flawless, carefree life because I've been sculpted with the ideals of propriety, intelligence, and felicity. That is the external me. Internally, I contemplate whether or not I should adhere to my parents' ideals because the image of "perfection" I have achieved is so tainted.

The perfection I possess begins with my smile. It is not the camera-type that fades after the photograph is taken. My smile is constant, always stretching across my face, making my eyes squint, even when I am downcast. It's no wonder that each time I attempt to have an effusive talk with someone about my conundrums, I never get beyond: "I am having problems." Even my friends doubt my sincerity because of my smile, which convinces them that the concept of me having concerns is an oxymoron.

I keep smiling out of reverence for my parents, the sculptors who have toiled too long and hard to make me who I am today. Although they have forced me to be an object in their exhibit, I have learned what I want to be ultimately—free. Still I must continue to smile, even if it's mendacious, because if I don't, I will disavow the gratitude I feel for the patience and love my parents have expended in trying to make me happy; I love them too much to take away their source of pride.

My piano is a source of pride for me. To convince myself that I am not at all living a flawless life, I return to my black Young Chang piano night after night to vent. I express anger at the world for not being able to decode the cryptic me, anger at my parents for refusing to release me from their strain. My piano playing is the only thing I do for myself and not for my mother and father.

Pounding each forte stanza on the black and white keys reveals my imperfect, dissatisfied self, and destroys my otherwise perfect musical composure. Each time I incorporate a part of myself into the music, my teacher ironically tells me that my piano playing is "monotonous" and that it's "terribly lacking in sentiment." She is also tricked by my misleading smile. How can a girl so perfectly happy produce something so gloomy and impure? I continue playing the piano to show my teacher and the rest of the world that there is more to me than the facade of my smile. I want to show that there is indeed imperfection within me because I will never allow my piano playing to be like my smile: an immaculate thing everyone expects of me.

I fight this battle between my internal and external selves because I know my flawless, idyllic image is tainted by my desire for freedom. I know the delicate piece of pottery my expert parents have spent years meticulously creating is cracked, fragile, and flawed. The question I'm trying to answer is whether I should fill these cracks to sustain the image—their artwork—or whether I should let the pottery crumble like Babylon and rebuild it myself.

roselyn**domingo** 17

Union City, California

My sister and I moved to California from the Philippines in 1992.
We are currently living with our relatives. My mother and brother
are still in the Philippines and my father is deceased. When my
teachers assigned me to write a reflective essay about my life, I was
embarrassed and afraid at first. As I explained about my life in full
detail, however, I started to understand and accept my situation.
Now I spend my leisure time writing about my experiences. I want
people to read my stories so they can understand and reflect on their
family values too.

Separation Anxiety

Looking back, I remember living with my family in the Philippines. We went to the park together, and my father carried me on his shoulders as we walked to the playground. He put me in a swing and pushed me, the wind breezing through my hair. Afterward, we had a picnic. My mother fed me, while my father made funny faces to make me smile. All that mattered to me was that I was with my family.

I was eight years old when I found out that my father was leaving the Philippines to go to America. Determined to provide a better future for his family, he was going to become an American citizen and petition for the rest of his family to come to America. A year later, he was able to send for my sister and me to come to America. Unfortunately, he could not send for my mother since they weren't married yet, and my brother was too young to make the trip alone. Had my brother left the Philippines, too, my mother would have been so lonely with all of her children gone.

Back then I didn't know exactly what was happening. I just obeyed my parents' orders, not realizing that I had left my mother and brother until I was already in the air where clouds were the only objects I could see outside my window. Wondering when I would meet the rest of my family again, I cried so hard that I thought my heart would explode. I couldn't stop my tears from rolling down, and my sister became irritated and angry toward me because of my continuous mourning. I was dolorous without anyone who could comfort me.

After spending some time with my father, he told me that he had to leave us because his work was going to be in Los Angeles. My sister and I had to stay in Union City with my aunt and her family. Every weekend, my father drove from LA to Union City so he could spend time with us. What I regret the most is not cherishing every moment I was able to spend with my father. A year and a half later, he developed cirrhosis, a liver disease caused by excessive consumption of alcohol over a period of years. He went to the hospital for frequent checkups. His condition worsened, and soon he had tubes in his stomach, and had to be careful when moving around. During the roughest times, he would even vomit clots of blood.

One night, my father and I were silently watching television in my room. He kept getting up to go to the bathroom to vomit, so I followed him to make sure he was okay. He vomited pieces of blood on the bathroom sink. I was frightened and worried. My father told me to call the doctor and our relatives. Everything happened so quickly; later, all I could remember was the sound of the ambulance. My relatives joined me and we followed my father to the hospital. He was shaking and he could not even speak to me. I did not know what to do or say to him. I cried, and I prayed for my father's health and safety, but my prayers weren't answered. He died in the summer of 1994. He didn't even live to celebrate Father's Day or to see his children grow up and graduate from school. He was a great person, a loving father, and a devoted husband, but for some reason, out of all the people in the world, he was the one who had to die so soon. I was filled with mixed emotions—mostly rage, denial, and sadness.

My father's body was brought back to the Philippines. My mother couldn't believe that her husband had died. They had so many dreams together. She was on the verge of giving up on the world because she had lost the most important person in her life. She didn't even get to bid my father farewell or tell him how much she loved him one more time. My brother didn't get a chance to spend time with him, either. He thought our father was sleeping when he saw him in the coffin. In spite of my father's funeral, I was glad that my family was finally reunited. I thought that I would be fine as long as I was with them, but I was wrong again. My aunt told my mother that she could take care of my sister and me in America so we could become American citizens in a few years. She said that later we could petition the rest of my family to come as my father had originally planned. My mom felt uneasy, but she agreed with my aunt, and said that this arrangement would be for the best. It was hard letting go, but I knew she left us so that we could have a better future and because she loves us.

It's been seven years since I came to America. My aunt and her family are my second family. My sister is eighteen, and she's applying for American citizenship. It will probably take months or even years until her citizenship papers are fully processed and approved. Right now, all I can do is write to or call my mother and brother. Every two to three years, my aunt arranges a trip so that my sister and I can fly to the Philippines during our summer vacation. I am thankful, but it is not enough. I see my friends and their families living happily together and I envy them. I pray every night that someday I can be closer to my family, but it's getting harder. I am so afraid of losing my family and never living with them again. I seek help but there is no one who can console me. None of my friends know what I am going through and my sister does not bother talking to me about our problems.

The only person who can give me comfort and relief is my mother. She understands the pain that I am going through. I try to stay strong but I'm losing faith. I want to live with my mother in the Philippines, but life there would be difficult. Being a single parent, she might not be able to provide us with an education. I might not have the opportunity to get a good job so I can provide for my own family. And I do not want to add to her problems. Then again, staying here in America means that I will have to continue being separated from my family. Even if I have better opportunities here, how good can life be if I'm not with my family? I need the chance to grow up with my family—a family that was taken away from me during my childhood. At the same time, I want to provide a better future for my family, so that they do not have to suffer the bad conditions in the Philippines, such as flood and pollution. I know that taking care of them would mean, in some cases, sacrificing my own happiness.

Right now, it's important for me to maintain my positive attitude, but I'm facing a difficult situation that's tearing me in two. This is my only chance to live, so I will do my best to enjoy life. I realize that God can take back his own creations to teach us to understand and appreciate the treasures we have in our lives. I can no longer see my father, but his soul, along with all of the memories I have of him, remains in my heart.

 janet**jun**20

Orange, California

> *I grew up in southern California, then moved to New York City at the age of sixteen to attend Columbia University. Besides writing, I am passionate about martial arts, snowboarding, films, and NY pizza. In my view, my family and my EMT-VJ girls are the two things that make life beautiful.*

Ghost Brother

Mother sings, *ja jang ja jang ooh ree ae-gi,* to my newborn baby brother, who is cradled in her pale, bare, and muscular arms. His cries are weak, small, so fragile I feel as though my breathing will smother them. I lay stiff and motionless next to my sister on my parents' enormous bed. *Janet! I'm cold!* I hear my sister's hoarse and frustrated whisper as she pulls on the huge mound of sheets that I hold tightly to my belly. The weight feels nice, steadying me, making me feel secure. *Mom! Janet stole all the blankets!* My sister whines in protest. I tighten my grip and shut my eyes.

Janet, sweetie, please share with your sister. Her voice does not change, it is still soft and lulling, careful of little brother in her arms. *She's older, please respect her.*

I softly moan, as if disturbed out of a restful sleep. *Ja-net!* My sister hollers; the spell of my mother's lulling voice is broken, Little Brother's cries echo loudly off the walls.

Girls, please. My mother's voice cracks, it sounds tired and strained, lacking its previous smoothness. *Please, girls, no fighting. You are sisters, the only sister you'll ever have. You must love each other and share with each other.*

I open my eyes.

Okay. Sorry, Mommy. I let go of the blankets.

Maybe even then my mother knew that we would never grow up with Little Brother, that he would be gone as quickly as he came. And so she decided to teach my sister and me to love each other fiercely, to know like we knew how to breathe that a sibling is irreplaceable, different from a parent, a friend, a cousin.

The record book in my head skips a few pages, pages that I can't see or read because I cannot remember. Then it stops in a dark, crowded, stuffy, and hot room. People are sitting, standing, squatting in every corner, on the floor, on the couch, on chairs. And the noise. The noise is never ending; chants and sobs, louder and then softer, like a symphony that can't make up its mind. *Jany-ah, look at your mother. She is so sad, what will you do?* A lady speaks softly in my ear and I can't see her. But I can smell her, mothballs and Dial soap. The sound of adult cries, new to my ear and different from Little Brother's, scares me.

Jany-ah, your mother is so sad. The lady points to another lady sitting on the floor. She looks thin, pale, and messy. When she lifts her head in a soft wail, I realize the woman is my mother. I crawl into her lap carefully, scared but sad because she is sad. Her cries get louder as I sit between her crossed legs and I feel hot wet tears drop quickly onto my neck, face, and hands. The hotness from my mother's body makes me uncomfortable and sweaty. She holds me tightly against her chest and feels pain. I search for my sister, but she is sitting on Uncle's lap, listening to him tell her something I cannot hear. I search for my father and cannot find him in the crowd of strangers' faces and bent necks.

My mother does not know that I remember these things, that I remember Joshua, feel him like a sad spirit wandering the hallways of our home. When I was nine she told me about him, believing I was too young to remember.

He was exactly two years and a day younger than you. He died of crib death when he was eleven days old. Her voice is soft and steady. I calculated in my head. His birthday was a day after mine. I wondered what went through my mother's head every year as she planned my surprise party, bought a chocolate cake, and sent out invitations. I wonder now if she was thinking of Joshua.

Does Mom have any pictures of him?

No. My mother looks away. We burned them after he died. She shakes her head and sighs. What did he look like?

Oh, he was handsome. My mother smiles proudly. *Very very handsome. He had big eyes, strong, round forehead like your sister's, and Appa's nose.*

I studied my father's nose that night at dinner. It was straight and dignified, not flat like my mother's or mine. A nose that signaled royalty and strength is what my mom always said. I looked at my sister's forehead and tried to put it together with my father's nose. But I still had no picture, no face, only fragments and the sound of a fragile cry.

A few weeks later I looked up "crib death" in the *Manual of Diseases and Syndromes* that was sitting on my sister's shelf . . . reports have indicated that the infant is more likely to suffer Sudden Infant Death Syndrome if lying facedown . . . I ran to my mother with this new information, reading it aloud to her.

Mom, look! It says that . . .

She cut me off as I read it, screeching, *Shik-a-ruh-wuh!* Noise to my ears, I don't want to hear it, shut up.

I dropped the book and ran to my room, hot tears already forming as I hid my face from my sister's startled expression. The desperation in my mother's voice at that moment was the same as the night baby brother turned into a spirit. When my mother told me to shut up, the first and only time, she told me that my words were empty like the way ghosts speak emptiness.

tina**shim**21

Huntington Beach, California

"Insomnia" is a personal essay I wrote in the fall of 1999 at Amherst College. I let a bit of my Korean culture sneak in. I don't like, at all, the idea of writing an all-encompassing book about my Korean American experience and heritage in full detail. I think that having a bit of my life is so much more interesting and personal. This piece allows a flash of insight into what it's like inside my head.

Insomnia

My best friend Cathy called me the other day, laughing through her noise as she told me she had spied a closet filled with blankets at a new friend's home, and realized it was a Korean thing. She had always thought it was just a weird thing of my family's that we should have so many blankets; further, that we should pile them up, carefully folded, one on top of the other, all into one specially denoted closet. But did all Koreans have a closet of blankets? She wanted to know. I felt sheepish for Koreans everywhere and had a raging instinct to tell her that it was a reaction from the Korean War and all that coldness so that she would feel guilty and stop asking me questions. I had to laugh, and then suddenly I felt so distant from home, talking to Cathy on the phone. I missed my closet of blankets.

Whenever Cathy spent the night or we rented videos, I would take her to our walk-in closet, tucked away in our yellow room, and have her pick out a blanket. Everyone's favorite was the thick furry red blanket, a type of blanket called *dam-yo* for Koreans, covered with dark pink blossoms and wide green leaves. It must have weighed five pounds. I thought everyone picked it because to Americans it was like the ultimate flannel sheet, verging on fur coat status, the heaviness creating an imagined heat more than generating it. Perhaps it just trapped heat better. I always picked two blankets; sitting on one, clutching my teddy bear in my lap, the other draped about my shoulders, tightly enfolding me like a real bear. My childhood was filled with draped blankets: over the furniture to dry, littered about sofas after cat naps, magically spread over me if I fell asleep while reading a book. If I happened upon freshly laundered blankets that had been quickly folded by my mother and left on the steps to be carried upstairs to the closet later, I would tuck my hands under the flaps and let the warmth pervade my body like hot tea.

Too many blankets can spoil a girl. In my dreams, with my eyes tightly clenched before falling asleep and cuddling a blanket to my chin, I was always a princess. It usually took me over an hour to fall asleep, so I would go through the whole gamut of princesses: I was one of the seven princesses, the sleeping princess, the Cinderella princess, even the princess with the seven dwarfs. But I never did connect the story of the Princess and the Pea to me. Not even when I would roll in between the many folded blankets in our closet, carefully piled like a sturdy tower so as not to topple if one of the lower blankets were yanked out like a magician's tablecloth. I was always fascinated by the idea that this princess's skin should be so sensitive that sleep would be impossible. Because I was a nasty sleeper myself: more often than not I would kick all of my blankets off so that my father would tiptoe in every morning before work to pile them all back on top of me. Or the small of my back would get hot, or my neck would get a cramp from the high pillow and so I would eventually, inevitably, slide off of the bed, yanking all of my blankets with me, and roll around until I was once more comfortable and fall asleep. Then, I would have to sneak back on top of the bed before my father came in. In high school I was certain that I had back problems, and after reading Jack Kennedy's biography insisted that a flat wooden board be placed between two mattresses in order to support my weak spine.

When I was in Korea the summer before college, before I would move away to school, taking as many blankets as I could with me, I had the delicious opportunity to sleep on the floor, every night. Hence the closet of blankets for Koreans: elaborate armoires filled with blankets that were spread out for bed and put back in by morning. I had not, however, accounted for the wretched heat of Korean summers, or the hardness of the ubiquitous linoleum floors. It was too much to bear. I would usually end up wandering to the living room and lie on the cool leather couches, constantly shifting because the leather would grow tepid from my body heat. After spending one particularly grueling weekend sight-seeing, I arrived late Sunday morning at my grandparents' home exhausted and ready to sleep. I took every blanket in the closet and selfishly began to pile the blankets, one on top of another, until a bedlike form emerged. I collapsed onto the blankets, sinking already limp muscles into unconsciousness. I don't even remember waking up. I only remember how sweet it felt to have only one linen sheet swathing me as if one had died, and everybody was silently treading past my pile like a funeral pyre.

Nowadays, the blankets pile on top of me. When my heater won't work, which is all too often here in these old dormitories, I take all of my blankets and spread them over my body like a picnic tablecloth. I huddle underneath, moving about to create warmth and occasionally poke my head out when I need some air. Usually the mornings are deliciously bright, and after I run off to the bathroom, I dance back to my bed and dive back under my blankets and spend at least a good, solid twenty minutes daydreaming about a perfect fantasy.

Currently I'm a first-year, biochemistry major at Boston University. Both my parents were born and raised in the Philippines. Writing started out as medium for emotional and artistic venting. Over the years, I've found myself inspired by people who make me see things in different lights or people who make me want to spit out all the emotions that they shake up inside of me. I'm very much for Asian awareness and I think this is a good opportunity to speak out as an Asian American girl who believes there's a common bond between all of us.

Daughter

Perhaps it is my overindulgence of my personal dramatics
That holds me back from trying
To be obedient enough to will energy in performing daily chores.
For to be a loving daughter is to be an obedient one
As one parent might explain to his child

Maybe it is simply the liberal environment in which I was brought
    up
That discouraged such meekness to anyone
So that I have, more than once, forgotten not to raise my voice
When I speak to her.
Such disrespect displayed in a daughter's attitude
Has clearly reflected her parents' own faults.
There is no love proved there, a warning to us all.

When I think of all this and realize how contrary a daughter I
    really am
I am pushed into accusing myself that somewhere,
I fell into the category of not being good enough.

In some way, I try to explain my fault with horrible explanations to
  her
When her eyes are closed in sleep
Many times in this situation I suddenly crouch next to her bed and
  squint critically
At her face and abdomen,
Checking to see that she is still breathing.
I hold my own until I see that she has inhaled and exhaled
And then re-collect myself
Right before realizing I had been crying.

gena s.**hamamoto**21
Irvine, California

*My family immigrated to America from Japan four generations ago.
Over time, my family has lost the Japanese language and many cultural traditions. Throughout my twenty years in Orange County, I
have constantly questioned my own validity as a Japanese American,
fearing that I was a "banana"—yellow on the outside and white on
the inside. Recently, I compiled a five-generation family history, and I
have come to realize my ethnic identity in more fluid, less static
terms. "Cultural Karma" is a reflection of this understanding of culture as it evolves through retention, inclusion, and loss.*

Cultural Karma

This hand
Placed over mouth
As graceful giggles slip through narrow lips

Holds no fan to cover blackened teeth
Has not burned with pain forming sticky cakes
Never poked by vines that grow tomorrow's meal
Does not brush beautiful calligraphy

Has held the hand of those who have
And still lingers
When I laugh.

julie**lu** then 14
San Diego, California

*I was born on September 7, 1985, in Oklahoma. I now live in San
Diego, California. Both of my parents came to the United States
from Vietnam. "The Answer" is a tribute to my grandma, whose
unforgettable stories, songs, and riddles fascinated me so much
when I was younger.*

The Answer

"Tell me a riddle, Grandma. Please. A new one this time," I said.

"Oh, all right," she said.

She was quiet for a few seconds thinking thoughtfully to herself
for a new riddle to tell me.

"The two of them sleep in separate rooms," my grandma
explained. "In the morning they open their doors to the outside, at
night they shut their doors."

"A table? People? Horses?"

At the time I didn't have the slightest clue what the answer was,
or even what the riddle meant. But I was determined not to give up.

"No, none of those." My grandma laughed. I laughed too.

"Don't tell me the answer, Grandma, I'll figure it out." I was
determined.

She smiled and waited patiently as I rattled off all of my ridiculous answers.

When I spent time with my grandma, I loved it when she told
me riddles. My grandma was never annoyed or too tired to tell
them to me. Although she couldn't make use of her arms or legs
while she was telling me stories, her voice was so animated when

she spoke. Her bed looked like a hospital bed. Climbing up the side of it, I'd sit right next to her head and ask her to tell me another one, another Vietnamese riddle. I loved hearing them because they had a flowing rhythm and they were so clever. When I was small, I used to think that my grandma's riddles were her secrets, and I felt so special that she would let me hear them and know about them too. I was always afraid that one day she might run out of new ones to tell me, and every time I asked, she would amaze me. Those were the best times I had with my grandma.

As I got older, I spent less and less time in her room. I soon forgot about the riddles altogether. I wanted something more to do than just play with my grandma. Other things started to interest me, like reading or playing with my friends. Occasionally I would stick my head into her room and see her lying in bed, staring up at the ceiling, and I could tell that she was sad and lonely. I felt sorry for her, but I would never go to her, because I didn't know what made her happy. Suddenly I felt like I was too old to ask for a riddle like I had when I was little. I would sometimes plan in my mind to go into her room and sit and talk with her, but I never knew what I would say to her.

In the end I always convinced myself that she didn't need my company. I convinced myself of this for a very long time. Even if she did want to talk to me, though, I knew there wasn't much she could do. Sometimes she would call out my name over and over again until she grew tired, and I still would never come to her side to see what she wanted. I would pretend not to hear her voice and go about my own way. Soon she stopped yelling because she knew I wouldn't come. I had other things to do, and I didn't realize then that life doesn't go on forever.

When my grandma died, I cried. I cried because my cousin cried and I stopped crying when she stopped. Outside I showed no emotions, but inside, I felt a horrible aching. When she was lying in her coffin, I touched her cold face. I wanted so badly for her to wake up. I wanted to have one last time to see her. I wanted her to come back and lie on her bed, so she could yell out my name once more time with great urgency; this time I would scramble to her room. I would express to her that I was sorry for treating her so poorly. I would do anything for her, and then I would beg her to tell me a riddle. And I would guess and guess while she laughed at my silly answers and together we'd laugh.

I bit my lip and tried to keep the tears from coming down. All of a sudden the riddle about the two things that slept in separate rooms came back to me with such odd clarity—as if she was telling it to me once again. I heard it over and over. I stood over the coffin for a long time, her voice and the riddle repeating in my head. And then I smiled.

I looked at her cold face, and whispered, "They're eyes."

jennifer**chen**21
Shrewsbury, New Jersey

I grew up in the United States as one of the few Asians in my small New Jersey town. My parents are from Taiwan. My parents divorced when I was three, separating East Coast and West Coast. I grew up with a love for reading and writing. When it came time for college, I decided I wanted to be a writer, which was difficult for my father to accept. I wrote "To Our Favorite Baby Doctor" to express feelings in words to my father that I couldn't speak out loud.

To Our Favorite Baby Doctor

My dad delivers babies for a living. A hundred snapshots of smiling tots standing near Christmas trees: *Love from the Joneses. To our favorite baby doctor.* We run into women at the grocery stores, women he's hovered over, delivering screaming red babies from their wombs.

My dad didn't deliver me. I was a complicated birth, one more twist of the umbilical cord and I would have been a goner. Twenty-three hours of labor minus my dad—only me, my mom, the nurses, and the obstetrician, who opened my mother's insides to pull me out. Chris asked me if I resented my father for not being there while I was born, if that's where it all began. The resentment, long silences, succinct (or nonexistent) letters, the dreaded phone calls (sighing when I hear his broken English). I don't know if that's where it all began but I suppose it's a start.

Age Seven.

I always get sick right before flying out to visit my dad in California. This time, 102 temperature. The stewardess gives me an extra ice-cream sandwich to cool me down. I smile at her because I love ice cream. I ask Mom if Santa Claus can find us since we're in the wrong house this year. She reassures me he will, and then she buys a package of gingersnap cookies and a half quart of milk. As we drive to our uncle's house, Mom asks if I'd like to see my dad tonight. I fiddle with the window knobs and play deaf. Later, Mom talks to Dad in hushed whispers over the phone. *She doesn't want to spend the week with you.* I put the groceries away quietly, pretending I don't understand big grown-up words. Mom kisses my cheek and then says that Dad will come by later to take me out to dinner. I ignore her and play with the bag of gingersnap cookies. I cradle it in my arms like a baby. When my dad comes to pick me up I cling on to my mother for dear life, begging her—

Please, Mommy, please don't make me go.

He's your father. I want to stay here. Don't make me go.

Cling to her neck like if I let go, I'll fall, and I can't fall. I fall into the leather seats of his car and make up my mind not to say a word. If I speak, I let go. No speaking. He takes me to a Rocky and Bullwinkle restaurant with skeeball games and strips of red tickets to win plastic prizes. I win some dippy prize I know I'll throw away. He takes me home and I run from the car into my mother's arms. I don't let go.

Age thirteen.

Braces, glasses, thick, awkward hair that shoots out like limbs. Pimples and a body that's bending out in weird places. I step out of the airplane terminal in heavy green pants, a matching shirt with a forest of green flowers. My favorite outfit. My dad greets me, minus a hug. He tugs my luggage to his blue convertible Mercedes. I sit in the seats gently, afraid to damage the perfect-looking car. I shut my eyes, willing myself to sleep. To tune out the classical music humming around us. To fade away in the leather seats. We pull up to a house five times the size of my squat ranch house on the East Coast, a place of familiarity, where I spent summers running through whipping sprinklers. This place is enormous, with white carpet, cold-feet marble, and space. And there's a baby grand piano in the living room. *Play the piano for me*. I stare at the enormous black instrument, about ten lessons under my belt, and I sit down and tap out a vague childish tune, my fingers wrestling to make something more pure, more Mozart. I stop, and he says nothing.

When my dad comes home, he checks his messages and I bury myself in a book. We shuffle around in the kitchen. Not speaking while I cook. Our meals are usually scrapped with my quietness and my dad's abundant broken English—he's grilling me on my academics, and why my mother isn't a good parent. He slides off my glasses because they're ugly and *why are your lips so big they look like pig lips, you know what pig lips look like. . . .* Inside, I'm a quivering, small child. Outside I nod and excuse myself into the bathroom where I lock the door and ball up, my knees to my chin, and cry. I try to imagine myself anywhere but here, maybe Bermuda, maybe my house, maybe my pink and gray room. He's banging on the door. *What's wrong? Let me in*. I push my body against the door. I vow never to come back.

Age nineteen.

My second Christmas home from college with my mom. It's early for me, 11:30 a.m. or so. My cordless Bell Atlantic phone buzzes. I grumble a hello. It's my dad. I brace myself for the usual talk of how I need to go to law school, business school, or any other school, instead of doing this writing, but instead his voice sounds tired and deflated, like a lifeless balloon.

I have cancer. He cries. And I don't.

My heart says, Cry, cry, don't you have any feeling inside?

He says, *Come see me.* I say *I can't.* I hand the phone off to my mom because I can't do this alone. They talk and I cry.

Honey, it's okay, don't cry. She's crying. It's okay. Inside I think that this is a dream. Outside, I'm crying uncontrollably.

I finally see my parents together around a hospital bed, and my mom does most of the talking while my dad stares at the ceiling. I think to hold tears back, and I pace or pretend to go to the bathroom because I feel safe there.

I have to help him to the bathroom. Unplug the IV stand and walk alongside him. His hospital gown lingers like open curtains and I see my father naked from behind and I can't close my eyes because I might trip on a cord. My mother and I look at each other and I think without her here I would be comatose. I help my dad back to his bed. The front of his gown opens and his penis dangles in front of me and the room smells like aspirin, chicken soup, and bleach. The woman next door rants, *Raymond! Raymond, where are you?* Inside, I'm having a nightmare. Outside, I sit down in the hard-as-rock, plastic, pale blue hospital couch and try to fall asleep.

My mom flies back to New Jersey without me. She has to go back to work. I visit my dad's office alone, the thousand Christmas babies are full-grown and I am no longer waiting for Santa. Dad rolls up his sleeves to reveal thick black veins. Chemo wears his body yellow. He asks me to send him some writing. I say I might, but I know I won't. I wait until we get to the airport terminal to hug him. "I love you" chokes me in the throat, and instead, I wave good-bye. When I get home, we talk. Inches of me sneak into the phone. Inside, I'm still confused, afraid to let myself slip out, trying to let go.

Outside, I fold up this paper and send it to my father.

My mom used to tell me life is just a blank book when you are born. Then you write all your strokes in it—calligraphy, drawing, spitting, whatever you want to do. It all depends on how you want to turn the pages.

—Actress Vivian Wu, quoted in *aMagazine* (April/May 2000)

anjelica**cruz** 19
Virginia Beach, Virginia

My parents immigrated to the States from the Philippines about six years before I was born, because my father was in the military. We moved constantly from place to place until we settled in Virginia Beach, Virginia. During our travels, I began forming questions about my identity. I was inspired to write my story "Fried Fish" because of the persistent strength and encouragement my mother gave me as I walked down the path to find myself. I'm still walking that path—with my mother right beside me.

Fried Fish

I am a girl. I am an Asian American girl. For a time in my life I was just an American girl and shortly after that I was just an Asian girl. Thus began my journey.

When I was younger I would sit at the edge of the driveway and play with my dolls while my mom cooked on the gas stove in the garage. I was never allowed to roam too far from my mom's sight. The garage would reek of fried fish or crabs and the smell would travel the length of the driveway and down the street. I used to hate that smell with a passion. I could never get far enough from the odor. No matter how many times I took a bath or washed my hair it always seemed to follow me around, kind of like the sound of my mom's singing. Her voice would make me cringe. She wasn't entirely fluent in English, so when she did try to speak, her heavy Filipino accent would often prevail. While frying the fish, my mother sang old Tagalog songs, which she had brought with her from the Philippines. The neighborhood kids, who would frequently walk by my house, would hear her singing and laugh. I was so embarrassed.

"Mom, do you always have to sing those songs?" I said, annoyed. "If you're going to sing, why don't you sing something a little more modern, something in English maybe?"

"Anak, those songs are a part of our culture," she said with a confident smile, disregarding my rude comment. "Culture is a very important part of our lives."

I shrugged my shoulders at this remark and went back to playing with my dolls. I never paid much attention to what she had to say. It all sounded like nonsense—I mean, how would my Filipino culture help me fit in anywhere?

"I'm an American," I thought to myself. "That isn't my culture."

I grew up in a white upper-class suburban neighborhood. It was the picture of perfect American life. The neighborhood was enclosed by white picket fences, each lawn was precisely cut into a trim neatness, and almost every household had exactly 2.4 children. That was my culture. That was my reality. I would often push my Filipino heritage to the sidelines while I tried to be more "American." In school I always felt like an alien compared to the other girls with their curly blond hair, light eyes, and pointed noses. I didn't look anything similar to them. I had dark slanted eyes, straight black hair, and a flat nose. As a child, I longed to be like those girls and at one point I made it my main objective to fit in with them. They would reject me, time after time, and I would go home crying to my mother. She was in the garage, cooking as usual.

"What's wrong with me, Mom?" I sobbed. "I do everything they do, and they still make fun of me."

"Just don't try so hard, Anak," she would say reassuringly in her broken English. "You're trying to be like them, but you're forgetting about yourself."

I didn't understand anything she said at the time and I really didn't care. I never did accredit my mother's opinion. After all, what would she know about living in the United States? She's not American like me.

"She's just babbling again," I mumbled to myself.

When I left elementary school, I became fed up with constantly being the social outcast. I decided, at that point, that my mom was right. Culture was a very important part of my life.

"I'm no longer American, I'm Filipino," I would say.

I became more aware of my "homeland" (meaning the Philippines) and made an effort to speak to my parents in Tagalog as well as I could. I thought that if I reached deep enough into my heritage, I would find out who I really was. I made new friends at school—new Asian friends. I went to every Asian function—rallies, picnics, meetings—and I joined all kinds of Asian associations. I had finally found a place where I felt like I belonged, but, somewhere along the way, I started to neglect my American background. I would make snide remarks about other races and I would take action on those remarks. Feelings of neglect that I'd grappled with as a child fueled my rage more and I resented anyone not sharing my dark skin tone. Fistfights among kids belonging to different racial groups became a recurring incident in high school, and somehow, I always seemed to get caught in the middle of them. On one occasion I was outnumbered and took a harsh beating. I had cuts and bruises all over my body. I ran home to my mother, crying.

"Anak, why are you trying to so hard to be something you're not?" she said, trying to hold back her own tears. She held my head in her arms and stroked my long black hair down to my waist. Her clothes smelled of fried fish and freshly steamed rice, just like they always did after cooking all day.

"You're trying to be like them, but you're forgetting about yourself."

Her words echoed in my mind. I found myself in elementary

school again crying to my mom because I was being teased at school.

"What am I doing? This isn't me," I thought to myself, while my mom held me and rocked me back and forth. She was crying, too. I could feel her tears fall on my shoulders, and they felt like drops of boiling water burning my skin. I lifted my head and looked straight into her eyes through the blood dripping from my head.

"So what do I do now?" I asked.

"You know what to do," she said, helping me clean off some of the dirt and blood I had accumulated during the fight. "You just aren't doing it, but you've known what to do all along. Come sit with me in the garage while I cook, your dad will be home soon."

I didn't quite understand how the smell of food frying and the sound of my mom singing would make my problems disappear. I sat there in the garage for an hour listening to the sound of the fryer occasionally drowned out by the sound of my mom's voice. We didn't say a word to each other. She just kept singing.

The next few days I moped around the house. I had no motivation to do anything. I didn't know where I was going and I didn't know who I was. I spent my afternoons sitting in the garage with my mom while she cooked and I listened to her sing. I never really took the time to actually listen to her. Every once in a while we would talk.

"You know, everything that happens in life is put there for a reason," she said as I stared at her blankly. "Sometimes we are just so busy we don't see what the reason is."

At times I would sit on the edge of my driveway again and listen to my mom sing old Tagalog songs while she fried fish in the garage. Her voice always sounded so beautiful, it seemed to float in the breeze as if she was singing to the world. She was never afraid, never insecure. She didn't always know where life would lead, but she never forgot who she was, and she never forgot who I was. I often reflect on my identity crisis and wonder why things unfolded the way that they did. It was my journey toward finding an identity—something I wouldn't have rediscovered without my mom.

rebecca in-young**chung** 18
New York, New York

> *I was born in Seoul, Korea, in the summer of 1982. My parents
> came to study in the United States when I was three. Two years
> later, they separated and I remained in the States with my mother
> while my father returned to Korea. From that time on, my relation-
> ship with my father, further confused by geographic and cultural
> conflicts, was something I found incomprehensible and at times,
> quite painful. I wrote "Collisions" during my junior year in high
> school, when pressures about selecting colleges and careers were
> running high. It allowed me to look back on the choices my parents
> made, and the way in which their decisions molded my life and
> allowed me to accomplish all that I thought I had done on my own.*

Collisions

I'm packing for the weekend, throwing books into my bag, when the
phone rings. It's my dad, and even while I'm consciously thinking
he's in Korea, just checking up on me since I never open my e-mail
anymore, something about the clearness of the lines, the closeness of
his voice warns me this might not be a long-distance call.

"So, what are you doing today?" He is casual, as if this were just
another phone call when actually it's the first time we've talked
since Christmas.

"I have plans with my friends . . . actually, we're getting
together to study for our exams on Monday."

"Wow . . . Hmm, listen, I'm going to this thing tomorrow
night. . . ."

"Huh?" I'm thinking, what does this have to do with me, whatever you're planning to do halfway across the world? But that
dread feeling; the clarity, the nearness . . .

"—at UH."

Oh.

"You're here?" I can see myself talking to my friends tonight, complaining about how my dad just shows up whenever he feels like it, without warning. They'll tell me he probably just wanted to surprise me, what a nice thing to do, they'll say. Well, maybe I'm just a hypocrite 'cause I'd say so, too, in situations like this, but we're talking about my dad and how this is happening to me.

"Yeah, so you seem pretty busy." Does he sound relieved?

"Yeah, I had exams on Friday, and I have more all next week," I say, only I have to figure out how to say this all in Korean and I end up stuttering so much even I would think I was lying.

"Hmmm, well, I'm leaving Tuesday morning. . . ."

"Oh. Well, I can cancel with my friends tonight—I mean, I can just go later, anytime." That's not what I was planning to say.

"Okay, great! Then I'll be there at two? Yeah, I'll be waiting, um, with Inhea." He mentions my stepmom's name deliberately; he thinks I don't like her, which is typical of him. He never listens and has the perceptiveness of a brick wall.

"Okay," I say. Then I scream excitedly to my mom, start pulling clothes out of my closet and laying on the makeup, rushing around the house, high-pitched. My mom gets excited, too, she's smiling and helping me pick out an outfit, which goes to show how crazy we both are—she, admitting anything in my wardrobe is nice and me, listening to her.

And still, seeing how happy my mom is makes me want to cry. It's not that she's glad to be near my father; she hates him with as much passion as her religion allows her. But she thinks my dad is here to see me, like he's being a decent father for once, and it's like this big guilt is lifted from her shoulders. That's the way mothers are: she thinks it's her fault I don't have a father because she's the one that fell in love with him, and she's the one that married him. She's the one that didn't sacrifice her entire life to stay with him so I could have a father. Sometimes, mothers will die for their children; the ones who survive always feel like they should've given more. So she hurts for me when he doesn't call, as if that shields me, and she gets happy for me, too, when he pays attention to me.

I check myself in the mirror one last time before leaving the building and walking down the steps like I used to when I waited for my dad to come by to pick me up when I was a little girl. As I descend, I can see two figures walking across the parking lot, waving through the shimmering heat. They are dressed in shorts and T-shirts, and suddenly I am uncomfortable in my pressed shirt and long pants. My dad's stomach is slightly protruding, but other than that, he looks so young that I am almost angry; he was twenty-seven when I was born, and I wonder if he has aged at all since then. My stepmother is so thin and pale, she looks breakable. She has the girlish proportions of a woman who has never borne children. She was forty when she married my dad, supposedly having been a career woman till then, but then she acts so submissive I can't see her as any kind of feminist. Instead, I imagine what dark or shameful secrets her past might hold, like, what she did with twenty years of her marriageable life. But then I think, maybe, she's just a testament of how fast time flies if you don't catch it and hold onto it for dear life. I think, also, of my mother in my room late at night when I got home from meeting Inhea for the first time. Is she low-class? My mother had whispered with deliberate apathy. The way she said it, I could tell that what she really wanted to know was if my father loved Inhea, or if this was just another something he was trying to rub in her face.

I'm trying to remember how I answered my mother as Inhea pulls me into an embrace. It's like hugging a pole and I feel sorry for my dad, the hopeful way he told me they wanted to have kids, the bravery he had to have mustered up to tell me that to my face. For a tender moment I think he really does deserve a second chance, a fair shot, since he's sure my crazy mother was the one that screwed us up. But then I think about how he lied through his teeth about having a girlfriend, and how he told me that he was married only after the fact, and how my grandparents cried when they heard about the wedding. And I feel hopeless rather than bitter that he's messed up more chances than anyone deserves.

So we sit at a park table in the shade and my dad goes to the vending machine to get some drinks. Inhea pulls her knees to her chest and asks me about college. I explain to her in Korean what college admissions in America is like, starting with technicalities, like what "early decision" means and how much GPA counts and what AP classes are. Then she asks me where I want to go to school, and I think about lying, just so I don't jinx myself. Instead I end up telling her how much I want to go to New York and become a writer or a journalist—I talk about passion and instinct and desire. My dad is back by now and he shakes his head as if it pains him that I want to make a living off my mind. He thinks I should become a doctor, a pediatrician, so I can make my brainless rounds every day and still have enough energy to go home and cook a nice meal for my family. He tells me earning a living by writing is too difficult. *You'll get ulcers*, he says, *you'll go crazy*. I want to tell him that that's what artists are like, mad as hell, but then I'd sound conceited and unappreciative and naive, so I just nod. It's not like he really expects his opinions to have much weight anyway. Then, suddenly, I panic—I'm thinking, here I am, bragging in my bratty way about all that I'm destined to accomplish, when I have exams in two days, and I should be cramming like a madwoman. After the panic swells down, I'm left with a gigantic headache, so I tell my dad and Inhea that I really should study for my exams, and they take me home. I tell my dad to come by Tuesday morning before he leaves and he nods before waving me off.

On Monday, I join my friends in the library, and they reassure me that the exam is three hours away, so I pull out my books, but then I tell myself it's too late. I sit at my cubicle and watch my cell phone instead. I gave the number to my dad and he said he'd call, and I can't believe I'm reduced to this—back at square one, waiting for him to call. People say that you can learn from your mistakes, but I think it's a lie, because life is regression. Every time we think we're moving forward, something grabs you and holds you back when you're not looking. Or maybe when you let down your guard, like gravity, so it's only things that are destined to fly that actually do.

My auntie calls later that night to tell my mom that my dad will be by the next morning to say good-bye. My mom says for him to come by 6:30, even though I leave the house at 7:15. He, verbatim, only wants to see me for ten to fifteen minutes. I'm irritated because this means I'll get an hour less of sleep time before a test, but I'm up at 5:30 picking out clothes again. Regression. At 6:45 I'm walking out the door when my mom stops me.

"Don't go yet," she says, half-pleading, half-commanding.

"Why not?" I wonder if we'll fight again now, waking the neighbors with our cursing.

"Because your dad's going to come."

"I thought you said for him to be here by 6:30." I'd actually daw-dled for fifteen minutes, just to make my dad wait. It hadn't occurred to me that he might stand me up the same way he forgets to call.

"I know, but you know he never listens to me." She laughs. *How charming*.

"Well, that's his problem. I don't even want to see him. I'm busy. If he's not here, that's not my fault. I'm leaving." I don't know what I'm hoping as I slam the door. I know I'll cry if he's not there, but I'm not sure I really want to see him either.

He's there, though, and he takes my hand and my backpack and insists on walking me to school. Needless to say, I'm embarrassed to be seen on campus walking hand in hand with a man who barely passes as my father. I'm also ashamed to be embarrassed because I'm supposed to be this mature adult, who grew up fine without a dad, but really I don't know what I am inside. We sit on a bench outside where my first class is and talk—pleasantly, really—about how an American education is so valuable, and how it has been so worth it for me to be far away from my family to be here. Then he gives me $500. I insist, I don't need it, and really, I don't feel like spending his money. Maybe I feel like I'm being bought, or maybe it's just that I don't feel close enough to him to be taking his money. Then again, maybe I just don't want to thank him like I know I'll have to if I take it, but whichever it is, I honestly don't want it.

But of course it gets shoved in my wallet. I bow to him to show my appreciation and I bow to him again when he leaves, after he gives me a hug. I think of the four days he was here, and how it threw me off right when I thought I couldn't be thrown; how I'd learned to thrive in apathy. One act of care was like poison, not the kind that causes permanent damage, but the kind that leaves your body out of whack for a few days, a week maybe, pulling you out of your safe and normal orbit for one brief collision.

anjali**blob**19
Oberlin, Ohio

I was born in Maryland and currently live in Ohio, where I attend Oberlin College. I am from a mixed ethnic background. My mother migrated from her homeland, India, and married my father, a Caucasian American man. Throughout my life, writing has been my consistent passion and outlet, my way of breaking silence and bearing witness to my experiences. This poem, "Funeral," serves as an account and remembrance of my friend, who died in a tragic car accident in 1998.

Funeral for Bryce

They lay on the street,
eighteen years
shattered with glass.

We piece them together
with praise, prayers, and hymns,
shiny shoes and a suit, crisp,
like the clock ticking.

I stare at it,
cold and stiff,
dressed for an interview
as if God were an employer.

Caked with makeup,
he is not the same
without acne,
greasy hair,
sweaty tennis shirts,
without his jokes
that pester to peaks
of helpless laughter.

I wish I could place
the memories of us
dancing,
laughing,
kissing in my kitchen
and place them in his pockets,
bury them.

It's hard to admit
I closed his casket
years ago.

 caroline**fan**19
Skokie, Illinois

Born in North Carolina, I grew up in Chicago. In past years, I have sojourned to Taiwan many times, which is why I feel an intense personal tie to Taiwan, the birthplace of my parents. I wrote "The Procession" when I was sixteen, and looking forward to a summer in Taiwan. I was motivated to write it while contemplating the last time I was in Taiwan, surrounded by my beloved relatives. I thought the tale was important because it examines bereaving customs in the United States and in Taiwan, as well as familial relations.

The Procession

Growing up in America, Taiwan struck me as being beautiful and yet quite odd. I still had not adjusted myself to the different time zone, but rather had fallen into a state of perpetual half-awakeness. The agile car glided down the highway and the scenery compelled me to the window. My flamingo-pink ice cream dripped pools of milk and sugar down my hand and onto the lap of the new dress Auntie had bought me. My two young boy cousins were playing a bizarre game of their own invention, most of which involved seeing who could attract and hold my twelve-year-old inattention. My uncle and aunt were having a flurried conversation in Chinese that had something to do with her kindergarten school. I could only comprehend bits and pieces, though. The trees were decidedly different from those in America and the terraced rice fields invited speculation. They looked like a giant set of steps to the heavens, man-carved out of the mountains, and I thought how funny it would be if one tripped on the way up.

We were headed toward my father's alma mater, Tung-hai University. The half-hour journey stretched out toward the horizon, with no intention of ending. My only disappointment was that they hadn't brought the new Game Boy along. Then a pretty flower car whizzed by on the opposite road, catching my roving eye. It looked like a Rose Bowl parade float, only not as large or elaborate. The flower car was proudly decked out in leis of pink, and the windows were fringed with green borders. I wondered if it was like a San Francisco trolley, and if I could get a ride somewhere. What is that, I questioned aloud in Chinese.

"Where?" asked my youngest cousin. I pointed down the road, but the dazzling incongruity had already vanished. "Oh, never mind," I breathed. It had disappeared faster than a butterfly. A little while down the road, I saw another flower car. This one was predominantly white and yellow, with red tufts and outlines and humongous pink flowers the size of shower caps under each window. This bauble was prettier than the last.

"That thing." I motioned.

"What?" my aunt inquired politely. I fumbled with the words, due to my lack of experience.

"That . . . that car with the big flowers—there!" She frowned noticeably and turned away.

Intrigued, I demanded to know what it was. My curiosity was aflame and I wanted an answer.

"It's something you wouldn't understand," she hedged. Now I knew already that the things adults say I wouldn't understand are the interesting ones that they don't want to explain. So I pursued the topic.

"Uncle, what's a flower car?" It was the best I could describe the phenomenon.

"Kailing, Uncle is driving," she patiently reminded me, brushing away my eager inquisitiveness. "Those flower cars are not pretty," she stated, attempting to put it in words I could understand.

"But why not?" I whined.

"Because they carry dead people!" she snapped, exasperated.

A subtle "oh" slipped from my lips. My eyes were liquid pansies of recognition. My cousins' raucous laughter startled me.

"Where? Where? I want to see too!" they clamored gleefully, climbing over me.

"Hush—don't speak of such things!" I cried.

The wind had just been knocked out of me. I shut my eyes and let go, letting their obnoxious chatter wash over me. And to think that minutes ago I had wanted to ride in a flower car, like at a carnival. The image of a cool black hearse crept into my mind and the contrast was so unbearable that I remained quiet the rest of the trip. A dark limo with tinted windows didn't give anything away, yet quietly announced its status—perfect for incognito movie stars, airport transportation, and . . . coffins. A somber metal bullet wavered, turning into bursts of red, yellow, green, and pink.

Two years later, I had the opportunity to return to Taiwan and sit in an actual flower car. I wore traditional white muslin, rough as my sorrow. My grandfather had died of complications due to

Parkinson's disease, and I flew overseas to attend his funeral. I glanced at the car, covered in white carnations with yellow and red roses as piping. It was all just icing, I determined, not very tasteful and visually overwhelming. The flower car was as out of place as a freak exhibitionist in a beauty pageant. The flowers no longer held my interest, just the funeral custom. It was impossible to decipher why anyone would choose to dress up death in such a cheerful fashion. The utter reversal of everything I had ever associated with the funeral process completely unnerved me. I trudged aboard the lumbering car, and then we were on parade.

rebecca**villanueva**21

Huntington Park, California

As a university student trying to understand poetic forms and techniques, I kept this poem secret. As the daughter of hardworking no-nonsense Ilocano parents, I kept this poem secret. But as a young woman who (like thousands of others) strives for identity and expression, I finally submit this poem to you. Pilipino culture is based on the vibrancy of oral tradition, whether in the form of storytelling or even tsismis around the kitchen table. However, I believe that out of respect for our American selves, we must remember to claim narrative authority on paper as well. This poem is about my mom. I wouldn't hesitate to say that my understanding of what defines the Pilipina woman comes directly, and almost completely, from her. She's loud, intelligent, religious, temperamental, and, without a doubt, the queen of her house. She dislikes my cooking, but I love hers.

Chicken Tinola

In my student kitchenette
I slice a thumb of ginger
into coins, chop chicken

with a dull cleaver.
Chicken skin is bumpy and yellow
like an old woman's legs,
blue veins rubbery, resilient.

The cold has gone around again.
I caught it in the library.
Sickness clings to the walls
of my throat and seals my talking
with soreness. I want to call you
to find out how exactly to make
that magic ginger soup, the one
that burns the insides clean.
You used to ladle a cup of its hot broth
into my Holly Hobby mug
and make me drink it as I scowled.

Now I want you to send me
the recipe, written in your
Old World penmanship.
I would tuck that index card away
and pass it down, a family heirloom
to withstand microwave pizzas
and sliced bread in plastic bags:
I would say,
"This is tinola.
Your grandmother
used to make it.
She was the one
born in Baggao.
It will make you
well again."

But even if my throat weren't sore,
I wouldn't call to ask.

Ours are recipes
too simple to write down.
Instead I let my hands remember them.
and I let my heart remember when

dinner finished, you, my Ma,
used to hold my face and kiss me,
your hands smelling
of dish soap and garlic
and ginger.

lei-ann**lawi** then 15
Honolulu, Hawaii

All my life, Hawaii has been my home. I live with my parents and two brothers and live close to many of my relatives. In 1994, my grandfather's death not only triggered the harsh realization of death, but also caused me to look harder and deeper into my own outlook on life. I wrote "Furikake" as a tribute to the many things my grandfather has taught me and the greater impact he has left on my life.

Furikake

Furikake to me is like the little bits of memories all put together to form a mix that tastes so good on plain rice. Without even thinking, I shower my wet rice with furikake, covering the opening halfway so that it doesn't all pour out in a river of harshness. It was a lesson my Grandpa had taught me long ago that has now become a habit. I don't even think about how he had cupped my pudgy hands in his, teaching me how to hold the container correctly, and how I had to use two hands to hold the bottle because it was too big and my hands were too small. All I think about is how this small habit of mine is such a significant memory.

I remember the days when I would run halfway up the pink stairs of my grandparents' house as quickly as I could and then run back down, remembering that Grandpa was always in the backyard. He'd always take off his gardening gloves and escort me back up to the house, saying, "Lei-ko, tell Grandma I'll be right up."

After I washed my hands for dinner, he would always be there, patting the seat next to him and inviting me to sit in the seat closest to the television. I'd plop myself on the chair and reach for the furikake bottle. Then he'd always pour it for me ("not too much, because you can always have more") and then I'd happily eat while watching TV. But this time was different. This time he let me grab the furikake bottle, and instead of taking it from me, he silently molded my hands to hold the bottle so that my thumb would be halfway over the opening. I could feel the warmth of his love flow from his crinkled hands into the tips of my cool stubby fingers with ease and patience. My hands were so small and cumbersome, my thumb barely reaching the opening as I held the rest of the bottle. I remember asking, "Why do I have to cover the hole?"

"Lei-ko Chan, if you don't, it would all spill out and your rice would be too salty."

Determined to make my Grandpa proud of me, I did as he told me. When it got to the part of actually putting the furikake on my rice, my little hand didn't have the strength. My hand slid off the container and I stared at it bewildered and confused. Grandpa smiled at me patiently, his compassionate eyes looking into mine with undying love and understanding. I tried a couple of more times until finally in frustration I grabbed the bottle with *both* my hands and lightly drizzled my rice, covering the hole just how he had told me. My heart glowed with a feeling of exalting satisfaction.

Since then my hands have grown. I no longer have to hold the bottle with two hands and, more important, I understand the significance of his lesson. It was something that I would take with me for the rest of my life, and something I will teach my own children. Putting my thumb halfway over the opening was always a habit, and I didn't really grasp the full meaning of furikake until he died. Ever since the first time he taught me that small lesson, I have held the bottle that way with one hand. Except for the one time right after he passed away, when the bottle slipped out of my shaking hands and I yearned for his hands to mold mine again.

At first I was angry at God (or whoever decided to take him away) because I didn't think it was fair for such a healthy, good man to die. I was also angry at myself. Why didn't I ask him to teach me more things, like winning strategies in Trumps or how to play golf? I thought that only the big lessons were worthwhile, without even realizing that he has taught me some of the little things that I do every day. I realized that when I do those little things he taught me, he is with me. I might forget how to play Trumps or be too old to play golf, but those little habits will always be with me. Even though he is gone, I know his hands are still molding mine, except they are in my heart.

Everyone has a lesson to share. Whether it is big or small, it is worthwhile in someone's life. The smallest memories can stay with you forever and affect you every day. Every once in a while, I smile, sprinkling furikake on my steamed rice. And I remember all that my Grandpa has taught me. I think to myself, furikake truly makes life taste good.

celena**cipriaso** 19
New York, New York

I always felt like I was on the outside looking in on my culture. I tried to fill that emptiness with my passion for writing, which has led me to study writing in New York. Working on a documentary about Filipinos, as well as getting involved with an amazing Pan Asian Theater group called "Peeling," I have learned how to be proud of my heritage. Flipping through the pages of Philippine history, sometimes I cry thinking about how powerful our struggle has been. I wrote "Kitchen God" at a time in my life when I was strug-

gling through my need to connect with my family history and my heritage. With the help of family and friends, that need is being fulfilled.

Kitchen God

I eat almost the same meal every day. In the morning I eat some eggs, mostly scrambled, and sometimes I have toast that's usually not toasted since my ex took the damn toaster. (I bought it, but he managed to sneak off with it when he moved out.) At noon I eat a sandwich again with untoasted bread. Sometimes there's meat on it. But I never eat pork.

At night, I eat instant ramen soup. I like boiling water over the stove and pretending I can actually cook. Ever since I moved out on my own, this is how I've prepared my meals. I've tried to cook before, but you're a lost cause when you burn spaghetti and risk burning down the house trying to make a grilled cheese sandwich. I dream of being a fantastic cook. Sometimes when I boil my water, I like to close my eyes; in a few moments, I'm in the kitchen with my dad again, the best cook in the world.

He could cook anything. To me, he was like Superman. When I was little, I would sit and watch. Cooking was like a religious ritual and the kitchen, his sanctuary. I barely saw my dad while I was growing up. He was always working long hours during the day, so we could keep paying the bills. The only time I spent with him was when I was sitting quietly in my chair in the corner of the room. He did everything in a slow measured fashion. Each spice, each ingredient, always had to be the right amount. Everything had to be perfect. In my eyes, this was what made Dad an artist.

We always ate his prized dish. The pig. The roasted pig, cooked pig's blood over rice, and pig's feet as snacks. I think if the Philippines had a national meat it would be pork. Pork used to be, without a doubt, my favorite food. It was my dad's favorite, too.

I yearned for him to teach me how to cook. Pulling recipes from my head as he did, I imagined the food forming magically beneath my hands. I wonder if he knew how closely I studied him, and that I always wanted to help him. I suppose I was scared to ask any questions.

My dad was a big man of few words. What he wanted, he always tried to communicate without saying. But I never understood him or knew much about him. I always wanted to ask him where he learned to cook roasted pig. Did his dad or his mom teach him? And why did Filipinos always have to have roasted pig as the main course at all their parties?

In our kitchen, there is a picture of my father proudly standing behind one of his pigs. He doesn't smile in it, but you know he's proud that all of the Filipinos waiting in line want to take a morsel of his dish, and that they will later smile and give him praise. If only he understood my unspoken words. He couldn't see that I was afraid; if I spoke and asked him to teach me, I worried that he would never let me watch him cook again.

One day I finally got the nerve to ask my father if I could help. He was making food for Grandma, who was visiting from the Philippines. He wanted everything to be perfect. I wouldn't stop bugging him, so he finally let me measure some of the ingredients. I didn't measure one of the ingredients right, and when he found out, he yelled at me and told me to leave the kitchen. The meal was ruined, and Grandma refused to eat. After that night, I stopped watching him cook. He wouldn't let me set foot in the kitchen again for fear that I would do something wrong.

And so I never learned how to cook. Even when I moved away for college, I was still obsessed with the notion of cooking. Maybe I could teach myself, I thought. I bought a Filipino cookbook and tried to follow all of the steps, moving around like my dad did, measuring as he did. But when I burned the pork and ruined the rice, I saw my dad's face, and he was laughing at me. Frustrated and angry, I cried and threw away the cookbook. And that's when, instead of trying again, I went back to buying jumbo packages of ramen soup.

janet**jun**20
Orange, California

I wrote my previous piece, "Ghost Brother," and "Sister Skin," because a story, a life, a memory, though painful, must be remembered; it must also be retold and reimagined if we are to give it meaning.

Sister Skin

Underneath our skin, silence and regret move us away from each other. I'll sit on my side, you'll sit on yours, and I'll hear you shuffling through bills and bills. My breathing gets lost among the papers. Water from my eyes collects like forgotten dust on your table.

I remember last summer, when we got high together on music and the sunrise; we were soul mates and sisters. Back then we thought the stars would always guide us home to family and to each other's midnight whispers.

Midnight whispers. I heard your voice when I was sleeping, muffled screams and bruised arms. But when I called the only voice was a recording on the answering machine.

We smoked menthols together on those drives home, watching the sunrise, hearing it break through the horizon. Now you smoke alone in a place that I can't touch, can barely see.

Words float around us eternally in purgatorial limbo, edging their way but moving nowhere. Our mouths open and smiles appear, but underneath our skin and flesh, waves of ache and bitterness wash us apart, shores of an island breaking in two.

I have been living in the Lower East Side, right outside of China-town, ever since I was born. Both my parents emigrated from Guangdong, China, and were married in New York a year before I was born. My own upbringing and the tacit taboos that are the undertone of my family and traditional Chinese society inspired me to write this story. "If" is about learning to be honest with ourselves and with the people we love. It's also about letting truth override consequences because it releases us in the end. It will hopefully encourage us to always look deeply, past the surface, as we search for meaning in our lives.

If

My hands, covered in tiny cold bumps, hang limp by the side of the chair. My face is sallow, and my mind, daunted by the imminent encounter. She was finally going to know. I was going to tell her right now. I was going to make her see what she never wanted to see, or could even imagine happening to her own daughter. Not that anything happened to me—just a realization.

I will find her by the sewing machine, her mind and her hands a fluid connection. Her brow is furrowed and beaded with sweat, and the machine, making a noise that never seems to end. Her hands deftly move up and down, wherever they need to be. She will not feel my presence as I suck in the air in loud gulps, nostrils flaring. My clammy hands slide down my plaid shirt, the one she made for me ten years ago when I hadn't found it embarrassing yet to wear homemade clothes. My legs grow wobbly, shaking uncontrollably. My hair is matted to my neck, and my eyes are starting to water as I know what her reaction will be. Again, I will question myself: Why did I have to do this to her? Why couldn't I just be the girl she wished I could be—obedient, shy, quiet, and perfect? Why did I have to make life so much harder for her? Before I can question myself any further, I know I have to stop. I've believed in that excuse for too long.

"Mom," I'd say, and I'd tell her. Short, succinct, and as painless as possible. She would stop working the machine, and there would be a silence I've never heard or felt. Her fingers and nails claw the cloth, the thread, wispy and frail in the afternoon breeze. She'd slowly turn to me and fix her eyes, those eyes that I wished I'd inherited, on my own thin slits that my dad gave to me. And she would ask me to repeat what I said. I'd say, "Mom, I'm gay."

For five minutes, we would stare into each other's eyes, searching. She searches for a glint of laughter, proof that this is another one of my pranks. Upon failure she will probe for the little girl she always thought she knew; the girl who had grown up without her.

Obviously, this was her dad's fault. This wasn't from my side of the family. Never!

Her mind would play these thoughts over and over again and faster each time. I would look into her watery-beyond-normal eyes, still searching for a sign of understanding, a hint of acceptance, and a signal of a motherly embrace coming on, only to find a black abyss, unrevealing and unfeeling.

"So, what are you telling me? This is a trend? This is what's in? This is cool?" she would ask. "Look at me, ah yeen! I raised you better than that!"

"Mom . . ." I'd begin, not knowing where to continue, and almost expecting her reaction. Waiting for her to accept, for her to recognize, that I was still the same girl. Still her little girl.

"Get out." She would say softly.

"What?"

"Get out." This time an octave higher. And then she is screeching, "Get out, get out, get out! I won't have it! What is my family gonna think?! They'll never know. Just go!"

I lurch forward, hoping to embrace her and to tell her it is going to be all right. I want to say the three words she was never taught. Words I always waited for. "I love you, mom!"

Jumping up, she reaches for me. I think she's finally letting go of traditional beliefs, prepared to accept the truth. My lips start to curl up in a relieved smile, and I await the hug I've always b een wanting. Instead, I would feel a sting come across my left cheek, sounding loud and ugly. My body is propelled to the floor. A silent cry reminds me of all the times she forgot to say she was proud of me.

I never said "I love you" to my father. I never hugged him before because I'm 5'10" and he's 5'4".

—Alberta Lee, activist daughter of Wen Ho Lee,
as quoted in an interview with
AsianAvenue.com

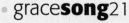 grace**song**21
Toronto, Ontario

My parents immigrated to Canada from South Korea in the mid-1970s, and I was born in Toronto, three years after my older sister. I credit three very special people—my family—for making me who I am today. Through thick and thin, they have always been my supporters. This piece in particular is addressed to my father. It is a letter that I have wanted to write for the past year. My last wish is for him to read it before he passes away.

I Love You, Dad (An Unsent Letter)

Dear Dad,

I don't know why I'm writing this letter to you. It's probably because writing is easier than making you sit down with me for a serious father-daughter talk, since it's difficult for me to freely display my emotions around you. We discuss politics, religion, and education, but I can't remember ever saying "I love you" and giving you a warm embrace. I guess I thought that getting good grades in school was the best way of expressing my affection. Then, three months ago, you were diagnosed with liver cancer and I didn't know what to say. I've watched you sitting on the couch with a blank stare out the window, trying to conceal your worries and fears.

Although we're close, we never had the kind of relationship where I could tell you about a new guy I met, or ask you for advice about problems I was having with close friends. Our relationship revolved around what was going on at school—for instance, how many scholarships I could obtain in university. You encouraged me to strive for excellence in all aspects of my life and you always tried your best to give me everything I ever needed or wanted. We've shared good times, aside from the roughest period of my life when our relationship nearly ended.

Looking back I regret the grief I caused you but I hope you realize that the tension between us was largely due to generational differences. I know that my naiveté was a huge factor, but it was the pressure of learning to assimilate into two worlds—bringing the mutually exclusive cultures (the East and the West) together—that was so overwhelming.

I didn't think you could understand what I was going through. Listening to your stories, it seemed like you were used to living according to a set of rules that everyone accepted. For instance, in Korea, students woke up bright and early to study and, not surprisingly, their typical day ended the way it began. They just studied more. Unlike our relationship, parents and their children shared the same mindset and methods of discipline, and the kids generally did as they were told. Immigrating to Canada wasn't easy. You set foot on foreign soil and immediately confronted new ideas. As traditional Korean parents you tried to keep your customs (the entire spirit) alive by teaching me the values your parents once taught you. Miscommunication led to confusion, and our relationship turned into a never-ending tug-of-war.

You put so much pressure on me to perform well in school. If my grades slipped the tiniest bit, it was time for you to pull out the "what-is-going-on-in-your-head?" lecture. You never failed to ask if I'd surpassed a smart Jewish boy who went to my school. ("Who got better grades this year, you or him?") And then we talked about my future. I thought that by becoming some big-shot lawyer, I'd be living your dream. You said that law was "in my blood" and went on about my "grandfather who was a great litigation attorney." I was glad that you thought I had the potential to become a successful lawyer, but you exerted so much pressure on me. I retaliated from time to time, yelling, "What if I don't become a lawyer! Will that make me less of a daughter?" But as usual, you ignored my emotional outburst. I usually surrendered, totally exhausted, with a pounding headache. I didn't see the point of arguing when it felt like everything I was saying was going in one ear and out the other.

The curfew you enforced also caused friction between us. My friends would constantly ask, "Why are your parents so strict?" My first reaction was to defend you and Mom.

"They're not that bad, they let me stay out later on some nights." Of course that was totally untrue.

I was always the first one to go home from a house party or a slumber party. I knew it was natural for parents to worry about their children, but you and Mom were so extreme, and I envied my friends, whose parents gave them more freedom.

Things started to change when I turned fifteen. Determined to break your rules, I was sneaking out of the house and meeting friends at karaoke bars and clubs. I experimented with beer and cigarettes, and started to hang out in predominantly Asian crowds. You forbade me to date because you thought it would distract me from my schoolwork, so I began to date people behind your back.

The guys I usually dated were either school dropouts or guys who were on the verge of failing out. My closest girlfriends were shallow, materialistic, and unmotivated to go to school. For some reason, though, I longed for their company. It was comforting to be in the presence of other young, second-generation Asian kids. They seemed to understand me in ways that you couldn't. When I came home, I wore a mask that concealed my true identity. Upon entering the house, the adventurous and humorous girl would disappear, instantly transforming into a quiet and submissive daughter.

I could see it in your eyes when I turned sixteen. You were worried. I was no longer the daughter you once knew. I had become somebody you barely recognized. To take control of the situation, you would deliver long-winded speeches at dinner table every night (if I were home). You eventually disconnected all the phones in the house, tore up all of my friends' pictures, and made me a prisoner in my own house. I kicked and screamed and spat evil words in your face; still, you didn't flinch. At the time I thought you wanted to make me miserable, when, really, you were saving me from failure.

In my self-absorbed state, I never considered the hardships you endured together so I was happy. You didn't make me pay for groceries, you paid my rent, and I never had to cook my own meals. While you and Mom were busy providing for me, I made you suffer.

I remember the night you told me to get out of the house. Mom cried silently, but refused to interfere, aware that it would probably cause more damage. In the heat of anger, I left home with one backpack slung over my shoulder, and you didn't stop me. Instead, you slipped away into your room, defeated.

Eventually, Mom found out where I was staying and, in a tired voice, she asked me to come back home. When I did, she burst into tears and told me that I was killing you. Every day, she said, you came home and walked straight toward the cupboard where the alcohol was kept. The condition of your liver worsened, but you didn't care. Drinking eased your mind and washed your sorrows away. You didn't say much to me when I came back, but Mom told me that you cried for the first time in a long time while I was gone.

Looking in the mirror, I saw an unhappy girl, fraught with anger, confusion, and guilt. I was headed in the wrong direction, and deep down inside, I knew that you were right. I needed to take control of my future. I needed new friends. I needed to start living for myself and not for others. At twenty-one, I haven't finished growing up, but

I'm changing for the better. Aware that all of my actions have consequences, I now know that if I'm not careful, life can easily turn into a reckless roller-coaster ride.

During the last couple of years, since you've been fighting your illness, we've switched roles. Now that you are weaker and more vulnerable, I've taken on some of your responsibilities. I seldom have time to hang out with friends because I'm so busy helping you and Mom buy this or pick up that, but I don't mind. It's my turn to take care of you. Sometimes I feel like the cancer is my fault, and that your drinking was intensified by my wrongdoings, but I've gradually learned to change my perspective. Dwelling on the past is pointless, and right now, I just want to make sure that you're healthy today and tomorrow.

Thank you for your unconditional love, and for saving me from following the wrong path in life. You never wanted to give up on me, and you have done everything in your power to see me grow up to become a responsible and caring adult.

In the past our struggles drove us apart, but now, our experiences have brought us closer than ever. I will never lose hope in you, Dad, just as you never lost hope in me. I love you.

Grace

Nora Okja Keller is the author of the novel Comfort Woman *(Viking Penguin, 1997). She lives in Hawaii with her husband and daughter.*

My Mother's Food
BY NORA OKJA KELLER

I was weaned on kim chee. A good baby, I was "able to eat anything," my mother told me. But what I especially loved was the fermenting, garlicky Chinese cabbage my mother pickled in our kitchen. Not waiting for her to lick the red peppers off the won bok, I would grab and gobble the bits of leaves as soon as she tore them into baby-size pieces. She said that even if my eyes watered, I would still ask for more.

Propping me in a baby carrier next to the sink, my mother would rinse the cabbage she had soaked in salted water the night before. After patting the leaves dry, she would slather on the thick red-pepper sauce, rubbing the cloves of garlic and green onion into the underarms of the cabbage, bathing it as she would one of her own children. Then, grabbing them by their dangling leafy legs, she would push the wilting heads into five-gallon jars. She had to rise up on tiptoe, submerging her arm up to the elbow, to punch the kim chee to the bottom of jar, squishing them into their own juices.

Throughout elementary school, our next-door neighbor Frankie, whose mother was the only other Korean in our neighborhood, would come over to eat kim chee with my sisters and me every day after school. We would gather in our garage, sitting cross-legged around a kim-chee jar as though at a campfire. Daring each other on, we would pull out long strips that we would eat straight, without rice or water to dilute the taste. Our eyes would tear and our noses start to run because it was so hot, but we could not stop. "It burns, it burns, but it tastes so good!" we would cry.

Afterward when we went to play the jukebox in Frankie's garage, we had to be careful not to touch our eyes with our wrinkled, pepper-stained hands. It seemed as if the hot, red juice soaked through our skin and into our bones; even after we bathed, we could still feel our fingers tingling, still taste the kim chee on them when we licked them. And as my sisters and I curled into our bed at night, nestling together like sleeping doves, I remember the smell lingered on our hands, the faint whiff of kim chee scenting our dreams.

We went crazy for the smell of kim chee—a perfume that lured us to the kitchen table. When my mother hefted the jar of kim chee out of the refrigerator and opened the lid to extract the almost fluorescent strips of cabbage, she didn't have to call out to us, although she always did. "Girls, come join me," she would sing; even if we weren't hungry we couldn't resist. We all lingered over snacks that lasted two or three hours.

But I didn't realize that I smelled like kim chee, that the smell followed me to school. One day, walking across Middle Field toward the girls' locker room, a girl I recognized from the gym class before mine stepped in front of me.

"You Korean?" she asked. She narrowed eyes as brown as mine, shaped like mine, like mock-orange leaves pinched up at the corners.

Thinking she could be my sister, another part-Korean, part-Caucasian *hapa* girl, I nodded and welcomed her kinship with a smile.

"I thought so," she said, sneering. Her lips scrunched upward, almost folding over her nostrils. "You smell like one."

I held my smile, frozen, as she flitted away from me. She had punched me in the stomach with her words. Days later, having replayed this confrontation endlessly in my mind (in one fantasy version, this girl mutated into a hairy Neanderthal that I karate-chopped into submission), I thought of the perfect comeback: "Oh yeah? Well, you smell like a chimpanzee." At the very least, I should have said *something* that day. Anything—a curse, a joke, a grunt—anything at all would have been better than a smile.

I smiled. And I sniffed. I smiled and sniffed as I walked to the locker room and dressed for P.E. I smiled and sniffed as I jogged around the field, trying to avoid the hall and other girls wielding field hockey sticks. I smiled and sniffed as I showered and followed my schedule of classes.

I became obsessed with sniffing. When no one was looking, I lifted my arms and, quick, sniffed. I held my palm up to my face and exhaled. Perhaps, every now and then, I would catch the odor of garlic in sweat and breath. I couldn't tell: the smell of kim chee was too much a part of me.

I didn't want to smell like a Korean. I wanted to be an American, which meant having no smell. Americans, I learned from TV and magazines, erased the scent of their bodies with cologne and deodorant, breath mints and mouthwash.

So I erased my stink by eliminating kim chee. Though I liked the sharp taste of garlic and pepper biting my tongue, I stopped eating my mother's food.

I became shamed by the kim chee that peeked out from between the loaf of white bread and the carton of milk, by the odor that, I grew to realize, permeated the entire house. When friends pointed at the kim-chee jars lined up on the refrigerator shelves and squealed, "Gross! What's that?" I would mumble, "I don't know, something my mom eats."

I also stopped eating the only three dishes my mother could cook: *kalbi ribs, bi bim kooksoo,* and Spam fried with eggs. (The first "American" food my mother ever ate was a Spam and egg sandwich; even now she considers it one of her favorite foods and never tires eating it.)

I told my mother I was a vegetarian. One of my sisters ate only McDonald's Happy Meal cheeseburgers (no pickle); the other survived for two years on a Diet of processed-cheese sandwiches on white bread (no crust), Hostess DingDongs, and rice dunked in ketchup.

"How can you do this to me?" my mother wailed at her American-born children. "You are wasting away! Eat, eat!" She plopped heaps of kim chee and *kalbi* onto mounds of steaming rice. My sisters and I would grimace, poke at the food, and announce: "Too fattening."

My mother had always encouraged us to behave like proper Korean girls: quiet, respectful, hardworking. She said we gave her "heartaches" the way we fought as children. "Worse than boys," she'd say. "Why do you want to do things like soccer, scuba, swimming? How about piano?"

But worse than our tomboy activities were our various adolescent diets. My mother grieved over the food rejected. "I don't understand you," she'd say. "When I was growing up, my family was so poor, we could only dream of eating this kind of food. Now I can give my children meat every night and you don't want it." "Yeah, yeah," we said, as we pushed away the kim chee, the Koreanness.

As I grew up, I eventually returned to eating kim chee, but only sporadically. I could go for months without it, then be hit with a craving so strong I would run to Sack-n-Save for a generic, watery brand that only hinted at the taste of home. Kim chee, I realized, was my comfort food.

When I became pregnant, the craving for my own mother accentuated my craving for kim chee. During the nights of my final trimester, my body foreign and heavy, restless with longing, I hungered for the food I had eaten in the womb, my first mother-memory.

The baby I carried in my own womb, in turn, does not look like me. Except for the slight tilt of her eyes, she does not look Korean. As a mother totally in love with her daughter, I do not care what she looks like; she is perfect as herself. Yet I worry that—partially because of what she looks like—she will not be able to identify with the Korean in me, and in herself. I recognize that identifying herself as Korean will be a choice for her—in a way it wasn't for someone like me, who looks pure Asian. It hit me then, what my own mother must have felt looking at each of her own mixed-race daughters; how strongly I do identify as a Korean American woman, how strongly I want my child to identify with me.

When my daughter was fifteen months old, she took her first bite of kim chee. I had taken a small bite into my own mouth, sucking the hot juice from its leaves, giving it "mother-taste" as my own mother had done for me. Still, my daughter's eyes watered. "Hot, hot," she said to her grandmother and me. But the taste must have been in some way familiar; instead of spitting up and crying for water, she pushed my hand to the open jar for another bite.

"She likes it!" my mother said proudly. "She is Korean!"

I realized that for my mother, too, the food we ate growing up had always been an indication of how Korean her children were—or weren't. I remember how intently she watched us eat, as if to catch a glimpse of herself as we chewed.

Now my mother watches the next generation. When she visits, my daughter clings to her, follows her from room to room. They run off together to play the games that only the two of them know how to play. I can hear them in my daughter's room, chattering and laughing. Sneaking to the doorway, I see them "cooking" in the Playskool kitchen.

"Look," my mother says, offering her grandchild a plate of plastic spaghetti, "noodles is *kooksoo*." She picks up a steak. "This *kalbi*." My mother is teaching her Korean, presenting words my daughter knows the taste of.

My girl picks up a head of cabbage. "Let's make kim chee, *Halmoni*," she says, using the Korean word for *grandmother* like a name.

"Okay," my mother answers. "First, salt." My daughter shakes invisible salt over the cabbage.

"Then mix garlic and red-pepper sauce." My mother stirs a pot over the stove and passes the mixture to my daughter, who pours it on the cabbage.

My daughter brings her fingers to her mouth. "Hot!" she says. Then she holds the cabbage to my mother's lips, and gives her *halmoni* a taste.

"Mmmmm!" My mother grins as she chews the air. "Delicious! This is the best kim chee I ever ate." My mother sees me peeking around the door.

"Come join us!" she calls out to me and tells my daughter, who's gnawing at the fake food. "Let your mommy have a bite."

It was a bleak, much-lamented fact of life that to a lot of folks in Pittsford, New York, I was a curiosity. I was used to being stared at when I was out in public. It was difficult not to feel conspicuous in the small, conservative town where the adults, like the children, didn't think twice before ogling anyone nonwhite or asking invasive questions—the most common one being, "Hey, what are you?" By the time I was a teenager, I had come up with a solid stock response that satisfied most people who just wanted to be indulged with a few titillating details on the "fascinating" other side of my American identity. And since I was almost always the token Korean girl, and I knew that my inquisitors didn't know fact from fiction, I "acted big" sometimes, speaking freely and haphazardly about things I knew absolutely nothing about.

Answering random questions from strangers while I was, let's say, checking out books at the library or shopping at the grocery store never threw me for a loop, simply because I assumed that we'd never speak to each other again. On the other hand, dealing with ignorance among my peers at school was a whole different story. Their comments were ten times more biting than any remarks I would hear from strangers. My heightened sensitivity to peers was definitely linked to the fact that I was trying so desperately to blend into the background. At school, racist slurs, immature "Chinese, Japanese, dirty knees, lookit these" chants, and twangy "Oriental" sounds that they associated with

China, Japan, and Vietnam (the only Asian countries any of my peers seemed capable of identifying off the top of their heads) followed me around in the hallways.

One year, racism sat in front of me in history class. To this day, I can envision the way Jessica's mouth would turn down whenever she passed my graded test back, her mocking eyes trying to feign pity. "Awwww, Vick! Your parents gonna whip you tonight for getting a 97 percent? You're disappointin' me." The girl whom I considered one of my best friends from elementary school sat on the other side of me. Not knowing what to say, she pretended like nothing was happening. I couldn't blame her, really, because I didn't know quite what to say, either. I waited to hear the last chuckle, the last fleeting glance from others who had been privy to the exchange, and it was over—until the next day, that is.

But people like Jessica didn't have to single me out. In fact, nobody else had to bluntly point out the countless ways I didn't fit in; I was, by far, my harshest critic. Whether I was in the girls' bathroom retouching my eyeliner, walking through the lunch cafeteria searching for my friends, or at home discussing politics over dinner with my parents and sister, I was constantly looking at myself from the outside. I was taking note of how I wasn't like the other kids, and simultaneously, I was deciding what I needed to change about myself in order to blend in.

At the end my freshman year, right before finals, Jessica still hadn't tired of harassing me, even if everyone else had. I was angry. I didn't know what I was going to say to her before school ended, although I'd rehearsed a couple of lines, which, I thought, if delivered with gusto, would send her reeling in shame. But when she passed back my last test paper of the year, instead of busting out with a profound statement that might shed some insight to others on racial prejudice, I took a cheap shot.

"At least I'm not flunking," I said, snickering, but I wasn't finished. "Summer school would rot." Everyone knew that Jessica was probably going to flunk the final and end up in the doghouse. Preying on her insecurity felt evil. Then again, revenge tasted hella sweet, too.

The title of this chapter, "Dolly Rage," was inspired by girls whose experiences as outsiders have given them a special insight into understanding the workings of society, as well as discovering the complexity of our identity as Asian American girls. That we haven't spoken out in the process of enduring insults, discrimination, and other forms of alienation in our environments can be misleading. Our silence might mislead many to think that we are passive victims who are not actively evaluating our place in the world. This chapter will relate most closely to readers who have felt pressured to decide when and if it's worth changing themselves in order to fit in with their peers. It will discuss a peculiar self-consciousness that stems from our unique standing as girls who often experience shifting priorities depending on location—whether we're at home, at school, or elsewhere in the world at large.

Reading the submissions, I became increasingly aware that either the world was changing a lot faster than I thought, or I had grown up in an unusually sheltered, monolithic environment. It was probably a combination of both. These girls were much further along in their journey toward self-awareness than I had been at the age of sixteen or even eighteen. Before I went to college, where I first began reading literature that trained me to look at my life through a gendered and racialized perspective, the deeper implications of Asian American female stereotypes had not yet entered my consciousness. For example, when I was younger, I didn't understand why people called me "china doll," "geisha girl," and "ornamental Oriental," beyond the fact that they thought I looked different and "exotic." Later, I learned that these labels carried a history, and that, in some people's minds, I wasn't just different from them—I was quiet, submissive (sexually), and mysterious.

We started a dialogue about stereotypes, and asked ourselves to what extent images of Asian women in film and in literature actually influenced us. As a women's studies major in college, I had done some of my own research on the representation of Asian American women in the media, but not once had I taken my investigation to the streets to find out firsthand how girls were reading these stereotypes. It wasn't until now that I was finally hearing their voices on the issue, and they went further than confirming my hunches that the stereotypes made them self-conscious. They told me why the stereotypes were so loaded, and why they were so desperate to derail them and claim the power to define themselves.

Contrary to popular myth, we are not unwitting objects of scrutiny. And there was a consensus on this—we would never describe ourselves as silent or docile. Nineteen-year-old Jenny Yan submitted an essay which included a powerful poem describing herself. Jenny wrote:

I am not
your China doll
your puppet
My face is made of colored flesh
Not of porcelain
Or colored cloth

My lips are not sealed shut
I laugh, I scream, I cry,
I am loud
I am bold
I demand my rights
I demand to be heard.

Doll imagery pervaded our writings. We used dolls as a metaphor, usually to represent the ultimate measure of perfection. We also used dolls to demonstrate our fierce longing to break out of prescribed, Eurocentric molds, which were based on the dominant views in our communities. We vented about the impossible ideals that could only sustain the life of something plastic or ceramic, but would never be achieved on our living, breathing, nonwhite bodies. We cursed the "mold," whether it took the form of the make-believe china doll, or the leggy, blue-eyed Barbie doll. In fact, I remember picking up *Allure* magazine, the resource of choice for the makeup-obsessed, while away on one of our family trips. The last thing I ever expected to see in *Allure* was an article aimed at nonwhite women who are trying to redefine beauty on their own terms. Then I caught a glimpse of a familiar name, and my skin tingled even before I had started to read it. Lois-Ann Yamanaka's piece dared to shake the average *Allure* reader's consciousness, as she illuminated mine. In "When Asian Eyes Are Smiling," our mentor Yamanaka sends an empowering message to all of us who are encountering similar stumbling blocks in learning to love our bodies and our selves.

"Dolly Rage" gives us the rare opportunity to share our memoirs with each other, and to illustrate the real-life struggles we've endured as girls who are constantly critical of our differences. This chapter provides Asian American girls, who feel alone amidst people who cannot fathom what they're experiencing, an outlet to express their emotions. Many of the girls who submitted their work for publication would agree that writing proved a powerful tool for venting, coming to terms with our rage, and raising incisive questions, which we've never had the opportunity to discuss in this type of open forum.

You'll hear stern, somewhat cynical perspectives emerge in the next few pages. To many of the readers, our voices may sound angry—and perhaps we are angry.

We are angry because we are aware that no matter how well we learn to master the art of blending into our environment, certain individuals will stare at us, point at our differences, and make us feel foreign. We are angry because the "model minority myth," as it relates to Asian American teen girls, glosses over our realities—the painful realities that are, by and large, invisible, because we're not given equal opportunities to express our views compared to Euro American girls. Sadly, we are the missing statistic in many research projects and market analyses.

So, what's the purpose of harboring angst and expressing rage? Interestingly, in the spring of 2000, I received an e-mail message from an anonymous cyber-male who, by happenstance, stumbled across the Web site that I'd created in conjunction with this anthology project. Apparently, he was upset that we appeared to be encouraging each other to bitch and moan about our problems. He wrote: "Expressing anger about injustice isn't going to bring you closer to understanding who you are or where you fit in. Asian American or not, *get over it and quit griping*. Oppression is universal." After thinking about his message for a little while, I felt the sudden urge to reply. I suggested that *if* Asian

American girls were indeed experiencing anger or frustration, expressing their feelings was the first step toward naming the problems we were facing and isolating the questions we were struggling with. And that the second step was either to reach for outside support, or to search ourselves for the answers.

Happy endings and other easy solutions are not what these girls seek in speaking out. We're looking for something—wisdom, perhaps—that can carry us through times of crisis. We are looking for reliable, lasting resources, such as mentors and support networks, to provide us with guidance. The focus of this chapter is directed at girls who, after experiencing various setbacks, have the courage to move forward on their journey. My personal goal is steadfast. I hope our dialogue helps us arrive in a safe place that ultimately allows us a clearer understanding of who we are and where in our communities we feel like we belong.

alaina**wong**19
West Windsor, New Jersey

Currently a student at the University of Pennsylvania, I'm continu-
ally amazed by the richness and diversity of the Asian American
experience. "China Doll" provides a whimsical glimpse into the
mind of a child, detailing the way girls may come to terms with
their Asian features, which so often contrast with the media-
defined ideal of beauty. My experiences growing up and slowly
becoming race conscious inspired me to write this story. I hope to
evoke a sense of familiarity and understanding from people who
may have also experienced these feelings.

China Doll

I wanted Princess Barbie, with long blond hair that you could brush and a beautiful shiny gown. She even came with a shimmery white tiara, which, in my eight-year-old mind, crowned her at the top of her Barbie world. My parents looked at me expectantly as I tore through the wrapping paper in childlike excitement. As the pile of shredded paper around me grew larger, so did my anticipation.

But instead of a beautiful princess with golden tresses, what I found was an unfamiliar black-haired "friend" of Barbie, who wore a floral wrap skirt over a pink bathing suit.

Disappointment passed over my eyes as I examined the doll more closely. With her dark hair and slanted eyes, she was a dull comparison to her blond friend. My other dolls were all alike and beautiful with their clouds of blond (or light-brown) hair, broad, toothy smiles, and wide-open eyes. Even Ken had a perfectly painted-on coif of blond hair and flashed a winning grin. I didn't think this new doll would go riding in Barbie's convertible with Ken. Why would he pick her when he already had so many blond friends to choose from? Besides, instead of a wide movie-star grin, her lips were curved into a more secretive, sly smile. I wondered what secrets she was hiding. Maybe she had crooked teeth.

I announced that I loved my new doll. I didn't want my mom and dad to feel bad. Maybe the store didn't have any more Princess Barbie dolls, so they had to buy me the leftovers, or the ones that no one wanted. I looked at the name of this new black-haired addition to my perfect Barbie family. Kira. Kira didn't even have shoes, though her feet were still arched up, as if they were waiting expectantly for their missing shoes. She seemed incomplete. She was probably missing lots of things beside her shoes. My other Barbies all had colorful plastic high heels to complement their fashionable dresses. Their outfits were perfect.

"Alaina," my mom said, "Get your things ready so I can drive you over to Sarah's house!" I threw the dark-haired doll into my backpack with the other Barbies I was bringing; Sarah and I always shared the latest additions to our Barbie collections. Everyone always said that Sarah would grow up to look like Goldie Hawn, some famous movie star. I didn't think I would grow up to look like anybody important, not unless I was like Cinderella, and a fairy godmother went Zap! so I could be transformed, like magic. Sarah's hair fell in soft waves down her back, while my own black hair was slippery and straight, like uncooked spaghetti. I bet Sarah had gotten the Princess Barbie for Christmas.

I liked going over to Sarah's house. Her mom didn't care if we ate raspberries from the backyard without washing them. The last time I went there, I saw my best friend pluck a juicy purple berry right off the bush and into her mouth. I was amazed that she didn't care about dirt. Sarah's mom let us taste cookie dough from the batter when she baked cookies. I guess only Chinese people cared about germs. My mother never baked cookies anyway. Baking cookies is what white mothers do all the time—they like to make things from "scratch" that turn out soft and chewy, while Chinese mothers buy cookies from the supermarket that are dry and go crunch, unless you dip them in milk. Sarah's mother made the best macaroni and cheese too. Obviously she made it from "scratch." I hoped I was eating lunch there today.

After we pulled into Sarah's driveway, I jumped out of the car and said good-bye to my mom. Inside, Sarah and I ran up the stairs so I could look at her new dollhouse. On the way, we passed piles of laundry warm from the dryer, toys spread out the floor in front of the TV, and newspapers scattered on the kitchen table. I was jealous. Sarah's mother probably didn't make them clean up every time someone came over.

Upstairs, I dumped my Barbies out of my backpack so we could compare our collections. Before I could even look at her dolls, Sarah turned to me.

"Look what I got!" she said proudly.

I knew it. Sarah had gotten the Princess Barbie.

And what did I have to show her? A plain Barbie friend with a funny name, Kira, in an ordinary bathing suit and a skirt that was just a piece of cloth that needed to be tied; it didn't even slip on like real clothes. My doll had straight black hair, no shoes, and worst of all, she didn't even know how to smile right.

"Well . . . she has pretty flowers on her skirt," Sarah said helpfully. "And she looks kind of like you!"

She did? But I didn't want to look like this strange new "friend" of Barbie. Everyone knew that the Barbies with the blond hair were the best. They were the original ones. And they always got to wear the prettiest dresses. I noticed something, but I didn't want to say it out loud. The best dolls, the most glamorous ones, were always the ones that seemed to look like Sarah.

"Sarah, honey," her mom called. "Why don't you help me bring up some cookies for you and Alaina?"

My best friend turned to me. "I'll be right back!" she chirped. "If you want to, your dolls can try on Princess Barbie's clothes," she offered generously.

Sarah skipped out of the room, her blond pigtails swinging around her head. I turned to my Kira doll, regarding her simple outfit. I highly doubted that Princess Barbie's costume would look right on her. Whoever heard of a black-haired doll with slanted eyes wearing a crown? Maybe it wouldn't even fit right. Hesitatingly, I picked up Sarah's Princess Barbie. She really was beautiful. Slowly, I slipped off her gown and dressed her in one of the extra doll outfits, a shiny purple top and silver pants. Princess Barbie continued smiling blankly at me. I was glad she didn't mind that I had changed her clothes.

Carefully, I buttoned my Kira doll into the glittery princess gown. No Velcro closures here; this dress was glamorous, like what a princess would wear in real life. The sunlight through Sarah's bedroom window made the dress sparkle, as if my plain dark-haired Kira doll was actually a princess. The doll's secretive smile began to comfort me, as if we shared a secret together. We both knew this wasn't her real gown, but maybe she could be princess for a day. Just maybe. I stared at her. Finally I placed Barbie's iridescent tiara on top of Kira's jet-black hair. And what do you know? It fit perfectly.

julia**wong**19
Monterey Park, California

During junior and senior years in high school, I had classmates who would put cosmetic tape on their eyelids to produce a fold in their eyelids to give them a more "Western" look. Recently, my family and I went to China and Hong Kong to visit relatives; while shopping, I noticed that the natives appeared more "Western" than I was—they were more slender, had blond hair, and looked boyish, like Calvin Klein models. These ideas around body image led me to write "Mirror, Mirror."

Mirror, Mirror

This is the third lingerie shop I've been to, and they don't have my size. It's not that I am too small. They have a plethora of bras for small-chested women, the majority of those bras being padded. Contrary to the United States, where the average cup size is a B or a C, in Hong Kong and in China, the average cup size was, unfortunately for me, an A.

Shopping was never this hard for me back home. Victoria's Secret and other women's clothing stores in the U.S. always carried something that fit me. I grew up surrounded by Barbie dolls and magazine cover girls like actresses Alicia Silverstone and Cameron Diaz; they were my main examples of beauty. My body type and figure might not be perfect, but then again, whose is perfect without the help of airbrushing and digital enhancement? I also grew up with another set of standards that went hand in hand with the common stereotypes of Asian women. I discovered that, as Asian American girls, we are supposed to be short, lightweight, petite, soft-spoken, and light-skinned, with long, straight, jet-black hair.

Growing up in the U.S., my body did not conform to these stereotypes. At the age of nineteen, I was short, but I was also relatively big-busted and thick (as opposed to thin). I wore large and extra-large clothes, but I wouldn't have called myself fat. I still looked good in my outfits, and I was really energetic. My mindset was, there was plenty of time to concentrate on my body *after* I got really important things, like school, out of the way first.

Then, for the first time in twenty years, my parents decided to take a family trip to Hong Kong to visit relatives. While we were there, we did plenty of shopping. The vast majority of the women in Hong Kong and mainland China had stereotypically petite bodies. At the trendy clothing shops, you saw only three sizes: extra-small, small, and medium. In the lingerie shops, you found padded bras for sizes ranging from 34 AA to 38 B in a profuse range of styles and colors. The largest size, which was available in only one style and color, was a 38 C. At home, I had never thought of myself as FAT, but spending a week shopping for clothes in Hong Kong was enough to give anyone a complex about their weight.

Now it's not true that EVERY Asian female is slim to the point of looking anorexic. There are clothes in a wide range of sizes in *some* stores; the difference between the stores in Hong Kong and the stores in Los Angeles is that, in LA, there is a wide range of sizes to suit the needs of the American female population. But since the majority of the population in Hong Kong is thin and petite, the majority of the shops carry clothing made to fit their proportions.

Being on the heavy side, it wasn't always hard going through puberty. It was awkward at times, especially when the teasing got out of hand, but the teasing was tolerable. The guys were insensitive and immature, and I knew that not all of us could be super skinny like those "popular" girls who had boyfriends. Still, the stereotype that Asians were SUPPOSED to be thin made me feel like I was a freak of nature. I wasn't what I was supposed to be. I didn't look the way a Chinese girl was supposed to look. After visiting Hong Kong and China, I became conscious of how this ingrained stereotypical "Asian girl look" came about. My insecurities stemming from weight in junior high were nagging me while I was shopping for clothes in Hong Kong. I comforted myself, thinking, "Hey, there's always the tailor." I would make the clothes fit ME, not just anybody.

I've come to terms with my weight better than my parents have. I know what kinds of clothes accentuate my body's strengths and minimize my body's weaknesses. Unfortunately, my parents believe that I will not catch a nice (hopefully, Chinese) boy to marry me if I weigh over 120 pounds and wear anything larger than size 8. "Ay-ya," one of my parents always says. "Why are you eating that? Don't you know that it has fat in it?"

Standards of beauty will always change, and these ideals will continue to vary between and among people of different cultural backgrounds. Like many Asian American girls, I wish to conform to neither the Western American nor the Eastern Asian ideals of beauty. For our own peace of mind, heart, and spirit, we need to set these standards for ourselves.

For a long time, I possessed two conspiring beliefs: first, that one's own physical beauty does not exist without the confirmation and approval of others; and second, that physical beauty determines one's worthiness for love. Now emerging from a particularly awkward adolescence as well as a number of agonizing heartbreaks, I'm coming to realize how self-destructive these beliefs have been. This poem deals with my personal unlearning. If I could go back in time and give myself, at thirteen, instructions for dealing with high school, college, and all the things these years brought on, I would say: "Read the poem 'Question' by May Swenson. Watch Oprah. *Drop the fashion magazines. And lastly, love yourself, love yourself, love yourself. You are the most beautiful as you are. You rock."*

for body

these calves
the taut backs of dolphins
diving in the waves
of comings and goings

this hair
blue-black shiny
lynched in a ponytail
down my back

this skin
a cake of brown cane sugar
tight and flexible
as a rattan basket

this stomach
soft as a ripe mango
where hide the seeds
of hunger and heartache

i have spent my life hating you
dreaming that a knife
could trim away the thickness
of thighs and waist

wishing that height
came in a bottle
that pilipino whitening soap
really worked when it burned

but you who carry me
never abandoned or quit me
enduring the blows
a battered and devoted wife

please show me the beauty
in my workhorse shoulders
my mountain province legs
my full moon face

please show me the beauty
in the smell of my bed
when i sleep alone and i
will try to see it

i promise i will try

cia_b talked so much in kindergarten class her teacher moved her to a new seat every week. she colored loaf of bread drawings just how they look in real life: brown on the outer part, white on the inside. she started a web site, generationrice.com, after she heard that to be an activist doesn't necessarily mean lifting your fist and joining rallies with placards. she calls herself neurotic, "wanting two mutually exclusive things at one and the same time," as sylvia plath wrote. she was born in manila, and yesterday, realized that she longs to return after her stint in new york city is over. that said, i hope you enjoy reading my story, "the pimple."

The Pimple

His face is so close to the bathroom mirror. I think he's inspecting some invisible crack, but he's getting ready to pop a pimple.

"I told you not to do that," I warn him for the umpteenth time. "It'll just leave scars on your face." He doesn't say anything. No matter how much I warn him, that pimple still has to go. "Did you call your mother back last night?" I ask, trying to change the subject. I can't keep telling him what to do if all he's going to do is ignore my advice, even though we're just discussing personal hygiene. He nods, still concentrating on which angle to take to pop the pimple, which is now red and angry. I'm still clinging to the side of the door hoping he'll give me more details about his conversation with his mother, who lives in Korea.

To remind him that I'm still waiting, I uncomfortably asked, "Did my name get mentioned?" This must have struck a chord because he finally looked at me. "Yeah—as usual, she asked if we'd broken up yet."

That question was expected, of course. His mother hates me. For the past three years we've been dating exclusively, and his mother has told him repeatedly to end our relationship because "there are a lot of nice Korean girls" she wants him to meet.

"The [Korean] girls don't have careers and they will take care of a family well, and they will take care of us when we get older," she'd say, as if she were threatening to disown him if he ignored the topic once more.

I've come a long way to get where I am today. I did pretty well in high school and attended an Ivy League university for four years. We met after I moved to New York City to accept an amazing job offer. Things couldn't have been better, and I thought that I had the perfect life—until I found myself campaigning for his mother's respect.

His mother doesn't like the fact that I have a career. ("Too independent.")

His mother doesn't like the fact that I have my own place. ("No family values.")

Her comments are endless. She detects flaws everywhere. I have a career because I want to fulfill my dreams, not because I have crossed off raising a family from the list of goals I hope to achieve in my lifetime. I got my own place because my job required me to move, not because I hate my family. He doesn't worry about these topics much. He tries to explain that it's just her Koreanness that makes her think a certain way, and he assures me that as time goes by, she'll soften up and accept me as the love of his life and his future wife. For him, ignoring problems will yield a solution.

This may seem slightly ironic; after all, I'm also Asian. As a Filipino-American born in the Philippines and raised in America, I haven't forgotten the importance of family values and traditions. I always thought that, as long as I was Asian, other Asian families would accept me. During times of emotional turmoil, my friends have tried to offer their advice. But they seem convinced that someday he will choose family over love. "Don't make too much emotional investments," they tell me, "or you'll just get hurt later."

Still concentrating on popping the pimple, he doesn't notice how depressed I have become, imagining what I should do next to please his mother. The relationship is not even about making each other happy anymore. It has become a cycle: he, telling me not to worry and, I, doing what I can to make his mother proud. I didn't plan that things would turn out this way. I feel like, in a way, I've become the pimple, only I'm receiving less attention each day.

I walk quietly back to the bedroom and start packing my things. I stare at the beautiful ring on my finger, loosen it, and leave it lying on top of the bureau. I walk past the bathroom and out the door, locking it behind me. Outside, I can see the yellow cabs driving recklessly. I can hear the fire truck's siren far away. I can feel the subway rushing beneath my feet.

All of a sudden, I feel free.

> There's nothing bad about venting . . . Anger is a propelling tool for me, it helps to move me toward what I wanna do, and helps me put things in action.
>
> —Sabrina Margarita Sandata, creator/writer of
> *Bamboo Girl* zine (Issue #7)

elena**cabatu**21

Hilo, Hawaii

"I Wanned fo' Try Biore" is another one of the first Pidgin poems I ever wrote. At the time, I was eighteen years old, and had just finished taking a Pidgins and Creoles class from world-renowned sociolinguist Suzanne Romaine. She taught me to see Pidgin's legitimacy through its linguistic systems. In my down time, in addition to writing and performing poetry, I enjoy working on my Web site (www.georgetown.edu/users/cabatue) as well.

I Wanned fo' Try Biore

Right afta I wen go back school on da mainland in '97,
One pimple remova ting came out on tv called, *Biore.*

Da tv said da pad supposta pull all da pimples outta yoa' nose.
  When look real fun, I wanned fo' try 'em,
But was kinda shame, especially being ind da mainland.
I neva like do 'em in fronna my rommates.

Took me one whole yea' fo' try 'em.
One aftanoon da following summa,
Me and my sistah was boa'd, only watching MTV, had *Say What?*
  Karaoke.
But dose haoles had call "karaoke" something diff'rent.
Dey tell, "CARRY-O-KEY."
Dey jus' doddo no know how fo' say 'em.

Anyways, my sistah wen fine da *Biore* in our step-maddah's
  make-up draw.
Da firs ting we wen do was peel off da pad from da plastic cova an
Put 'em on our nose.
Da ting no was staying,
But you know how anybody can get excited ova dea pimples,
  especially da ones on da nose
So we was jus' holing 'em so da ting would stick.
Afta five minutes our aa'm was getting sowa so we wen finally read
  da box.
Da box said, gotta wet our nose befo' we put 'em on.
No wanda da ting neva stick!
As soon as we wen wet 'em, da ting wen stick real fas'.
Shoulda read da box firs', den we no weould get sowa aa'm.

We wen waid longtime because we wanned 'em fo' work good, eh?
Laddah on, my sistah wen say, "We go take 'em off."
We wen go to da mirrah.
My sistah waz firs'.
We wen read, peel from da edges.
When she wen peel 'em,
Ho, her eyes was all waddaring an' she was kinda screaming.

Den she wen peel 'em off at da tip a da nose.
Jus' like we wen read 'em on da box.
And guess what?
Na-ting, as my Filipino gramma would say.
Neva get one ting on da pad, only da hea' from on toppa da nose.
Ho, she waz bummed,
But my turn was next.
She tol me, "No fo'get from da tips, eh?"
Peel. Waddah. Scream lillo bi'.
Na-ting!
Ah Shit!
Waste time!

meggy**wang**17
Los Gatos, California

"For Those Who Love Yellow Girls" resulted from my overanalytical mind interacting with my rowdy personal life. Irate and confused are two feelings that naturally lurk in my head at any given time. This piece was written in response to an innate feeling that the "Asian fetish" was wrong, conflicted by so-called logical arguments that tried to turn the "Asian fetish" into an "Asian favoritism." I'm sure there are people out there who will protest that I'm making mountains out of molehills, but hey—hopefully somebody will find something here that can be taken to heart (or brain).

For Those Who Love Yellow Girls

It was the middle of my junior year when one of my acquaintances (of the tall, male, chain-smoking variety) let it be known that he was interested in me. The feeling was not mutual, but I was vaguely flattered and, as a result, entertained drunken late-night calls and flirtatious gestures in history class. In this state of Relationship

Limbo, word spread over to my neck of the 'burbs that said boy had a long history of affairs with Asian girls.

These Asian fetish types are not at all few and far between, and the topic has been discussed before in many admirable essays ("Hear Me Roar" by Stephanie Han comes to mind) about the link between "rice lovers" and their mental images of subservient, tiny-footed Asian women. Which brought this question to mind: Is there a difference between a fetish based on such stereotypical ideas and a non-Asian person whose dating history consists mostly of Asian females—like, is one more innocuous than the other?

This was the question I posed to *Slander* zine's Mimi Nguyen's politically progressive mailing list, which is "dedicated to both critical theory and practice, especially around issues of race, sexuality, gender, nation and capitalism." First came the "I've been there" stories—not just from other Asian women, but from other women of color who have had their own stereotypical images to contend with (black men pursuing lighter-skinned black women because they are "better" than darker-skinned women, the fiery Latina image, etc.). Next came the other explanations for why such racially homogeneous dating might occur. One person suggested that if the "said white person [lives] in an otherwise white area where the only racial 'minorities' tend to be people of Asian descent," and if this person tends to identify more strongly with the culturally oppressed, it is possible that the person might just prefer to date nonwhite people, because maybe he thinks that it's more "culturally enriching" to date a nonwhite person. Aesthetics are another issue. Looks do matter in our largely sexually oriented society, and if yellow girls float your boat, who is anyone to argue? Perhaps an attraction to colored females is a reaction against narrow, Barbie doll beauty standards?

At face value, it's a nice thought—"radical" individuals who interweave politics with attraction. However, there are many gaping pitfalls within this politically agenda'd rationale. One is the assumption that racism is something that can be "risen above" through a romantic relationship. With this convenient worldview, personal interaction conquers stigma for the benefit of one's own self-esteem as well as for credibility amongst others. (Ever heard anyone protest, "I'm not racist! I have black friends!"?). It's insulting, not to mention ridiculous, to expect a Chinese Significant Other to provide a culturally enriching experience akin to taking a "Native Mountain People" boat tour in China (a fun tourist pastime, as I noticed this past spring).

I asked a few female Asian friends for their opinions on the issue, but was unable to solicit any thoughts from the two Caucasian young men who had, in asking me out, also professed their "love for Asian women." Instead, a friend told me to check out a Web site entitled "Sell-Outs and Asiaphiles," a self-proclaimed alternative to pornographic, "geisha girl"–devoted Internet domains. The site seems to be written, at first glance, by a levelheaded, articulate individual who separates himself from Internet perverts by giving a few definitions of "philia" (attraction to characteristics) and "fetish" (attraction to objects). One page in particular, entitled "Why I Date Asian Women," justifies physical attraction by saying, "Gentlemen prefer blondes . . . [so why can't I prefer girls with long black hair?]" The question is interesting, but ignores the underlying problem of long black hair as a *symbol*. Throughout Western history, long, silky black hair has been exoticized as a symbol of the sexy Orient. Is it possible that there truly is no link between such history and his aesthetic taste?

Although the "blondes" comparison piques my interest, the "Asiaphile Myths" section (also headlined: "What White People Say") is much more blatantly suspect. At the top of the screen, the self-proclaimed Mr. Asiaphile states, "It is amazing some of the things white people say when they see an Asian 'girl' with a white man." Below, he lists many of the degrading comments he and his Asian girlfriends receive, such as, "She must be a wildcat in bed!" By showing such quotes, he allows himself to ignore his social status—gee, look at those crazy, wacky white people! What will they say next?—simply because of his partner. Mr. Asiaphile, looking for redemption in the world of cinema, also lists a number of movies in which Asian women are paired with white men, claiming that "the image of the Asian Woman with the White Man is imbedded in our culture; no other interracial couple is shown as much." I suppose he sees nothing strange with the recurring themes in the films listed: white man = freedom from internment camp/a miserable life in a dirty Third World country/oppressively old-fashioned Asian family/etc.

Selective attraction to "Asian characteristics" and a desire for Asian women as objects are closely related and cannot be disguised or brushed over by romantic dressing. The problem is ignoring the parts of societal and historical context that determine person-to-person interaction AS WELL AS racial domination. It is not enough to be wary of the mullet-headed thug who proclaims that he likes to date "Orientals" because of their "slanty eyes and instinctual subservience." Paranoia is not advised, but caution is. Analyze your personal interactions.

> I was teased mercilessly. I went to public school, and the kids called me "Risa Ring." Kids would come over to my house, and it would smell like Chinese food, and that was embarrassing. Or if I had friends over, my dad would say, "Tell them to go home" in Chinese, right in front of them.
>
> —Lisa Ling, cohost of *The View*, in a *New York Times* article called "Asian 'It' Girls Say So Long, Dragon Lady" (May 21, 2000)

◢ • alison**park** 18
Woodside, New York

I was born in Chicago, Illinois, and currently reside in New York City. My poetry has appeared in The Nuyorasian Anthology, *edited by Bino A. Realuyo, and* The Asian Pacific American Journal. *As the daughter of Korean immigrants, I am interested in many issues that arise as a first-generation Asian American. "Maybelline on Maple Street" delves into the identity of an adolescent girl growing up in an upper-middle-class, white, suburban town in the U.S.*

Maybelline on Maple Street

Jeannie Hampton
Of 7492 Maple Street
Who lives down the block
Walks her dog down Washington Avenue wearing
Candies slides
skin-tight Paris Blues jeans
a Bongo mango-colored
   halter top
cherry-flavored lip gloss and
Maybelline mascara.
Her dog is a cocker spaniel
And his name is Blondie
Because his fur is the shade of sunlight
That Jeannie's hair is.

Everyone knew she wanted
   Tony Maughum,
First-string runningback for
   the Hawks,
From the way she pursed her
   lips
And swayed her hips
When she passed him in the
   hallway. She bragged
And told us in the locker room
That she had blown him away
With her stunning smile
And fabulous lines
Under the bleachers
During half-time.

But everyone knew he wanted me
"Asian girls are the

hottest," he said
With a knowing wink that
    would melt any girl's heart
In the lunchroom
Last Friday. He watched me
over Jell-O the color of the
    Astroturf
On the football field outside.
I smiled, unsure, maybe I was
Popular?

I tried to ignore Jeannie
    Hampton
In the corner of my eye
And instead I picked at my
    salad
While she lifted her hands
And used her middle fingers
To tug at the corners of her
    eyes.

jennifer**l**i21
Silver Spring, Maryland

My parents moved to Silver Spring, Maryland, from Taiwan in the mid-1970s. In high school, I got tired of defending myself against stereotypes and dealing with racist situations. In college, I started reading wonderful books and zines that dealt with being Asian American, and they inspired me to write about my own experiences. "Best Friends" deals with issues with which I finally came to terms after leaving home.

Best Friends

Up until high school, I never gave much thought to what race my friends were.

My friends were people with whom I got along, and they liked the same things as I did. It never occurred to me that I should separate them into categories. It just happened. Suddenly, I had my group of Asian friends and my group of white friends.

As a Chinese American girl bred on white rice and macaroni, I was torn between what appeared at the time to be good and evil. As a punk rock–loving feminist, I felt at ease with my white friends. When I was with them, I was an anomaly—an Asian girl, with pink-streaked hair and Doc Martens. I didn't fit into the stereotypical idea of what an Asian girl was like. I admit, I liked the shock value; in a way, this was my way of making them think twice about labeling people again. On the other hand, I felt like a reject among my Asian friends. Falling victim to my own prejudices, I believed that I was the ugly duck in a flock of future doctors and engineers. Math and science weren't my cup of tea, so I automatically shut myself off from them. I knew my parents wanted me to be more like them, but I wanted to be a rebel instead.

My best friend at the time was a white girl who liked lizards and cartoons. We met in ninth grade, and for the next four years, we were inseparable. At lunch, we sat in a mismatched group of riot grrrls, goths, and computer nerds. The music we listened to, not the color of our skin, is what separated the groups (or this is what I believed). As the lone Asian, I felt the need to defend myself from time to time against racist comments from "well-meaning" friends. I would laugh the comments off most of the time, attributing their hurtful words to their lack of knowledge, as opposed to hatred. They didn't quite know what to make of me.

The relationship between my best friend and me was tumultuous. We shared and did everything together, but, deep down, there was a part of me that felt like she had used far too many racial slurs. Everyone at school used to call us twins because we had short hair, glasses, and we dressed alike. One day, while we were going to class, she burst out, "Maybe if I painted my skin yellow, dyed my hair black, and had slanty eyes, we could be twins." I stared at her in shock, not believing that the words had come out of her mouth. This, I thought, from a girl who supposedly understood me the best. For the first time, I noticed how blond her hair was and how bright her blue eyes were. I flashed back to the time when she once told me the reason her sister didn't like me—I was a "Mongoloid." I also recalled numerous times when she had referred to her mother's boyfriend as a "spic." In all of these instances, I had simply shrugged off my discomfort and ignored my feelings. I wanted so desperately for her to be the person I could confide in and depend on, but suddenly, I was faced with the knowledge that her words weren't just naive, they were dangerous ideas that she believed. My friend Susan also happened to be there, and she instantly picked up on my feelings.

"Is that supposed to be funny?" Susan asked.

"I was just kidding. Jennifer knows that I'm just playing around," my best friend retorted.

"It's not something that you should kid about," said Susan. "How can you say all that stuff about yellow skin?"

"Sorry, I thought it was funny."

After the incident, our friendship pretty much deteriorated. Instead of spending more time with her, I immersed myself in college applications and studying for the SATs. I was incredibly angry with myself for not having the courage to speak my mind to her. I was afraid of knowing the full extent of her prejudices and chose to protect myself instead. She went from being my best friend to being someone I couldn't even look in the eye anymore. I avoided her in the halls, and after we graduated, I lost touch with her completely. I was torn over the fact that she probably didn't even know why I was mad at her, since I never really voiced any of my objections. I wanted her to realize that she was a racist, but I was too afraid to bring it up. And I wondered if it was even fair to use the term *racist* to describe her.

I eventually decided it would be healthier if I just let everything go. Sometimes I thought that I was at fault because I never brought up my feelings with her. I reminded myself that this was a single experience—my best friend did not reflect the views of the rest of my friends or of an entire race. I couldn't resent anyone else for her behavior. This girl made me aware of how narrowly I viewed people, too. I was busy sticking people into boxes based on appearance. In the end, I realized that I should consider this as a learning experience and put it behind me.

oliviachung 19
Silver Spring, Maryland

I watched the spoken-word group I Was Born With Two Tongues perform and was inspired by their style of reflecting on personal experiences. This piece flowed from my desire for self-expression and hopes of challenging other Asian American girls to question their definition of beauty. I am a second-generation Korean American, born and raised in a loving family in Silver Spring, Maryland. Currently, I'm a sophomore at the University of Pennsylvania, pursuing interests in activism, writing, and hip-hop. My ultimate goal is to keep it real and selflessly live for the Lord.

Finding My Eye-dentity

Olivia, you wanna get sang ka pul?

I'm driving my mother to work, when she randomly brings up the eyelid question. The question that almost every Korean monoeyelidded girl has had to face in her life. The question that could change the future of my naturally noncreased eyelids, making them crease with the cut of a cosmetic surgeon's knife.

You know your aunt? She used to have beany eyes just like you! She used to put on white and black eyeliner every morning to make them look BIG. Then she went to Korea and got the surgery done. Now look!

She looks so much better! Don't you want it done? I would do it . . .

I think this is about the 346,983,476th time she has brought this topic up. Using the exact same words. You would look so much more prettier with bigger eyes! she says. *You know, because they look kind of squinty and on top of that you have an underbite, so you look really mean . . .* She explains while narrowing her eyes and jutting out her jaw in emphasis of her point.

A couple of years ago, I would have taken her suggestion seriously. I remember reading a section of *Seventeen* magazine, where the once-did-funky-makeup-for-100-anorexic-white-girls-on-runways beauty expert revealed the secret to applying eye makeup. As a desperate preteen girl seeking beauty advice, I remember it perfectly. Put dark shadow right over the eyelashes, light powder all over, medium shadow over the edge of the crease of your eyelid. That's where I always tripped up. Crease? Umm . . . excuse me? These so-called beauty experts never gave me enough expertise to figure out how to put makeup on my face without looking like a character in a kabuki play. I tried to follow the beauty experts' advice. But I decided it wasn't working when people asked me if I had gotten a black eye.

My friends suggested training my eyelids to fold with tape. *My mother did that and now she has a real crease, one of my friends told me*. I, however, never learned the magic behind that, and always felt too embarrassed to ask. Another friend once excitedly showed me how she had bought a bottle of make-your-own-eye-crease glue from Korea. I let her try it on me too. I could barely open my eyes, thanks to the fierce stinging sensation resulting from the glue that got on my eyeball. And when I finally did take a quick glimpse of myself in the mirror, I saw a stranger with uneven eyelids.

The first time I remember being insulted was when I was little. . . .

In kindergarten, I believe. Oh, it was classic. A little blond kid pulled the edges of his eyes out, yelling, *Ching chong chinaman!* I, being new to this game, could only make a weak comeback. *I'm not Chinese. . . . I'm KOREAN*. I remember feeling a confused hurt, realizing that I looked different and not understanding why being different was bad.

Couldn't we all just get along? I had learned that God loves people as they are, as different as they are. I learned that He looks at the heart, and that it really doesn't matter how a person looks. I think my belief in this, combined with my fear of a sharp object cutting the skin above my eye, kept me away from the *sang ka pul* surgery. Yet, I continued to receive comments on my "chinky" eyes, and I always emerged from these situations feeling confused and angry . . . without ever really knowing why. Why couldn't I be accepted with my so-called chinky eyes? Why in the world were they even called "chinky" eyes? If they meant to insult Chinese, all the Chinese people I knew had huge eyes. With the crease.

As I grew older, the childish "ching chong"s came with less frequency. Still, the magazines continue to give me unhelpful directions on how to apply makeup. Still, I witness my own friends getting the surgery done in an effort to be "more beautiful." Still, my mother continuously confronts me with the dreaded eyelid question. *You wanna get* sang ka pul? I always answer her with an *are-you-crazy?* but simple *no*. All the things I wish I could have told her come flowing on this page with my pen. . . .

Umma, my mother, don't you see that my noncreased eyes are beautiful? Asian eyes are beautiful. Your eyes are beautiful. My eyes are beautiful. Asian is beautiful. After all these years of wanting to open up my eyes with tape and glue and surgery, I have opened up my eyes to a different definition of beauty. A broader definition of beauty, one that embraces differences and includes every girl, who can hold her head up, *sang ka pul*-less and chinky-eyed, because being *Asian is beautiful*.

Since my birth in '83, I've come to love eating cereal at midnight, rubbing my feet in grass, and—my nostrils. My most vivid memories are from my elementary school days and it's thanks to my nostrils that I am able to remember exactly how my first grade teacher smelled, the smell of jungle gym bars, the hint of dirt left on my fingers after falling on playground gravel. All these things remain clear and unaltered in my mind and I love writing about them.

Nostrils

"Sarah? Why are your nostrils so big?" Asking innocently, Lauren pointed at her own nose, white in every way.

"What, these?" I looked down at my nose and shrugged.

"Yeah, look—look at mine," and she pointed again. Her pink nail polish was coming off. Maybe she bit her nails.

I paused between every few strokes of red to look up at my tablemates. At the far corner, a WWF shirt disrupted the diluted pink flesh of Sean Kaplan. He was dirty. I picked up a green crayon, then reconsidered, grabbing the white to see if I could make a lighter shade of brown.

"Hey, wanna see me color my tongue?" David asked us with his taste buds exposed and saliva in danger of dripping. White boys were dirty.

Lauren Katz took a rubber band and expertly pulled her hair back. Pretending to reach over really far to grab a yellow crayon, I looked at Lauren's nostrils. I decided Kristi's were prettier. The wooden door opened and the breeze swept the smells of glue sticks, construction paper, and Magic Markers around the room. White mothers did this all the time, especially the blond ones. Kristi's mom towered over Mrs. Rogovin and spoke in hushed tones as I watched their mouths move, fascinated. White women always had extra-sticky lips that parted in waves whenever they spoke. Kristi Placek's mom always wore earrings. Today was hoop day. They swung and hit her neck, glancing sunlight off in cyclic directions. She nodded her head according to what type of okay was being said, her head dipping and tilting, accompanied by appropriately placed uh-huhs and mmms.

When they finished their courtship dance, Kristi Placek's mom hurried over to our table, her heels stabbing the floor tiles. Contact between the floor and her shoes produced internal rhythm and I wished she would walk forever. She stood behind me and made various noises, composed of car keys, pennies, and worn gum wrappers. I could smell the cigarettes through those ivory white teeth. I looked up.

They were beautiful. Narrow ovals bordered by perfectly tanned skin loomed over me, breathing the same perfume-infested air that I breathed. Subtle freckles adorned the bridge of her nose, set symmetrically between sea-green eyes that jangled when she blinked. Why didn't I have freckles? Chunks of blond ripped across my vision as she leaned over to plant a plum red lipstick stain on Kristi. The coins in her pocket shifted and the sunglasses obeyed the careless flick of her wrist as she repositioned them to sweep back the yellow to reveal the natural brown. I think I liked the brown better. My eyes followed those nostrils out of the room. It took two slams to shut the door, making a deep-throated groan as it forced itself into the doorway. I guess they didn't fit quite right.

That night I stood in front of my mirror and slightly pinched my nose. Maybe if I held it long enough it would stay like that. The will of a six-year-old child could not be tamed. But I let go. It was getting hard to breathe.

I need to be out there because when I was growing up, I never saw someone that I could relate to on TV, something where I could say, "I want to be like her." So now, with me out there, I want the Asian kids to say, "Hey, maybe I can follow my dreams and go into the music business and be like CoCo!"

—Musician CoCo Lee, in an interview that appeared in
aMagazine (February/March 2001)

kim**mckee**16

Penfield, New York

When I wrote the following essay I was fifteen and just coming to terms with being adopted and Korean. All my life my school has been full of Caucasian people and being Asian kind of sticks out. Last year another Asian friend of mine accused me of "being white." I asked him how I should be, considering I've grown up in the suburbs almost my entire life, and only lived in Korea until I was five months old. Putting things into perspective, I've realized that being Korean American gives me a unique identity.

The Other Sister

Ever since I can remember, people have given me strange looks. They look at me, then ask me to repeat my name. With a name like Kim McKee, they most likely expect to see a curly redhead with freckles. Instead, they see a petite, Asian girl. And they're surprised.

Living in a suburb of Rochester, New York, has not been easy. There's such a small Asian population, so the cultures are almost invisible. In my high school you can probably count the number of Asians on one hand. Like me, many of them are adopted kids.

Before I switched schools last year, one of my friends couldn't understand how I could be related to my Caucasian cousin, simply because I was Asian. I explained that I was adopted, but he still had a difficult time making the connection. That incident annoyed me, not due to the fact that he looked at me differently, but because I'd expected him to "get it"; after all, one of his good friends was an adopted Korean, too.

Few things make me angrier than when people stare at me while I am with my younger half sisters. To give you an idea, one of my sisters just so happens to look like the "model" Caucasian—I mean, she has blond hair and big, blue eyes. When we're together, adults have the audacity to gawk and stare at us. I'm suddenly reminded of people's general lack of awareness about international adoptions. My sisters haven't necessarily made the distinction that I am Asian, but I sense that they know something about me makes me different from them. For instance, I remember when my blond-haired, blue-eyed sister, now six, used to ask me why I was black when she was a toddler. It was frustrating to have to explain.

"I tan easily, and I'm Korean," I answered.

She's just a kid, I told myself. It was unrealistic for me to expect her to know that these comments were bothersome. But I wished her mother had helped clear things up by explaining that I was Asian American, and that Asians did not come here from the same continent as Africans. Her mother made no attempt to help me teach my sister the difference.

My appearance draws a lot of attention and people have commented on the fact that I don't look like anyone in my family. Usually people say that I have an "exotic" beauty. I wouldn't mind it so much if they didn't follow this statement with some mention of the phrase "china doll." My first impulse is to scream, "I'm not Chinese!" But they don't seem to notice a difference—growing up, I've noticed Caucasians and other racial groups tend to group Asians together. They assume Vietnamese is the same as Korean, and Korean is the same as Japanese. People in my family have jokingly called me "Chinese girl" and I'm secretly offended by their remarks. How can my own family be so insensitive, I wonder. I understand that they're only joking, but why can't they imagine how it would feel if I made a mockery of them?

Others might think that, by now, I'd be used to getting weird looks for being an adopted Korean American girl, but I'm not. And I don't see why I should be. Everyone claims Americans are open-minded, but I could argue the opposite. I'm gradually learning how to tell the difference between curiosity and hostility—I guess it's fair to say that people stare out of curiosity, and their remarks about my background are meant to be compliments. It's not like they're always calling me "slanty-eyes." But I look forward to the day that I'll stop having to explain and teach others all the time. A time when people truly begin to see me for who I am—me—and not as someone who's different from them on the outside.

anonymous
Location unknown

> *This "note" was mailed to me with no return address. It was scrawled across three pages of crumpled, lined paper. The sender titled the piece herself.*
> —V.N.

Breakup Notice

Brad,

I'm sorry we ended up fighting again. *I hate this.* We're always arguing about something every time we see each other when we should be enjoying the little time we get to spend together. And I know you think I'm the one who needs to relax all the time.

When I found out that Sara didn't invite me to her house because her dad is conservative and he only likes her to hang out with certain people, it totally pissed me off. But what really bothered me was how you didn't think I had any reason to feel totally alienated and different. Even after I told you everything else her dad has said about issues concerning race. If we're to stay together, you HAVE to try to understand what it feels like to be me in these situations. Actually, I take that back. You should want to know what it feels like to walk in my shoes, in general. I mean, I'm curious to know what your life is like, too.

I'm starting to figure out why I think I "jump to conclusions" when I'm hanging out with you, our friends, your family, and my family. I think when you brush my feelings off and tell me to relax, and you refuse to talk things out with me, a brick wall goes up between us. You trivialize things and it totally bothers me! I feel so alone when you say I'm jumping to conclusions. The more you insist that life isn't like it is (that people aren't sometimes racist or closed-minded), and that I need to change my attitude, the more I feel alienated. From you. From Sara. And I want you to know how important this is to me.

I don't fit in with your family. It's like your dad doesn't have anything to say to me other than the fact that he fought in the Vietnam War, and your mom looks really uncomfortable when she has to make small talk with me, saying you have a lot of plans ahead of you, blah blah blah. I never know what to say, so I don't say anything. And then when I spout stuff in your face about how weird all this makes me feel, you get frustrated. You think I'm crazy. But I talk to you because I think we should talk about this stuff. Because if I can't talk to you about these things, then I am alone. And I can be alone, by, like, being alone. (Don't interpret this to mean anything except that I want to put everything out on the table and not hide issues like these if we're together.)

I know you feel like I'm pushing you away but I think it's the opposite. I'm trying to open up to you. I'm not paranoid, and I'm really still annoyed that you even said that to me. You know how I feel. I just want to make things work. But I can't feel this way when I'm with you—I hate when we fight, but if we try to hear each other out, we can grow closer. Is this making sense to you? I hope so!

(Just so you know, I'm waiting for Sara to apologize or something. God, as if she wouldn't have been offended, if the roles were reversed!!!)

Call me, OK? I wanna talk to you about this. . . .

Me

My parents are from Taiwan, but I was born in New Jersey. We moved to Ann Arbor six years ago, and adjusting to the social life was difficult. I didn't fit in with the other Asian Americans who lived in the area as they'd been living in the States much longer. In high school, although many considered me to be "pretty," I never thought I was as good as other people. And I gradually fell into depression. This is my story.

Anorexic

My mother tells my father that I've been diagnosed with depression. My father tells me this is okay. That maybe God in all His holiness let this happen so that I could help others. One day, he says, I just might help a little girl like myself get over something like this. Because not everybody knows how it really feels unless they've gone through this, and since I have, I can be compassionate toward them. He tells me to pray. Pray, Alice. Pray. Ask him to help you and make you better. *Pray.*

And then he points to my waist and tells me it's too thick. He says that I should lose some weight. I don't need him to tell me.

Something has agitated him. Someone has contradicted him and he is offended. Someone has not lived up to his expectations. Perhaps, this time, someone is late. And, perhaps, someone doesn't agree with him on his stupid point. It will begin innocently and change directions quickly. His eyes bulge. His mouth snarls, and his face becomes strained and red. He pounds the table. He is trembling and looks flushed from holding his anger inside. Suddenly he hurls it all out.

Worthless. Undeserving. Don't try hard enough. What kind of man would want you? Your husband would fire you. Failure. Look at Paul Chen's daughter. Look at yourself. What are you going to do with your life. Lazy. Expletive. Nothing. Take a good look at yourself, he says, you're so ummotivated—why can't you just cheer up, I told you cheer up. You're not "sad," you're just lazy. The only reason you hate going to school is because you stay up all night. You watch TV, so you are tired, and you don't want to go to school in the morning.

And then he says, Go to church. There is nothing that that stupid doctor, that stupid psychiatrist, can do for you. They just want your money. Don't believe a word they say. Just believe this. What your father tells you. Your father loves you. Pray. God will heal you.

My mom walks past me and I'm sitting on the tiles of our kitchen, holding a big stainless steel kitchen knife and the second part of a second Subway sandwich. I am eating and I am crying. And crying and eating. My mom walks past me. Why don't you just control yourself? Why can't you control yourself? But drug addiction and alcoholics and cigarette smokers, that's different. My mom walks past me and she sees nothing. She hears nothing. I scream at my mother. I tell my mother. I tell her again and again. I'm screaming and sobbing hysterically. I scream screaming.

No one knows what goes on behind closed doors. They will say to me, you have such a great haircut, I want one just like yours, and they will say to me, where do you get all your clothes, you're so stylish, and guys will stare at me and approach me and try to hit on me. But wherever I am, I am conscious of the fact that Asian girls are supposed to be thin and small-boned. And I am conscious of the ring of fat that encircles my waist. And Asian girls are supposed to wear only a size 1 or size 2. And I think about all the Asian girls with their flat chests and hipless butts. *This fat around my stomach.* All the Asian girls with those padded push-up bras and their little flat butts complain loudly to each other, "I'm so fat," including my cousins, who are all skinny. I feel this fat that's mine is like a tube of rubber tied around my waist and I feel these two breasts, which are mine are heavy and 36 B. And, when I am finally alone, I stuff another bowl of noodles, another bowl of rice, another piece of fruit, and I ram another muffin, another cracker, another cookie, another plate of leftovers down my throat. I am bloated. Crying. I am hurt and wounded and happy and disgusted and then I am soiled and dirty for my sins.

I open the shower door and I turn on the hot water and watch as the mirrors and the glass cover with steam.

I stand under the showerhead and feel the hot water running over me. My face stings. My body stings and I wonder how much I will be able to get out this time. When I am done, I will rinse the floor and wash my body with Dove-so-pure-it-floats, and there will be no evidence. Tomorrow I won't eat breakfast—just half a cup of coffee—and I'll eat half my lunch. Tomorrow I will go to school and I will sit in class in my jeans, so tight they hurt. And I will struggle to breathe and to look people in the eye. Tomorrow I will sit in class and suffocate through more than half of it and wish to God, just let me die. Tomorrow I will pretend that nothing is wrong and that everything is fine and no one will suspect. No one. No, because I am not a walking skeleton, and I'm not white, and because I'm the president of our Asian American club, and I'm an Asian American feminist, and because I am so strong.

> Growing up, I always knew that I never belonged and never fit in. Instead of dealing with the pain, I just immersed myself in a lot of school, classes, theater and just ignored it for a long time.
>
> —Actress Mingna, in an article that appeared in
> YOLK magazine (Issue #4)

➤ • naomi**irie**20
Cleveland, Ohio

i was born twenty years ago to my japanese mother and japanese-canadian father. my piece is a memoir about one of the subtle but painful ways my perceived differences were ridiculed while i was a child. i wrote this piece my junior year of high school, before i really began understanding what it meant to be asian american. since

*then, my life has been and continues to be an evolution of con-
frontation, realization, education, respect, and acceptance. i am
now realizing how being asian american affects my life in the
largest and tiniest of ways, and where there was once doubt there is
now understanding and a growing sense of pride.*

rice cakes rice cakes and cereal: a memoir

it is routine for the sisters to get dropped off at the local library
after school. they stay until their father can pick them up after
work. each day the sisters shuffle through the library, their heads
low, dark bangs hiding their eyes. hastily, they enter the children's
section. they take the farthest table in the farthest corner of the
room. quietly, they lay out their textbooks. they do not talk. they
are quickly engrossed in their books.

they do not hear the creaks encircling them around the table
made by a group of young boys. one of the boys tries to mimic the
sounds of their language. they are not imitating japanese; they
sound like a bunch of drunken idiots. their voices are kept low, so
as not to be a disturbance to the librarians. the sisters do not raise
their heads. the boys continue with their misplaced accented
words. they pull at a sister's black braid. pulling, until she lets out
a cry. the boys snicker in disgust. "what's the matter, you jap
bitches, can't even handle a little tug?" their fun done, they leave
just as quietly as they had arrived.

a sister remembers once watching the mother cook rice and fish
for dinner. rice is rinsed once. twice. once more. the sister asks
why they have to go to the library every day. she tells the mother
about the boys. the mother looks up, stops washing the rice.
"ignore them. that is all. they will stop. what else can be done."
four times. perfect and white.

soon the father will come and pick the sisters up. they rise and
begin cleaning the table. they can see the father waiting for them
near the entrance of the children's room. they move toward him.
the boys see the family.

"hey, you chinese?" they ask. the father turns the other way, holding limply onto the sisters' hands. "how do you make rice cakes? they taste good?" the boys laugh. only when the boys say, "see you later, you japs," does the father tighten his grip. he leads them to the car. they go home. the sister heads for her room. she leaves the light off and sits on her bed. it seems everyone is laughing at her. she tries to think of something, anything that might stop the tears. but she cannot. and rather than stop the tears, she encourages them.

sitting on her bed with a stained face

linh**ngo** 16
Walla Walla, Washington

I am at the tender age when one thinks she is invincible enough to take on the whole wide world alone. My Chinese father was born in Vietnam, and my mother is a Vietnamese native of Vietnam. Currently, I am living on campus at Whitman College. Writing my story helped me to reflect and deal with conflicting emotions that were never truly resolved. By sharing my story "The Lawsuit" with you, I feel as if I'm letting go of unnecessary baggage that belongs to the past.

The Lawsuit

Athena, Oregon. The population was about 1,500. My parents were looking for a gas station to buy, and the real estate agent brought them to Athena. Instantly, they fell in love with the place. They imagined themselves owning a family-operated business. Across the street, there was a local high school, and they saw their children growing up, sheltered and protected from the corruption found in the city. Unfortunately, we seemed to interrupt this small, lazy-atmospheric town by moving in. As far as I could tell, we were the first "real" Asian family there.

People in Athena saw us not as the Ngo family, but as the "Oriental people who owned the gas station." My parents didn't understand this. To them, we were just Americans like everyone else. Race was not an issue. All they wanted from Athena was to fulfill the typical American dream—you know, the classic dream of raising a family and obtaining a source of income. As I sit here typing these words, I wonder. Can we find the values of this American dream anywhere any more? And if so, is this dream limited to those of European descent?

My parents ran their business differently than the previous owners had. For one thing, they wanted to conduct it like a family-run business. And seeing that my parents, two uncles, and two close Caucasian friends of our family (who did volunteer work for us) were healthy enough to work, my parents decided to fire the employees, whom they'd inherited from the previous owners. Big mistake.

For as long as people could remember, the name of the convenience store had been "Fred's Market." What a funny name, I heard my parents discussing once. Personally, I don't think they've ever met a Fred in their life. Thus, there went Fred's Market, and in came "Athena One Stop." My parents were so proud of our little store that they even got a loan to replace the old washers and dryers in a tiny laundromat that was connected to our store. But it became clear to us that we were like a huge tornado that was sweeping into town, disrupting it from its sleep. Later, a lady told me that the changes that were brought on by our arrival made a lot of people mad.

Instead of making business, we ended up scaring people off to our competitor. There were always rumors going around the school about our store.

"Don't eat there, the food makes people sick," they said.

"That Oriental guy who owns Fred's Market has his gay lover working there," I heard.

Since when did my dad become gay, and how come my mom didn't know about it? My family took these statements lightly, but I knew they weren't all that happy inside.

One day, a health inspector stopped by to take a look around the place. He walked in with an attitude, and a while later proclaimed, "You yellow people don't know how to do dishes." I am still able to visualize my parents standing there, paralyzed in shock that a state worker could be so narrow-minded, and that he could act in such an uneducated way. But they kept calm, and tried not to make a scene, even though I saw my mom accidentally releasing a few tears.

The man continued his attempt to make my dad feel incompetent. "You yellow people don't know how to run a business," he said. "You should look for another job."

The health inspector wrote down some other false accusations about our store, and did everything he could to close it down three times for noncompliance. During his visits, he threatened my parents, telling them that he could catch faults in a brand-new hospital kitchen, and that eventually he would also shut down our store. The man went even further to tell my parents that they should buy a bolt and lock my five-year-old brother into the back office, because we were running a business.

It pains me to think about how this experience affected my parents. My mom's heart was broken. Due to stress, she gradually developed ulcers. My dad was a very proud man, but his spirit was also broken. We were getting closer to bankruptcy, and he began to feel like he was too incompetent to care for the family.

Imagine our situation. My parents came to America less than twenty years ago with nothing. After they met each other and fell in love, my brother and I were born to complete their concept of happiness. Afterward, everything they did was for us. Their motivation to raise their social standing stemmed from wanting us to receive all of the things that they lacked when they were younger. Then, in an instant, everything they had been working toward—and everything they had accomplished—was fading before their eyes. They were trying to hold on to what they had, but it was useless.

The closing of our business was considered a scandal in the

small town of Athena. We were already viewed as pariahs, but this event finalized it. Not knowing what to do, my parents took legal action against the state inspector. My dad wanted the best lawyer he could find, so he hired one for over $60,000. We had witnesses take the stand, such as a police commissioner and a Protestant minister, and all of these witnesses were white. More than a year later, after a long, draining process, justice was finally delivered in court. We won the case and gained compensation for our loss.

In spite of what happened, my family feels no resentment against Caucasians. Although some of the people we encountered were pretty mean, we met others who were kind to us and who did everything for us. They supported us, and they constantly held us in their prayers. At times, when people get hurt badly, they have a tendency to generalize about things, like when an entire race is blamed for the actions of a single person. My parents taught me to do the reverse. They pointed out that regardless of one white man's mistake, we should be grateful for the rest of the white people who helped us through our difficult time. It's been over a year since the lawsuit ended, and my family has sold the store. We are moving on.

 debra**yoo**18
Schaumburg, Illinois

I wrote this poem in reflection of a real memory I have of two young boys calling me a "chink" on the bus ride coming home from school in second grade. It was the first time I had ever heard the word. I didn't know what it meant or what its connotations were, but somehow it still greatly stung me. It was my first encounter with racism, and I will never forget it.

INNOCENCE

The first day of kindergarten.
The classroom, filled with happy children.

A sea of blond and brown heads.
　　And yes, one head of black.
　　Me.
I didn't care. I didn't notice.
　　But everyone else did.

I walk in the classroom.
Whispers follow, buzzing with gossip.
Secrets float from child to child.
　　I tensed, everyone was looking
　　At me.
They stared. I stared back.
　　Why was everyone watching me?

I see a boy about my age.
Pulling his eyes at the corners.
Making them sharp and pointed.
　　I realized, he was making fun
　　Of me.
But why? Because of my eyes?
　　I couldn't understand.

That first day was horrible.
Girls giggling, boys pointing.
No one who would be my friend.
　　I noticed, they were staying away
　　From me.
I almost cried. Tears sprang to my eyes.
　　But I kept my pride.

I boarded the bus for my ride home.
I felt safe, finally, at last.
Two boys sat in front of me.
　　They turned. "Chink," they said.
　　Me?

Chink? The word brought sadness to my soul.
   Dejection crossed my face.

That first day hurt me.
Hurt my core, my only being.
But I finally realized.
   People were prejudiced
   Against me.
It came like a tidal wave. Smashed my spirit.
   My eyes opened to the harsh world around me.

nina ji yun**baek**19
Amherst, Massachusetts

I live in Massachusetts during eight months out of the school year, and I live in Korea for the remaining four. Societal ignorance was my inspiration for writing "Chalk Marks." I see and hear all sorts of comments from people suggesting that Asians are stupid because they can't speak English, or that the majority of Asians just can't speak English, period. From a young age, I was told I wouldn't make anything of myself because I was Korean. Now I'm proudly working toward a major in psychology with a minor in English.

Chalk Marks

When I was a little girl, everyone always told me that I could be whatever I wanted when I grew up. A doctor, a writer, a lawyer . . . but the only thing I wanted to be was white. Growing up, I never saw Asian people who had prestigious careers. Those jobs were all being taken by white people. Every doctor I had ever seen was white and none of my teachers looked like me. As far as I could tell, Asians were behind deli and liquor store counters. This convinced me that, in order to become what I wanted, I had to be white.

In elementary school, I was the only Asian child. Unlike most Asian families, mine did not live in New York or LA. We lived in a small suburb of Indiana, not by choice, but because my father's job was based there. Although we lived in a small, mostly white community, making friends was not too difficult. Surprisingly, most children were accepting of me, and my cultural differences didn't seem to affect them. In school, however, I wasn't liked by all of my teachers.

One day when I was in the third grade, I found a Hello Kitty pencil on the floor. Later that day, one of my classmates told our teacher that her Hello Kitty pencil was missing. Remembering the pencil I found earlier, I took it out of my desk and gave it back to the girl. My teacher accused me of stealing the pencil. Even after I explained that I had found it on the floor and didn't know whose it was, she called me a liar. I was shocked. She didn't call my parents, but the damage was done.

The next year wasn't much better. A little while after the school year had begun, my teacher made me take the chalkboard erasers out to the playground to dust. Every day ten minutes before school was over, I would beat the erasers. If I didn't finish in time, I would miss the bus and have to call my father to come pick me up. I didn't want to make him angry, so I would hurry as fast as I could. Sometimes, my teacher would hold me back on purpose, knowing that I would miss the bus. I realized early on that none of the other children had to perform this chore, so I gathered the courage to ask my teacher why I was the only one that had to do it. She glared down at me and told me it was because I was different.

I wasn't white, and cleaning up after people was probably the only thing I'd ever end up doing with my life.

On the bus ride home, I began to cry. I couldn't understand why she had been so mean to me, and I was too young to know what racism was. So I believed her. I never told my parents about what my teacher had told me, or about the chore that I was forced to do. I wanted so much to be white. I longed for blond hair and blue eyes. I would sit in front of the mirror for hours, staring at my Asian eyes and plain black hair. After a while, I couldn't even recognize myself. I didn't want to be different anymore. I wanted to be like everyone else around me. I would pray every night for God to turn me into a little white girl, but in the morning, I was always still the same little Korean girl.

Although my fourth grade teacher's voice was always in the back of my mind, I still managed to excel in school. My name appeared regularly on the honor roll, and I was in the talented and gifted program, but I did these things mostly to please my parents. It didn't matter to me what kind of grades I got. After all, I thought, a cleaning woman doesn't need an education.

The winter of my fifth-grade year, my father got transferred to Korea. For the first time in my life, I was surrounded by people who looked like me, but that didn't change anything. I still didn't think I would get anywhere in life unless I was white, and I believed that all Asians suffered the same affliction. I was stubborn and refused to change my mind. It's much easier to believe what you're told rather than to prove that what's being said is wrong. But someone changed my mind.

In junior year of high school, I was put in an advanced placement English course. English had always been my best subject, so this didn't come as a surprise. My English teacher was a tall, sixty-something white woman. She was soft spoken, but very articulate and intelligent. It was even more unusual that she seemed to genuinely care about her students. She took the time to talk to each student at least once a day. Even me. Through her dedication I discovered my love and talent for writing.

One day she asked me to stay after class. After everyone had left the room, she handed me a piece of paper. On it was a poem I had written. She told me that she had never received the essay I was supposed to have turned in that week, but instead, got my poem by mistake. I felt my cheeks burn as I read it. These were my private thoughts, and I had never meant for anyone to see them. She told me that she had never read anything so passionately written by such a young person. Then she asked me if I would bring in more of my writings for her to read, and I was embarrassed but intrigued at the same time. I was curious to hear what she had to say. The next day, I came into her classroom after school. I handed her a notebook full of my writings. She read some of the pieces and we talked about them. She asked if she could take my notebook home with her over the weekend, and assured me that she would not show my work to anyone.

On Monday, I appeared in her doorway once again. She beckoned to me and shooed the other students out. She told me that she thought my writings were very good and asked if I'd considered submitting something to the school's literary magazine contest. I said no, and told her that I really wasn't that good at writing. I probably wouldn't win anything, anyway. After multiple attempts to convince me to submit something, she asked me why I was so down on myself. I took a deep breath and then I told her what my elementary school teacher had said to me all those years ago.

At first she was very quiet, but after a while she said, "You know what that teacher told you was wrong, don't you?" I didn't say anything, so she continued. She told me that there was nothing stopping me from being whatever I wanted to be. It didn't matter if I was white or not. The only thing that was stopping me was myself.

I decided to submit one of my poems to the literary magazine on the day of the contest's deadline. Three weeks later, I heard my name announced—I was the first-place winner.

For the rest of the school year, my English teacher and I remained close. She helped me with my writing, but most of all, she helped me raise my self-confidence. When I learned that she would be transferring to a school in Germany, I was devastated. I wanted so much for her to be there when I graduated from high school.

On her last day, we exchanged yearbooks. I took up two pages thanking her for everything she had done for me. We said good-bye, and when I got home I read the message she had written in my yearbook. It was short, but what she wrote has always stayed with me:

"You have brilliance of mind and wisdom of the soul. You will go far in life. I have confidence in you."

I will never forget the way she touched my life.

sandy'ci**moua**19

St. Paul, Minnesota

Nyob zoo (hello in Hmong). In a nutshell, I am a first-generation, Hmong American, college woman. My parents are from Laos, but I'm not. "On the 16" was written as an attempt to create meaning for moments in my life that could be dismissed as mundane. I hope to continue producing art and writing as a form of adding meaning to my life. Currently I am passionate about women's issues from the Hmong perspective; specifically, the cultural authenticity of Hmong pageantry and the social construction of beauty.

On the 16: Episodes

10 P.M., February 2000
Valentine's Day weekend

Tired, young, sagging bodies are sitting or standing behind me and in front of me. I am the only Asian—the only Hmong—on board, but of course I don't realize this at first.

A scrubby, ashy-looking black man gets on. He sits in front of me, turns around, and smiles. He reeks of urine, sweat, and musty alcohol.

I smile back.

The bus hits a bump and continues on its regular route. He turns around again and begins to speak. To me.

"You Chinese?"

"No," I reply.

"Yes, you are—you're Chinese."

"No, I am not. I am Hmong." My inner alarm is ringing, "Get out of here." I ignore it.

"Yes you are, whyyoulyin'?" He insists that I am Chinese.

"No, I am Hmong," I repeat again. Annoyed, I'm eyeing the front section of the bus, where people are oblivious to our dialogue.

All of a sudden he gets up. Swiveling his body around, he sits next to me. I am pinned between him and the cold bus window.

"Yes, you ARE Chi-neeese!"

He's drunk.

"I can tell by your legs."

I cover my lap with my school bag. *Embarrassed, angry, and ashamed.* Wait, ashamed of what, I wonder. The bus comes to a halt.

"I need to get off," I say. "This is my stop."

"Oh, lemme walk you home."

"Nah, that's okay, I can walk myself home." I try to talk casually and play it cool.

"No, I'm gonna walk you home." The bus rushes past my stop and I sit paralyzed in fear.

"No."

We stop talking or I stop talking to him. *Pretend he doesn't exist.* I feel naked in his gaze. He keeps on talking. I stop listening and look at the other passengers. They look at me and I plead with my eyes. No one helps me. It is as if, all of a sudden, they have selective vision and they don't see a tired, old, sad, drunk man harassing a young, scared Asian woman. I have no choice but to wait.

I stay on the bus until we're already downtown, where it makes a U-turn. By this time the man has passed out. I scurry to the front, angry tears streaming down my face, and I can barely speak to the bus driver.

"C-c-can you please drop me off?" I stutter.

He looks at me and mutters impatiently, as if something is my fault. At my stop I get off the bus and shuffle home. I'm still ashamed and my questions beg for answers.

Why didn't I run?

Where was my voice?

I think my upbringing made me a tougher person. I believed that there was no physical hardship I couldn't endure, no mental hardship that I couldn't cope with. So it made me tough.

—Actress and film director Joan Chen, in an
interview with AsianAvenue.com

khamphian**vang**21
Milwaukee, Wisconsin

With every change, every beginning, and every end, I learn something new and wonderful about myself. I learn that I am stronger than I believe myself to be. The world has many obstacles, but every time I jump a hurdle, I am excited about having to face what comes next. It wasn't easy growing up in a place where I felt like I didn't belong. But I've learned to embrace what it is that makes me different. Every day I write a new page in my life, and "Salt Bread" is only Chapter 1.

Salt Bread

You grow up in this land called America—"the land of the free" and "the land of opportunity." But you don't really know or understand what that means. The ways of life in America seem familiar to you and you go with the flow of things. As a child growing into adulthood, things change. Perspectives change.

Life is about getting your clothes dirty, playing with friends, and eating cupcakes on a Sunday morning before going to church. At school, you are treated "special." All the teachers are eager and willing to help you out. You and some of the other kids, who are just like you, are taken out of the regular classroom for two hours every day. At one o'clock in the afternoon, after recess, you and the other kids, who are just like you, line up in the hallway with books under one arm. The kid behind you always tries to push you off the black line in the tile floor pattern. Rocking back and forth, you try your hardest not to let your feet slip off the black line.

"Stop!" You shout at him, wrinkling your brows. Then you snicker and giggle along with the rest of the kids. When the teacher comes out, everyone falls silent. The teacher looks at you, turns her back, and then starts walking down the hallway. That is your cue to follow.

Trailing the footsteps of the giant, you all walk quietly with your heads down. The pattern of the waxed floors doesn't interest you anymore. There are ten of you in the stale room. "ESL" is what they call it. You don't know what it means. The teacher is nice; she shows you a few pictures, and you're supposed to recite words after her. You roll your tongue flawlessly. Only the perfect English pronunciation is allowed. You don't dream of speaking it any other way.

At home, Mom and Dad talk in a strange language, and you respond back to them in that same strange language, stumbling on some of the words. It starts to feel weird to speak that strange language. Thank heavens they don't make you talk like that at school.

Your grandma sits by the window. She's sewing. You silently laugh at her for wearing those big pink bifocals. You'll never know just how she makes such beautiful artwork from pieces of colored thread and white cloth. Looking at them always makes you smile.

"I'll teach you someday when you get older," she says, pinching your cheeks.

You take a moment to gaze at the piece of cloth in her delicate hands. It feels like magic. Then you take off your backpack, throw it on the couch, and run off to play with the other kids. For dinner you scarf a bowl of rice with a side dish of greens and fried pork skins.

Suddenly things around you start to change once again. The kids at your new school are strangers. Everything and everyone is different. In the hallway, a kid at your school calls you a "chink." You glance in his direction, but you don't say anything. You just keep walking to class.

You find out that chink means something horrible, something you don't like. When you get home, you look in the mirror, and suddenly, you notice something different about yourself. Your skin is tinted yellow, your hair is jet black, and extremely straight, your eyes are smaller than the other kids' eyes, and your nose is flat. The other kids at school don't look like you. Some are brown and others are white. But they don't talk like you talk to your parents in that strange language. All of these things are confusing, but you keep quiet.

During lunchtime, you hold your books under your left arm while trying to balance the lunch tray in your right hand. Your black eyes search the lunchroom for an empty seat. Smiling, you walk to the table where your friends were sitting. Is the last seat taken? You glance down and see someone's feet reaching from the other side, resting on it. You don't understand. It feels like someone is squeezing your little heart so tight you can't breathe. You walk up the crowded aisle to the last table and sit down. With your feet barely touching the floor, you sit there and stare straight ahead. You try not to look at the table where the other girls are sitting. They're talking and laughing together. At that moment, you wish you were like them. You hate yourself. Grabbing a piece of bread, you slowly nibble the crust. Your vision turns blurry. You try to hold it all in, but you can't. A tear falls down your cheek and soaks the bread. The salt stain stays on your lips, but the rest seems to fade like a dream.

These days you wake up extra early to iron your clothes and pile on makeup. And when your mother sees you, she yells (in that strange language), "You're wearing too much makeup."

Humming to the new Jewel song playing on the radio, you pretend not to hear her. When everything seems just right, you quickly run up the street waving your arms to catch the yellow school bus before it turns the corner. You sink into the plastic dark green seats, relieved that it didn't leave without you. Once inside the yellow-tinted rooms of the tall brick building, you walk straight to your group. You talk in that strange language, while catching up on the latest gossip. You laugh and giggle at what people are saying, and no one else around knows why. You carry on as if the other kids aren't in the room at all.

When fifth hour comes along, you stand in the never-ending lunch line talking in that strange language you once only spoke at home—sometimes loudly, on purpose, just to see how others react. You laugh when they give weird looks to the person standing next to them. Looking across the room, you glare at those like you who refuse to acknowledge your similarity or are afraid to. They are always working a little bit harder to be accepted, and to fit in, but even they are never really accepted.

All the while, you're wrapped up in your little world. It's all you have and everything you know. It never occurs to you to think about your future. You realize that there will always be people who will judge you based on your appearance. This realization has changed you forever.

Every day is a struggle and it never seems to end. Every day is a constant battle to find out who you are. Your voice is the only thing you have. Sometimes it's not always heard, but you learn to deal with it.

Once in a while, you sit at home gazing into the mirror at your reflection. And you give yourself a smirk and wonder how the hell they came up with such a thing. You can sit there for hours just thinking about how cool it is that this silver piece of glass can reflect the smallest detail. You wish it didn't because you are trying to hide that zit on your chin. You make funny faces at yourself and stretch your face every which way. You wonder, what do people see when they look at you? Who do they think you are? Who do they think they are—those people who stare at you and speak to you in that tone? You grow sad thinking about those whom you will never know, and those who can never know you.

I am Filipino, even though when people see me, they think other-
wise. My parents are originally from the Philippines and they came
here in the 1980s. In 1993, I came to the "land of opportunity." My
experience during my first year in the U.S., going to school with
"Americans," and trying to assimilate and be like them inspired me
to write the following piece.

"Ching, Chang, Chong!"

A skinny, bucktoothed, eleven-year-old Filipino girl enters the United
States of America on September 1, 1993. Like other immigrants who
come to the "land of opportunity," she is overwhelmed by her sur-
roundings. Fortunately, she understands English and she needs only to
improve her vocabulary and to enunciate her words in the "American
way." She and her sibling watch Barney, the purple dinosaur, in order
to learn the basics of enunciating words the "American" way to avoid
sounding funny to the "American" kids at school. After getting lost in
the hallways and in the sea of new "American" faces at school, she
sits quietly in the cafeteria and daydreams of coconut trees, dirt roads,
and her friends, who are back at home in the Philippines. In her
English Speakers of Other Languages (ESOL) science class at Sligo
Middle School, she watches as her teacher slowly enunciates the word
fire *to her multicultural class. The teacher explains the word* fire *by*
lighting a Bunsen burner, and, pretending to burn her finger, she yells,
"Ouch. Fire is hot!" Fire is indeed hot. So, how, you might wonder, did
this girl, who was one of the top five students at Baguio City Seventh
Day Adventist School in the Philippines, end up in such a silly class?

I felt like I'd been sentenced to prison and, like a prisoner, I
learned lessons that would contradict my parents' and even Barney's teachings.

* * *

"Sticks and stones may break my bones, but words will never harm me." Whoever coined this chant probably never heard the words I heard at school. Vanessa was a frizzy-haired Hispanic girl in my gym class who just loved to put me down because I looked Chinese. She called me "Ching Chang Chong girl," "Chung Ho," and many other "Oriental" names. I suppose, to Vanessa, if you were a skinny, pale, and so-called slanty-eyed person, you qualified as Chinese, and if you were Chinese, these were the degrading names you deserved. And she wasn't picky. She called all my Asian friends "Ching" names. I was very timid back then and I didn't have the courage to fight back. Eventually ignoring her, I didn't care what names she called me because I knew who I was. And I wasn't like her.

Whenever she would start calling me names, I used my imagination and saw her as a piece of dirt talking to me. Because of all the name-calling in Sligo Middle School, my skin grew thick, so thick that "words" like Vanessa's couldn't harm me.

From what I can tell from my experiences at Sligo Middle School, whoever said, "Beauty is only skin deep," was wrong. Parents, teachers, and Barney said so—they were wrong too.

If someone's appearance doesn't matter, then why did Vanessa call me all those names? Why did some unknown girl in the cafeteria point at my brown boots and giggle to her friend that my boots were from Payless? They didn't want to be friends with the "Ching Chang Chong girl" who wore no-name-brand shoes. That I was a nice person didn't matter; they judged me by my cover. So, learning that people are like books, judged by their covers, I've learned to present my cover well.

I learned the meaning of hard work from honors-level classes in Sligo Middle School. Although I didn't want to leave the comfort of Clifford, the Big Red Dog, books in ESOL class, I wanted to tackle some more challenging classes. After I began raising my hand and answering my ESOL teachers' questions in fluent English, they finally placed me in advanced classes. My honors classes were challenging, but I survived them. In sixth grade, it took me longer than the other kids to complete my homework, and I remember staying up late until it was finished. I loved the quiet nights when everyone in my house was already asleep, while I was still at the kitchen table reading about the Egyptian gods. Sligo Middle School was my little prep school, where I learned all about assimilation into "American" society and what I'd have to do to prepare for high school. Sligo molded me into what I am today—an eighteen-year-old girl who withstands racist taunting, who dresses well, and who knows how to work hard.

It's June of 2000, and I recently graduated first in my high school class. It's been about seven years since my Sligo Middle School experience and indeed things have changed. No longer are people who are skinny, pale, and have slanted eyes called "Chinese." They are now known as "Asian." Finally, people have realized that China is not the only country in Asia. The name-calling in middle schools has probably stopped now because of how Pokēmon, Buddha beads, T-shirts with Chinese characters, Japanese anime, thong sandals, Mulan, Jet Li in *Romeo Must Die*, along with many other exports from Asian countries, have assimilated into the American culture. Perhaps now, many Asian kids, including the skinny immigrant Filipino girl or boy who looks "Chinese" won't have to hear chants like "Ching Chang Chong."

alice**chung** 17
Ann Arbor, Michigan

Part of my goal in sharing the next poem is to educate people about the stereotype that people have about Asian women. One factor that aggravated me was the constant pressure to be skinny. It seems that most people, both male and female, have bought into the idea that Asian females are supposed to come in one size only: XS. This piece expresses my frustration with this stereotype—one that manipulated me too at one point during my illness.

94.6

94.6 Because I am
5'2" and that's how much I should weigh.
They just don't tell me. They say
I'm underweight and they're lying.
They only tell you you're not fat because they are
worried that you might be big boned and try to kill yourself
with anorexia or bulimia.
Then your parents could sue them and they'd
have to pay and everything.

How society influences people and all that crap
That's all shit. You do it because you want to be thin.
You do it because you want to look good.

You do it because it makes you feel good.
And all of you out there who are overweight. If you had a little
commitment, you'd be
able to deal.

I don't listen to society. I don't conform. I know I can get sick.
But I deal. I can control
myself. And I do.
I deal.

With having a raw throat and the fumes of
half-digested food.
(I chew peppermint flavored
gum) I deal.
I deal because I want to. So when you see me.
See what I want you to see.
So when you look at me, see Me thin and in control.
See me as Beautiful and
Listen to me when we talk.

"millie"

Location unknown

> *The sender attached the following note with her submission: "Hi to the person who reads this. Thank you for this book. Please accept the following story. If you publish it, credit me as Millie."*   —*V.N.*

The Barbarian

Barbie's head is made of rubber, the kind that collapses if you squish your thumb in the center of her face. I called her "Alien Barbie"—I dug my thumbnail deep into the center of her face until the inner walls of the hollow plastic head would touch. At times Alien Barbie's face would stay in this awesome, grotesque, distorted mound, with one eye and a cheek where her nose should be—that is, until I decided to mold her face back to perfection. My older sister never abused Barbie as I did. She was more merciful since Barbie was her property.

Sometimes when my sister wasn't home, I'd slide the top drawer of her bureau open and peek inside. That was where she kept her collection. I'd take Malibu Barbie (she had the squishiest face of all), and I'd pop her head off. Carefully, I slid my index finger into the neck-hole; at once she became a much more lively, self-deprecating puppet. "Digit Barbie" was cool, but Alien Barbie was still my favorite. My sister would have my head if she saw Digit Barbie. She didn't understand why I had a fascination with taking the doll apart.

I loved manipulating Barbie. Seeing her limbless, headless, with a distorted face. I liked the disembodied head, and especially, seeing how the peach-colored hole hugged my yellow finger, like the two parts were somehow built to fit together.

At school it was too taxing to imagine Sue and Margaret without flowing blond hair. Sometimes when I braided it during recess, I felt the mess of windy curls tickling my fingers and wondered what would happen—what my sister would do to me—if I decided to give Barbie a haircut when I got home. And, while I wouldn't have been surprised if air came whistling out of their heads if I smushed their faces in, I was sure there was more than just air inside those oval peaches.

I studied Alien Barbie and wondered how anything about her physique could be linked to the grotesque. The schoolgirls, with their twinkling blue eyes, swelling chests, and long, slender calves, which moved in that carefree, white-girl walk, would never understand what beauty is. Because to know what beauty is, is to know what ugly looks and feels like.

My sister was ignoring me after school one afternoon. It was the calm before the storm. As predicted, my mom later yelled at me for being irresponsible and insensitive.

Barbie's face had turned a sooty gray from too much handling. Her head wasn't sitting properly on her neck, and I'd popped her legs on to the wrong sides of her body when I'd played with her the last time. Oops.

I told my sister to chill out. She'd get a new Barbie soon enough—Hawaiian Barbie was out on the shelves, and she came with accessories. This girl came with her very own lei, a brush with a pineapple on it, and some other stuff, I think. Silently, I wondered how squishy Hawaiian Barbie's head would be.

I don't remember when exactly I got tired of mangling my sister's Barbies. I think it's when I noticed my own body bubbling out in weird ways, getting taller, and getting slightly wider. It might have been when people started telling me that I was looking like my mother more and more. And my mother is prettier than any damn doll I'll ever see sitting at some toy store.

Lois-Ann Yamanaka is the author of Wild Meat and the Bully Burgers, Saturday Night of the Pahala Theatre, Blu's Hanging, *and* Heads by Harry. *She was born in Ho'olehua, on the island of Moloka'i, and lives in Honolulu with her husband and son. The following article appeared in the September 1997 issue of* Allure *magazine.*

When Asian Eyes Are Smiling
BY LOIS-ANN YAMANAKA

Kala's got droopy eyes. She's been stretching out the skin with Scotch tape and Duo eyelash glue since the seventh grade. As a Japanese-American girl growing up in Hawaii, Kala, my sister, learned early to hate the way she looked—her eyes especially, slanty and rice-y in her mirrored reflection.

She has what we call single eyes: the piece of skin that hangs from the brow is smooth and taut, and very different from the *haoles*, or whites, who have deeper-set eyes with a distinct fold above the lid. Double eyes, in other words. Kala wasn't alone in her quest to look more like a white girl. We all longed for eyes like those of Cheryl Tiegs, Cheryl Ladd, or Natalie Wood, whom we watched in late-night reruns of *This Property Is Condemned.* And we would get those eyes by stretching and pulling and then taping and gluing the skin of our lids back into a self-made fold.

Now, 12 years later, Kala and I are in a plastic surgeon's office in Honolulu, where I live. The doctor looks at me first, and I wonder if he's thinking, "Does this one want the fatty tissue from her chin removed?" Then he looks at Kala. "Hmmm. Sagging eyelids. . . ." He sees. He's heard the tragic Oriental-eye story a hundred times before.

When we were teenagers, Kala would give her three sisters the haole eyes that all Oriental girls wanted. (And we were Orientals back then, though we've come to be defined as Asian Americans, another neat category for all of us. We were Orientals with our own aisle called

Oriental Foods in every supermarket in town, as though every other aisle was Occidental Foods.) She would put a dab of Duo eyelash glue on a toothpick, make a thin line over my lid, then lift the skin slightly into the glue. "Don't blink," she would warn, "or you'll get an uneven, bumpy line." And in a minute, I had double eyes.

On our sisters, Melba and Claire, she used pieces of Scotch tape and would carefully place a thin strip in a well-formed arch right over their lids. When the skin folded over the tape, their double eyes rivaled Donna Mills's: Where God didn't, Kala did. She made visible creases (medically known as the supratarsal folds) for all of us.

And then we'd have *haole* eyes. No more Oriental eyes, dammit— slant eyes, seeing-through-venetian-blinds eyes, kamikaze eyes, your-ancestors-started-World-War-II eyes, Nip eyes. We had double eyes, thank you very much, even if we couldn't wet our faces when we went to the beach, lest we emerge, eyelids sagging, glue white and bumpy, and pieces of Scotch tape floating like shiny dead minnows in the tide.

In school, my friend Melanie stretched her skin out so much that she was forced to pull more and more of it into the tuck, until the red veins under her eyelids were exposed. Her eyelashes stood straight up, and all the way through high school she never got a really good blink during daylight hours. Then there was Nina, who explained to us the uselessness of curling our eyelashes after we had glued our eyelids unless we wanted to pinch the meat in the process and risk an eye infection. And Suzanne, Nancy, and Debbie, whose parents financed clandestine trips to Japan for eye operations the summer of my junior year in high school. The three rich and popular girls returned with the puffy surprised look of double eyes for a fabulously tapeless and glue-less senior year free of supratarsal oppression.

"So you need blepharoplasty surgery?" the doctor asks Kala.

"Yes."

"Both eyes need some work," he says. He hands my sister a photo album of his blepharoplasty successes. We gaze at all the Asian faces in the album, a lineup of *haole* wannabes, page after page of beautiful "before" faces without smiles. Why did they do it? And then the "after"—women smiling for the camera with their eyes healed but still slightly swollen six months after surgery. So many faces: a classic Japanese, a porcelain Korean, flawless Chinese features.

A sad realization came over me as we flipped through the doctor's book. We were all Oriental girls who had never seen our faces in a magazine, on TV, or in the movies, unless you're talking Suzie Wong, Fan Tan Fanny, or Mrs. Livingston. The only roles available to beautiful Asian actresses were riddled with Charlie Chang-chop-suey talk and stereotypes; Juanita Hall as Madame Liang in *Flower Drum Song* was African-American. Agnes Moorehead, Katharine Hepburn, and Shirley MacLaine were *haole* with heavy eyeliner. They didn't count.

When Kala was home in Honolulu last Christmas, we counted the blepharoplastics in our aerobics class (mostly Japanese nationals), on interisland flights, and the streets of Chinatown. (And contrary to what *haole* America thinks, we don't all look alike, and we can tell a Japanese from a Chinese from a Korean from a Filipina from an Indian). We can also tell who couldn't afford a top-notch surgeon like the one Kala went to see and was forced to go to the butcher Korean doctor. He flies in twice a year and lines up hordes of Asian women who all suspiciously begin to have the same surprised expressions.

Kala earned a cosmetology degree a few years back in San Francisco and learned how to contour her nose with brown and white eye shadow—her own Japanese nose, she thought, was too flat. She learned to draw dark eyeliner on top of the glue on her eyelid, creating the illusion of even more of a fold. Now in the doctor's office, she sees my reflection in the plastic sheeting covering the photos, and it's almost identical to her own. She closes the photo album. The look she gives me makes me sad. In her eyes, I see all the Asian girls and women who have mutilated themselves in the hopes of looking white. "I think I'll treat Mommy to Las Vegas with this money instead," Kala finally says, deciding against the surgery.

"Scotch tape was made for wrapping Christmas presents," I say.

Kala really doesn't look as droopy as she thinks. She's Japanese-American beautiful, and her face alone gets us a good table at a crowded restaurant or into the faster lane on the freeway during rush-hour traffic.

She grimaces. "That's the magic of Scotch tape," she muses. We get up to leave the building. "The transparency."

She's right about the whole notion of our feeling invisible in the eyes of others. For us, it was the lack of images of ourselves in magazines, literature, movies, and pop culture that made us want to be otherwise, Orient to Occident, yet we were so utterly visible and transparent in our attempts.

Kala, who's now back in San Francisco, sends me magazine articles on Josie Natori, Tina Chow, Gemma Kahng, Naomi Campbell, Anna Sui, Jenny Shimizu—every one an affirmation. I send her copies of books by Maxine Hong Kingston, Chitra Divakaruni, Nora Okja Keller, Cathy Song, Jessica Hagedorn, Gish Jen, Cynthia Kadohata, where we see our own faces.

We recognize our lives in movies, television, and plays because of actresses such as Ming-Na Wen, Gong Li, Joan Chen, Margaret Cho, Tia Carrere, Lea Salonga, Tamlyn Tomita.

Our Asian-American eyes, open now and knowing, are fixed on images and words that mirror and help shape our definition of self. Kala and me, we're starting to like what we see.

Who are you?
How do you define your identity?

Who are you?
How do you define your identity?

Language. Brush with death; survival story.
Learning to love the self. Clear self-image.

Finding My
Voice

awakenings
... discovering
the

inner
girl

To what extent has being Asian had an impact on our adolescence? Did we have Asian friends when we were growing up, and if so, what made these relationships unique compared to relationships we had with our other peers? Did we all confront racism and discrimination? How did other Asian American girls cope with the idea that they were different, yet the same, as their non-Asian peers? And most important, how did these experiences finally help them to come to grips with their identity—as a girl, as an Asian American, and as just another American teenager?

These were the questions I had originally outlined in my book proposal for *YELL-Oh Girls!*—the questions I was determined to find the answers to in the process of collaborating with girls on the anthology. After rethinking these questions about three months into the process of receiving girls' submissions, I realized that I had made some general assumptions about what Asian American girls were thinking, saying, and doing in their lives. No doubt my assumptions were derived from my own subjective experiences, which, I quickly realized, didn't mirror any sort of "normative" Asian American female experience. We brought unique perspectives with us, and as a listener and as a reader, I needed to come out of my own boxes of thinking. I needed to let these girls, who exhibited various gifts, perspectives, and goals, define themselves in their own words.

In my proposal, I noticed that I was guilty of replicating the same stereotypes that I was criticizing others for. My approach to the project suggested that we, as Asian American girls, in fact envisioned ourselves as different—as Asian first, and as American, second—but the degree to which being Asian shaped our self-image depended on certain variables (age, location, ethnicity, socioeconomic background, etc.). Later, after I realized my grandiose boo-boo, I felt like I'd committed one of the five mortal sins. But most of all, I wondered how my attitude was any different from that of countless people who, when I was growing up, presumed I knew the slightest thing about what it meant to be Asian. In fact, I remember how frustrated I became when someone saw me as less American than they were, just because I wasn't white. It was through their lens that I saw myself. It was by answering their questions that I heard my voice.

One day, in high school, in the middle of a forty-minute lecture about "Far Eastern" cultures and traditions, my global history teacher asked me to help him teach the class about "my culture." I stared at him, and looked at the article he had just handed out, which was meant to "give us a flavor" of what life for Korean teens was like. It was about the latest phenomenon among Korean youth; desperate to get into the few top-notch colleges in Korea, girls and guys were locking themselves in rooms in preparation for their entrance exams. The article cited the sudden increase of suicides, which was becoming the most popular way out for students who failed to get into one of the top institutions. Reading the biased, Eurocentric article, it came as no surprise that my peers were walking away with such warped ideas of people whose parents or grandparents came from countries besides the "Land of the Free."

He asked me to approach the board and teach the class five words in Korean. I would write the word first in Korean, and then I'd give them a direct English translation. Forget the fact that I was blanking out on anything I'd learned at Korean school every Friday night; I didn't want to go up and teach. Even if they saw my role as a being the Korean spokesperson, I saw myself as a student. An "American" student who didn't know any more Korean than Carlo did Italian—but did Carlo, whose parents were semirecent Italian immigrants, get called on to teach us his language? No. I was dumbfounded, literally, and couldn't think of five words. Mom, *um-ma* (which isn't even the formal translation, it's slang); Dad, *ahpba* (again, slang); Sister, *uni* (correct translation, incorrect spelling) . . . two more, I thought. Rice cooker, *bap soht* (of all words I could think of, why did I choose that?). And, the fifth word. I couldn't think of anything and the silence was ringing in my ears. Dummy, *bah-bo*. I ended up being the world-class comedian that afternoon. People laughed at me, but I got over it.

The Korean language was a source of trauma for me. I pushed it away and refused to talk to other Korean elders, even though I knew it was the only language they understood. Perhaps I would have made an effort, albeit a reluctant one, to communicate with them if every time I opened my mouth they didn't give me that famous dirty look. ("What a shame, you should learn to speak your language.")

Now I think about these experiences, and I wonder how I've come to use American-English to communicate my ideas, and to describe who I am. By senior year, my frustration with the dry, monotonous junk we were doing in AP English class led me to experiment with creative writing as a means of self-expression in the privacy of my bedroom. As I saw my thoughts scrolling out of the printer, I noticed that I'd integrate the meager proper Korean, gutter Korean, and *ban-mal* (casual slang) I'd picked up during my youth. I began to rely on my "other language" when English failed to contain my thoughts. I began to understand the hybridity of my own language, and gradually, it became clear to me that English and Korean enabled me to form the sentences, which allowed me to color my subjectivity with greater accuracy and power—not simply as an Asian American girl—but as ME. An individual who had dozens of quirks ranging from the ethnic to the just-plain-zany.

As I read the submissions, some of which appear in "Finding My Voice," these thoughts guided me and kept me from giving in to the tendency we all have of listening to each other's voices through the filter of our own experiences. What I found was that we were all wrestling with language, trying to somehow find the words to portray ourselves, and that the task of self-reflection through writing proved a daunting challenge for girls who had never used writing to navigate their identities. My role as the editor was to read, to listen, and to encourage them to keep on scribing.

That said, I encountered girls who were discovering the power of the pen, and who demonstrated courage and determination to push the boundaries of the written word in coming to finding their voices. Some girls had a difficult time thinking of something to contribute to the anthology and looking at their lives through a new perspective. Often, the awakening that came along with this unconventional writing assignment was jolting, and many didn't know where to begin. Tammy, sixteen, explained to me that she was worried that she wouldn't have anything to say, but after reading through the submissions guidelines, she realized that there were topics she wanted to explore. She wrote: "The challenge to write [about my identity] really encouraged me to keep trying to discover new things about myself that I had been unaware of." Lynn, of Brooklyn, New York, also thought that tackling the project was helping her to find her voice. She wrote, "As a seventeen-year-old Asian American girl and aspiring writer, I understand how difficult it can be to find a voice, and this book is a wonderful platform for us to make ourselves heard."

Then there were the girls whose only challenge was choosing which essay, story, or poem they wanted to send in for review. Three girls who jumped on board early in the submissions process were superstar scribes; Diya Gullapalli is a journalist/editor, Meggy Wang is a feminist and creator of a zine called *Mad Girl's Love Song*, and Sarah Chang is a writer/poet whom I'd discovered through the Asian American Writer's Workshop's CreateNow program. Within days of roping them into the project, they were inundating me with all sorts of provocative "works-in-progress" (poems, dialogues, memoirs, and song lyrics), which the girls had generated during the past year. While Diya, Meggy, and Sarah appeared to be normal, everyday teen girls, I couldn't help but think that they were unusually perceptive; they articulated their thoughts and passions like seasoned literati, well on their way toward mastering the art of soul-searching. But I reminded myself that these girls, however remarkable they were in their own ways, were embarking on their journey through adolescence along with the multitudes of other Asian American girls.

While young writers polished their impressive repertoire of creative writing, novice writers were looking within themselves in search of their stories for the first time ever. Some of the most heartrending, free, and fearless voices belonged to closet writers, whose submissions usually took the form of letters, confessions, e-mail messages, and diary entries. But again, these girls felt comfortable using writing as a means of self-expression, even if they'd kept their passion a secret.

The process posed steeper challenges to those who felt that language posed a threat in the process of trying to harness a "voice" that could adequately reflect their emotions and experiences. The guideline flyers reached girls who were first-generation immigrant girls, whose first language wasn't English. This is where irony glared at me, the editor. I was encouraging girls to speak out about their experiences through writing—meanwhile, the thought that there would be girls whose struggles were manifested in the language barrier hadn't occurred to me. At the same time that I was grappling with this unresolved issue, I was hearing from girls who considered English to be their native tongue, but who also felt that, at times, words failed miserably to express what they were thinking and feeling. Kaye, fifteen, wrote: "Words are slipping through my fingers. I want to write about my experiences, but English, the only language I know, isn't letting me say what I want to say. I wish I could contribute something, and I'm frustrated that I can't."

I sensed frustration among girls who felt as if language imposed severe limitations on their ability to locate the right words to express the complexity of their experiences. And I watched in awe as their frustration turned to determination in seeking the words, which chronicled the progress that they were making. Often, after reading someone's first draft, I found second and third drafts in my in box week after week until girls felt they were satisfied with their self-portraits. After a while, I expected the shifts in tones, colors, and textures that came with each revision. To me, this movement echoed the insatiable need to recreate and redefine ourselves to keep up with our changing world.

In the next few pages, you will hear self-affirming stories from girls who have gained knowledge and insight after weathering the storms of adolescence. They're awakened, entering a new consciousness, and finally breaking through the cloud of questions which no longer prevents them from embracing the qualities about themselves they once viewed as "different." The contributors are sensitive to the constraints of language, but like warriors, they continue to seek and claim words that enable them to speak out.

The chapter concludes with an essay written by Elaine H. Kim, professor at University of California, Berkeley, who is revered for raising cultural awareness through community organizing and activism, as well as through her support of independent, creative projects that contribute to the cause. In a candid, dynamic narrative, Kim's writing depicts how hardship, accomplishment, and self-love have guided her on the journey toward finding her voice. Together, we celebrate all emerging young writers who are learning to love the differences which enhance their perspectives as girls, as Asian Americans, and most of all, as human beings.

A subjectivist adviser, traveling storyteller, and cynical idealist, sometimes I wonder how these all fit inside one petite Asian mind, forever searching for a voice to express their thoughts. At this point in my life, all I can say is that I am Caroline Fan, a nineteen-year-old Williams College student and food fanatic. Every day I become more fluent in expressing who I am, incorporating new aspects and ideas. I wrote "Chinglish" as a reflection of some of these discoveries.

Chinglish

Language is a barrier to me. I grew up silent, but bursting with the glimmering desire to describe everything I observed in the closest detail. I scrutinized people sitting across from me on trains, attempting to read their life stories from the lines on their faces, the wrinkles in their clothes. I turned an empty car into a joyous amusement park for a family of ants, with the windshield converted into a gleeful water slide park. I would trace the interior features of our station wagon with the intent to discover its secrets, to script a story worthy of a childhood afternoon.

I remember being four, having just returned from a half year's stay in Taiwan, where I had attended school and immersed myself in Mandarin, shedding the English language of my birthright. When I returned, I spoke haltingly, in a language I now call "Chinglish," a bit of Chinese and a few parts of English, communicated with the anxiety of someone lost on the street. Preschool was rough: I was brimming with stories to be told, in all the languages I contained, but they were silenced the day I climbed to the top of the playground and triumphantly yelled out, "Wo zhe She-Ra!" Yet somehow, no one wanted to play. I immediately resolved to set aside my other tongue, intending to pick it up again when it was convenient, when I had friends. Years passed, and my English progressed, but I remained ever silent; and when I spoke in class, it was with a pounding heart and quickened breath that let the words tumble out and scatter in the wind. I knew that if I ever faltered, I would be reminded at recess, at the water fountain, and during day care. So I spoke rarely, frustrated that everything fascinated me and that my vocal descriptions lacked the substance of my written poetry.

But no one should ever settle for imprecision. Words carry an almost holy weight that I have lugged around in an attempt to hide my unspoken thoughts, only to try to expose my feelings through writing. And after having mastered the English language, I tried to help others communicate their ideas effectively in my high school's Writing Center. The process of revision is something I have never feared. Tutoring my peers, refining their essays, correcting their grammar, and sharing their ideas only strengthens my writing and belief in the power of words. I plan to harness this force to become a writer. I speak up in class now and chase my goals directly.

Much of this change is attributable to my visit to Taiwan a few summers ago, where I recovered my Chinese heritage, which I had thoroughly neglected. I fell in love with the embroidery of the language, the silk of my culture. I participated in the speech contest. My friends and I spent numerous hours exploring every nook of Taipei, whether "cutting prices" with market vendors or visiting museums. I delved ever deeper into the ancestral pool, and the waters welcomed me. I can only say that the wounds are healing. I am sewing my fragmented soul together again, and I could never leave one half for another for it would only tear me apart. I have rediscovered a focus and love of learning that had seemed to wane after high school started and all my friends spent their Saturdays at the mall, while I was cloistered indoors, repeating character after Chinese character, trying to get the pronunciation exactly right. Today I am proud to have served as a translator for my Chinese painting and calligraphy class. My mother always said I would thank her for prodding me to go to Chinese school, someday. Now is a better time than any to take the words that have been rolling around in my head, in all my harmonious languages, push them out of my mouth, and into the light.

> I would tell girls who struggle with articulating their feelings in English that fluency is not necessary for self-expression. Sometimes the simplest of words are the best for conveying the most universal of emotions.
>
> —Dina Gan, Editor in Chief of *aMagazine*

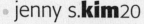 jenny s.**kim**20
Sanford, Florida

> *I did an independent study project on Asian American women writers my first year of college, and wrote a paper on voice as resistance and empowerment in text, and the social implications for race and gender activism. I based this idea on Maxine Hong Kingston's* Woman Warrior *and Joy Kogawa's* Obasan; *imposed silence has always been a social, cultural, historical way to keep marginalized people down. Asian American women carrying a double burden must learn to be purposefully angry and to shout. This essay traces my own challenging but rich experience in finding my own voice.*

Kim Chee and Yellow Peril

I was born with a temporary blue spot right above my butt, a trait universal to all Koreans at birth as descendants of Mongolia. I have low ethanol tolerance. I like kim chee. I think the IMF (International Monetary Fund) is a collective of power-hungry Western expansionists feeding off Korea's ravaged economy. So maybe I'm Korean.

But I stutter, blush, and bite my lip when I can't express myself in Korean. First-generation Korean immigrants give me hostile stares; shaking heads are what I get when I accidentally use the familiar tense instead of the formal with an eighty-year-old Korean woman. And I thought I did well by bowing at a ninety-degree angle. It was not so much the linguistic slipup that merited the "ba-bo" remark (meaning "idiot," suggesting incompetence). It was *their* perception that I was just another overassimilated ingrate with a blasé, disloyal attitude toward age-specific respect. "Another/An other" Americanized daughter who couldn't speak the mother tongue well enough.

Go back to where you came from. I heard this so much while growing up. I used to say the same thing to the migrating birds from the north every winter.

For some reason, I equated "American-ness" with "whiteness" throughout my childhood. Calling myself "Korean-American" instead of a categorical "Korean" was seen as a treacherous sellout, as if I unconsciously wanted to be white more than anything else. My parents' generation called me a "banana": yellow on the outside, white on the inside. But I was insistent on this hyphenated identity, mainly because I felt that I was a *type* of American (i.e., Korean as adjective, American as noun)—a cultural hybrid. I knew African-American and Latino children born in the U.S. like me were also "American" in terms of citizenship. But collectively we would always be the Others. Why else would whites dominate the mainstream culture of the Gap, McDonald's, and TV sitcoms?

In kindergarten I thought I was funny when everyone laughed after I said "I like kitchen" (I mispronounced "chicken"). But then I grew curious about why kids used their index fingers to extend their eyes horizontally when I approached them, and I didn't understand why extending *my* middle finger vertically got me in so much trouble. I didn't want my mom to pack pickled radish in my Strawberry Shortcake lunch box anymore, because it stank up the cubbyholes. I wanted PB&J sandwiches like "all the other American kids," even if milk gave me the runs. Self-definition was an ambivalent process, and it still is. When I was nine, I became the fourth-grade heroine and the apple of my father's eye for giving a classmate twice my size a black eye for calling me a "ching-chong bitch whose stupid parents stole American jobs." At the same time, I grew irritated when my parents' friends reminisced about the difficult days upon arriving in the U.S. (they were trained as nurses and accountants in Korea, but because of language barriers, they did janitorial work). With an internalized self-denigrating attitude, I thought, *This is America. Just get used to it.* Barbie dolls were scary-looking and ugly to me but I still wanted creased eyelids and big, demure, Western-looking eyes.

One time for an elementary-school Christmas party, all the students were supposed to bring enough baked goods or snacks for everyone. I told my mother that she could just pick up some premade cookie dough on the way home and we could bake them. But no, she said that that was "cheap" and that I should think about everyone else, and suggested that it would be nice to bring something different for them to enjoy. I started panicking when she opened a package of wonton skins and prepared ground-beef filling for *mandoo*, Koreans. Although I absolutely loved them, I couldn't bear the thought of the other kids spitting them out and saying, "What kind of nasty chink crap is this?" I just wanted something that was considered "normal," so that maybe people would forget that I had slanted eyes, and so people would stop asking what my last name was (people thought "Jenny Kim" was like "Mary Ann"). Most of all, I wanted to be *American* and not just "Gook Girl." I took the foil-wrapped tray of mandoo to school and was tempted to chuck it over the playground fence, except my mother had spent so much time making them. The party was full of home-baked goods, from fruit-filled pastries to burnt cookies with too much baking soda—all "normal" food in my eyes. Embarrassed, I quietly set the tray down and inconspicuously tried to take off the foil. A pack of wolves couldn't have converged toward the tray any faster. The teacher fought for a plateful to share with the school secretary, who later begged my mother for a recipe. Although the teasing and annoying questions didn't completely end, it didn't matter to me anymore what "normal" was. My mother's mandoo was the winner that day, and that was more than normal for me.

I didn't understand any of this—it was never easy at all. These small but personally significant events equaled a "culture clash," which was very much situational and dynamic, and worked itself out into split identity. I think the protagonist of Maxine Hong Kingston's *Woman Warrior* describes this cultural schizophrenia well:

> Chinese-Americans, when you try to understand what things in you are Chinese, how do you separate what is peculiar to childhood, to poverty, to insanities, one family, your mother who marked your growing with stories, from what is Chinese? What is Chinese tradition and what is the movies?

In Kingston's novel, the protagonist receives culture as something not explicitly taught in a cut-and-dry manner—but rather as something that is learned through observation and oral tradition. However, her search for coherence and meaning is frustrated by the lack of explanation of past and present differences:

> Never explaining. How can Chinese keep any traditions at all? The adults get mad, evasive, and shut you up if you ask. I don't know how they kept up a continuous culture for five thousand years. Maybe they didn't; maybe everyone makes it up as they go along.

Nobody "told" me that the woman in the family serves herself last. I watched my mother bustle around the kitchen after rushing in from a full day of work, not even taking time to change her clothes. When the dinner was ready, she would scoop a heaping mound of fresh, hot rice for my father first, then my younger brother, then me. Then she'd scrape together a small handful from the bottom of the rice cooker and take the smallest piece of fish for herself, insisting she wasn't hungry. When I was younger and couldn't finish my food, I'd give my plate to my mother, not realizing what I was doing. I was giving my mother the leftovers, something she grew up with as a postwar Korean female—the generation that knew firsthand that things, dignity, family and friends, peace, and national unity, could be taken away at any instant, and that women were taught to put themselves last. Hearing about her impoverished childhood made my eyes sting, my privileged conscience uneasy, and my own childhood stories pale by comparison. For her, scraping the rice pot sometimes yielded nothing, and humble survival came down to accepting leftovers from your own—it was one of few constants provided in the former precarious world of hers. (Old habits are hard to break.) Yet, my mother told me not to stand there with both hands open, meekly waiting for things to happen. An ambitious and generous woman, she even chose the name Debbie (meaning "industrious") when she immigrated to the U.S. Nothing gets accomplished sitting down, she says. I was left with this contradiction and a half-eaten bowl of rice. Watching, waiting, and never understanding.

At home, in Flushing, New York, at church, or at my relatives' houses, I don't have to monitor myself. I'm steeped in a culturally saturated environment, and I've learned to embrace it and even to crave it after being away from it for too long, like eating kim chee and rice after weeks of pizza, Americanized ramen, and other college food. I sometimes feel an instinctual impulse to "find my people"—there's something to be said about commonalities. At the same time, however, there's a tendency to feel suffocated in its deeply historical sphere—there are so many expectations from the older generations (and obligations, considering the sacrifices made), and the parents' desire to live vicariously through their children's success.

It's unnecessary, unconstructive, and impossible even to attempt to quantify the Korean versus the American in me; it's not as easy as doing an autopsy to find kim chee next to a Big Mac in the gastric lining and declaring the corpse Korean-American. At times it is existentially dizzying to try to separate and count how many times I ran around East and West, cultural reality and fiction. It's a rich, textured, and complex existence—I've begun to see Korean and American cultures as two fluid worlds that sometimes mesh, sometimes conflict, but always form the identity *I* claim.

I was born in Boston to Indian parents, and I lived in and loved that city till I was eighteen. Then it became clear that I needed to go west. Maybe this poem is about starting to love myself without someone else, or maybe it is just a breakup poem that I wrote when I was seventeen and angry at the world. I just know that I love Marvin Gaye, and the way things were juxtaposed at that time in my life was nothing less than poetic.

MARVIN GAYE/THE TRIALS OF BEING

as a child/ he danced to marvin gaye with his mother
it was they two in the kitchen

you told me a couple months ago you was on a marvin gaye kick—
two weeks straight and nothing but/ she between your sheets and
     i on the other line
/nothing but
later/ we—our tongues—dancing to a different tune on your mat
     of dishonesty
wonderin if she too could learn to develop a passion
for late kitchen nights on a tiered tape deck
and learn to wonder
what's going on . . . ?/

missed your voice and kinky hair/ wondering
what's goin on . . . ?/

though I could keep walkin/ keep stompin/ to my chick tunes
or my urban life beats . . . alla which you didn't get/ you couldn't
     see/
still years later blindly flailin your arms and feet

tryin to keep time/
yet tryin to keep it this time/
but you don't really try that hard/ emotional tire marks still left
    burnin
from that hot wheels track/
at thirteen years in freedom finally/
watchin porns and talkin shit
I wouldn't hit you
But you couldn't afford to take the chance
at sixteen you thought you were old/ walked outta the house
with the future in your step
at twenty you still remember those late kitchen nights
and the last time the only real woman in your life ever beat the shit
    out of you
/i wouldn't hit you/ but you couldn't afford to take the chance/
but still you lie to a woman woman like me/
such a woman/ not to be a victim/
how many whole people do you need holdin on to the pain of scars
    on your body/ as my
hands/hands/her hands/ womans hands/ touch these hidden marks
    beneath your
whick whick whack facade and camel cigarettes/
dancing soft and slow/ with our feet skidding the floor/
at seventeen i still terrified of men/ of your body of a man/ of the
    conception of man
'cept marvin gaye

don't get me wrong
i'm too strong to crumble/ got too much in me/
you and your sexual healing/ nothin comparin to how I would
    never trust you again/
butthenagain fuckin with me is something unpredictable/ you're no
    fuse to my bomb don't flatter yourself
but I'll explode/
/woman woman I'll explode/ with the wholeness of a person and

the radicals
of an intolerable world/

just like the TV today/ the tube/ yup I saw a documentary on your
   main man/
said he was sick when he asked what's goin on/ so sick of the
   world/
sounds familiar/ has he teary eyed and choked pondered
- i teary eyed and choked thought of you for the first time in awhile
/i saw your trajedy/ your self-made trajedy (maybe handed down)/
i wanted to call you tape it for you tell you I understood even
   though I don't
i've been waitin for your familiar buzz against my hip
/the sound of your page beggin and hatin an explanation for being
   the

tasty   indian   side   dish

i didn't know the trajedy in marvin gaye's life
shocked to find out
his heart pierced with his father's bullets/
cried in my head   a little/
you learned to protect yours from the best of them/
you got that organ armor/ to save you from the mental gunshot
   wounds
dancin too close for comfort/ (not close enuff)
with a woman woman

diya**gullapalli**19
Reston, Virginia

A sophomore at the University of Virginia, I can't believe my teenage years are almost over. My family is from India, and we currently live outside of Washington, D.C. My story isn't remarkable by any means; the trauma of growing up in America as a first generation Indian pales in comparison to the struggle that my parents experienced when they immigrated here. Theirs is the real success story, and theirs is the journey that speaks of true difficulty and hardship. When I write about my experiences, I never forget that no matter what, my life is a fortunate and comfortable one. This is just my small way of thanking my parents for it.

Funny Girl

"So, Diya, has your family arranged a suitable husband yet?" Michael asked, nonchalantly. We were sitting around with our friends during lunch. My friends all turned to me, trying to be inconspicuous, but eager to hear how I'd respond.

"Yes, actually we've obtained his biodata through the classifieds already—tall, fair, MD, with a green card," I promptly replied, knowing the kind of answer he wanted to hear.

"Hmmm, that sounds good, but what about his caste? You should make sure he's not an untouchable," Michael shot back with a twinkle in his eye, proud of all the Indian trivia he was dredging up.

"Oh, of course he's a Brahman," I mock assured him. "What kind of Indian girl do you think I am? But I'm not sure if we can provide him with enough dowry—he's asking for two cows, a sheep, and my family's hut. It's a little over the top."

"Huh, well, don't worry. I'm sure you'll think of something," he said, patting me on the shoulder as I finished my sandwich.

Conversations like this were the norm with my friends in high school. I would never discourage their gentle teasing, because I knew they didn't mean to offend me. Instead, I would egg them on, offering quirky little stories about my Indian experiences, so they didn't think that my lifestyle was different from theirs and that my culture was so personal and serious that it couldn't be shared.

In high school, my general attitude was: "Anything for a good laugh." I was always an eager beaver when it came to sharing my cultural observations even if no one asked. Something nagged me about the idea of compromising the value of my heritage by constantly making fun of it, but I felt that, as the only Indian kid in my group of friends, it was my duty to be the Indian ambassador of sorts. I thought I should offer them insight about my culture, even if this meant extracting snippets that I knew they'd find funny. I knew that part of what they liked about me was that I was in the position to give them the go-ahead to participate in this banter. I was the green light that allowed them to race onto a new cultural highway—to take license to poke fun at our differences without looking around for the censorship police to pull them over.

I'm not sure when this became a habit. It might have been when my family moved from New Jersey, the state with the highest concentration of Indians in the U.S., to Virginia. Alarmed by the growing number of South Asian immigrants filtering into our hometown, Edison, my parents decided to move to the D.C. metropolitan area; this region that was fairly diverse yet still not so concentrated with minorities that it stopped feeling like America. My parents were concerned that if we stayed in New Jersey, we might make only Indian friends and forget to integrate into mainstream, white society. So we were transplanted just past the Mason-Dixon Line, barely placing us in the South, and there we began a new lifestyle, which was a culture shock in itself. When we moved to Virginia, it was hard to identify with the clean-cut, friendly, white, suburban kids we encountered in middle school and in high school. They were nice and well-educated, but fundamentally different in their very American upbringing.

"So, you're Hindu, right?" a girl asked me on the bus during the first week of eighth grade. She sounded like she was trying the word on for size, and this annoyed me for some reason. I was impatient with her attempt at being polite, and the incident just sped up the enlightenment process.

"Yes, I am," I quickly responded. "My family goes to temple, but we're not that religious. We eat beef and celebrate Christmas and stuff."

"Huh, cool, because I know you pray to cows or whatever," she said a little more confidently.

"Well, sort of. The cow is a sacred animal in India because it provides milk, so it's a metaphor for the maternal figure. But it's also a beast that bears load and helps with farming. It's not just a cultish icon—it's really practical too."

I felt like an authority all of a sudden, empowered to say anything on the topic of being Indian, because no one else really knew the facts. At first I hoped that I could educate kids when they'd ask timid questions like these, clarifying the vague notions they'd picked up. Eventually, though, I abandoned this approach for a more laid-back one, because I noticed that when I was self-deprecating about Hinduism and India, kids felt more at ease. Subconsciously, I decided that if these kids were going to imitate the stereotypes that were being portrayed in the media, I would too. It wasn't the kids' fault they were ignorant, especially if their only exposure to Indians was in the form of Abu of Abu's Quickie Mart in *The Simpsons*, or the Indian immigrants on *Seinfeld*, or even Madonna, with her trendy bindi obsession.

Although this "When in Rome, do as the Romans do" approach was easy to execute, it was just a shortcut to the accurate, real depiction of my culture. I was scared of being the oddball—the one whose culture alienated her because it wasn't something that could be shared. Determined to assimilate, I went to the extreme. I began giving out bindis to girls who asked me about the "dots." My mom helped fashion some headgear for some boys in my neighborhood who wanted to name their band The Suburban Turbans. So she might feel what it was like to be Hindu, my friend accompanied me to temple; the priest tied a string around her wrist to remind her of her visit. And when I invited my friends over to eat Indian food, I would instruct them on how to eat the brown and red curries with rice.

As I moved through high school, the pressing need to feel accepted gradually faded. Catering to people's amusement through this "Indian humor" and trying to please everybody was exhausting. None of the other Indian kids in my high school dared so blatantly mock everything like I did; at first I thought it was because they took themselves too seriously and couldn't lighten up. I eventually realized, though, that their seriousness wasn't a bad thing at all. Instead, I viewed them as having a true appreciation for the complexities of Indian culture. They were never asked the kinds of questions about arranged marriages or castes that I was being asked, because people respected the lines that they had drawn. On the other hand, I acted like I approved of the ridiculing. I began to feel self-conscious about the mocking, which, in the process, was making me resent my friends, but I knew I was the one who was instigating the whole cycle.

"Let us to be going to the Kwikie Mart, little Indian girl," my white boyfriend declared while we drove home one afternoon. He was using his best taxi driver accent. "I will like to be taking you to this place of beef jerky obtainment and perhaps to be procuring a Slurpee as well."

I sputtered out a laugh, but then I asked myself, When did the joke go so far? I started to get a little angry and very confused by this seemingly irrational irritation. *Who is this guy?* I thought. He has no right to just make fun of things—I mean, has he ever asked me about the true meaning of my background?

Then I realized that I had never expected this level of sensitivity and cultural understanding from my friends and, at some point, they stopped thinking that they needed to consider these issues. It was when I arrived at college that the final pieces of the puzzling identity fell into place. After five years of making mainly non-Indian friends, I went to the University of Virginia, where I found a community which reminded me of the one that had made me feel so comfortable as a child in New Jersey. I attended Indian Student Association meetings. I took Hindi 101 with thirty other South Asian kids. I began dating an Indian boy and making mainly Indian friends. For my high school friends that came with me to college, it was a surprising change. They had never realized that despite all my efforts to share my culture with them, being with other Indian kids was still easier for me. I think it took a long time for me to realize this too.

I grew satisfied with my Indian friends, because I felt like we had a lot of things in common. Instead of having to constantly explain the obvious, we shared subtle nuances, which were so real to us, yet so impossible for us to describe to others.

I began to drift away from my white friends because it was difficult to explain what was really happening with me, and why I thought that I could relate to Indian kids so much better. I began to ask myself whether I was becoming "more Indian." But clearly, the bonds between me and my white friends went beyond the ethnic differences we joked about; at the end of the day, they were still people I could vent to.

"So, when did you become a fob?" my friend Karen asked me over the phone one day, using the fresh-off-the-boat abbreviation that I had taught her. I was doing an internship on Capitol Hill through a newspaper called *India Abroad*, and the sixteen other interns were also Indian.

"I know—it's so weird, isn't it?"

"No, not really, you're meeting different kinds of people. But what are the kids like? Are they cool? Are they fun?" she asked.

"Some of them are. But some of them are typical, uptight, Indian kids who can't relax. I'm realizing that my UVA Indian friends aren't the 'typical' Indian kids either, because they're so laid back and fun."

"But so are you, Diya. It's just that you can be friends with different types of people. I don't even know if your UVA friends can do that, no matter how relaxed they are with each other," Karen replied. "They seem so prone to only hanging out with Indian kids and you're not like that, even if you incorporate them into your circle of friends."

"Maybe—it's kind of interesting that you can see all that," I said.

Conversations like these made me remember why Karen and I were so close. I loved my non-Indian friends, but I was not just learning to appreciate them in a different capacity. I stopped putting myself in the ambassador's seat. I stopped trying to make them as Indian as me because, of course, they would never be Indian. But that's not the point. Instead, I'm trying to be myself in the whole sense, not just in the ethnic sense.

To me, this understanding is a sign that I'm coming to terms with my own heritage and how it applies to the way I interact with people. Unlike Indian kids who are convinced that non-Indian kids will never be able to relate to them, I know that resentfulness is as wrong as any other kind of separatist attitude. No one expects you to be anyone but yourself, or to share anything except what you want to share. As for the future, I've learned that, white or Indian, people will love me for who I am.

I'm not struggling to define and label myself any longer, I learned to love the fact that I came from such a diverse place and to be grateful for the opportunities my parents gave me. I've learned life is not about categorizing yourself and other people. It's all about acceptance.

—Actress Lucy Liu, in an article that appeared in
LA Parade Magazine (October 22, 2000)

jennifer**wang**17

Melville, New York

I am a high school senior in Dix Hills, New York, who emigrated from Beijing, China, at the age of seven. My favorite subjects are physics and computer science, and I enjoy reading, writing, and sleeping during my nonexistent spare time. Influenced by various summer programs I've attended, "Orientation Day" was written hoping that it would foster a greater understanding of Asian teenagers and their search for identity. My goal is to become a research scientist.

Orientation Day

Someone spiked the air, I'm sure of it.

It's summer, yet I'm sitting in the auditorium at one of the greatest universities in the world. Fear and anticipation are oozing from the seats, the walls, and the heavy stage curtains, which are stained the color of fresh blood. A thick carpet of yellow, brown, and red hair covers everything in view.

The director, a gaunt woman with cropped blond hair and the gait of a track star, saunters over to the podium. She opens her mouth and reluctantly releases a word every few minutes, holding them captive in her mouth like lonely prisoners. We are welcomed to the program, introduced to the counselors, explained the rules, and then we are generally oriented—all within the window of sixty interminable minutes.

"And now, we'd like to hear something about each of you," she intones. "Please stand up and introduce yourselves."

Something about myself? How do I summarize, in thirty seconds, everything, which adds up and equals a neat little bundle called, Me? How do I present myself in a user-friendly format, complete with "Help" buttons and batteries? Who am I, and why do I matter to any of you?

First of all, I am a girl who wandered the aisles of Toys "R" Us for two hours, hunting in vain for a doll with a yellowish skin tone. I am a girl who sat on the cold bathroom floor at seven in the morning, cutting out the eyes of Caucasian models in magazines, trying to fit them on my face. I am the girl who loved Connie Chung because she was Asian, and I'm also the girl who hated Connie Chung because she wasn't Asian enough.

In sixth grade my health teacher announced in a dictatorial

voice that all female pubic hair was curly. And I watched in horror over the next two years, as mine grew straight. During that time I also first heard the term "chink," and I wondered why people were calling me "a narrow opening, usually in a wall." People expected me to love studying and to enjoy sitting in my room memorizing facts for days and days.

While I was growing up, I did not understand what it meant to be "Chinese" or "American." Do these terms link only to citizenship? Do they suggest that people fit the profile of either "typical" Chinese or "typical" Americans? And what or who determines when a person starts feeling American, and stops feeling Chinese?

I eventually shunned the Asian crowds. And I hated Chinatown with a vengeance. I hated the noise, the crush of bodies, the yells of mothers to fathers to children to uncles to aunts to cousins. I hated the limp vegetables hanging out of soggy cardboard boxes. I hated the smell of fish being chopped, of meat hanging in a window. I hated not understanding their language in depth—the language of my ancestors, which was also supposed to be mine to mold and master.

I am still not a citizen of the United States of America, this great nation, which is hailed the destination for generations of people, the promised land for millions. I flee at the mere hint of teenybopper music. I stare blankly at my friends when they mention the 1980s or share stories of their parents as hippies. And I hate baseball.

The question lingers: Am I Chinese? Am I American? Or am I some unholy mixture of both, doomed to stay torn between the two?

I don't know if I'll ever find the answers. Meanwhile, it's my turn to introduce myself. Ms. Gaunt Director smiles a loan-shark smile; it was meant to be reassuring, I'm sure. Eyes are on me, taking in my every move. Is the judgment of strangers harsher than that of friends?

I stand up and say, "My name is Jennifer Wang," and then I sit back down. There are no other words that define me as well as those do. No others show me being stretched between two very different cultures and places—the "Jennifer" clashing with the "Wang," the "Wang" fighting with the "Jennifer."

wendy m.**thompson** 18
Oakland, California

I was born in Oakland to a Chinese immigrant woman and an African American man. I am the oldest of three daughters and identify as a mixed-race woman of color. I currently attend the University of California in Santa Barbara, where I am learning that to be a person of color means retaining a sort of invisibility in the eyes of white society. I am currently working on themes of forged/forced identity from the perspectives of young women of color and the biracial identities of those people who come from Asian and African American parentage. I wrote the following out of my frustration and ongoing battle with not belonging to either community.

Going Undercover

I am a lot like my mother. Together, we are a pair of chopsticks. When taken apart, I am the side that's brittle, the side that leaves little splinters in your mouth.

The other day I was on the phone, arguing with her about life—that is, about her, about me, and about the fact that I'm neither modest enough nor Asian enough. And I yell at her about how being Asian isn't easy when you're African American as well, and you've got dark skin and kinky hair. I tell her that my appearance isn't what Asian America has ever looked like, and that Asian America has never claimed us mixed-bloods as her children.

"Asian" isn't something you can wear, hear, or smell—and it's not something you watch racing by on the freeway. To me, being Asian is something more real and more frightening.

Frightening, especially when I find myself in a situation where I wish I could tell someone off, but because I've been conditioned to stay quiet, to take the blame, I stand there and let the person spit all in my face. Being Asian is something deep inside, which is why I get so angry when I see people trying to sell it on the streets to tourists, or market it in tattoo parlors and henna shops. Suddenly, everyone is decked out in Chinese characters, and they're wearing my fucking language on their body. They are the same ones who think that just because they're reading stacks of Asian American history books, and they're eating dim sum, they're mastering step one toward understanding the Asian American experience. (These people aren't multicultural, they're ignorant.)

Were someone to ask you to identify an Asian American woman, I'm the last person whom you'd envision. I'm too different, too rebellious. I'm plotting revolutions instead of getting a 4.0 so I can get into an Ivy League college. And I've forsaken practicing the piano so instead I can help galvanize my people to overthrow the white, racist, patriarchal system.

That said, I will never be quiet.

Refusing to be silent doesn't only disturb my mother. It bothers everybody on her side of the family. My father's side, the African American one, is more tolerant, yet equally dysfunctional. As a result of having endured bitter, painful experiences, while also buying into some of their own self-deprecating stereotypes, some of my (black) male relatives have chosen to intermarry with other ethnic groups, mainly Asian Pacific Islanders. Don't ask me why. It's a question I cannot answer by myself but, as an undercover Asian American woman, I intend to use my life lessons to start putting the pieces of this puzzle together.

I call myself an undercover Asian American because to many people, I look "just black." As a youngster, this made me feel all the more frustrated, since all I wanted was to be "just Asian." My mother's prejudice toward black people (not including my colorless father, of course) intensified my desire to be Asian. So I tried to hide the black side of me.

At the same time, whenever anything "Asian" was imposed on me, I rebelled. It was in part because I still did not have a healthy understanding of my ethnicity. I wasn't like all the other Asian kids whom she compared me to. I couldn't relate to them; the little rice bowl haircut, traditional upbringing, and repressed sexuality. Their experiences were different from any of mine. I mean, at one point, my parents tried to give me a bowl cut, which turned out to be a natural disaster; kinky hair doesn't fall straight, so we discovered. The other Asian kids and I did have something in common, apparently—my parents were strict as hell, too. My parents are like a lot of Asian parents. They're restrictive, demanding, in the closet about sex. They told me that I wasn't allowed to date until I turned twenty-one. Of course, in defiance of their rules, I went out with a black boy at the age of fifteen and lost my virginity. It was too quick, too easily taken, and, as expected, my mother didn't have consoling words in my time of depression.

I look back now and see how Asian I really was and never wanted to be—we ate Chinese food, I grew up in a "silent" house, I wasn't allowed to listen to rap music, and I couldn't wear clothes too big or too tight. I was tired of piano recitals, having a nine o'clock curfew, and not being able to date. And when I sought unity with black kids my age, I was consistently turned down. They didn't think I was "black enough" and told me that I "talked like a whitegirl." The fact that they thought I was selling out infuriated me. It was insulting, being called a wannabe whitegirl from one side, and then being told that I "must be black" from the other side. I was torn in two; rejected by everyone. It was my own choice to belong, and it was everyone else's choice to exclude me.

When I was young, I developed a habit of avoiding black people. I wanted to be the opposite of all that was poor, bad, drunk, and easy. That's how the other part of me is displayed and misrepresented in the mainstream—we are portrayed as fools and whores in music, in the media, on television. My mother, who grew up with prejudices toward African Americans, never changed her perspective, even after she married a black man and bore three black-Asian daughters. She put down black people in front of me, and since I looked more African American than my light-skinned sisters, these twisted comments and remarks were direct blows to me and my self-image. Afraid of falling out of favor with my own mother, I tried to be as "Asian" as I could. I shunned part of myself and rejected all ties I had with people in the black community. It was a long road back toward accepting both sides of my identity.

Now I see my identity as something that fluctuates as necessary. I am African American, I am Chinese, and I am a rare, unexpected similarity, which prevents the communities from completely going to war with each other over their differences. At the same time that I am like my mother, I am like my father. I am also the desire for change.

I am the angry one, who asks controversial questions, which are left unanswered. I am part of the revolution, and I embody the negative and the positive. I challenge people who believe all Asians look the same. I am the revolutionary, the passive worker, the infiltrate, the outsider. I am all of these things because I am complex, human, and I am real.

When I think of my Asian American identity, I think of Chinatown and picture steam rising above roast duck and pig limbs hanging in the window. I recall memories of learning my mother's language, and then, as a second grader, telling her to stop communicating to me that way because "in America, we speak English." But I know, deep down inside, we are alike. I will not have full-blooded, Asian children. I will mother third-generation, mixed babies and, because I think it's important to preserve culture, I will teach them to speak the language that my mother passed on to me. My identity is too precious for me to forget, and I will not obscure it.

I acknowledge that I can no longer pass for anything else. I am a strong woman, a self-aware woman—an Asian American woman, who also happens to be African American. With this face and this history, I will not go unnoticed. I have one foot in each community and I will never forget who I am.

I am *both* Chinese and American, a product of history and present circumstance, and if I choose to devalue or reject either side, I will never be able to experience myself as a whole person.

—Claire Chow, author of *Leaving Deep Water: Asian American Women at the Crossroads of Two Cultures*

 erika**kim**20

Northridge, California

I was born in 1980, and currently I live in Isla Vista, California, although my family lives a few hours away in a suburb of Los Angeles. I seem to share my last name with the entire Korean population, but I read that there are 274 Korean surnames, so I'm obviously wrong. A university course and two really hot T.A.s set the stage for my interest in Asian American studies, especially in examining the special circumstances women of Asian descent must face.

Analyze This

Recently, I had a conversation with a friend of mine, a Chinese-American woman who is also my former roommate. She asked me how I saw my identity. In other words, Who was I? It had been difficult for her to reconcile her Chinese self with her American self. Her query stemmed from the few things she knew about my past experiences. And without thinking, I told her that I had never been confused about my identity, and that I am who I have always been.

Later, that discussion came back to haunt me on some sleepless night. Already prone to insomnia and nightmares, I was staring up at my cottage cheese–type ceiling, listening to a depressing medley of songs that I'd picked solely for the purpose of brooding. I thought about the time my friend asked me if I had grappled with any problems concerning my identity. I replied no, without any consideration. I realized that I did have issues regarding the formation of my identity after all.

Before college, I never thought about what it really meant to be a person of Korean descent living in America. Although I've never had many white friends, I have had many white acquaintances, at least half of whom considered me an honorary white person. This bothered me, and I informed them that carrying this label was an affront to my Korean identity. I mean, it was obvious that I wasn't white. This became extremely clear to me when, for example, I bought my first makeup foundation and the saleswoman told me, "You have yellow undertones." While I was growing up, I also remember feeling self-conscious about the differences that existed between my family and the families of my Caucasian friends. My parents owned their own clothing store, whereas my white friends' parents were doctors, lawyers—all professional people. Because there were so many glaring differences, I resented it when someone like Susie Westing put her arm around me and said, "You're my favorite nonwhite white person."

It was in college, however, that I took Asian American studies and became more aware of Asian and Asian American issues. It was like my eyes were opened. Suddenly I was outraged at the stereotypes on television, when prior to my "awakening," I used to fall asleep while watching television. After an all-night drinking binge, I watched a rerun of the television show *Xena: Warrior Princess*, because I had seen an Asian woman in the adverts. I waxed poetic about how great the actress was. Then I started to think about it: she's a Korean woman playing a Chinese woman. This sort of thing didn't used to bother me, but now I contemplated the idea that "white people think all Asian people look the same." I started to dislike the episode, but I could not write it off completely, because the character was compelling and beautifully portrayed.

I became increasingly aware of Asian American issues, but meanwhile, I started to feel more alienated from myself. Soon, even the smallest things became issues for me. I was annoyed with my male Caucasian friend, Andrew, for telling me that I was "exotic," and that he would receive a lot of attention from his family if I was his date to his sister's wedding. I started to think any white guy who had a proclivity for Asian women automatically had an Asian fetish. I started to feel more pressure to associate with Asian people, and I felt guilty when I had a crush on a white guy, because of the debates over the politics of interracial dating and miscegenation among Asians and Caucasians.

Who am I? I guess everyone asks herself that question at one point or another. Sometimes I ask myself that question, and I really don't care one way or another if I give myself an answer. But other times, I really think about it, like, I step outside myself and I analyze. I just HAVE to have an answer. For starters, I'm a twenty-year-old female living in California; coupled with the fact that I'm Korean American, I'm just like thousands of other twenty-year-old Korean chicks. But your identity goes beyond when you were born, or where you live or who your parents are. I mean, don't we all shape our destinies just by virtue of who we ARE? For me, my identity isn't only entrenched in my ethnicity, nationality, age, etc., etc. There are heaps of other Asian girls out there, and we're approximately in the same age group, and yet, I don't know anyone who shares my interests. My roommate, for example, was completely intolerant of my Celtic, Bulgarian, and Arabic music. The only other Asian woman I've ever met who was as deeply interested in mythology and fairy tales (in a larger social framework) as I am I found the Internet, two years ago in a single, random encounter.

Moreover, I don't believe in love or marriage, but I've been involved with someone for an extended period of time. How that works can constitute a manifesto longer than the Unabomber's. I've been told that I am sarcastic and cynical, but I do not agree. Well, maybe I do, but I have to deny it out of principle. I have liberal views on sex and sexuality, many of which have resulted in castigation by others. I would rather stay at home than go out. My favorite movies are *Heavenly Creatures* and *Once Were Warriors*, but I've never even seen *E.T.*, the *Star Wars* movies, or *Independence Day*. I like to collect Powerpuff Girl paraphernalia. I want to have five kids one day, but I'm afraid of messing them up. I am as mercurial as a pit bull, I can talk to you in a very congenial manner one day, but I can curse at you like a Wapping waterman the next. In high school, I was the girl who read Camus, Sartre, and Sophocles for fun; I would have been a bigger dork had I not also managed to earn the nickname "druggie," as well as the reputation for being prone to violence.

I'm a living, breathing stereotype, and a walking mass of contradictions who also happens to be Korean American. I used to think of my identity as being a split between the Korean and the American sides, but I realize now that it was wrong to divide myself like that. I used to blame either of the two sides for my personality and diverse interests, but not anymore. I've accepted that, beneath it all, I'm just one Asian girl among countless others, and aside from having a few of my own quirks, I'm fairly normal. Ultimately, THIS is who I am, twenty years in the making, and millions of years of evolution on my back.

I'd talk to my cousins about what life's like in America and explain, describe, show pictures and still know that they'll never get it because they haven't been here. Talking to Americans about India is the same— it's always partial. As a storyteller, I'm aware that there are limitations in communication.

—Author Jhumpa Lahiri, in an interview by Vibhuti Patel
(*Newsweek International*, 9/20/99)

kamala**nair**19
Rochester, Minnesota

I'm currently a sophomore at Wellesley College. My parents are originally from India, and they left in 1976. I was born in London, and we moved to the States when I was almost three years old. Throughout my childhood, I constantly felt as if I was caught between two vastly distinct worlds. But my sense of alienation was something I never really acknowledged or talked about. Writing has always been my primary form of creative and personal expression. So, at eighteen years old, it seemed only the natural way for me to tell my story.

Learning to Love My Skin

When I was little I used to wish I had blond hair and blue eyes. I would stand in front of the mirror with my eyes closed, hoping that if I wished long and hard enough, my skin and hair would have magically transformed when I opened them. I did wish for a long time, and when I finally opened my eyes, I had transformed. But not in the way I had once hoped. I saw my reflection for the first time, thick black hair and beautiful brown skin, and I felt indescribably happy.

If you asked a seven-year-old girl to make a wish, she might say that she wanted a new dress, a pony, or the latest Beanie Baby doll. When I was seven, what I wanted more than anything in the world was to belong. During the day, I attended an all-white school, where I studied American history and played with my white friends. I came home in the evening and, over a dinner table, laden with heavily spiced curries and red-hot pickles, I discussed the *Bhagavad Gita* with my Indian parents. At age seven, I was caught in the middle of two vastly different cultures.

On the playground during recess, one of my third-grade classmates called me a "blackie." After I told the teacher what had happened, she smiled pleasantly, and said, "Well, at least you never have to worry about getting a tan." Running home as quickly as my knobby knees could carry me, I proceeded to scrub my skin violently with soap, hoping that, by some miracle, I could scrub away its offensive shade of brown. My intense scrubbing dissolved into broken sobs. This was my first startling introduction to the truth—I was different from the other kids, thus, I would be treated differently.

My parents always used to tell my sister and me that we could do whatever we wanted to do, and we could be whoever we wanted to be. I never doubted that this was true. After all, this was America, the land of opportunity. I looked at my girl cousins in India who were married off the minute they finished their studies, and felt overwhelmed by my good luck.

But later, after listening to my mother's advice, I wasn't as confident as I had once been. "When everyone else works one hundred percent," she told me, "You have to work one hundred and ten percent." I could not understand this double standard, this flaw in the so-called American dream.

So I decided I would create a loophole, and beat the system. Maybe if I walked, and talked, and acted like everyone else, nobody would know the difference. I turned myself into a carbon copy of my white classmates, folding up my Indian self and tucking her away in a locked drawer to collect dust. Just like everyone else in elementary school, I wore spandex, I tight-rolled my jeans, and I listened to New Kids on the Block. I kept my Indian origin proudly under wraps, like a well-kept secret, trying hard to ignore the fact that my brown skin was a telltale giveaway.

As I entered middle school, I continued my crusade. To me, conformity was key; it was the only way to bridge the division between my classmates and me. I thought I related to the stories about white teenage girls when I read *Seventeen* magazine. And when the popular kids teased the brainy chess club captain or the chubby computer whiz because they didn't fit into the mold, because they didn't know what it was like to be cool, I laughed along with them. I didn't realize then that my behavior was only a cover for the shame I felt inside for not having the courage to be different, to embrace my identity.

After being inspired from a trip we took to India one summer, my sister started to wear salwar kameez to school. She read the autobiography of Mahatma Gandhi, and she converted to vegetarianism. She also began meditating, even attempting to sleep on the floor (a stint that lasted about a week). I pretended to be scornful of her, but in truth, I was jealous of the happiness she was finding in her culture. While my sister was finding herself, I was embarrassed of anything Indian—from my parents' accents to the samosas my mother sneaked into my lunch box. It upset me when my friends could not understand my parents, when I understood them perfectly well. Once, a man rushed frantically up to my mother to inform her that her forehead was bleeding (she was wearing a bindi), and I was mortified. So, I did everything I possibly could to be accepted (short of crimping my hair), even if it meant sacrificing my culture. And it was working.

After seventh grade, everything changed. My father was offered a job in Minnesota, so we loaded our belongings into our big red station wagon and drove halfway across the country. I was furious. How could my parents uproot me from my home and my friends and drag me to this strange, unfamiliar place? I didn't care that my father, who grew up in a tiny village in India, was going to be a physician in one of the leading health care centers in the world. All that mattered was that everything I had worked so hard to build, the acceptance I had finally found, was slowly unraveling before my eyes.

My mother brought me to register for school. We walked into the building, and the woman standing behind the counter took one look at me, and blurted, "So, you'll be signing up for the ESL [English as Second Language] classes, right?" Her words stung, and I coldly told her no, taking small comfort in her surprise that I spoke English with a perfect American accent. I dreaded the day I would have to begin school.

My new classmates proved harder to win over than my old ones. Maybe it was because we were at the height of adolescence, the time in our lives when we are the cruelest and least empathetic. The kids were not used to my brown skin and thick black hair. I defensively turned up my nose to their stares and ignorant questions, because that was the only way I knew how to cope with them. I had to find a new tactic. A new identity. So I fell in with a group of girls who dyed their hair pink, listened to grunge music, and called themselves hard-core punks. I was angry at the world, so why not show it? I would be the champion of nonconformity. In all the pictures of me in eighth grade, I am glaring at the camera.

High school signaled a revival of all things preppy, and I went back to wearing what everyone else wore. But I had changed. Although my high school was pretty homogeneous, I started noticing yellow, brown, and black faces popping up here and there, like worms poking their heads out after the first rain. I began to pick up the fragments of my fractured childhood self, slowly piecing together a self-portrait. I still did the things that the other kids did; I joined clubs, performed in school musicals, played on the tennis team, and I attended football games and dances. But I did these things with energy and passion. I no longer felt an urge to hide behind my perfectly pressed Gap and American Eagle outfits. At home I was asking my parents questions about India, genuinely interested in what they had to say. I started corresponding with my cousins in India, and was surprised to find that we had a lot in common. But what surprised me the most was that even as I accepted my Indian culture, my friends did not reject me. I knew I would never be prom queen, but I realized that my classmates actually respected me more when I finally learned to love myself, brown skin and all.

College is opening doors for me. In joining the South Asian Association I have found a community of people who are straddling two deeply distinct cultures, just like I am. We all went through that same harrowing search for identity—some of us still are. But in each other, we find comfort in knowing that we are not alone.

I wrote a zine called Tennis and Violins *and compiled* Riot Grrrl Review. *Currently I live in Florida and am studying women's studies and political science at the University of South Florida.*

Zine Grrrl

Words are just a vehicle for whatever someone is thinking. Although I always had words to transform my thoughts into communicable reality, the meaning of my identity was unclear to me throughout my childhood and early adolescence. Words and ideas are also cyclic. Sometimes, writing itself will inspire me to think in another direction, and reading and hearing other people inspires new thoughts.

I began writing zines when I was twelve years old. My first few zines were just for my friends. At the time, I was very absorbed in magazines like *Teen.* (These magazines were my handbooks for navigating my way through the intense peer pressure in middle school.) Most of these early experiments revolved around makeup, trivia I obtained from the *World Book Encyclopedia,* and other superficial information. As everyone knows, most magazines for teenage girls revolve around social acceptance, so that was on the forefront of my personal agenda.

At age twelve, I probably fell under the self-erasing category of anglophile. My mother is white; my father is Chinese. My father has always worked very hard at his restaurant, while my mother stayed home. As a result, I can't speak Chinese, and I am less familiar with most Chinese customs than other Chinese Americans may be. I was also raised to achieve. My mother was a teacher, and I often spent my time at home filling out educational workbooks. I didn't see my father as often, but when I did, he always gave me a speech about the importance of education and success. I was lucky to have such devoted, caring parents during my formative years.

However, I feel that my upbringing, compounded with 1980s American cultural values, was not advantageous in the formation of my ethnic/biracial identity. I equated beauty with whiteness; I linked beauty to social acceptance; and to me, social acceptance was another test of success for me to achieve.

I was always trying to be as white as possible. In one school picture, my family joked about how surprised I looked because my eyebrows were raised high. For years, nobody knew the reason my eyebrows were raised was because I tried to make my eyes look more round by opening them as much as possible. I used the lightest foundation I could get away with. I plucked the eyebrows I inherited straight off my father's face into thin, indiscernible lines. I curled my straight eyelashes and preserved them in mascara. In the last few years, I have met adult anglophiles. They are not just people in Asia getting cosmetic surgery on their eyes. Sometimes, they are just as subtle as I was. They envy me because I am part white, and it makes me sad. My desire to be a blue-eyed blonde is now a sad memory I have. I slowly realized and accepted the fact that I was setting myself up for failure over and over.

For a long time, self-denial was the only intelligible response I had to the identity questions looming in front of me. This began to change slowly when I was thirteen. In 1992, the presidential elections were big news. I kept abreast of the whole campaign with keen interest. By doing this, I came to the firm conclusion that I agreed with a liberal social agenda. I eagerly identified as pro-choice, feminist, pro-gay rights, etc. My zines changed into sociopolitical criticism. Identity politics was a door for me to articulate my own identity. For the first time, I began to think about my ethnicity as a serious piece of my identity and as something that shaped my entire formation as an individual. I started criticizing other kids who called me "chink" as racists. I was beginning to assert myself.

The Riot Grrrl movement blew up in the early/mid-'9Os. I identified as a part of it quickly, and my zine reflected my radical feminist views. From Riot Grrrl, I also branched off into punk rock. Zines are taken fairly seriously in punk and Riot Grrrl. I found a large audience for what I wanted to say. Riot Grrrl launched me into the world of feminist theory, but both punk and its feminist microcosm were predominantly white movements, so I had yet to find my platform for other facets of my identity. One day in 1995, I got a flyer in the mail from Mimi Nguyen (who writes *Slant* zine now). It was addressed to "Punks of Color." Mimi was compiling an anthology zine by nonwhite punks. She asked potential contributors to write about various issues concerning ethnicity and race, especially within the punk rock subculture. I was so excited. I wrote some pieces about being mixed race and about how Asian women's sexualities are exploited through stereotypes. It was a huge turning point. I felt very empowered, knowing that there are words (like *assimilation* or *fetish*) that convey some of the issues I face, and it is my opportunity to explain the meaning and result of these experiences.

I haven't put together a new issue of my zine in over two years, but I still learn new things about other people and how this affects my niche in the world. In 1996, I decided to put together an Asian American zine anthology. Submissions trickled into my mailbox over the next several years, as my project spread by word of mouth. I was startled by the diversity of my sample. For example, an Indian girl wrote to me. I had never really even considered Indian people as "Asian" until that point. There were first-, second-, and third-generation Asian Americans. Some of us assimilated into the white mainstream; others resisted. All of us had other components that formed our social identity, like class, sexual identity, family, religious faith, location, etc. I am certainly not the first person to comment on the diversity of Asian Americans, but putting together my zine anthology was my first exposure to this diversity. Some white people with good intentions commented on how I "didn't seem Chinese," and I did have a concern that maybe other Asian people would think of me that way, also. Even my father thought I was "too American." At that point, I felt firmly comfortable identifying as Chinese and Asian American because I saw that there was no ideal Asian American figure. We share issues; that is the bottom line.

After Heavens to Betsy released their 1994 album with the song "White Girl" on it, white privilege and race became critical issues in Riot Grrrl, and naturally, a lot of nonwhite grrrls came out of the woodwork. Real discourse about racism in Riot Grrrl and punk rock was created, and in it, I found understanding individuals I could confide in about these issues.

I don't live around many Asian Americans, so the bonds I formed with other Asian Americans through zines are irreplaceable. Several of my best friends today are people I met through the zine network. Zines were a huge part of my life. Reading them inspired me; writing them validated me; and trading them fostered community.

> I'm not uncomfortable with being singled out [because I'm Asian]....
> I'm proud to be who I am, and their support feels good. I consider
> myself to be Chinese-American, that's who I am...my father is from
> China and my mom's from Hong Kong, and I am first-generation.
>
> —U.S. Olympic gymnast Amy Chow, in an article that appeared in
> Blue Jean Magazine (May/June 1998)

Who We Are: South Asian Girls Speak Out
A Roundtable Discussion

Diya Gullapalli, eighteen, of Reston, Virginia, completed a summer internship in the India Abroad Program based in Washington, D.C. At the end of the program, she conducted her own roundtable discussion with some peers, in an attempt to explore the issues which have had a critical impact on the decisions they're making in their lives. As South Asian American girls, they engage in a dialogue in search of answers that will bring each of them closer to finding their voice, as well as their place in contemporary society.

The Girl Gang
Uma: A junior at Princeton University
Mona: An India Abroad Program adviser who went to University of Illinois, Urbana-Champaign

Shanti: A senior at University of Illinois, Chicago and the vice president of student government

Marian: A junior at University of Maryland, College Park

Sonja: A student at the University of Minnesota

Barnali: A sophomore at Stanford University

Maunica: A senior at Louisiana State University

Commentator Diya Gullapalli: A sophomore at the University of Virginia

On South Asian American Womanhood

Diya: Uma, the other day you said that you think that Indian men don't respect girls who have an opinion or who are outgoing.

Uma: Well, it's not necessarily girls who have an opinion—it's just opinionated girls. Actually, I had a long talk with Arun [male friend] while we were walking over here, and you heard the words he used to describe the type of person I am; that statement, "girls like you are the reason I used to stand in the corner at dances at school." He didn't mean it in a bad way, but Indian men (although I do think that it's a "men thing," in general) are very intimidated by girls who seem really independent and really strong-willed, like they don't need a guy to fall back on. And that's something that's hard to deal with as a South Asian female.

I mean, I was telling my dad that this was something I learned during the summer, and I said to him, "You know, you should be happy that I am this way." But it's going to be a lot harder for me to find their [concept of the] ideal Indian husband because there are very few Indian guys who are willing to put up with me.

Diya: So, what are you saying? Are you saying there aren't any other Indian girls who are like you then?

Uma: I don't know. I think I've definitely come across individuals who are as opinionated as I am, even in this group, but I think that there are certain things that I'm opinionated about that a lot of Indian girls aren't. My attitude about guys is very different; for example, I'm willing to be like "boom, boom, boom"—have a big fight, have a big argument. I'm not willing to ever submit my opinion or ever change the way I act for a guy.

Mona: So do you think that's because you feel secure about who you are?

Sonja: Actually, I think it's more of a knowledge thing, like I think there are certain things I'm very opinionated about because I know a lot about them. Like sports. And when I'm not taken for what I know and they treat me based on the fact that I'm a girl, I get pissed off. For instance, in the Indian Student Association at my school, when I first came to college, I started making friends with the guys, and it's not even that the guys were intimidated by me. But I'd start talking about sports to make friends with them, and even then, they kept dismissing what I'd say with an "Oh, but she's a girl, but she's a girl" attitude. And it wasn't even that they were intimidated by what I was saying as much as it was that they just didn't appreciate it. Anytime I said anything else, like when I expressed an opinion about politics or anything substantial, like on mass culture, I was cut off too. Sometimes I can't even finish a sentence, which makes me more adamant about how I feel.

Mona: So do you think that, for Indian women, being strong-willed is a defense mechanism?

Maunica: Well, I never went to India until a few months ago, so I'll put that out there. When I went to India, I always heard the notion of soft-spoken Indian women, gender issues, all these problems in India which are all over the media. I went there just curious about it. And when I went there— these women in India, they are strong women. They are scary. My brother, who's a big guy, like 6 feet one, went to these temples, and he was scared of these women. He stayed out of their way. I think Indian women, in general, are really, really strong. I think our moms are inherently strong because they take the burden of the house, and in America, they take the burden of jobs, and now we are taking the burden of education, as well as trying to be equals to our South Asian American male partners. So I really admire South Asian women for this strength. What I studied in India was the concept that Indian women are strong, but they have to submit to their father, brother, husband, whatever.

Sonja: Maybe it's that submission makes you stronger, because the more you're put down the more you have to fight.

Marian: Well, I think what our mothers have is a different kind of strength. But in terms of us, right now—I think a lot of times we're not respected for the traditional chores because we're not doing anything related to keeping the house together, since we don't have one. We're doing things for number one, not for our husbands, or our brothers, or our fathers. I think a lot of South Asian guys expect South Asian girls to care, because their mothers were very smart, but their mothers still cared about them. Like my mom, she's a really smart woman, but when she did anything, it was for us. My mom always told me, "I'm doing everything for you guys." Meanwhile, I'm here for myself, and not so that I can get a good job for my children.

Shanti: I think that for our mothers' generation, it was that they were embedded in Indian culture so they were expected to follow tradition. But for us, it's like we're struggling with the Indian culture and the American culture. Like, I know my male relatives in this country expect me to be assertive when necessary, but when it comes to Indian events, I'm supposed to act passive and feminine. It's a constant struggle. And it's tormenting. I'm one of the more assertive Indian girls on campus, and to a certain extent, guys are just scared of me. And, Uma, I don't know—this summer I feel like I'm struggling with issues of femininity. I've never felt feminine before, but this summer, I have. I've always been the biggest tomboy, and this summer, I've been quiet, acting "like a woman."

Diya: Why? Why are you trying to do that?

Shanti: I just want to be in touch with my feminine side. Can you blame me for that?

Uma: But what is not feminine about having an opinion?

Shanti: Look, I go to a school where so many Indian guys have essentially told me, maybe not to my face, that I'm not feminine because I'm assertive. And now I come here, and I haven't been assertive at all, and I've been getting these vibes from these guys, who are like, "Oh, you're cute." It's sick, but it's like the experiment is working.

Uma: But you know, that's what propagates the stereotype. A lot of times, I know you're struggling. And I'm thinking, as I go to the guys and ask things, Do you think I'm overly abrasive? What's the matter with me? But it's like, when do we stop drawing the lines? We are the ones doing this to ourselves.

Shanti: I know. I have a headache because I'm frustrated. I want to be assertive yet be considered feminine at the same time yet I'm surrounded by eight or nine Indian men, who, as soon as I'm assertive . . .

Maunica: But what happened to just being yourself and being happy? Why does it have to be about Indian men? I think that the road I've taken is, if Indian men want to be that way, then screw them. I don't want to be with them.

Barnali: It's very interesting to hear all of you say this because my experience has been so opposite. People always say, "You're not assertive enough." My parents, especially my dad, are very big on, "Oh, you're a woman and you can do anything." And he's really trying to drill that idea into me. He says, "Oh, the reason you're not into math and science is because society doesn't foster women to be good at that."

And I'm just like, "No, *I don't like* math and science." My dad tries to justify things by saying, "As a woman, you're disadvantaged." But I've never really felt disadvantaged in that respect. Hearing Shanti say she's too assertive—most of my guy friends are like, "Oh, Barnali, speak up."

Diya: Are they Indian guys?

Barnali: Yeah, actually a lot of them are.

Maunica: Well then I think you're very fortunate.

Barnali: And I don't really even think I'm that quiet. I just need time to open up. And last night when we were all sitting in our house in Georgetown, I was finally opening up and Uma was like, "Oh, Barnali's being sarcastic." So when you say being assertive is looked down upon, I think my experience has been that it's so highly valued.

Sonja: When does the narrow-mindedness stop being the older generation's problem, considering boys in our generation are propagating it too? I think we can all agree that it's happening to us.

Mona: And, you know—it will continue to happen. But we are the generation that has the power to make that change. When we are fifty years old it might be different, but we have to do that groundwork now. We're in transition.

Maunica: And just to go back to this, if Indian men don't want to change, then as they see all their good women leave to be with people of other races, they'll start to realize it. I think they're already developing inferiority complexes.

Marian: And also I think you should remember that if you want to be quiet and not say anything, there's nothing wrong with it. If you're comfortable with it, and that's the way you want to be, then you should never feel like you're in a situation where you feel forced to be assertive. But the most important thing is that we should never feel like we can't say something. I mean, I only speak up when I'm really passionate about something, and if I'm not passionate then

	I don't really care all that much. But if we are, then we should all speak up.
Sonja:	But this situation sucks because even when we speak up about things, we are not listened to . . .
Mona:	I come from a family where my mom and my dad do talk about the things that are important, but my dad does everything. He handles the expenses, and he taught my mom how to do everything, from balancing a checkbook to driving a car to buying groceries here. And granted, she's better now, but to me, she still says, "No. You don't speak up loud, you don't stay out until two in the morning because you'll be considered a prostitute." An example: I don't wear lipstick. Did you guys notice? Then my mom says, "Ugh. You don't wear lipstick? You're not going to find a man." Excuse me? The more she says things like that, the more I do what I want.
Diya:	Okay, so I've been dating someone for a while who's twenty-two, and all his friends are done with school and are older. Contrary to the sweet but stupid Indian girls you guys think they like, these boys are just, like, "Those girls are idiots." I mean, they have no patience with that. And maybe I've just found someone who likes me for my personality, but I don't know if he's just the exception to the rule. Also, I think that Indian boys want too much. Like, they want a beautiful, smart, interesting, stable, maternal, and strong woman, all at the same time. They want a girl who is Indian, yet American, liberal, but not too crazy. The list just goes on and on.
Maunica:	When Indian boys ask me, "Why don't you date Indian boys?" I don't want to say it. But the truth is, Indian boys want a mom. And I just can't do that for them. It's just such scorn, like, "Oh you don't want me so you must be a bitch. Or, you must be arrogant because of it."
Shanti:	And I also think it's so sad because Indian girls don't unite. It's a competition, and a catty, petty battle.

Making Choices for Our Future

Sonja: Well, I really think we're breaking in to a lot of new fields. My sister went into academia. She's a math professor.

Uma: It worries me, though, because after this summer I want to go back and do so many things, but I wonder. Will they listen to me in my Indian community because I'm a female? And that bothers me. My mom is a professional, and she's amazing. She's raised my sister and me to be strong and intelligent people. At the same time, my mom is always there. She has opportunities to travel, but does she? No, she'll be there when my sister and I are, even though we're in college. My dad is gone every week traveling. When are things like that going to stop? When will those roles really reverse?

Marian: I just think that when I see my future, I want to stay at home. But the good thing I like about that is that I have the choice to do that. I'm going to get my law degree and everything so I could prove it to myself that I could do it, but I want to volunteer my time to immigration law. But I think that unlike our moms, we have the choice to decide if we want to stay at home, if we want to be single, if we want to be fifty-fifty. But I think that even though some Indian girls and some Indian guys don't let us fully take advantage of that, I still think we're really lucky.

Maunica: It's interesting because my dad is the one who taught me how to cook. My mom would tell me to be quiet and all that, even though she's very loud. My brother on the other hand, who is twenty-five, has regressed to being a chauvinist. I went to India with all these white feminists who were like, "Indian women need to get liberated." But I don't know if they understood the culture. One of our speakers was an Indian woman and she talked about how liberation is a double burden because as a woman becomes successful, gets a great education, a great job, she still needs to play the other role. When she comes home at five, and her husband does too, she is the one who has to cook dinner and serve the whole family. And what she explained was that she's liberated and her daughters are too, but in some ways she wants to go back to the old way because this is just too much work in India. The men aren't doing anything there, but they're not doing anything here, either! There are all these programs to educate women, but you need to educate men, as well. I tell my brother that all the time.

Sonja: Yeah, and continuing on the lines of professionalism, for me to look into an Indian person's eye and say, "I'm an English major," I feel so bad. I see my reputation in their eyes fall to the ground. Indians are just so afraid of risk.

Maunica: See, I love that though. Because these aunties who want to marry me off to their sons, as soon as I say that I'm an English major, they just look away.

Sonja: But it's still bad because it's equated with being not smart, i.e., the person who couldn't make it into med school. The person who wants to be a teacher.

Barnali: Oh my god—going to Stanford, I get that all the time from Indian parents. You go to school in the Silicon Valley and you're not a comp sci major? You don't want to become a dot-com millionaire? Their respect for me falls since they know I go to a good school, but they see me as not fulfilling my potential. It's like I have a gift that I'm not using, even if I have other interests that I want to pursue. As if I'm wasting myself.

Sonja: I mean, granted that in America professions like medicine and engineering are respected more, but I think it's magnified in the Indian community.

Uma: I think this is a problem for both Indian girls and guys though. But I think the whole notion of professionalism can still be gender quantified. Exactly what Maunica said, get a job, but at five, come home and let your husband watch TV while you cook.

Barnali: But here, going back to what Marian was saying about staying home with the kids . . . I think if I ever did that, my dad would be so disappointed in that choice, because of how hard my parents have worked to get me where I am. He's upset my mom didn't work for twenty years; he thinks that she wasted time. My parents got married late, and then she chose not to work. Marian says she feels like she has a choice. I don't. Because I feel like so many people are expecting so many great things from me. And if you're sitting at home with your children, you aren't taking advantage of everything out there.

Uma: Well, I want to put a totally different spin on all this. I pictured myself married with a career and successful and powerful. But I can't picture myself in my wedding at all. I have no concept of what my husband will be like, or what my ceremony will be like. I remember in high school, sitting around with my white friends and hearing them talk about their weddings. And in my office, my intern coordinator is getting married in September, and she talks about her wedding. Indian traditions are so foreign to me—I can actually see her Christian wedding so much clearer than I can see my own.

Diya: I think it's going to be hard for our generation to plan our futures—not just for Indian girls but for girls in general. We're so assertive, and we want to do everything, so when it comes time to choose, it's going to be impossible. My mom stayed at home with us because she wanted to, because those were the only years she'd be able to watch us grow up. My dad teased her about getting a job, which she did when we were older, but he knew it was the right choice too. With us, it's going to be that much harder, since we've been raised to be so independent.

Uma: But Diya, looking at my mom, she didn't ever choose. She
          was perfect. She was fantastic. She avoided traveling too
          much, but other than that she was a total professional,
          working nine to five. I was a latchkey kid; I came home
          and made myself a snack. It just all depends on that guy—
          my dad is so accommodating. I wonder if I'll ever find a
          guy like that.

Sonja: But see, look. My mom was expected to go into my dad's
          office as a nurse without pay and work. Full-time eventu-
          ally too. So she was professional, but she wasn't paid. And
          she couldn't work unless it was for my dad; it was very
          submissive like that.

Maunica: But the thing about South Asian men is that even though
          they respect your assertiveness to a certain extent, they
          really don't see you as an equal.

Uma: I think my dad feels like my mom is an equal.

Diya: Okay, I need to wrap things up. Is there something anyone
          has wanted to say, but didn't know how to work into our
          conversation until now?

Maunica: Well, I just wanted to say that I think everything we said
          today is really important and I'm glad it was documented.
          We need to stick together and understand where each other
          is coming from.

michelle**chang** 17
Novato, California

*I was born in March of 1983. That makes me a Pisces according to
the Western horoscope, and I was also born in the Year of the Boar.
Currently, I live in San Francisco with my parents who are from
Taipei, Taiwan. I wrote this piece, "Identity Crisis," as a reflection
of my inner conflict and continued struggle to define myself as a
Taiwanese-American girl.*

Identity Crisis

Being Taiwanese American is supposed to give me all the benefits of two rich, vastly different cultures, when in reality, every cultural influence from either side makes it impossible for me to be accepted by the other. Everyone who is Taiwanese considers me American. Everyone American considers me Taiwanese. It's like standing with one foot planted on a side of a crack that continually widens with time. For every time I thought I actually belonged to either side, there have been five times when I've felt entirely lost, bereft, and on my own. When I begin to feel comfortable in one environment, something brings me back to reality. I don't fit in anywhere.

"Do your parents encourage you to speak your opinions?"

I sit, listening to the teacher in an orange chair in the warm classroom, half asleep from yesterday's grueling six-hour gymnastics workout. Leaning over the desk with my head down in my arms, I try not to attract attention to myself; I am content to listen to, but not participate in, the discussion of a book. Slightly interested, I hoist my head up to watch the other students' reactions. Of course, the ones whose parents have encouraged them to form opinionated minds are the first to respond.

Someone answers, confidently, "My parents were extremely oppressed and not allowed to voice their opinions, so they try to encourage me to always say what I think."

Well, then, that was profound, safe, and politically correct. Intelligent, creative, thoughtful answers like these scream, *I'm trying my hardest to let you know I see everyone as an individual and I know that everyone is equal.* Their preposterous self-righteousness makes me want to laugh, but instead, I put my head back on the desk and I close my eyes.

I consider the question, too, but what could I say?

"Well, actually—no, not really. My parents' opinions were suppressed; therefore, they silence mine as part of traditional Asian beliefs. I supposedly have no opinion, because as my parents' daughter, I have no right to an opinion." Besides, according to my parents, it's not right to talk about personal, family matters. And now I'm wide-awake. My teacher's question has reminded me once again of my inner conflict: I don't belong here or there.

I'm going back to Taipei this summer, just as I have every summer since I was born. I still speak Taiwanese and Mandarin Chinese with an atrocious American accent. I still bring my old, ratty clothes, because the decrepit washing machine at my grandmother's house bleaches stripes on my T-shirts. It's still hot, and mosquitoes plague us throughout our stay. Now, when I go back, I sit down at the dinner table, view the food, and swallow hard against what tries to come back up. My grandmother looks at my sister, my brother, and me with suspicious eyes that seem to gaze right through my mind. She looks at the food that is unfamiliar to us, and infinitely familiar to her. I am unable to finish it, and she turns to my grandfather and my parents, and says, "bi-gok gin-na" (American children) in the tone of disgust people use to describe a homicidal Satan worshipper. Then she looks at me as if I cannot understand anything but American English, even though she knows I do. My parents bow their heads in shame, and I'm also ashamed for something that I can neither help nor change.

And if it's not my grandmother showing me that I don't belong here, the sales clerks in shops and department stores will remind me. I'll walk in Shinkong, a huge department store, trying my best to imitate a humble, unassuming, quiet, Taiwanese girl. I don't say a word, because the moment I open my mouth, my Americanized Taiwanese will give me away. Just when I think I'm blending in and nobody notices, the saleswoman will approach my parents. After asking if they need help, she opens her mouth to converse with me, does a double take, and then says to my parents, "*Ta shr chong mei-guo lai de*." (She's from America.) She never tries to see if I understand.

When I return from Taiwan, ready to start a new school year, I hope that I'll be accepted here, where I live. All I want is to have a place where I can be myself; I want time, sleep, friends, and some freedom. But I'm not normal, because my parents have tried and continue to try to make me truly Taiwanese; this is a far cry from being a typical American kid.

If I get a 99 percent on a test, they ask me where the last 1 percent went. Anything less than an A− is considered flunking. Despite my hard work, high school makes it nearly impossible to continue getting A's in all my classes. I'm constantly compared with my older sister, and what makes it worse is, she's too smart for her own good—or mine. My parents compare our report cards and our class schedules every semester to determine whether or not I'm doing well enough. My parents remind me that if I don't get "good" grades, *"Li xi-ya"*—I'm dead.

The generation gap that separates teens from their parents makes communications difficult; in my case, it's more than twice as bad, not only because my parents are extremely conservative, but because they're extremely conservative even for Taiwanese parents. They seem to think that they can raise us exactly the way their parents raised them in Taiwan; the fact that we're living in the United States a quarter century later apparently means nothing to them. Even though I was born here, I go to school here, and I spend eleven months of every year here, I'm supposed to be 100 percent Taiwanese. Clearly, it doesn't work, and it's obvious that I don't belong in Taiwan. Regardless, they continue to try to make me into something I'm not.

Imagine being unable to lock (or even close) your door for any reason, ever. Imagine being punished for listening to WILD 94.9 radio, not because of the sex and violence contained in the lyrics, but because the music is a sign of how "American" you've become. Imagine being treated as if you were less important in the family because you are a girl and because your last name will be lost when you marry. Imagine having to listen constantly to sexist or racist or homophobic ranting and getting punished for expressing an opposing viewpoint. Imagine a place where staying silent when you disagree is not enough; you must vocally agree and submit to their power. Imagine having to follow a course of action that will lead you nowhere, simply because your elders are always right—even when they're wrong. Imagine living in constant fear of being disowned by your family were you to do something wrong. Imagine having your entire life plotted out for you without your opinion or consent. Any deviation from a prescribed path is impossible.

Imagine all this, living in a country supposedly built on liberty and equality for all, while going to school in a supposedly open-minded environment, where independent thought is encouraged. The home environment inevitably has an impact on everything else, especially school. For instance, how can I participate in class and present opposing views when it's expected that, at home, I shouldn't have an opinion at all? How can I choose my own classes, my own path, make my own decisions, when my parents have already made them for me?

Living in the U.S. has instilled me with more American than Taiwanese values; I think we should develop strong, personal opinions and foster creativity. I believe in freedom, equality, and nondiscrimination, wherever these issues might be problematic. Unfortunately, for me, my parents have been more successful than they know in inscribing certain Taiwanese ideas in me. I feel uncomfortable talking to anyone about my personal problems, or even presenting my own ideas. I'm never happy with anything less than perfection. I see things skewed through the window of my own experiences.

People tell me that I have to be positive and that I will come to a conclusion about my conflicts; in the meantime, I don't know what to do. Someone once told me, "Everybody faces these issues to some extent, but it's the choices you make that solve them."

I just need to find the choices that are right for me.

Elaine H. Kim is Professor of Asian Americans Studies and Associate Dean of the Graduate Division at the University of California—Berkeley. She has written and edited a number of books on Asian American literature and culture. She cofounded Asian Women United of California, Asian Immigrant Women Advocates, and the Korean Community Center in Oakland, California.

Then and Now: Finding My Voice
BY ELAINE H. KIM

I love fortune-telling of all kinds—Chinese or Korean astrology, palm reading, tarot cards, the I Ching. I have visited Buddhist temples and shamans in Korea. Once I waited in line for an hour among crowds of anxious mothers right before their children's school entrance examinations for a popular *jomjeangi*, or fortune-teller, with the stage name Spring Wind to interpret my *saju*, or configuration of year, month, day, and hour of birth. He took one look at my four birth animals—horse, dragon, tiger, and dog—and said, "Who is this man?"

Apparently, my *saju* would have guaranteed success and happiness to a man, but for a woman they suggest disaster. More desirable than fierce tigers, fiery dragons, and horses that run fast from hearth and home would have been the comely rabbit, the diligent rat, or the gentle sheep, he said. They make better wives and mothers. This is no doubt true. Women fortune-tellers, on the other hand, have looked at my *saju* and exclaimed, "You must have lots of fun in your life!" This is also certainly true.

This year, the Korean Community Center in Oakland sponsored a fund-raising party on the weekend before Halloween. We featured a DJ, food, and ten amateur fortune-tellers, most of whom were community activists. Since I was on hand early, I asked one of the fortune-tellers to tell my fortune. Among other things, he said that whatever shaped my goals and ideas happened to me between the ages of twelve and seventeen. This struck me as all wrong, because that period—the period between junior high and high school—was the unhappiest and most difficult period in my life so far. The fortune-teller was born in Korea and had never experienced being a teenager in the U.S. Maybe he thought me fortunate to have been living in the U.S. during the devastating Korean War of the 1950s and figured that I had been somehow inspired by the peace and prosperity that Americans, by comparison, enjoyed back then. I told him he was dead wrong, but he kept insisting that age twelve to seventeen was a watershed period for me, according to his numerology figures.

During and for several years after the Korean War, our house in suburban Maryland was often filled to brimming with Korean refugees to the U.S. who needed a place to stay. My parents were scraping by themselves, and I never seemed able to catch the attention of my harried mother, whom I remember standing for hours over the sink, steam curling the hair around her face, for she had to figure out how to stretch the tripe and vegetables far enough to feed a crowd. At times, there were wall-to-wall beds in both bedrooms, with no way to get across the room except to walk across the beds.

The other challenge I faced between the ages of twelve and seventeen was the disjuncture between the people and culture inside and outside our house. People inside my house spoke Korean, ate Korean food, and talked about what was going on in Korea. By the time I was twelve years old, 3 million Korean people had been killed in the Korean War and 10 million families had been permanently separated by the U.S.-USSR's division of the country at the 38th Parallel. Outside our house, though, no one knew much about or seemed interested in Korea. Most people who had ever heard of Korea thought that it was a state in Japan or China. I was used to being asked if I was Chinese or Japanese, as if there could be no other choices. My father said that the printing press and gunpowder had been invented in Korea and that a Korean marathon runner had won a gold medal in the 1936 Olympics, disproving Nazi Germany's insistence on the superiority of the white race. But no one at my school had ever heard of such things. Instead, I was taught that all of the world's great inventions and discoveries were made by Europeans and Americans.

I went to junior high and high school in the so-called "good old days," but I always think of that period as anything but.

While some might recall the 1950s as a time of easy upward mobility and material comfort, it was a period of violence and outright discrimination for many people of color. African Americans were forced to live in segregated neighborhoods and had to enter "white" establishments by the service entrance, if they were allowed in at all. Of course they were then as now victimized by the police, which arrested and harassed them just for being black. I still recall the "help wanted" ads in the newspaper, which read "jobs for men" and "jobs for women" and "jobs for whites only." That was many years before the civil rights movement and the 1964 Civil Rights Act that made it unlawful to discriminate against people because of their gender or race.

Although Asians, unlike African Americans, were allowed to live in white neighborhoods, my brother was taunted and beaten by gangs of white boys on a daily basis. I was harassed from primary school through high school by people holding the corners of their eyes up and calling me "chink" and "Jap." When our family members jumped into the car for our occasional vacation, which consisted of driving around in the Smoky or Blue Ridge Mountains, we worried about where we would stay, since we, along with blacks and Jews, were not welcome at the tourist homes along the way. Signs reading Gentiles Only were propped in every window. As a girl, I was not invited into white folks' homes, and when I was, the classmate's mother would tell me to go home and admonish her daughter not to bring me in again.

I think I was the only Asian in my class in high school. I know I was the only Asian female. In those days, most Americans treated Asians as foreigners. They often asked me when I came to America and when I was "going back." They complimented me on my English, unable to imagine that English could be my native language. I was treated as a perpetual outsider.

Determined to be "popular," my goal was to become a cheerleader. In that racial climate, for an Asian American girl to become a cheerleader was a near impossibility. Even Jewish girls were usually not chosen. Many girls wanted to be cheerleaders, but for me, the big white sweater with a huge chenille letter and megaphone meant instant recognition as a real American. I worked harder to become a cheerleader than at anything else, including schoolwork, because I thought it would prove that I wasn't a foreigner and that I deserved to be popular. I closely observed and then practiced cheerleading routines at every spare moment. I never passed the mirror in my parents' living room without doing some routine. When I was finally chosen to be one of the school's ten cheerleaders, my parents were puzzled that I would want to jump around and yell in front of people. But by that time, I had decided that whatever advice they could offer me about living in America was off-base. For instance, when I complained about being called "chink" or "Jap," they advised me to tell them that I was Korean, as if that would solve the problem.

I believed that being chosen to be a cheerleader was a major life victory for me. In a way, it was, just because it proved that I could do the almost impossible. In other ways, though, it sent me down a long path of digression. I could sit like a kind of pathetic mascot at the lunch table with the popular girls, wishing that my eyes were big and blue and my hair blond and curly, hoping that no one would ever see my parents, wanting to be something other than what I was. When I think about how I was then, I regret the relationships, the ideas, and the experiences I missed while I was wandering, lost down that lonely road toward a dead end.

The difficulties and confusion of my teenage years inspired me to want to learn about history when I grew older. I feel very fortunate to have lived long enough to learn about the history of U.S. racism and American women's and people of color's struggles for equality and social justice, which helped me better understand the circumstances of my teenage years, what happened to me, and why I responded as I did. Learning about the history of the U.S.'s involvement in Korea helped me understand why my parents came to a country that treated U.S.-born Korean Americans like me as foreigners.

It may be just as possible for a person's goals and ideas to be forged in difficulties and challenges as in comfort and happiness. So maybe the fortune-telling numerologist was right about my teenage years shaping my life's goals and ideas. These experiences may have stimulated me to work to educate people against racism and sexism. This work has helped me better understand myself and appreciate others.

Girlwind

what ha... ...some
you done to... ...injustices
...tried to...

Change

Emerging Voices for

Racist... ...woman...
sexu... ...essive...
Eco... ...of's

Good girls don't talk back, and they *never* yell.

People told me this all the time when I was growing up, but there were definitely some mixed messages, because I also heard the opposite.

If you don't speak up for yourself, nobody will. In America, we have the freedom to shout. You have a mouth, *so use it.*

The last time I remember hearing the latter was two years ago. For as long as our church has been open, we've been aware that there is a racist man who lives nearby. He has pulled childish pranks, like leaving nasty notes in the church mailbox, but he's never lashed out violently, so members of the Korean community never felt it was necessary to confront him. Then one day, the pastor discovered that the signpost had been vandalized. The words "Go HOME, Chinks" were spray-painted across it.

My parents phoned me at my apartment in New York City, where I was living at the time. Infuriated by the racist offense, my dad insisted that I write a letter in protest to our city newspaper and alert the television stations. I was surprised by my reluctance. Normally, I would have been all over this.

"Well, I'm not there, and I don't know the details about what happened—I really think YOU should write the letter," I explained. I knew what his response was going to be.

As one of the church elders, my dad was concerned about maintaining calm among the church congregation. It was critical that church be a peaceful environment. And by speaking out, he risked disturbing the peace. Even worse, he didn't want people to view him as a rabble-rouser.

"Well, you know, you are better at this sort of thing. . . . Daddy doesn't know how to write those kinds of letters."

I resisted the urge to show him the pile of cards that he and Mom had sent to me during college. The most heartwarming, eloquent, beautiful notes I'd ever read—a clear sign that for years I'd underestimated my parents' ability to put their thoughts and feelings into words.

As usual, when he doesn't feel like he's making progress in our conversations, he passed the phone to my mom. Likewise, she was outraged by the racist incident. I suggested that maybe she and Dad could get the pastor to mobilize other members of the church, call the press, and protest. Television camera crews had panned the graffito for a few seconds on the evening news, and a reporter interviewed a police officer at the crime scene, but nobody from the community had been quoted. I told my mom that, since the topic was already attracting media attention, it probably wouldn't be too difficult to get a reporter to cover their side of the story. They just had to make some noise.

I felt guilty about putting pressure on them to change their behavior, and I was making the solution seem easier to execute than it was. In my heart, I understood that my parents' beliefs were largely based on cultural tradition. But I also thought that these same beliefs were partly formed by habit. A bad habit.

When did we passively accept the idea that, while it was totally appropriate for me to yell and scream in the name of equality, it was totally absurd for my parents to yell (or to even write a missive, for that matter) about their grievances? Up until now, I'd been their delegate, speaking for them on cue.

My parents said that the older generation felt like their voice didn't have credibility "outside," and what they had to say would never sound persuasive enough. It wasn't a lack of compassion or cultural understanding that compelled me to challenge my parents on this issue. I just wished that they could experience the powerful, liberating rush and the gratification that come along with speaking out and engaging in activism. It pained me that they always heard their words filtered through mine. They only felt the joy secondhand.

In college I told them stories about Asian American men and women who were raising hell in literature, politics, and in popular culture. Later I discovered that, while I was gone, my mom was burying her nose in my course readers and textbooks. She especially liked Hak kyung Cha's *Dictee* and Nora Okja Keller's book *Comfort Woman*, she said, because she felt like she could easily imagine the settings and the characters. But even though both of my parents were captivated by modern Asian American movers and shakers, something stronger held them back from wanting to come out of their real-life comfort zone. They simply did not feel confident about engaging in political activism— I mean, beyond going to the voting booth on Election Day.

Eventually, I stopped pushing them. But all of their reasons for staying silent inadvertently made the fire within me grow stronger. On the day they asked me to write that protest letter, my mother told me something that made my insides stir.

"That's why your generation is different," she said. "You aren't the hope for change, you *are* change."

On one hand, I was relieved that I had reconciled this case of mixed messages. As a girl, I have agency. And as a girl, I am discovering different ways of expressing myself and, more specifically, of voicing my anger. When I am roused to anger, I can be powerful. When I choose to be silent, I can be powerful too. The power to change the world resides within me.

The skill of political self-expression was being mastered by girls who were much younger than I. Forward thinkers from all over the country sent me their mini-manifestos, political zines, and dramatic monologues documenting their fight against oppression. They engaged all kinds of controversy, calling attention to homophobia, racism, sexism, classism, size-ism, environmentalism. These young women were incredible—their courage, and their commitment toward improving the environment and raising social awareness about certain issues.

The last part of the anthology is a tribute to them, as well as to the

Asian American activists who, from the front lines, laid down the first bricks of possibility that now line our path. U.S. Representative of Hawaii Patsy S. Mink and her daughter Wendy Mink are two such role models whose work has transformed the lives of many. Each of the women's stories chronicles the challenges and victories they experienced on the road toward discovering their passion for political activism.

This chapter was the only one in the series that came together effortlessly and seamlessly. Passionate voices sang freely, and the writings fell into place. Movement from the first selection to the last was constant, relentless, creating a whirlwind effect—each fearless voice feeding it and adding to the momentum. Here we are, caught in a girl-wind. The forecast: swift, self-empowering, and fierce—capable of transforming lives and prompting others to action.

There is no better way to present the last portion of our project. Like the weather, and like the growing-up journey, the dialogue we've initiated in *YELL-Oh Girls!* has no ending point. "Girlwind" marks the last chapter, but it also marks an ongoing, wide-scale movement among Asian American girls who wield their pens to express themselves, as well as to engage in activism.

Hear the emerging voices of our Asian American sisters. They are the women warriors of tomorrow. Whether the speaker's cause is to fight for women's equality, to preserve the environment, or to dismantle stereotypes of Asian Americans in popular culture, she seeks justice. She dreams. And together, we unleash the spirit that rouses us to perform our work, so that others might also dare to change the world.

mai-linh**hong**21
Annandale, Virginia

The following poem is concerned with "history." It's in the voice of someone who's fed up with the commodification of history and culture to the point where she fantasizes about a world without either— where nothing comes from anywhere. The question I am asking others is if it's even possible to have or share culture without its being filtered through a third medium, be it a corporation or the media.

Ginseng from Starbucks

Soon in the suburbs
there will be no more coffee.

Newsweek says holistic
Asian living is the rage this
year. You want tea bags
tucked in bamboo crates,
shipped from a village in
California. Housewives,
buy your ginseng from
Starbucks and wear
chopsticks in your hair.

At Barnes & Noble,
a book will help you
raise your baby sensitive
and wise. Place
magnets by his temples
to stimulate blood flow.

I decline.
No packaged

monsoon winds will start
my morning. My coffee
shall be bitter, not exotic.
Chinese beaded bracelets
look like sacrilege and
cannot bring me luck.

I imagine
years later,
Amy Tan's descendants
will teach their children
Starbucks. A cup of
ginseng tea a day chases
your spiritual fears
away—that is Chinese
wisdom, daughter.

My children will believe
culture is for sale at
Pier 1 Imports. They
will think of history only
that it happened long
ago. Before this comes
to pass I will say:

Let me raise my children,
far away. I will teach them
to see nothing in the mirror
but themselves.

There will be no
Santa Claus, no
feng shui lanterns, no TV.

Come afternoon we
will drink coffee, black.
What we do not swallow
will disappear in steam.

I will not tell them where
coffee comes from.

This world is as it
has always been, children, but
it will end with us.

To me success means effectiveness in the world, that I am able to carry
my ideas and values into the world.

—Author Maxine Hong Kingston, as quoted in
Words of Women: Quotations for Success

 alaina**wong**19
West Windsor, New Jersey

*I love the written word, and often write as a way to unleash the
thoughts, which clutter my brain, as they come together at the tip of
my pen to form spirited musings. I fully believe in the importance of
standing up for causes that one feels strongly about, and in the
importance of Asian Americans exerting their voices in society. We
have been silent for too long—there has never been a better time to
dispel the model minority myth. Whether by writing letters of protest,
taking political action, or simply speaking out, it is important that
we do so.*

Just the Tip of the Iceberg: Letter to the Director

Like many other Asian Americans who live in this media-
saturated country, I often feel conflicted after taking note of the

ways in which we've been misrepresented. I'm appalled that people in the media, often people in the majority, think that they can take advantage of Asian Americans and other minorities because we won't speak out against them. On the other hand, I value creative freedom. So it's hard for me to determine whether I should support or dismiss these causes. I've always believed that it is best to choose your battles wisely, because it is impossible to fight them all. However, I've realized in the past year that choosing one's battles means (or *should* mean) ultimately choosing to *do something*, rather than passively sitting back and refusing to do anything.

The recent controversy over the *Mr. Wong* animated cartoon on Icebox.com, a flash-animated Web site, prompted me to find out more about it. I don't know exactly what motivated me all of a sudden. Perhaps I was just tired of sitting back and doing nothing while Asian American organizations across the country were sending out pleas to others in the community to join them in protest of the racist show. I finally realized that passively agreeing with the protesters, and griping about the problem to people around me was getting me nowhere. Furthermore, the fact that the cartoon seemed like a personal affront to my surname also could have pushed me over the fence into activism. Whatever it was, I'm glad that I chose to get involved in the protest against *Mr. Wong* because, in this case, the line between creative freedom and blatant racism had to be drawn.

I sent the following letter to eCompanies, the primary sponsor of Icebox.com, in protest of the *Mr. Wong* cartoon. My hope is that it will inspire others to get involved in Asian American causes. The first step toward shedding the model-minority stereotype is to take action. In view of the ways in which the media has reinforced negative stereotypes of Asian Americans, Icebox.com is unfortunately just the tip of the iceberg.

July 20, 2000

Jake Winebaum
Sky Dayton
eCompanies
2120 Colorado Ave., 4th Floor
Santa Monica, CA 90404

Mr. Winebaum and Mr. Dayton,

I would like to formally voice my support of the National Asian Pacific American Legal Consortium (NAPALC) in their protest against the cartoon *Mr. Wong*. By sponsoring Icebox.com and thus supporting the airing of this racist and derogatory cartoon, eCompanies is making a clear statement of its disregard and lack of concern for the Asian American community. As you may know, Asian Americans, who are at the forefront of the Internet industry themselves and are also a growing consumer demographic in this country, have voiced their concerns and discontent with *Mr. Wong*.

The cartoon's perpetuation of negative racial stereotypes, such as physical features, is especially insulting and detrimental to the welfare of Asian Americans because of the widespread lack of counterportrayals in American media. The eponymous title character of *Mr. Wong* is depicted as a hunchbacked, bucktoothed servant, forever subordinate to his superior Caucasian boss. Furthermore, the title of the third episode in the series, "Yellow Fever," is an outright reference to the term "yellow peril," a derogatory phrase used to refer to Asian immigrants. In response to Icebox's claim that they are "a revolutionary entertainment network dedicated to developing cutting-edge, original animated content," I would like to point out that, by reinforcing and lending credence to some of the oldest, outdated, and hurtful stereotypes of Asian Americans, Icebox is clearly not being original.

Mr. Wong's accent, and the way Miss Pam ridicules his speech, is offensive in and of itself. In addition, the fact that Mr. Wong's voice is provided by "writer" Kyle McCulloch, a non-Asian individual, is further demeaning and offensive. Mr. McCulloch is creating and mocking the accent deliberately. This situation is eerily reminiscent of the nineteenth-century minstrel shows that were widely deemed as racist to African Americans. In the first episode of the cartoon, Miss Pam even refers to Asians as "yellow people," using a term in blatant disregard and insensitivity toward more than half of the world's population. On the cartoon's Web site, Mr. Wong is referred to as an "eighty-five-year-old Chinese house boy." If I may ask, since when is an eighty-five-year-old referred to as a boy? This proves that the character is unquestionably meant to demean Asian Americans and perpetuate racism—upholding the stereotype that Asian males will forever remain "boys" in American society, subservient and unequal to their white peers.

Steve Sanford, CEO of Icebox.com, defends the cartoon by citing creative freedom. Yet, there is a difference between creative freedom and blatant racism toward such a large part of the Internet community. The company has also defended the cartoon by offering that the vice president of production is Japanese American. This, however, does not excuse its offensiveness—Icebox is merely resorting to the belief that it is acceptable to make racial jokes about one's own race. If the Icebox executives were more culturally sensitive, they would know that it is possible to be racist against one's own race. The truth of the matter is that it does not matter what one's race is—blatant racism and racial "humor" is offensive and unacceptable, regardless of the source.

Last, I take personal offense to the cartoon because not only does it stereotype the whole Asian American community, of which I am a part, it does a disservice to the thousands of people who share my surname. Just think of how you would feel viewing an offensive cartoon entitled *The Winebaums* or *Mr. Dayton*, which depicts a host of stereotypes commonly used to characterize those who look like you, none of which are true.

As a student at the University of Pennsylvania, and an officer in Asian Pacific American (APA) organizations on campus, I appeal to you to carefully consider the ramifications of your support for the *Mr. Wong* cartoon. It is up to you whether or not to discontinue the cartoon, or to modify it in some way. However, I strongly urge you to put an end to this offensive display. The APA community may be forgiving, yet with continued disregard for our interests, we refuse to be silent much longer. I hope that you will take our concerns into consideration, much of which is long overdue. The Asian American community is eagerly awaiting action or, at the very least, a response from eCompanies concerning the *Mr. Wong* cartoon.

Sincerely,

Alaina Wong
University of Pennsylvania
Fundraising Co-Chair, Chinese Students Association
Managing Editor, *Mosaic*, Penn's Asian American Literary Magazine

Asian people in general I think were considered to be more quiet, less articulate, and not as prone to entering fields that require a lot of communication. We'd pick fields like medicine or science because they're analytical and require less personal interaction. Now though, I think you're finding that in terms of the media, Asian women are becoming known for being assertive and outgoing. Many of us are now choosing this field and so in a lot of ways I think that image is changing.

—Jeannie Park, Executive Editor of *InStyle*

tressa anolin**navalta** 18

San Antonio, Texas

A Texan by birth, Filipina by heritage, and a military brat, I am currently a freshman at the University of Southern California. As a lesbian (and a Catholic, Asian American lesbian, at that), I have had a very interesting life, so far. I've even met my idol, Gloria Steinem, who is a very confident and strong woman. Since my "coming out," my life has taken a complete turn for the better and I am only now beginning to learn who I am, who God really intended me to be. I aspire to be a human rights lawyer and part of my life's work is the legalization of gay marriages.

One in Front of the Other

We march.
Our hearts provide the beat to which
my feet your feet our feet
march.
Boom-boom-boom-boom.
"Dyke!"
Yeah, so what.
"But you're Catholic. You're Filipino. You're YOU."
And?!
I march on, annoyed, perturbed.
I hold my sign high; Sappho would be pleased.
"Sinners!"
God, where do these people come from?
Boom-boom-boom-boom.
What color do you bleed?
Red. Yellow. Rainbow.
Choose one—call me what you like.
I am queer. I am Asian.
I am, I am, I am.

I "came out" in the spring of my junior year of high school. Perhaps I should set the scene: large Texan city with sprinklings of Filipinos, richly Roman Catholic, and, consequently, ridiculously conservative. So where's a queer gal like *me* gonna fit in?

Church.

Of all places, church had to accept me. Unfortunately, this only lasted until the winter of my high school senior year but three extremely good things came out of it. I learned to listen to God, to fight what I believe is wrong in the Church, and to love; I found someone to love. The separatist in me drives me to see the difference between homosexual and heterosexual relationships but the truth is if love is there, it doesn't matter who's radiating that fire. After all, love has no gender.

We all have different reasons for falling in love. I fell in love with her heart. Together, we formed such a formidable team that no one dared to question our morals. It's always amazing to see the link love forms between two people because this link never breaks, even if the couple breaks. You should admire one sometime. It's a sight to see.

My queerness is a gift from God. But being born a queer Catholic Asian is a curse, for me, at least. Restrictions bombard me every minute of my life. There is no respite in my life as a gay Asian, especially a Catholic gay Asian. When I was a child, I used to wish I were a different race because it seemed like my friends had fewer restrictions on their lives. Nowadays, I know that some rules were for my own good but restrictions on my heart and on my body were not.

I love being Asian. The smells from the kitchen before potlucks, the traditions during holidays, the clothes, the people, the music, and the languages always intoxicate me. Imagine how incredibly boring it would be if everyone were white or black. Yellow or red. Gay or straight. Although most Asians' smiles quickly turn to disapproving frowns when confronted with homosexuality, I still cannot help being drawn into my culture. These colors, smells, and sounds—this is me.

I have been told I am going straight to hell for who I am. *Putang ina mo*, how can people do this to their fellow human? And this, also, from the woman who sponsored me during my Confirmation (a Catholic sacrament in which we are "confirmed" in our Catholic faith). Yet, I feel the fire of the Holy Spirit in me every day. Is this the fire that awaits me at the end? If so, then I welcome it with open arms.

To you homophobic people, what drives you to condemn us? Is it born within you to single us out, to point your grubby little fingers at our pride parades, our public displays of affection, and our work? I am driven to dismantle your stereotypes because I am everything but the things you consider to represent a typical lesbian. I don't bash men. I don't dress like a man. I'm not even angry! (Frustrated, yes, but angry? Far from it.)

At times I feel like a walking abortion clinic. This isn't because of the abortion part, but because of the protests that occur at those clinics. (And while I'm staunchly pro-life, I do not in any way condone violent protests.) Thankfully, no one has become violent with me, but I am aware of the dangers as the daily news is filled to the brim with hate crimes directed at gays.

And so I enjoy women. Is that a crime? Is it a mortal sin? We all have crosses to bear, but this isn't mine. My queerness is a gift. It is branded on my Asian identity. I'm in love and she happens to be a woman. Try to blow me up. Just try it. I'm already on fire, baby—and in the meantime, I'll continue marching, one in front of the other. *Boom. Boom. Boom-boom.*

 l.w.18

Austin, Texas

> *In a letter, L.W. wrote: "Amy Tan's book was groundbreaking, no doubt, but people think that because it's so popular, it reflects all Asian Americans and their lives. But there are stereotypes within her work that people don't seem to think twice about, which really bothered me."*

After the Credits Rolled

"Weh-weh-waverly-ya!"

A favorite baby name for
Asian girls born in 1995 from
The Joy Luck Club

The "Asian American film"
based on
the "Asian American classic"
which made the bestseller's list

which made my shit list.

And just for the record—

I take best quality crab when eating
I have best quality heart when loving

White men aren't white knights
I'd freak Russell Wong over Andrew McCarthy any day
Not all of our mothers and grandmothers were
peasants or concubines
battered or suicidal

I'm in lusty love with a tender, Asian guy
and we'll never live in a lopsided house

Nope! No swan feathers, here. (*So soh-ree.*)
Mom tells me real-life stories in plain ole English

And just between you, me, and Hollywood's Old Boys Club

Geishas, picture brides, bar girls,
dragon ladies, sex kittens
mothers, daughters, wives harboring dark "Oriental" pasts . . .
WAKE ME UP
I'm bored to tears at 18

(Beside, the fat guy sitting in the back is snoring.)

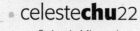 celeste**chu**22

St. Louis, Missouri

My awareness, sense of identity, and activism were slowly cultured,
although perhaps if I had had publications such as this while I was
growing up, I would have come to these realizations sooner. A lot of
the work I've done in the Asian Pacific Islander community has

been aimed at empowering women to become dynamic, intelligent, and articulate leaders in their chosen profession. My involvement in the anthology was spurred after editor Vickie Nam saw my student profile in an article that appeared in aMagazine *called "Big Activists on Campus."*

Learning by Example: Youth Activism in the New Millennium

Yuri Kochiyama, a wonderful example of a humanitarian, activist, and feisty lady who was a vital figure in the struggle of Asian Pacific Islanders, once said, "Education is consciousness-raising. Education is learning about history; often history that is not taught by those in power. And the young must learn the truth and continue the struggle." The truth began for me when I first understood that I was API. Did I learn it growing up in a predominantly upper-middle-class Anglo-Saxon neighborhood? No. Was it when I went to high school with about a dozen other APIs and joined the diversity appreciation group? No. Rather, I learned about what it was to identify as an API because of the Asian American Mentor Program (AAMP) at Pomona College.

Thanks to the help of my API mentors, I learned how to think about the way my ethnicity in this country is perceived, how I can go about learning more about my API identity, and what it is to be a person of color. And in the process, I found a supportive community that I had not felt in such a way before. It is like finding $20 in a pair of pants—you were not looking for it and it was something that was always there, but now that it has come to light, you can revel in your new gain. To celebrate the discovery of my API identity, I became an AAMP mentor. This was my first opportunity to recognize the needs of my college campus and produce programs to address those issues. For my last two college years, I was an Asian American Resource Center intern, where I created new programs like Developing Leadership Skills in Women of Color, which consisted of panels of colored women in academia, film showings on courageous women leaders, and a weekly discussion on race.

College is a fantastic time to get involved in any area that you may have not been exposed to in the past; there is a particular kind of freedom of expression and exploration that is steeped in the (hopefully) open and eager minds of classmates and professors. However, I thought that in medical school, the precious time, energy, and resources found in college would be left behind just like dorm food. I knew that people who devote their lives to community service and activism do not stop their diligent and often thankless work, and others find ways to incorporate these good deeds around their work schedule. Yet, as a medical student at a top-notch school, I was unsure as to how to incorporate activism for the API community into the memorization of all the nerves in the body and making sure that I was sleeping at least seven hours a night. Therefore, I was quite relieved that APIs do not stop their work simply because their location and workload change; activism does continue on into graduate schools. One of the best examples of the continuing presence of graduate students on the API activism scene is the APA Medical Student Association (APAMSA), a national organization of API students in health-related schools and physician advisers. APAMSA's mission includes providing a network of students and professionals to combine into a powerful public and political voice. Also part of the mission is the culturally competent care of the API communities that raised us. As the new membership vice president, my new role in APAMSA is to get more people involved, whether it be a new chapter at their school, finding donors to support APAMSA's projects like the Hepatitis B project, or increasing our membership pool. It suffices to say, APAMSA is a fantastic link to continuing the work I have done for and within the API community.

The reason why I regurgitate my résumé is not to tell you what to do with your time nor receive kudos for work I have done nor shamelessly promote the various institutions to which I belong. I share my story to demonstrate that awareness and acceptance of your identity, and that work to promote understanding of the culture, can happen anytime, anywhere. Whether you examine me from the outside by observing the shape of my eyes or you observe me from the inside by the values I hold, I am an API, and this knowledge has allowed me to see myself as a person of color. Even if you just learn more about yourself, you are creating good in the world. Yuri Kochiyama also said, "all humanity can be affected in a positive way if everyone took the time to raise their own consciousness." So, as stated by my colleague Kim Ta, you can still be an activist and "not live off of a nonprofit salary." You do not have to drop everything to be an activist. Blend it into your own life, in whatever career you choose. Each of us makes different priorities in our lives; you can make activism *a* priority if it is not feasible to make it *the* priority.

However, it is not just what we do that progresses the movement of APIs. We should always recognize that the hard work and devotion of people of color gave us the foundation and momentum to carry us through our battles. What state of affairs would the human race be in without the likes of Gandhi, Cesar Chavez, Norman Mineta, Martin Luther King, Jr.? Those with name recognition are not the only ones making a difference. A small grain of sand can make a magnificent pearl given enough time to develop; imagine the string of pearls created if all of us took the time to donate our grain of sand. This is the conceptual basis behind the activist musical group A Grain of Sand, who gave voice to the struggles of activists in their songs from the birth of Asian America when they sang:

It's been throughout the ages,
We have seen it move in stages,
They can chip away until it's gone.
We can decide to make the rules,
Or decide to play the fools,
We can be the player,
Or merely the pawns.

By yourself, you are just by yourself.
Together we can all take a stand.
By yourself, you are just by yourself.
Just look at my children walkin' hand in hand.

leanne**nakamura** 17
Kaneohe, Hawaii

My parents, Lorene and Waring Nakamura, grew up in Hawaii—
my mother in Kahaluu, and my father in Honolulu. Editor Vickie
Nam approached me after she saw an article about me in the
"Local Hero" section in the August 2000 issue of Teen People. *In*
writing "Global Impact," I hoped that other girls who read my
piece would think about the things that they care about, and create
a project close to their hearts that can change their community.

Global Impact

When I started dedicating my time toward community service, I
would often hear the comment, "You're just one drop in the bucket,
how can you possibly think you can make a difference?" It wasn't
just strangers and acquaintances who questioned my reasons for
getting involved in the community, it was also a question that I
occasionally asked myself.

Growing up Japanese American, my mother always taught me
humility. "Never be too proud," she used to say. I decided that
activism did not conflict with modesty, wondering, "How can I
possibly think Leanne Nakamura can make any type of difference
in the world?"

A year ago, I struggled with self-doubt. Was I actually making a
difference? As I contemplated volunteering at various organizations, I continued to question my commitment. What if I wasted six
years trying to make a positive impact on people's lives, and I
didn't accomplish anything? Was all that hard work for nothing?

When I turned to newspapers, radio, and television shows, I noticed how the focus was always on teenagers who were getting in fights, murders, and accidents. The media seldom directed the spotlight on teenagers who were improving the community.

After volunteering for a children's summer camp in 1994, I wanted to find more ways in which I could get involved in the community. Volunteering was something I wanted to do all the time, not just during the summer, so I joined Key Club (a community service club), where I worked with a diverse group of people, mainly organizing local events. When an environmental project surfaced, my first thought was, "Eww, bug bites, dog doo-doo, bugs, mud, bugs, dirt, bugs, itchy weeds. And did I mention bugs?" Besides, I thought that Hawaii was beautiful enough already, and that the environment didn't need any help. After all, I thought, I lived in paradise.

Every day I wake up to the sound of birds singing in the morning. When I drive through Kahalu'u, I face luscious green mountains; the heavy rains call me to witness sparkling waterfalls as well as the colorful rainbows that are left behind after the storm.

My opinions changed when my life crossed paths with Y.E.S. (Youth for Environmental Services). In 1998, I attended a convention where I listened to them deliver speeches that transformed the perspective I had on my role in the world.

Being a member of Y.E.S. made me realize that I had to help preserve paradise. We are taking paradise for granted, and our environment is slowly deteriorating. During the convention, I remember seeing two pictures which will remain with me always. One showed a person dumping rubbish into the stream in someone's backyard, and the second revealed a little plant struggling to grow amid trash and weeds.

While I still wanted to help people, I discovered that by helping the environment, the environment would inspire others to strive for a better world as well.

I also joined the Castle High School's One World Club in 1998. In the following year, our adviser, Mr. Erik Kenner, brought my attention to the fact that fishnet was causing erosion on Kualoa beach and endangering marine life. The nets captured and entangled the creatures, leaving them on shore until they eventually died. "No one is doing anything about it," he said to us during a lunch meeting.

When nobody else wanted to take on the project, I volunteered. Mr. Kenner helped me with the first step of the project: to obtain information on how to start cleaning up the beach. I called the list of contacts nonstop, walking around my living room with the telephone cord around my neck and the receiver pasted on my ear. After two weeks of making calls, someone actually returned my message. Unfortunately, in this case, persistence didn't pay. The voice at the other end told me that I shouldn't pursue the cleanup mission.

"There's no fishnet there!" the person insisted. "We searched the entire beach, and it's gone—the government must have taken it away."

As president of Student Actions and Values for the Environment (S.A.V.E.), a grassroots organization whose goal is to clean up the island of Oahu, I organized a team of twenty volunteers to clean up the beach; I was not going to tell them that they couldn't. So, instead of a fishnet removal, we had a general beach cleanup. In the process, however, Mr. Kenner found fishnet buried under a layer of sand. We scrambled to find knives so we could cut the ropes that were tangled with the netting.

The "men" on our team congratulated themselves for physically hauling the net out of the water, but the "women" knew who *really* did all the work. We used our brawn *and* brains to untangle, cut, and dispose of the fishnet. With the combined efforts of strong male *and* female Samoans, Hawaiians, other Asians, and U.S. Marines, we pulled the entire three-ton load of fishnet out of the beach. We organized a follow-up cleanup every three months following that first cleanup, and it took us approximately half a year to remove the rest of the nets.

Making changes our environment began with a complaint. Whoever said complaining was a bad thing? In our situation, it was the first step toward making a difference. Thinking back, the most exciting, rewarding aspect of the entire project wasn't that we were cleaning the beaches; we were educating volunteers about beach erosion. We were also learning the true value of being volunteers, who were taking responsibility for the environment. In the end, all of us walked away from the project with a piece of the earth in our hearts.

> Sometimes I wish Hollywood would take more risks with casting. . . . Why can't a person of color be the main character on a show that doesn't have anything to do with what the person looks like?
>
> —Actress Lindsay Price, in an article that appeared in *Teen People* (June/July 2000)

jean**phan**19
Rosemead, California

> *As they fled Vietnam with my two brothers in tow, my parents held the hope that the child in my mother's womb would not have to endure Communism's grasp on freedom. Born on 1980 in bustling Los Angeles, I was the symbol of my parents' strength and courage. I wrote "Screening Asian Americans: More Asian than American?" as a response to the exhausted stereotypes of Asian women depicted in the mass media. I seek to make a difference by screaming in the face of adversity and having my voice heard.*

Screening Asian Americans: More Asian than American?

As an Asian American, movies and television shows are constant reminders of my minority citizenship. It's rare to see an Asian American character in a blockbuster film delivering lines in fluent, American English, while appearing comfortably acclimated to the American culture. I find this representation offensive because I don't speak Chinese, nor do I know kung fu. And, I eat burgers and fries just as often as the average American—a fact that might surprise you, since people of Asian descent on the big screen are practically never seen eating everyday, Western grub on the big screen. We are always shown eating typical, "authentic," Oriental food—usually rice—using chopsticks. (How clichéd.) Just for the record, I didn't learn how to use chopsticks until I was ten, and I prefer to use a fork.

So, what does this mean to me? To be honest, I feel alienated. As a child, I rarely saw any Asian people on television or in the movies, and if I did, they were sort of like stage props serving as people in the background. The majority of the lead roles are scored by beautiful Caucasians with blond hair and blue eyes. It's no wonder that as a child I wanted to hang out with white people; like how Slater, a Latino teenager, tried blending in with everyone else in the hit television series *Saved by the Bell*. I even found myself attracted to Caucasian males in my younger years because of the stereotypes embedded in the cartoons I watched. I mean, remember Prince Charming from Cinderella? It's still difficult for me to imagine a nonwhite Prince.

At one point I even wished that I could be seen as "normal," like white people. Being normal meant that I could somehow have blond hair and blue eyes, so that I, too, could be rescued by my blond-haired, blue-eyed prince. The harsh reality surfaced, though, when I realized that I wasn't white and could never be perceived as being white. I was the typical, run-of-the-mill Asian girl living in the background of the television show called Life.

It's hard to relate to what's being produced by the media these days. Take Jackie Chan movies, for instance. Yeah, Chan is a great martial artist and all (can you name an Asian actor who isn't?), but his characters seem defined by the fact that he knows kung fu and speaks choppy English.

Would he have become the Asian American blockbuster king he is today if he spoke perfect English and preferred performing Shakespeare? Would the moviegoing public shell out eight bucks to watch his movies if he looked like a "whitewashed" Asian man who couldn't jump-kick if his life depended on it? Not to mention his resemblance to actor Jet Li, who is another martial artist (surprise, surprise). You can just hear people asking themselves, "Are these guys brothers or what?" And, why not? They both have stereotypical Asian features: small eyes, heavy accent, and that classic coif Bruce Lee made famous. The impact of these stereotypes has hit so hard that some people have questioned whether or not I'm half white just because I have unusually big eyes and because I am fluent in English. And other people have actually come up to me and asked if I could teach them a few karate chops. Being both Asian and American, this comes with the territory.

These images have had an astounding effect on Asian Americans, too. I realized this when, in my communications class, a fellow Asian American announced, "My English isn't very good—as you can see, I'm an FOB. (Fresh Off the Boat)!" Then he started laughing. His English wasn't that poor, and I never would have guessed that he was a recent immigrant based on his speaking skills. It was obvious to me that the stereotypes in the media had affected him. He acted out the part beautifully and with gusto. He had become exactly what the stereotypes said he should be: an immigrant, an FOB, a cliché.

In light of all this, there are Asian actors who appear to defy stereotypes—but even they fall short of making a difference. Take Lucy Liu, for example, who plays the role of Ling Woo on the hit series *Ally McBeal*. Ling is a strong, independent Asian woman, who is employed as a prominent attorney, with a kick-ass wardrobe to boot. Sounds pretty good, right? Well, not for long. Take a closer look, and you'll discover that she's also a catty bitch who serves as arm candy to Fish, her white boss. Fish did not hire Ling based on her merits, but rather because he was turned on by her exotic, sex-kitten attitude. Talk about reinforcing yet another chronic stereotype of Asian American women!

Regardless of how much you differ from a stereotype, people will always see you in light of how you "should be" according to the images carried through television and movies. Think about how many hours an individual spends in front of the television compared to how many hours an individual spends having a real conversation with someone. The lack of communication between people of diverse ethnic backgrounds prevents us from actually getting to know each other based on one's character, as opposed to one's skin color. If we all just stopped watching television long enough to speak to and understand each other, we might be able to dispel myths and stereotypes. The problem is, most people have gotten used to stereotypes, and they view people who diverge from the norm as troublemakers. Furthermore, it's obvious that stereotypes sell; otherwise, you wouldn't see these images portrayed repeatedly in the media.

The nation is growing and the population is becoming increasingly diverse. One can only hope that there will be a wider range of TV shows and films, which project new ideas of what is "American" and what is "Asian American." Perhaps then we will finally see the old myths and stereotypes fall away, making room for real progress.

april bonnie**chang**21

Chapel Hill, North Carolina

Born and raised in the south, where I go to eat my mom's stir-fried collard greens. The Revolution has relentlessly challenged my identity as an Asian American and as a female, and it is for this reason that I feel compelled to write about my experience in activism at Wellesley College, an all-women's institution. It is important that I write about my experiences with activism to document for my Asian American sisters and the broader Asian American population that activists do exist in this community regardless of how we might be portrayed.

The Revolution

There are two reasons why I absolutely must be vocal, stubborn, and aggressive: I'm Asian American and I'm female. With these demographics, I am railroaded into silence before a conversation has even begun. You could say that I've lived the majority of my life unconscious. Not only was I unaware of my own identity as an Asian American, but I was completely oblivious to the insidious forces that were working against me—stereotypes, presumed passivity, immunity from my vitriol. The more aware I became of the walls surrounding me, the louder I spoke to make my voice audible, and the more boorishly I behaved. I wanted to break all the stereotypes that could possibly be applied to me. Meanwhile, my rage continued to grow. I spent time venting in what are essentially unproductive ways, until the Spring of 2001, when my activism was no longer limited to individual battles in my daily life. I have long harbored the energy and outrage necessary to fuel a protest, but it was not until certain events came to pass at Wellesley College that I felt compelled to make my outrage manifest.

I spent the first year and a half of my college career on the ever-progressive West Coast at Pomona College. Although Pomona students were involved in their own struggle for Asian American studies, the college did offer a few courses under this heading, and one of them was Asian American psychology. By some act of serendipity, I was able to push my own internalized racism aside and sign up for this course. The impact this course had on my self-concept and identity was significant, concrete, and phenomenal, and it is for this reason that I became adamant about developing Asian American studies as a formal academic program when I arrived at Wellesley College.

Asian American psychology. Some might be so ignorant as to ask if such a thing even exists. In fact, I signed up for the course during my borderline Asian-in-denial days, and I believe that part of the reason why I did so was to find the answer to this very question. I was curious to find out exactly what scholars were purporting to be the psychology of an Asian American. What I found in that class, however, was more than just the meaning of the term "Asian American psychology"—I found my identity, and I found a sense of belonging that I had never thought possible. From within the four walls of that packed classroom, I gained a clear picture of my place in American society. Moreover, I was faced with the reality and universality of my own experiences. The very private conflicts I had experienced growing up at the intersection of Asian and American cultures were exposed and recognized as predictable facets of the Asian American experience.

It is imperative that other Asian Americans have the same opportunity that I did—the opportunity to realize that the Asian American experience is a shared one. Institutional acknowledgment of the very unique experience of Asian Americans not only validates the existence of a distinct culture belonging to Asians who are also Americans, but also helps to solidify societal awareness of an Asian American community. Wellesley College's egregious deficiency in this academic field became a significant source of discomfort for me once I enrolled in the college, and, thus, I sought to help this critically acclaimed college usher in a more complete curriculum. I began by joining Wellesley Asian Alliance (WAA) as the Asian American studies representative. From the time it was established, part of the purpose of WAA was to push for the development of Asian American Studies at Wellesley.

During my first semester in this position, I started small. Over the years, the fight for an Asian American studies major had been progressing, albeit slowly, and it was agreed among former Asian American studies representatives that at this point there were a few areas in which our efforts could be concentrated. Thus, I worked on those key areas, which were very controlled, calm, and patient means of lobbying for Asian American studies. I talked to faculty, encouraged student interest, surveyed students about their interest and willingness to take Asian American studies courses, and encouraged students of Professor Elena Creef, the only Asian American specialist on campus, to write letters of support when she was evaluated for tenure in the fall of 2000.

Much of WAA's hopes and dreams for a more fully developed

Asian American studies program rested on the tenure of Professor Creef. Thus, when it was announced that Professor Creef had been denied tenure, my activist motor kicked into high gear. Significantly more was at stake in this decision than the fate of a professor's career. The little that does exist of an Asian American studies program depends almost entirely on Professor Creef's courses. It was therefore a significant blow to Asian American studies–supporters that Professor Creef was denied tenure. With the decision to let Professor Creef go, the college essentially had decided to negate years of efforts to diversify the curriculum and complete the college's American studies program. In response to this affront to Wellesley's much-touted multiculturalism, I began brainstorming with other concerned students.

By the time the spring semester began, many students were quite outraged at what we came to see as a continued neglect of multiculturalism and, particularly, of the Asian American community at Wellesley. In response, WAA called a meeting for all concerned individuals to plan direct actions to respond to the decision regarding Professor Creef. At this meeting, we began to discuss the many wrongs we felt we had suffered at the hands of Wellesley College and soon drew up an extensive list of our grievances, followed by a list of demands that we wanted the college to fulfill in response. It was at this time that the Wellesley Asian Action Movement (WAAM!) was born.

I suppose I have been one of the more passionate members of the resultant movement (a.k.a. The Revolution) and I feel that my heart and soul are encapsulated within it and its goals. For me, The Revolution itself has become as important as the concrete things for which we are fighting. A fellow "revolutionary" once asked me why I continue to be involved in the movement when it is so exhausting: in other words, why am I so passionate about it? I actually had to stop and think about this question, and it became clear that a large part of my own stake in this movement is simply that I want to ensure that people see that Asian Americans, and particularly Asian American women, can be loud and aggressive. Indeed, organizing the movement has been exhausting, frustrating, and often depressing, and there have been numerous times throughout this revolutionary roller coaster that I have considered resigning. What has kept me going, however, is my rage-motivated concern that this movement that is led by Asian American females be loud and visible. I want to be there to guarantee that it is.

The Revolution is more than a fight for overdue resources. It is a fight to shock people into seeing that Asian Americans can be more than hardworking stalks of bamboo that bend and sway with ease at the blows of societal punches. It is an opportunity to shove yellow skin into the faces of the media, "the majority," and the college—all entities that have a history of selectively forgetting the existence of my skin tone. My aim is to force it down the throats of mainstream America that yellow means power and strength. Yellow can no longer connote cowardice as it did in the days of yesteryear.

Concretely, the purpose of the movement is to obtain certain resources for the Asian and Asian American community on campus. More abstractly, however, the movement has been a challenge to the administration to force it to evaluate the attention, or lack thereof, that it gives to people of Asian descent. I believe I speak for all involved in this movement when I say that one purpose of The Revolution has been to hold a mirror up to Wellesley College and force it to examine its own imperfections. Unfortunately, out of pain and neglect, we the students have had to take it upon ourselves to show Wellesley the institutionalized racism it propagates. I realize that my words may give the impression that Wellesley College revolts me. What I find revolting, however, is not so much the college as it is the ignorance fostered by American society, which allows such fine institutions as Wellesley to believe that they aren't racist.

oliviachung 19

Silver Spring, Maryland

I am appalled to find people who think racism no longer exists in American society today. This piece recalls evidence from the past awell as personal experiences in hopes of showing such people that racism, whether subtle or blatant, most definitely exists and most definitely affects them. As a student, I actively speak out against social injustice in search for a brighter and harmonious future.

Untitled

At first glance, they looked at my face and prepared themselves in advance
For what kind of person I am, an *Asian*.
I watched them uncomfortably guess my "original" nation.
Chinese? Japanese? Malaysian?
This is the overplayed scenario like the replayed songs on the radio,
Over and over like there ain't no end to it yo

Since the first day of school I heard it.
Ching chong chinaman chinky winky twinky
DO YOU SPEAKEE ENGLISHEE?
From the first moment, I felt it.
Can you really see through those eyes?
Oh how cute, two oriental girls. Are you twins?

I listened to their ignorant remarks as their sharp words **pierced my heart**
I allowed them to form my identity and tell me who I was
Bruce Lee, Michelle Kwan, Yan Can Cook and so can you!

Because pigeonholed, it was all I was told.
Aren't you gonna be a doctor?
All Asians are good at science right?

So now you're thinking,
"What? Things like that don't happen to me. I hear no evil, I see no
   evil, hear no evil, see no evil . . . no evil."

You tell me you don't know what it means to be Asian,
born and raised in a white nation, you're third generation,
"I've never *seen* discrimination.
I've read about Hitler and his evils of intended entire elimination of
   Jews.
I've heard about Rosa Parks with the blacks at the back of the bus
   laws—to obey, she refused.
But me . . . I've never *seen* discrimination, never *felt* racial humilia-
   tion, never *experienced* segregation.

So you know you're Asian if you leave your shoes at the front door.
That's your definition of tradition. You consider yourself Asian on
   this one condition!

I am who I am, I be who I be
I am who I am, I be who I be
People will see me for me and award me for ability,
Praise me for attending ivy league
Hire me for working so hard, so hopefully
Holding onto a vision of my future reality . . .

But . . .

What if they fire me?
Look at Dr. Wen Ho Lee—
Maybe innocent, maybe guilty
Targeted unfairly 'cause of his ethnicity

"You know dem chinese. They're either restaurant owners or spies"

I despise the lies seen in society's eyes

See, even though
I am who I am and I be who I be
People *can't* see me for me.
That's the reality.

Can you hear the evil? Can you *see* the evil?
The sugarcane harvesters, sweatshop workers, picture brides, interned Japanese Americans . . . all the immigrants who came with high hopes seeking liberty stretching from sea to shining sea, singing my country 'tis of thee, sowing seeds of strife in hopes of better life . . . sacrifices and sweat, sacrifices and sweat, sacrifices and sweat, and sweat

These people faced persecution in the form of piercing painful prejudices pointing at them at every place . . . political pariahs, unable to speak their piece, unable to
speak peace.

That is why I get offended when you ask me where I'm really from.
That is why I fight for justice while obstacles continue to come.
That is why I call myself Asian American.
I am who I am, I be who I be
See me for me,
Then you'll get the reality.

So my big thrust when I go on interviews with the Korean media is to say, "You must—when you see that your children are interested in the arts—push them toward that, encourage them, inspire them because it is through the arts that our voices will be heard."

—Author Helie Lee, in an article that appeared in *AsianWeek* (June 28, 1996)

___ • mia chan mi**park**

Chicago, Illinois

> *Chicago is my home, where I am grateful to have the opportunity to sing, drum, and write songs in Kim (a pop-rock, punk-out, all-female Asian band); drum in Pook Nury (Korean female group that plays traditional Korean and modern Western drums); volunteer in Asian community organizations; co-own a CD duplicating business called Dig It All; teach kick boxing and cohost Chic A Go Go!, a Chicago children's variety show. "Waving Fans" talks about some of the challenges I've faced as a member of a female Asian American rock group.*

Waving Fans

Fans and critics often ask us if we face Asian female stereotypes in our profession, but the more challenging question is, when have Asian women NOT been labeled as exotic, submissive, quiet, and servile? Part of Kim's mission is to update and overthrow these antique stereotypes by rocking the world!

When I tell people that I am the drummer for an all–Asian American female rock band, I don't expect to be taken seriously. There aren't any other bands like Kim in Chicago, let alone in America, so I don't expect the masses to comprehend that, YES, women rock, and that, YES, Asian American women also rock . . . and we rock hard, dammit!

What I do expect from the uninitiated is that they give respect to my band mates and me for taking creative risks and for being committed to raising social awareness. I sometimes notice that when people hear about Kim for the first time, they respond blankly or with a humored grin, especially men.

This summer I was passing out Kim flyers at a Korean language class for our show at the Chicago Chinatown Street Fair. Two male students, a Korean American and a Caucasian, just did NOT get it.

Imagining Asian American girls engaged in aggressive self-expression was too taxing for either of them. They laughed, and asked super-stupid-obvious questions like, "You guys are a rock band?" after I'd just explained, "Here's a flyer for our rock band."

The Korean American guy wanted to know if we sang in English. "Of course we do, we're an American band!" I retorted. The white guy looked smugly at the Korean American guy and sneered, "Yah, right, an *American* band."

Standing up to leave the room, I looked at both of them and sang my heart out: "WE'RE AN AMERICAN BAND! We're coming to your town, We're gonna party down, WE'RE AN AMERICAN BAND!"

Okay, so idiots like these guys obviously don't understand that Asian Americans don't have to sing in Asian languages to play music. On a deeper level, I'm sure they discredited our band even more because we are women. Neither one of these shallow fellows came to our shows, which is fine by me. Still, I would have loved to prove to them that their minds could use some blowing, and if any-one could do this, we could!

I thought about my encounter with the two guys again—the white guy, in particular. I wondered what his Korean American wife would have thought of our band if she had actually listened to our music. But when I was explaining Kim to her and her ignorant husband, clearly, I ended up wasting my breath trying to legiti-mate our band. I remember how she just sat there looking at me with this blank stare.

I just kept thinking about how much I would have LOVED to teach this woman a few guitar chords and throw her on stage in front of hundreds of curious music lovers. She'd know in an instant why I think being in an Asian American band, and kickin' it with other Asian American women rockers feels so comfortable, so empower-ing—and, well, pretty fucking cool.

I grew up in Whittier, California, and I just received a BA in American literature with honors from UCLA. Currently I'm enrolled in the selective New York City Teaching Fellowship, where I am simultaneously working on a master's degree in education and teaching sixth grade in Brooklyn. After I complete the two-year fellowship my goal is to make documentary films on issues concerning urban youth. "My First Film" was inspired by my determination to start a celluloid revolution in Hollywood.

My First Film

I've always been obsessed with movies. As a child, watching movies felt like living in another world, even if it was just for a few hours. When the movies were over, I was forced to confront reality. I would often pretend that my life could merge with the lives of characters I saw in films. When I was four, I pretended that Elliot from *E.T.* and Arthur from *The Sword in the Stone* were my two dearest friends who regularly attended my afternoon tea parties. When I was twelve, I identified closely with Eugene Morris Jerome, who was a budding writer conflicted with his bicultural identity, from *Biloxi Blues*. It didn't occur to me that my protagonists were all boys who looked nothing like me.

Eventually I became tired of living in these celluloid worlds. By the time I reached adolescence I started hating my life. When would my life be as good as the movies? I often wondered. The only thing that was supposed to look anything like me on TV or in the movies was that fobby guy in *Short Circuit* or Abu on *The Simpsons*. Both of these characters were played by white men, whose accents weren't like mine, or like anyone else's I knew, for that matter.

Would I ever get to experience the sort of adventure those prepubescent boys had in *The Goonies*? When would I ever undergo a personal transformation like those teens in *Dead Poets Society*? And when would a South Asian girl from East Los Angeles ever get her chance to capture the world's attention?

I quickly realized that there was only one way for me to this. I had to make my own movie.

It's been six years since I came to that realization, and I haven't shot my movie yet. I have a script and a plot, and I've been consulting with many different production companies. I keep having to change my script around to accommodate the Wall Street bankers who will fund it. But in the meantime I have a somewhat solid synopsis.

My first film is going to be one of those cops and robbers movies. A pure testosterone flick with pimps and hos, violence and ultraviolence, sexual violence, and sexualized violence. There will be no plot development, no three-dimensional characters—just random, naked women and guys, who allegedly have penises as big as the guns they carry.

My first film will be real. No fantasy at all. A documentary, in fact. A day in the life of Mark, a Korean pimp who lives it hard. And Gaya, a Bengali cop from East Los Angeles who will do anything to protect other women, even if it means being topless for three-quarters of the movie. Costarring real sinners in the flesh.

The Wall Street bankers want all of my characters to be white or black or of some marketable ethnicity but I've convinced them that if this is going to pass as real life, we'll have to stick with a Korean and a Bengali. It's all being contested. Of course, my movie is going to be a documentary, but it's all scripted, so maybe "mockumentary" is the real word for this movie. But everyone will be made to think it's real. Kind of like *Dateline*.

Gaya is about sixteen years old, muscular, tall, with frizzy black hair. She has unsightly hair on her arms and on her upper lip. It's a dysfunction that comes with being Indian. She looks nothing like Amanda Peet in *The Whole Nine Yards*, her inspiration for becoming a topless warrior. At first I was uneasy with the idea of asking a minor to take her clothes off. And who ever heard of a sixteen-year-old cop anyway? But this fifty-year-old exec at one of the production companies, Tom, convinced me to turn Gaya into a special agent. And as for my reluctance in asking underage actresses to take off their clothes—he told me to watch *American Beauty*. I realized that gratuitous underage nudity could possibly win us an Oscar for Best Picture and hundreds of millions of dollars in revenue. Then it also occurred to me that instead of having one sixteen-year-old girl take off her clothes, we should have two eight-year-old girls take off their clothes, and that way we'd be even more successful than *American Beauty*. But I think I want my mom to see this film so we draw the line with one naked sixteen-year-old. Of course, this idea was the source of much debate with Tom.

"I didn't think you were hung up on morals," Tom said to me, his teeth clenched. "*American Beauty* wasn't trying to be moral. It wasn't supposed to be moral. That was the point."

"This is not a morality issue," I cried. "This is something else. This is about the removal of human dignity."

"Femi-nazi." Tom shook his head, then went about his business.

I was so upset, I couldn't articulate myself anymore. If Kevin Spacey was a black man chasing after a naked blond sixteen-year-old, do you think America would have accepted this misogynistic bullshit? Fuck no. And this isn't even about hating men. This is about humanizing women. But I'm not here to rant and rave about *American Beauty*. Sometimes when I get a little too angry I tend to go off on tangents. So back to my story.

Mark is a Korean pimp who markets drugs and hos to finance his big-time underground computer-parts business. He aces SAT classes in his spare time. Gaya is ordered by the LAPD to seduce him into a drug bust. Gaya meets Mark in a bar. Homeboy never gets any action, so when he sees Gaya, he thinks, "Aha! There's that ho who flashes her goods everywhere. I'm gonna get me some of that tonight!"

Gaya notices Mark and busts out with an English accent to seduce him. In a drunken stupor she finds herself onstage, singing a song by Boy George. The big twist, however, is that Gaya is really a man. After they go upstairs to her apartment, they start making out, and then flop! Out comes Gaya's penis.

Mark is stunned.

"Don't worry," she consoles, "my breasts are real. Just like Jaye Davidson's in *The Crying Game*."

The film continues with a graphic sex sequence. Gaya is supposed to carry on with the drug bust, but she's fallen for Mark and hides him from the LAPD. And then there's a countertwist. Mark is really a stone butch lesbian, trying to pass as a man in a patriarchal society, which doesn't allow him to transcend gender and sexual boundaries. The ultraviolent pimp and ho movie turns into a psychosexual thriller with random rebellious genitalia coming at you in every direction. And what's more rebellious about this movie— the nudity and the sex come to a spontaneous halt. The sex, nudity, and random genitalia were just eighty minutes of fluff, which was needed to please the distributors. Conveniently, eighty-one minutes into the movie Gaya realizes that not wearing clothes in a Hollywood movie is counterproductive to her feminist agenda and leads to the societal degradation of women.

Then my first film reveals its true self, a political manifesto. Once Mark and Gaya reveal their true sexual identities and engage in some violent lesbian intercourse, they team up as partners, determined to save women in Hollywood. They get ahold of several different synopses of projects in production and decide to figure out which one will do the most damage. Among them, they find a Korean prostitute with a heavy Oriental accent who falls for a fat-ass white guy (as seen in *Waking the Dead*); a Korean woman who plays a Chinese Canadian who falls for a sociopathic white guy (as seen in *Double Happiness*); exotic South Asian women who dance around naked for three-quarters of a film (as seen in *Kama Sutra*); prepubescent Chinese girl off the boat gives dorky white man a massage and a boner (as seen in *Two Days in the Valley*); Chinese woman who can't speak English fucks Richard Gere and gets him into jail (as seen in *Red Corner*). The list goes on and on and on.

Finally Mark and Gaya have a winner. They find themselves on the set of *Very Bad Things* and just before the Asian sister is about get killed, they kill all the white actors, who are about to fuck her over. Then they jump out of the screen and kill every man and woman in the audience, who has paid $7.50 each to watch an Asian woman get naked, fucked, killed, and chopped up into pieces. The credits roll.

Of course, this story is completely different from my original synopsis. There wasn't any sex or nudity in the original. There were no transsexuals, no hot lesbian action sequences, no Korean pimps, no rapes, no Bengali topless cops, and no flashy genitalia. My first film was supposed to be my life story, a coming-of-age drama about a South Asian girl who grew up in struggle on the East Side. Unfortunately none of the production companies were interested. For six years I had a crazy idea that I'd be able to hand my script to someone with dignity, and tell them, "This is me. This is who I am." What a load of crap. As I see it, the only good news is that my ending stays. The celluloid revolution is about to begin, although I'll have to work in chains for a while.

So then you ask yourself where's the leadership? The leadership is going to come from people who have the capacity to identify with what their heritage is, but understand that is not all that they are and not all that they want to be.

—Activist Angela Oh, Clinton-appointed member of the Advisory Board of the Initiative on Race Commission, in an interview with the youth of KYCC (Korean Youth and Community Center)

rupal**patel**20
Ann Arbor, Michigan

I am a student at the University of Michigan. My mother and father emigrated from India during the 1970s and eventually settled in the state of Michigan. I have a twin sister, with whom I

struggled in white, middle-class suburbia as a child. My conscious-
ness emerged during my university experience and I was inspired to
write this piece from my observations. I plan to pursue public pol-
icy and law centered around racial and ethnic minorities in the near
future.

Coalition Building Among People of Color

It amazes me how difficult it is to mobilize Asian Pacific Islander (API) college students around issues of racial inequality—espe- cially those who attend the top twenty-five institutions in the United States.

We've been so wrapped up in our success that we are blind to our history and to the millions of brothers and sisters who still remain underprivileged in this country. We have bought into the media portrayals of "successful" APIs—the CEOs, internet start-up masterminds, and other science and technology geniuses. I will not devalue the celebration, but why forget about the Chinese immi- grant brought over in the bottom of a ship as recently as 1997, trav- eling for hundreds of days across foreign waters, to be subject to subhuman working conditions and income in cities like New York?

Why not speak out about the U.S. government and businesses that continuously grant entry permits to thousands of APIs across the waters for their own economic purposes while white Americans discriminate and attack us for "stealing their jobs"? Does the white man have us so deep and comfortable in his own pockets that we choose to stand by? We need to critically think about why we only hear the success stories of our people on television and radio and why we never hear about the effects of poverty in the many urban areas heavily populated by API communities. Black and Latino communities have success stories just as we do, so why do we only hear about them as impoverished? It is intentional on the part of U.S. media.

We as APIs are pawns in the game of racial inequality. Let other minorities think we are treated better than they are so they will direct their anger at us rather than those who actually hold a place in the power structure. Then, force us to believe that we are more successful—the "model minority"—than other nonwhite communities so we can aid the white man in oppressing them. It is pure genius if you think about it and we as APIs have been falling into the trap. Every API has been victim to the brainwash including myself and every API has either suffered or helped others suffer because of it. We must overcome this forced socialization and remember how other communities of color aided us in achieving a better way of life.

The civil rights movement of 1965, initiated and led by the black community, granted us certain rights in addition to their own. It was their energy, commitment, and sacrifice that gave us our opportunity to claim and fight for our rights. Issues such as affirmative action, minority retention, and ethnic and black studies are our issues as well. How many Southeast Asians and Pacific Islanders are in the top twenty-five institutions? How many are retained and how many are given the opportunity to be admitted despite their inadequate educational opportunities?

As APIs who are presented opportunities, it is our responsibility to critically assess our part in societal race relations and do all we can to help our people and others as well. No one has ever made it on his or her own. Someone sacrificed and spoke to help each person achieve. It is up to us to do the same and we need to start today. Organize with the API community and organize with other communities of color. Only as a collective will we force change.

kristina sheryl**wong**21
Los Angeles, California

I am the Webmaster and creator of a popular mock mail-order bride/Asian porn site spoof called www.bigbadchinesemama.com. A published writer and active performing artist, I've guest lectured in university classes up and down California and at various arts and APA conferences. Later this year, I will be a subject of a documentary on "Revisioning the Dragon Lady." Currently I live in LA ("Hell A") and San Francisco and do a damn good Guns N' Roses medley on the karaoke.

A Big Bad Prank: Broadening the Definition of Asian American Feminist Activism

"I am an anti-geisha. I am not Japanese, I am Chinese. There is a difference between the two, you know. I have gigantic size 9 feet, crater zits that break out through my 'silky skin' before and after and during my period, and a loud mouth that screams profanities and insults and my mind. I have a little potbelly, I have an ass that needs to go to the gym. I have hangnails and calluses and blisters and baggage (emotional, historical, and whatever the hell else kind of baggage that is keeping HIM from taking a chance on someone who actually gives a shit about herself). . . . I am a beautiful animal." (From my "Memoirs of an Anti-Geisha" link on www.bigbad-chinesemama.com)

It all started because I was feeling like I never had ample means to represent myself. College graduation approached, the real world peering over the horizon. What was my college career but a mishmash of theory, half-read books, a dozen hangovers, papers written in one night, a bit of modern dance, and some daydreams about stardom hiding in the back of my head? I worried about my unhealthy fear of computers making me pretty unemployable. And my classes, which were winding down to the final few days, were driving me nuts. Asian American studies, which had previously been enlightening, had become repetitive and numbing. I was getting sick of dissecting Asian women stereotypes with the same classmates quarter after quarter. My senior project was approaching and I winced at the thought of writing one more paper in a night to be seen by only me and my professor, and to find its fate tossed away in a recycling bin. For my senior project, however, the medium was broadened from type and paper; I could create anything—a documentary, exhibition, research paper, or other medium that would reflect a culmination of my studies.

I was surfing through Asian women's Web sites for an Asian women's writing class. I noticed some Asian girl Web sites were bannering, 'This is not an Asian porn site!" at the bottom of their splash pages. With the presence of Asian women on the Web probably being 97 percent Asian sex sites, statements like these were made in defiance to the cross-traffic from people who fell upon their sites in search of porn. Then I had an idea. To trick people mid-pursuit. Why not willingly intercept the efforts of nasty men and school them?

I wanted to skip academic rhetoric altogether and just screw with people. I would trick my audience into visiting me by marketing my site as porn! Slip in a little critical theory and social analysis—voilà! I would find the perfect audience, a mix of people who are and are not educated on Asian American and social justice issues, in an accessible, changeable, malleable, though, most of all, humorous format. I wanted to do more with my education. I wanted to spark a dialogue with people who might not choose to go to college or take Asian American studies and women's studies. I wanted to take a stand for myself. I wanted to debate with people, and for people to debate among each other. I chose to use the format of a mail-order-bride Web site as a response to the blatant racism, Western stereotyping of the East, and sexist attitudes that are typical of Asian sex sites.

If you have never been to one of these sites before, let me offer you a preview. First, generate a list of stereotypes for Asian and black women ("black" I say specifically because in the world of porn women are stripped of political identity). For black women, you might enter words like "Big Mama," "Big Booty," and "Rump Shaker" into a search engine. The results are usually all black porn sites. For Asian women, you might enter words like "exotic," "demure," and "petite" and get Asian porn sites. For Latina women I have found that entering "Latina" into the search engine yields enough Latina porn sites to skip the guesswork. Then examine the imagery and language used to describe black women in porn sites. The layouts are crude, the women are emphasized for their "big booty" and ability to "fuck like animals." And then look at sites featuring Asian women. They are described as "horny sluts," "sushi-to-go," and are featured alongside "chopstick" font and Chinese characters. East and West are almost overemphasized and in all the pictures the men are white and occasionally black. Take a tour of a mail-order-bride/Thailand-sex-tour site by entering "mail-order bride" into a search engine (by the way, here you will see my site listed too). Study the language and the sections of the site—how the women are said to be "a fantasy," "exotic," and "faithful." (This is why I picked the subversive title of "the Big Bad Chinese Mama"—to mix up racist expectations of pornography). In particular, look at the "Frequently Asked Questions" section. The procurers of the site answer such pressing questions as "Why are Eastern women better wives for Western men?" and "Do these women speak English?"

It was a difficult process. Not only did I need to learn HTML with no background in computers, I was constantly asking myself how much of my life I should divulge to an audience that would be adverse to my site. I did not set out to praise "Asian American" identity, expose the hidden realities behind Southeast Asian women forced into the sex trade industry, or attack "the Man" as the root of the problem. My goal was only to satirize the blatant racism perpetuated by Orientalism and to spoof anger itself. However, I make a playful critique of all three of these and am often misconstrued as putting forth a brutal and confused argument. I spoof a mail-order-bride catalog in my link "The Harem of Angst," finishing it off with a "not so exotic" collection of "brides." I also answer "Frequently Unasked Questions"—questions from actual bride sites answered on my terms. I also spoof Orientalism in photo-shopped, two-headed china dolls, and present my take of Arthur Golden's *Memoirs of a Geisha* in my "Memoirs of a Anti-Geisha." There are also sound bites of prank calls to "Introduction Service," porn studios, and massage parlors. So much of putting up the site was getting over the fear of having my image seen by people who might be looking for porn and trying to predict my audience's reaction. Nevertheless, all the panic paid off.

My site launched, my professors were supportive, and the reaction has been tremendous. I have also done extensive guerrilla marketing to draw more traffic to my site. All of the tactics are intended to draw in both Asian audiences who may or may not feel camaraderie with my work, as well as non-Asian audiences. My tricky tactics include placing line ads in the adult classified section of the *New Times LA*, spamming to porn-swapping clubs, linking to Asian American organizations, intercepting the efforts of pants-down surfers in chat rooms, and sticker campaigns via my exhausted color printer. I keep an unedited guest book to monitor my feedback and reflect upon the reality of my audience. As anticipated, much of the feedback is negative. And every couple of weeks, a lone appreciative note of feedback will come and bury itself between "Fuck you, gook, shut up!" and "Asian women ARE sluts." Despite criticisms that my site shouldn't pass for academic material, some universities are eating it up and adding the site to their syllabi. Most of them are attracted to the radical way I am representing race and gender. Others are intrigued by the "no-fear" policy I have in addressing people who are and aren't in the community. And not just Asian American Studies classes, but media/journalism, art/design, and women's studies classes have all invited me to speak. I have given guest lectures in these classes and have been invited to speak on panels.

Do I think I've met success in my project? Consider a guest book message I received:

"In my experience in Asia, Asian countries find it as almost a birthright to exploit their own people by defining 'class.' Asians have a strong dislike for one another but given a common enemy they will band together. So, all you white people (like myself) who are angry and/or complain—my advice to you is to just leave the Asian swine alone, they will destroy each other. . . ."

So the site fails as a perfect spoof because not everyone is laughing. My audience is addressed abrasively and is left feeling accused, defensive, and insulted. The material hedges on being more scathingly political than lighthearted and amusing. I seem to drop the names and incidents of racial discrimination and world globalization, but only leave more questions unanswered. I do not edit crude comments in the guest book, leaving them open to debate, but this only creates more anger and frustration. Maybe I should do what any sensible Webmaster would and delete the foul messages in an effort to keep them from coming back. Maybe I should do line-by-line responses to the messages, and show people who are posting who's the boss. Maybe I should remove the guest book altogether, leave my own "message," without allowing feedback to taint the impression I am trying to make. But is that what social dialogue is—only engaging the voices of those who can speak articulately? Only engaging the people who are interested in the issues rather than those who refuse to acknowledge the problems in race relations? There is no point to try to hide the problems of race relations, to delete the reality check, and cover up the hate that is a reality in our community.

And although the site's URL is www.bigbadchinesemama.com, too many visitors confuse it as www.all-asian-people-conveniently-defined-in-one-website.com. People write me every day telling me how my fierce opinions are incorrect. Anyone from a man who claims to be in the KKK, a black man who spent a night in a Thai whorehouse, a white woman who is dating a South Asian man, and an Asian man who has not experienced racism—all sign my guest book and claim to have a better understanding of Asian women than I do. But I am only representing myself. My hope is that more Asian women will take advantage of the Web to intercept the overwhelmingly negative presence we hold on the Web. We need to stop waiting for other people to speak on our behalf and start building the spectrum of voices that actually exists. And I am definitely the last person on earth qualified to speak on behalf of anyone other than myself.

marites l.**mendoza**18
Pasadena, California

My parents came to the United States from the Philippines in 1974 and have struggled ever since to climb the socioeconomic ladder and to make a life for themselves and my three sisters. Pasadena, California, is my hometown, but right now I'm attending the University of California, Berkeley, studying English and political science. I never really liked to acknowledge my Filipino identity because assimilation is the key to success in America, but I realized when I got to college that it's unavoidable when interacting in society. I'm still trying to figure out who I am and what I want to be.

Model Minority Guilt

There it was.

My palms were sweating, my mind was racing, and I couldn't bear to put my eyes on the page, much less my fingers on the typewriter. For most students, the most painful part of college applications is the essay, or reporting an especially low SAT score or GPA. For me, it was Checking the Box.

Statistics from UC Berkeley's and UCLA's booklets said I had a 50 percent and 75 percent chance, respectively, of getting into both schools based solely on grade point average and test scores. Too bad the grids didn't factor in race. Supposedly, race wasn't supposed to be a factor anymore in UC admissions. But I still felt that being Asian American was more of a liability than an asset, regardless of my academic records. In my mind, this was the year admission committees would institute a de facto affirmative action in response to falling minority admissions, leaving Asian Americans out in the cold. As random as Berkeley and LA admissions were already, this added factor threw any stat out the window.

On paper, I was an above-average student, or as above average as one gets coming from one of California's neglected urban public schools. But nothing in my application jumped out and said "admit this girl NOW." In the days of affirmative action, I would have been on the losing end when compared to the thousands of other minorities vying for a spot at Berkeley or LA. How was I to convince admissions committees to choose me over a minority who may or may not be as qualified as I was?

Here was the dilemma: my last name is Mendoza. What do you think my background is when you first hear that? Latina? Hispanic? Would you even guess that I'm Filipino? More importantly, what would Berkeley think? I played the imagined dialogue between admissions committee representatives in my head over and over:

ADCOMM 1: Look at this applicant. National Merit Scholar, president of Asian American Club, founder of battered women's shelter . . . impressive.

ADCOMM 2: Yes, but how about this girl—went to a disadvantaged school in LA, scores are not that high but her grades are stellar, middle-class family, very involved in the community and in school . . . she didn't check the box, but I'm pretty sure she's Hispanic. Think of all the obstacles she had to overcome to get where she is!

ADCOMM 1: But we only have one more spot left!

ADCOMM 2: The Mendoza girl should get it then! We only admitted fourteen Latinos so far . . . it wouldn't seem fair. Let's just make it a round fifteen.

ADCOMM 1:   True. And it'll raise minority admittance figures. Hopefully that'll shut those liberals up.

So, what to do? Mask my ethnicity for this one time and not take my chances? There were no traces of my background in my application or essay; no membership in the Asian club or acceptance of any Asian awards. All I had to do was leave the box blank and leave the rest to the readers' imaginations. It wasn't lying . . . it was merely omitting an item that was optional in the first place.

The more I thought about it, the more I tried to rationalize. Among the Asian American populations at the top two UC schools, how many were Filipino? We're a minority within the group as it is; we could use more representation in the state's public universities. I was no wealthy Asian American who attended private or "blue ribbon" public schools, either. I received the same half-ass education that many minorities in California receive. So in a way I was doing a favor to the Asian American working-class community . . . right?

But there was still that tugging feeling in the corner of my mind, the corner that holds my sense of ethnic pride. Why should I even have to hide my background? If I get into a school, I want them to want me for all I am, including my ethnicity. Even more, why the hell should it matter if I'm yellow, white, black, or brown? It was all very vexing, to say the least. Despite all my reservations, there was one cold hard fact that would dictate my decision. I wasn't going to let myself get rejected from schools I felt I deserved a spot in. If not checking the box meant an extra boost in the process, then I would use it. God knows California education hadn't given me a boost in any other respect.

So I sent the application for Berkeley, LA, and San Diego, box unchecked.

I finished my first year at UC Berkeley a little over two months ago. Throughout that year I was astounded at the sheer number of Asian American faces I passed by each day. And I was ashamed at the absence of anyone nonwhite and non-Asian.

This is not to say that I felt my actions were the sole cause of a homogeneous student body. I did feel, however, that I somehow stole a space that rightfully belonged to a minority who could have given some color to a campus that falsely prides itself on its diversity.

But do I regret trying to mislead admissions into thinking I was Hispanic? Oh, hell no. I have to watch out first and foremost for myself. But I feel for the hundreds of thousands of minorities who also got gypped by the California education system and now have to hide or exploit their ethnicities, just to get a quality education.

I direct this tirade to all the politicians and conservative voters in California. I resent the fact that quibbling, mostly white officials dictate what happens to public education in poor urban areas populated mostly by minorities, when many of those politicians were educated in affluent private schools. I resent that the system puts us in subpar schools as children and then expects us to compete against each other for a spot in college, not to mention students from better schools. I don't want your affirmative action; yes, it puts us on the same "playing field" in college, but minorities walk on that field facing opponents who have new uniforms and world-class coaches, while we don't even have a locker room. If you really want to be fair, try providing inner-city children with the same tools and opportunities presented to kids in wealthy suburbs.

And for those who say minorities just have to "work harder" to get where whites and some Asian Americans are now, I say stop pitting everyone against us with this "model minority" shit. I refuse to be your poster person for policies that don't give support where support is needed.

Congresswoman Patsy Mink was born in Maui, Hawaii, in 1927, and is of Japanese descent. Representative Mink has devoted her entire adult life to public service. Currently, she serves as a member of the U.S. House of Representatives from the Second District of Hawaii. High on her list of concerns are gaining economic equity and gender equality for women. She resides with her husband in Honolulu, Hawaii, and Washington, D.C.

Like her mother, Wendy Mink has devoted her adult years to the study of politics and is actively concerned with women's issues. Mink was born in Chicago in 1952, and grew up in Hawaii. She says she has been a feminist all her life, and she has worked for the Equal Rights Amendment, welfare rights, reproductive rights, pay equity, and sexual safety for women. She is now a professor of politics at the University of California, Santa Cruz.

Excerpts from *The Conversation Begins: Mothers and Daughters Talk About Living Feminism*
BY PATSY MINK AND WENDY MINK

A Mother's Story

I became interested in Democratic politics through friends who pulled me into party workshops and seminars. One thing led to another, and soon I was elected to the state legislature. Campaigning took a lot of time, and much of my political activity in those early years I did alone. Equal pay for equal work was one of my early achievements. Male legislators got up on the floor and ridiculed the legislation ("Equal pay?"), but in 1957, they voted for it. We took pleasure in the fact that Hawaii adopted the bill six years sooner than the nation. As a representative, I helped open up state government after noticing that it was always the same people who served on important commissions. "A lot of talented people want to serve," I said. "Give them an opportunity." In all, I served three terms in the Hawaii legislature.

When I first ran for national office in 1959, I lost by 8 percent. Losing felt awful. It's terrible enough to be rejected by just one person, but to be rejected by thousands you thought were in love with you is devastating. That's why most people don't run for office. You can run again only if you believe strongly that you have something to contribute. After losing, I said, "Never again," but soon I reentered local politics and was elected to the Hawaii state senate in 1962. In 1964, a seat opened in the U.S. House of Representatives, and I decided to seek national office. This time I campaigned for federal aid to education, which became law my first year in Congress. As a representative, I pushed for equity in education. . . .

Wendy, in sixth grade when we moved to Washington, D.C., expressed little opinion about my politics during her teenage years. While attending the National Cathedral School, she went through a rebellious period—the usual stubbornness and resistance against the school's authoritarian discipline. She didn't dare miss classes, but when special events were scheduled, she'd slip off to Georgetown instead. The school would call and say, "Your daughter missed such and such, and we don't know where she is. You'd better look for her." We'd find her, looking self-conscious and conspicuous, hanging on the corner with a group of kids watching the crowd. She was also politically active—mainly against the war in Vietnam. Once she got to college, she began to appreciate more of what I had done and the changes I had advocated.

Wendy is far ahead of me now and much more radical in her politics. I consider her an activist, but I don't know what did it—perhaps osmosis and my constant lecturing on the fundamental principles of equity. I've probably been tempered over the years, so she's going to have to take my place as a rabble-rouser. Wendy has continued my work in the different but equally important arena of academics. She has certainly, at great risk to her future, become a champion of those principles on the campus. She was involved in a successful Title IX discrimination complaint regarding a campus rape because she felt that the victims were not accorded proper protection, nor the rapist adequate punishment. She is an uncompromising firebrand. I have to admire her.

I think Wendy has found satisfaction in her life. She has found her niche and is growing with it spectacularly. The University of California has given her many responsibilities, which she carries out with great relish. Recently head of the system-wide affirmative-action committee, she served as conscience for her coworkers regarding issues of equity, justice, and fairness. As a parent, I am proud of her academic achievements and proud that she is not just an academic. . . .

I am a feminist—one who cares about the role of women in society—but I do not believe the women's movement is broadly enough based. In limiting itself to a certain segment of society, it leaves out the rest. Millions of women, such as those on welfare, are not connected to it, but I don't see the feminist movement getting involved in welfare reform; women of color are the only ones who care about this issue. I would like to see preschool childcare become part of the official educational programs so that childcare workers' pay is comparable to that of teachers. Childcare workers are currently paid less than animal-shelter employees. Why aren't feminists campaigning for better salaries for childcare workers? Is an animal more precious than a child?

The women's movement still focuses on middle-class white women, which I don't see changing. The "glass ceiling" is an upper-class ceiling for those aspiring to be bank presidents and executives, not those who can never rise above the minimum wage. The majority of people working at minimum-wage jobs in the United States are women. That's the glass ceiling I am committed to doing something about. American women must stand up and be counted. The new women in Congress have absolutely made a difference—forty-nine is better than twenty-nine—but to get more women into office, it must be easier for women to run. If we could just persuade women to support more women candidates, more would win.

Politics has kept me on my toes. To continue in it, one has to look to the future. I hope to look to the future. I hope to stay in Washington as long as I can, but the moment I can't compete physically, I'll quit. I don't think I paid my price for my dual role as career woman and mother, but a supportive husband made it easier for me to do what I had to do. After forty-three years, John and I are still married. He has served as my manager for seventeen campaigns and is still at it. . . .

I have no regrets. My greatest achievement has been balancing my family and my career—taking care of my parents when they needed me and being available for my daughter. You do your share and others will be willing to do theirs. You can't be a casual observer of your life; you have to be prepared to commit a whole lot to make it work.

A Daughter's Story

Growing up, I never felt alone, but I did feel different—both from people I went to school with and from people in my own family. This stems, in part, from the fact that I am mixed-race. My father is the only white person in my mother's extended family. Also, my mother is a professional, which was very unusual when I was growing up. Many of my classmates assumed that I was different, and lonely, because I didn't have a "real" mother. They assumed that my mother was unavailable to me because she worked outside the home.

In truth, much of the time she was gone from home, I was with her. We went shopping, to political rallies, to coffee hours. When I was in elementary school, I would often go to her law office after school. She shared a suite with my grandfather. My grandmother worked for him, so I would hang out with them. My mother was always active in politics, even when she was practicing law. I wasn't lonely when she wasn't around, though; I was usually with my cousins or with friends. It wasn't as if my parents made a choice to pursue a public life at the expense of a private one; they took me as many places as a four-year-old could reasonably go. I was completely integrated in their lives.

My mother was elected to Congress when I was twelve. I was proud of her, but I had always felt proud of her. Her fame was just a part of who she was, so it seemed natural to me. But moving to suburban Washington, D.C., was a culture shock. The fact that my mother was Japanese, against the Vietnam War, and a feminist in a culturally conservative town didn't win me many friends. Discrimination in Hawaii had shown itself in silly things, such as other Japanese American kids assuming I didn't know how to cook rice because that wasn't part of my complete genetic profile. They were not unfriendly; I just had the sense that they saw me as different. Not until we moved to Washington did I experience out-and-out racism and learn what it was to be "other" for white people.

At first, we lived in Arlington, Virginia, and I went to a public school there. Under Virginia law at that point, miscegenation was illegal; *Loving v. Virginia*, a landmark case, had not yet been decided. This was 1964 and 1965. The white kids called me a "Chink" and told me to ride in the back of the bus and made fun of me for not dressing like them. (I wore knee socks instead of nylons.) Once, in high school, I agreed to accompany a friend on a blind double date, and when the guy showed up, he threw a tantrum, saying, "I am not going out with any damn Filipino." Other people treated me as an exotic, asking me when I learned to speak English or if I wore a grass skirt all the time in Hawaii. To some I was a Jap; to others, a Chink. As Vietnam heated up, the word "gook" was added to the arsenal.

I spoke out against the prejudice. I answered it. But that is what you live with if you're not part of the dominant culture. You find ways of coping by learning to direct your anger in creative ways like politics or the arts, or you repress it, or you explode. I chose the political path, attending my share of civil rights marches and antiwar marches not only to express my feelings but also to participate in some process of public political education. Sometimes, I reported instances of prejudice to my parents, and they would get angry and want to intervene on my behalf. Other times, I wouldn't tell them, because I didn't want to spread the anger any further.

They taught me to try to put things in perspective by insisting that racism is an unfortunate pathology in our society, which we might work to get rid of, but it wasn't about me; it was about other people's myopia. Talking with them about my experiences with slurs and discrimination helped me to get rid of the immediate aftertaste and to decide how to cope with my feelings. Early on, I decided that fighting inequality would be a central part of what I ultimately chose to do with my life.

I was different from my friends in a political sense. Most of them had come to their politics through rebellion; I didn't have to work toward my politics that way. For my friends, going to a march was a defiant act, whereas my parents would say, "Can we come along?" Sometimes I rebelled against parental discipline (once or twice I didn't call home and missed curfew on purpose). But my parents were not very strict, and I didn't present many challenges to them on those fronts.

From the age of twelve, I was politically active on my own terms. My first antiwar march was in April of 1965, on the Mall in Washington. I went with my father and was converted to the cause from that moment forward. As a high-school student at the National Cathedral School, I helped organize mobilizations against the war and marches against hunger in Africa. With friends, I put out an underground newspaper, I wrote a lot, and I debated these issues in debate club. The administration of the school and the majority of students were utterly hostile, but there were fifteen or twenty of us who could be very persuasive.

As a student at the University of Chicago, I became involved in antiwar activity; we marched up and down the streets, waiting for Mayor Daley to send out the clubs. I directed a voter registration drive and was an organizer in the community where I lived. In 1972, I transferred to Berkeley, where I knew I'd find a more culturally and socially diverse student body. I also imagined that there would still be some political vitality there. But although there was some third-world organizing, the antiwar activity had basically stopped. The Me Generation and a lot of drugs and taken over.

Joining the women's movement was a natural move, and as soon as things started happening with the younger branch of feminism, I knew I was allied with it. How I wanted to connect directly, I wasn't really sure, but I always thought of myself as a feminist. Fairly early on, I was involved in the choice issue. In 1970, I interned in Senator Kennedy's office, where I worked on the issue of abortion statues in different states and how women's rights were balanced against the medical-necessity arguments. I have sustained an interest in reproductive rights ever since. . . .

As a professor I have continued to be politically engaged. I chaired the Status of Women Committee for six or seven years; I do a lot of work on sexual harassment; and though I teach politics, I make it a point to teach courses that count for women's studies credit. I teach a course on women and the law, or feminist jurisprudence, and another on U.S. social politics, which is a race, class, and gender course.

I think that everybody who considers herself a feminist is at least fundamentally contesting the sex-gender system and the power and domination under which we live. But there are many different feminisms and many different feminist agendas, not all of which are happily reconciled with one another. Being a woman of color in a largely white movement means that there have been plenty of moments when I felt exoticized or regarded as marginal to the conversation, or even the exception that proves the rule. Not wanting to separate myself from feminism has meant struggling to find ways to build bridges—bridges that can bear the weight of differences among women. I am not yet satisfied with what we have achieved. . . .

My mother is a highly regarded and effective legislator. I hope that the kinds of policies she cares about actually come to pass. Serving as a member of Congress is shockingly exhausting work. I'm always concerned about her working too hard. She gets a lot of pleasure out of her work, and that is not what I object to. I worry about the long-distance travel, the relentless schedule, and her long hours.

My mother was a good mother in that she always let me know that she cared and that, in a fundamental way, I came first. Many things claimed her attention, but I knew that I was her first priority. If I needed her, she would be there. We were not particularly close when I was in high school; I wanted distance to create my own independent way. I wasn't rejecting her. I was just finding myself. I think it is important for a daughter to carve out her own path. Not that my mother wanted me to be like her; she always made it perfectly clear that I should do what I want to do. She conveyed a sense that I needed to make my own choices. A good feminist model, she taught me that while it may not be easy, living your life in accordance with your own expectations is perfectly possible and terribly rewarding.

Epilogue

When I was putting the proposal together for this anthology, I encountered many skeptics. They wondered if Asian American girls would be interested in this type of book. Moreover, they doubted that I would be able to organize a scaleable team of girl writers who were capable of generating enough relevant, well-written stories addressing issues surrounding culture and identity. ("Do you *really* think Asian American girls are thinking about themselves critically at that age?") The lack of statistics from market research and analyses indicating that Asian American girls represented a viable consumer group made it that much more difficult for me to package *YELL-Oh Girls!* in a way that would win many people's support. I had to conduct independent research by going out in the field to find other credible sources.

We need only go back a couple of months to find an example where people relied on flawed "research" to legitimate executive decisions—research which, according to leaders in subsequent debates, failed accurately to reflect the voices of Asian American girls. Last spring, toy manufacturer Mattel, Inc., launched the "President 2000" Barbie line. Company spokespeople suggested that an Asian American Barbie, for various reasons, would not appeal to girls of Asian descent, and that these observational inferences legitimated their decision to omit the doll from the collection, which included an African American, Latina, and Euro American version.

It is fair to say that the e-mails I was receiving from girls during and after the debate offered different interpretations of what was *really* going on. The company's attitude reflected a general lack of knowledge when it came to knowing and understanding the needs of the Asian American–girl consumer group. Stereotypes fueled their decision-making process. And no real effort was being made to gather more reliable data. I am aware that many of the girls who wrote to me about their grievances also directed formal protest letters to Mattel. Let's hope somebody—anybody—at the company was taking notes.

So, then, how are we to gauge the progress of Asian American girls if we do not actively engage with them? More specifically, how can we as a community inspire girls to express themselves and talk about the conflicts they face? In what ways can we dismantle stereotypes that continue to stifle our voices? And how can we build more channels of communication with young women in our lives?

In the last days before I am scheduled to deliver the final manuscript to my editor, the list of questions I've compiled since the book's genesis is still growing. I have often wondered, who am I to ask these questions? I am not an adolescent psychologist or a counselor. I am not a professor, a lawyer, or any sort of teen "expert." I am just another Asian American girl. Curiosity and passion led me to seek others' insight in the process of making sense of my place in the world. That said, my stake in this project was never to present an all-encompassing narrative or finished portrait of Asian American girls. On the contrary, this work is unfinished—it invites others to carry the torch and carry on.

YELL-Oh Girls! signals a movement among girls who are tired of being spoken for. And for those who are seeking guidance and support from peers, family members, and mentors, it's a way of reaching out. It outlines reasons why we should initiate and support more collaborative creative projects that showcase young emerging artists. It presents a wide-lens snapshot of our outspoken, diverse, and dynamic community, and it's an endeavor that will set millions of wheels in motion, starting an ongoing dialogue that will hopefully bridge cultural and generational divides. As the editor, and as an Asian American girl, I feel blessed to have been a part of this amazing work, and I pray that *YELL-Oh Girls!* will fill pockets of possibility with brilliant ideas. That it will spur each of us to think about ways we can prolong the conversation we've started here—one that led so many girls to come together, to speak out, and to be heard. In my heart I believe that this book is the first of many victories to come.

PERMISSIONS AND ACKNOWLEDGMENTS

Grateful acknowledgment is made for permission to reprint the following

"My Mother's Food" by Nora Okja Keller. Copyright © 1997 by Nora Okja Keller. First published in *New Woman*, September 1997. All rights reserved. By permission of Susan Bergholz Literary Services, New York.

"Then and Now: Finding My Voice" by Elaine H. Kim. Copyright © 2000 by Elaine H. Kim. By permission of the author.

Revised poem "Who Is Singing This Song" with lines from "Breaking Silence" by Janice Mirikitani. Copyright © 1999 by Janice Mirikitani. Reprinted from *Shedding Silence, Poetry and Prose by Janice Mirikitani*, Celestial Arts Publishing, 1993. Reprinted by permission of the author.

"When Asian Eyes Are Smiling" by Lois-Ann Yamanaka. Copyright © 1997 by Lois-Ann Yamanaka. First published in *Allure*, August 1997. All rights reserved. By permission of Susan Bergholz Literary Services, New York.

Excerpt from "Welcome to Washington" from *Asian American Dreams* by Helen Zia. Copyright © 2000 by Helen Zia. Reprinted by permission of Farrar, Straus and Giroux, LLC.

"Patsy Mink and Wendy Mink: A Mother's Story and a Daughter's Story" by Patsy Mink and Wendy Mink, from *The Conversation Begins: Mothers and Daughters Talk About Living Feminism* by Christina Baker-Kline and Christina Looper Baker. Copyright © 1996 by Christina Looper Baker and Christina Baker-Kline. Used by permission of Bantam Books, a division of Random House, Inc.

Artist Credit
Annie Than (Than-Trong Kim Duyen), 19, of Toronto, Canada, is enrolled in the graphics communication management program at Ryerson Polytechnic University. She created the line drawings introducing each chapter herein. "Art is a mirror of who I am, what I'm thinking, everything that's in my soul. Even though I live in a very westernized world, my parents have kept the Asian-Vietnamese blood in me strong."